DISTURBED

DISTURBED

book three

KATIE LOWRIE

TO YOU,

THANK YOU SO MUCH FOR READING MY WORDS

Author's Note

This is the second edition of Disturbed and is the follow on from the
second edition of Disease.
There are new chapters, new POVs, and some other changes inside.

For any content warnings you may need, please head to my website.

P.S. A quick heads up: the vocabulary, grammar, and spelling of
Disturbed is written in British English.

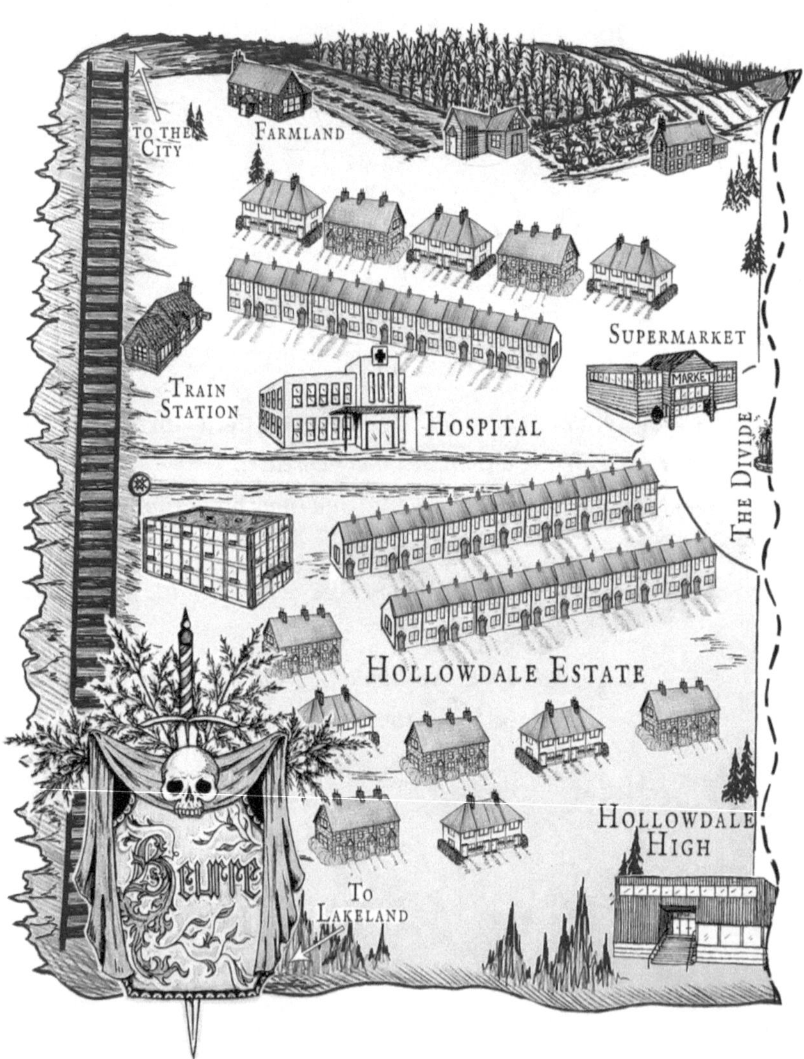

TO THE CITY
FARMLAND
SUPERMARKET
MARKET
TRAIN STATION
HOSPITAL
THE DIVIDE
HOLLOWDALE ESTATE
HOLLOWDALE HIGH
TO LAKELAND

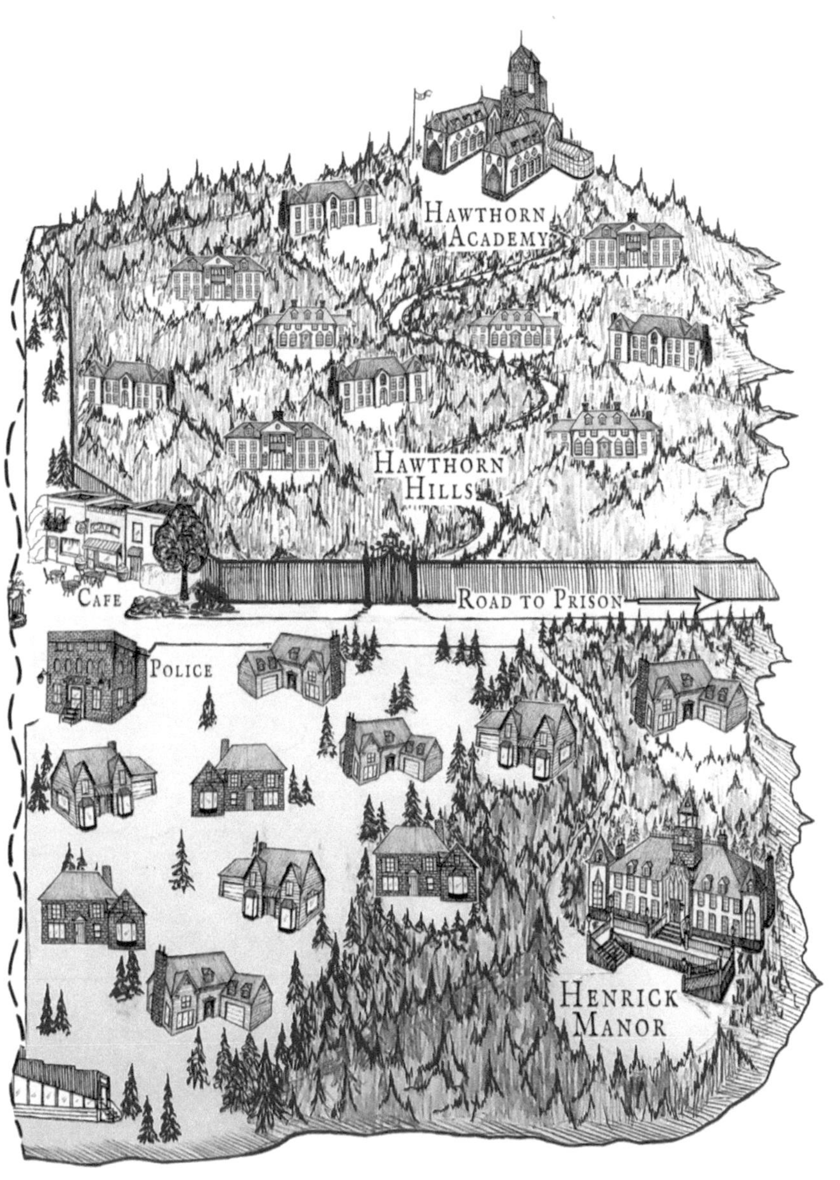

Hawthorn Academy
Hawthorn Hills
Cafe
Road to Prison
Police
Henrick Manor

DISTURBED

adjective -
emotionally or psychologically troubled

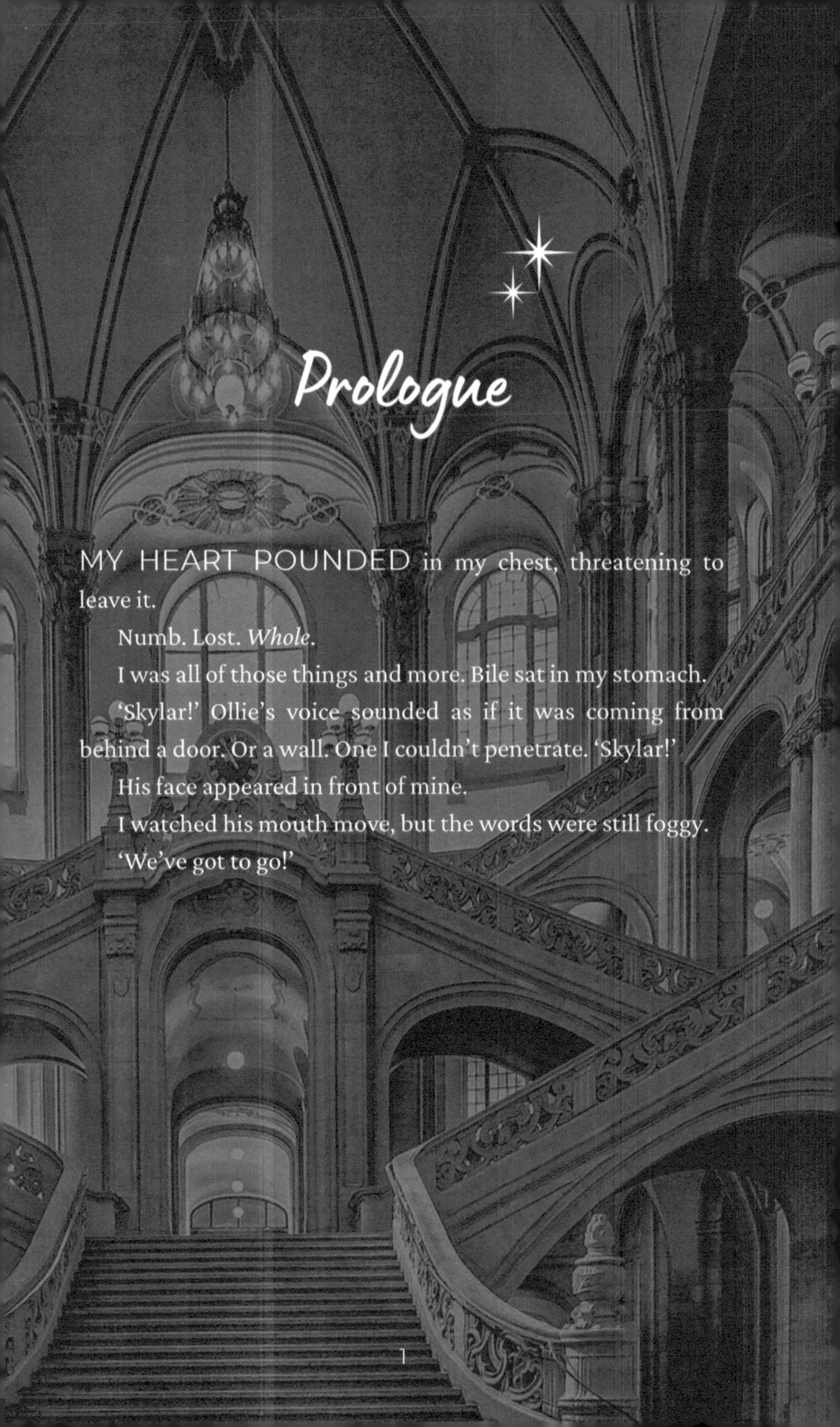

Prologue

MY HEART POUNDED in my chest, threatening to leave it.

Numb. Lost. *Whole*.

I was all of those things and more. Bile sat in my stomach.

'Skylar!' Ollie's voice sounded as if it was coming from behind a door. Or a wall. One I couldn't penetrate. 'Skylar!'

His face appeared in front of mine.

I watched his mouth move, but the words were still foggy.

'We've got to go!'

One

GRIFF'S FACE looked the same, if a little bruised, and I smiled, thrilled to be in his presence even if we were in the dank hospital.

'How are you feeling today?' I asked.

The first time I'd visited him, he looked so small in the bed—the bright white sheets had swallowed him as he lay sleeping—and even though a week had passed since the shooting, I still wanted to shield him from the world.

'You look better!'

'Cheers, Clouds. You don't look so bad yourself.'

'I look like shit, Griff. No need to butter me up,' I replied, sending a small smile his way. Being around him made me happy. Yes, he may be my family, but he was also one of my best friends.

'Nah,' he dragged out. 'You look a tad tired, tis all.'

The aftermath of New Year's was a blur, and I still hadn't come to terms with any of it. The one thing I remembered vividly: the gunshot that had rung out throughout the hall and disrupted the peace. A second gunshot came after the first.

The one that shattered everything.

The first shot had hit Griff. The second, Clover.

'I am tired,' I replied, rubbing my face. 'I'm not sleeping well.'

'I bet.' He nodded. 'Not much better in this place. There's someone on the ward who constantly shouts about not wanting to be attacked by the soldiers, poor guy. I'm hoping I get to leave soon.'

The paramedics had grazed Griff's shoulder, and the paramedics had rushed him to the hospital, where he had made a pretty speedy recovery. In typical Griff fashion, he acted like a cheeky patient with every nurse assigned to his care, and flirted his way to an extra pudding every evening.

'I doubt they'll keep you here much longer.' My words sounded hollow—I had no clue how long they planned to keep him there—but Griff appreciated them, regardless.

Clo hadn't been as lucky.

They were both staying in the hospital I'd stayed in after my stabbing. A *private* hospital I'd since found out and cost a fuck ton of money. Goes to show how little attention I paid while in residence, as I'd stayed three weeks and hadn't realised somebody was paying for my stay there—in a room all to myself no less.

'Have you heard the latest from Ollie?' Griff asked, and I shook my head. Things were weird between all of us and since the gala, even though he'd barely left my side, Ollie existed in his own spiral of hurt, trying to figure out how his family had lied to him his entire life. And who had lied to him, and what they'd lied about.

It would be some time until he rooted out where the deceit started. To know how long the family had let it fester.

'I've not spoken to him today,' I said. 'Why? What's going on?'

Ollie was staying with his father at the house on the

Hawthorn grounds, and I was staying in my dorm at Hawthorn alone. Leo was staying in his suite in the staff quarters. The same Leo who had told me not so long ago he was falling for me, yet could no longer make eye contact for more than a second.

I needed to get him alone, needed to corner him somehow and find out what he knew, because after everything Orlando said at the gala, it was apparent Leo knew a lot more than the rest of us.

Then there was the issue of Orlando himself.

' ... out on bail.' Griff's lips turned down, and I shook my head to clear the cobwebs.

'Sorry?'

He took a deep breath and repeated himself. 'Orlando's out on bail.'

Of course he fucking is.

Back at the academy, after the ambulance took away Griff and Clo, Detectives Smith and Saunders arrived at the scene full of questions. My dislike of them grew with each passing month, and the way they swanned onto the scene and inserted themselves into the aftermath pissed me off even more.

They questioned me—the two of them still believed I murdered a girl, after all—but I didn't say a word about any of it. Fuck them and fuck their opinions of me.

For Orlando to be out on bail, major money had to have changed hands.

Back before I started my scholarship at Hawthorn Academy, I used to think that having money, significant money, would change my life for the better, but after spending so much time around the truly wealthy, I wasn't so sure how true that opinion was anymore.

Money had hurt the Hawthorns more than it had saved them.

'Does that mean he'll be on Hawthorn grounds?' I asked, worried I'd have to look him in the eye for the foreseeable future, wondering what he knew about me, what he'd seen.

The constant thought of Orlando swirled through my brain on repeat, never ceasing. When alone, and trying to sleep, questions rushed to the forefront of my mind and I had no answers for any of them.

Questions like: What memories had I shared with Orlando? Or: What if the moments I loved with Ollie weren't Ollie at all?

So far, Ollie and I hadn't sat down and discussed it, but we would soon. Everything had got so twisted so fast it was hard to see a way out of it all without something imploding or exploding—that something being me.

'Not sure.' Griff shrugged. 'Ollie said he'd made bail, and he'd tell me more when he comes to visit tomorrow.'

'Fair enough. Has Leo come to see you at all?' I asked, deciding to stop pussyfooting around the question I wanted the answer to most. I wanted to know if he'd visited Griff, and maybe more importantly, I wanted to know if he'd seen Clover.

'Erm …' Griff turned away to face out the window, the sheepish expression covering his face clear even from his side profile. 'Not today.'

'Yesterday?' I asked. I'd badger him until he gave me a straight answer. I didn't give a shit anymore. 'Day before that?'

'No and no,' Griff said, looking me in the eye. 'He's been busy.'

'Oh, he has, has he? Cause I've seen him around campus, and let me tell you, the boy didn't seem busy at all. Nope. If anything, I'd say he was avoiding moi.'

Griff coughed, then said in a low whisper, 'He's busy with Orlando stuff, but he's told me not to say anything.'

'Why would he tell you not to tell me?'

Griff rubbed his chin, a distant stare in his eyes. 'He wants to speak to you about it himself.'

'How generous of him,' I said in a droll tone. 'To talk to me, he'd have to look at me, wouldn't he?' I sounded like a whining teenager and all I'd need to do was stamp my foot to fit the bill. I truly believed we'd shared something special and were on the cusp of something ... more.

'I'm sure he will soon, Clouds. He's a little messed in the head right now.'

'Aren't we all? Clover's barely conscious, and you're trapped in here because you were both shot! Then Ollie's having to deal with the fallout of having a SECRET twin he knew nothing about!' I ended in a frustrated scream. Sure, Leo was having a hard time, but fuck, he wasn't the only one.

'I get it, Sky. Give him time.'

'Fine,' I huffed out, crossing my arms across my chest. Talking about Leo made me angry and sad in equal measure. 'No more talking about arseholes. How are you?'

'I'm okay, I promise.' He smiled at me, his dimples showing. 'I can't wait to get out of here.'

'Surely you're not champing at the bit to get back to school?' I laughed. Nobody was rushing back to the academy, surely? Multiple students had died since I started and they still hadn't brought the murderer to justice.

Even though we all had a pretty good idea of who the murderer was now. Or at least I was certain I did.

'I am a little. I feel so useless here. I want to help you figure out all this Sanctum stuff, and I can't do shit from here.'

I nodded. The boy had a point. So much was still unknown

about the goings on at Hawthorn, *The Sanctum* being one of the biggest mysteries.

'I get you, but I also want you better.'

'I want to go see Clo,' he whispered. Since they were both admitted, the hospital staff hadn't allowed Griff to see her much, as they didn't like too many people entering the ward she was in. They'd wheeled him down to see her a couple of times, but not enough. Not like she'd known, anyway, seeing as she hadn't stopped sleeping since being admitted. Not that I'd say that part out loud.

'You'll be able to soon, I promise. I'll make sure it happens. Or, maybe more like, I'll convince Ollie to pay somebody.'

He smiled slightly, the shadow of his former self staring back at me. I'd become so accustomed to seeing Griff with his usual cheeky grin, I didn't know how to behave without him cracking jokes. He reminded me of a lost child; vulnerable and afraid.

'I'll hold you to that,' he said. I moved closer to his bed and pulled him into a tight hug. The fact I'd nearly lost him pinched my gut, and I'd barely had him in my life long enough. He was the only family I had besides Cora, and I didn't want him to disappear. The boy got me. We were scarily similar for two people who had experienced entirely different upbringings.

He squeezed back, surprisingly hard for somebody laid up in a hospital bed, but then again, he was a skilled swimmer with super muscles hiding underneath those clothes.

'Sky.' Griff pulled himself back from my hold, forcing me to look him in the eyes. 'I'm so glad you're my family. You know I love you, right?'

His eyes were uncertain, his watery gaze causing emotion

to rise inside of me. We'd never been so open with one another. Never been so honest. Not in a serious way, at least.

'Yeah. I do,' I told him. 'And you know I love you right back, yeah?'

'Course I do,' he said, his tone once again lighthearted, as if he wasn't sad and choked up two seconds prior. 'I mean, how could you not?'

We both laughed and hugged again before we settled down to watch a film. The rest of the time spent together was in a comfortable silence, neither of us needing to talk to fill the space.

One thing I knew for certain in this life?

Griffin Cooper was one of the best.

Simple as.

Two

SCHOOL STARTING BACK UP WAS both a blessing and a curse.

I wanted to get back to normal. Wanted to learn enough, study enough, ace my exams and get the hell out of dodge when the year ended, leaving Hawthorn and all of its shit behind me.

But being back at school wasn't the same.

Not without Clover. Not without Griff.

Not to mention the fact I'd still not spoken to Leo—and not from a lack of trying. At my lowest point I'd even messaged him asking to meet, and the bastard had left me on read.

It also wasn't the same because I spent a lot of time pondering what times I had shared with Ollie and those I had shared with Orlando, if any. In the week since the Orlando revelation, it had become obvious from a couple of things I'd said to Ollie and his responses that some of our moments together hadn't happened the way I thought they had.

Clover should be beside me. Living with me. Studying with me so we'd both get to escape at the end of the year. To leave the grasp of Hawthorn Academy and the gargoyles and ghouls that lived among the debris and decay.

Okay, okay. They lived above the entrance.

Everything was tainted now, and I didn't know how to come to terms with it on my own.

The entire school was required to attend an assembly on the first morning back, so I made my way there on dragging feet, not wanting to hear anything Ms Hawthorn had to say.

I took a spot in the last row of the rack seating, and Ollie took the empty spot next to me. It was as if a silent agreement existed between the two of us to watch out for the other while everything remained so up in the air.

Ollie leaned down and murmured in my ear, 'Wonder what the old bat has to say.'

'No idea,' I murmured back. 'Reckon she'll mention the events of the gala? Some students were lucky and weren't there to witness the fuckery.'

'Maybe she's going to pretend it never happened,' Ollie said in a dark tone. He had a point. Only a handful of students were witness to it, so maybe she wouldn't mention it at all. The local newspaper, The Beurre Banner, hadn't even posted an article about the shooting or Orlando's appearance. Just a small piece about the gala itself and the wealthy people who had attended.

I shrugged, not having the words to reassure either of us, as we waited for Ms Hawthorn to make her way across the stage to the microphone stand in the centre.

A hush fell over the room when she made her appearance. And what shocked me the most? Orlando by her side, walking in step with her. The pure smugness on his face set my blood boiling, and I knew whatever news Winifred had to impart wouldn't be good for us—for me.

The students who hadn't yet heard about the existence of

Orlando all gasped and fell into whispers. Heads turned in unison to where we were sitting.

Ms Hawthorn got to the microphone and made a small cough into it. All heads snapped back in her direction.

'Students,' she said, her voice at its normal level, assessing the room with her piercing gaze. 'I have an announcement.'

The room stilled.

'My son, Orlando,' she said, waving an arm in his direction, 'will now attend Hawthorn Academy as a student in the thirteenth year, and I hope you will all make him welcome here. He will be my eyes and ears at the academy.'

'Wonderful,' I said to Ollie out of the side of my mouth. He bristled next to me, his knee moving up and down, the agitation needing an outlet.

'Do not let him near you,' he warned. 'You'd think Leo would've at least given us a heads up about our new classmate.'

Our eyes went over to where the staff were sitting on the stage. Leo sat on the far right, his face as attractive as the last time I kissed it ten days ago.

Had it truly only been ten days since I last kissed him? Ten days since I called him mine—at least in my head—even though we'd never truly defined our relationship.

His eyes locked with mine, and he averted his gaze, turning to face Ms Hawthorn and Orlando. Orlando's mouth moved, but whatever words he spoke weren't computing in my brain.

' ... wait to study here.' Orlando smiled, showing off his straight white teeth, and a chill ran down my spine.

Ms Hawthorn must have paid off a lot of parents and law enforcement higher ups to make it happen. Or maybe she'd paid for an excellent lawyer.

Orlando should have been in prison awaiting his trial for

attempting to kill Clover rather than at some private school his mother owned. He should continue to hide away, the way he had his whole life. Joining the students and studying here like he had done nothing wrong didn't sit right, surely?

Like he hadn't shot a pupil.

Like he hadn't drugged me at the party in the woods.

Like he hadn't nearly drowned his twin brother.

Like he hadn't nearly drowned me.

Because deep down, my gut told me Orlando was responsible for it all, even if I had no proof—yet.

I needed an hour alone with him. An hour to interrogate him and get him to spill all. But nobody—meaning Ollie—would let me be alone with him to find out for definite. He did his best to stay with me at all times, probably to keep me away from Orlando, and maybe from Leo, too.

Everything was so up in the air, and although I knew Ollie meant well, it still stifled me. Even though he'd apologised to me back before the gala, things still weren't back to normal between us. Not that they ever were. The guy had used me in a revenge plot, after all. We'd never had a normal.

No matter what happened next, I would speak to Orlando.

Alone.

And no fucker was going to stop me.

Three

OLLIE and I were sitting at dinner on the last day of the week when holding back became utterly impossible.

'I'm going to talk to Orlando alone.'

'Don't you think you should talk to Leo first?' he asked, his fork paused halfway to his mouth. 'We know nothing about Orlando or what he wants. What if he wants to get you alone so he can hurt you? We've got no way of knowing anything about his mental state.'

'He won't,' I replied, trying to sound confident, but not sure I achieved the desired effect. My gut told me Orlando wouldn't hurt me—at least not in the physical sense. He never had before. Or maybe he had. How the fuck was I to know without asking him?

'How can you be so sure?'

'I can't. But I've been alone with him before and nothing bad happened.' I shrugged and returned to my food. The dining hall always served good food, but since Orlando became a student, the food had got even fancier. As if Ms Hawthorn was attempting to make up for lost time and giving her son the best of the best.

'Yes, and look what happened then!' Ollie shouted, his face flushing a deep red. 'He's hurt you every time.'

'We have no way of knowing,' I whispered, knowing my words were true, but not sure what I meant. For all I knew, the times I'd seen him were when he'd harmed me.

I had no proof otherwise.

'No, Skylar. I'm putting my foot down.'

'You're putting your foot down?' Was he for fucking real right now? Who did he think he was to dictate my actions? We weren't even a couple.

'Yes,' he bit out, his anger growing. 'You will not see him alone and that's final.'

We finished our meal in silence and once I'd emptied my plate, I excused myself and went back to my room. My head killed, like somebody had taken a brick and pounded at it.

In the same spot.

Repeatedly.

I went to my bathroom, opened the cabinet above the sink, and grabbed some ibuprofen and threw them in my mouth, swallowing the tablets dry. When I closed the cabinet door, I caught sight of myself in the mirror and didn't like what greeted me.

Limp hair and the purple bruised hollows under my eyes that let anybody who glanced my way know I lacked sleep lately.

Once back in my room, I paced, unable to stop myself, livid at Ollie. How dare he think he had anything to do with my actions? The bastard had done as many bad things to me in my time at Hawthorn as anybody else—maybe even more.

Mid-pace, something sitting on the shelf above my bed caught my eye, and I stepped closer to get a better look.

Oh, yeah! The tiny message in a bottle Leo had given me for

my first Christmas at Griff's parents' estate. Back before shit hit the fan.

What did Leo say when he handed it to me? That he'd let me know when I could open it?

Huh. At no point during our relationship had he mentioned it. Maybe he'd forgotten about it like I had, seeing as it was a relatively unimportant thing in the grand scheme of life here at Hawthorn.

Maybe whatever it said inside the bottle would convince him to talk to me.

Yes, I wanted to talk to Orlando, but talking to Leo should be higher on my priority list.

Can I open the message in a bottle now?

It didn't take long for him to reply, which surprised me, seeing as he'd avoided every other message I'd sent him since the gala.

Sure, Stutter. And I'm sorry in advance.

Leo Hawthorn would never give out an apology without having thought it through first. Whatever was written on the paper inside the bottle, Leo considered it apology-worthy, and that made my stomach drop. Ever since Orlando had shown up at the gala and said what he had about Leo, every moment between us had become shaded and I didn't know how to come to terms with it all.

I grabbed the bottle off my shelf, being careful with it. Be just my luck if I broke it or smashed it at the pivotal moment.

I'd propped up the card—the one from the box the bottle came in—and I hadn't glanced at it since the day I got it.

It read:

Merry Christmas ...

I placed it down and picked up the bottle.

Gently, I uncorked the stopper and realised I wouldn't be able to get the paper out without some tweezers.

Back into the bathroom I went to locate my make-up bag and once I found it, I rooted through until I found the only pair of tweezers I owned, with a pug face at the top. A distant cousin gifted them to me for Christmas one year. You know the type of gift—one from somebody who knows fuck all about you but is needed to give you *something* so they show up with a beauty set. *What a stellar gift.*

I took them back to my bed, sat down, and held the bottle as close to my face as I could without seeing double. The thin and tiny piece of paper inside wouldn't be an easy grab.

Good thing I loved the game Operation. It was one of those fun games anybody could take part in even if they had little skill, but the real highlight? It only needed one player. And growing up, those were the games I liked best.

Channelling my inner love of the game, I got the tiny piece of paper out of the stupid glass bottle and placed it in my hand. It was the same size as the paper on the inside of a fortune cookie and it took a lot of careful manoeuvring to open the darn thing.

My fingers trembled, unfurling the piece of paper in stages, the sweat from my hands making everything harder. Even holding it made me nervous. What on earth could be on there to make Leo so shit up?

The note made my blood boil.

I can't wait to finally meet you, Little One.

I stayed frozen to the spot, my mind whirling. Of course Orlando had chosen this note, no doubt about it.

What had Leo said when he handed it to me?

'The note inside is real, but don't open it yet. I'll let you know when.'

Well, the bastard never had. He'd never mentioned it again, allowing it to collect dust on my shelf. Every time he'd visited, did his eyes go to it? Did his deceit ever bother him, or did he think of me as something to play with? Make the new girl fall for a lie and laugh at it behind her back. Again.

My phone was in my hand before I even registered that I'd thrown the bottle onto my bed with the stupid little note next to it and picked it up. Fuck him for avoiding me. Fuck him trying to stop the conversation from happening. Things were going to happen on my time and not anybody else's.

My room. Now.

A knock sounded on the door, small and timid, like the coward standing behind it.

'Let me in, Stutter.'

Either the boy had teleported outside my door the moment he'd received my text, or he'd already made his way to my room the moment I'd asked if I could read the bottle. Probably the smartest thing he'd done in weeks.

I opened the door, not wanting to catch his eye, and turned my back to let him into the room. I couldn't even glimpse at him without fury filling me. The red mist returned —and I didn't know how to get it to leave without exploding.

'Skylar.'

My name broke me. He only ever used it if he wanted me to listen, truly listen, to what he had to say.

Until the gala, I saw myself in a relationship with Leo in the future. I could envision it. See it in my mind and feel good about what the next steps held.

All I could muster out was, 'You knew about him.'

He didn't deny it.

'You knew about him and at no point did you think to tell me? At no point during whatever we had did you think it'd be kind to fucking tell me the truth? What the fuck, Leo? I thought we—' I stopped myself. 'It hurts.'

I looked into his eyes for the first time, and the pain I saw there gutted me further. I'd be picking up my innards for the foreseeable future if he kept assessing me like that. The pain. The sadness. All of it. It was like a vice around my heart—around my very soul—and I couldn't glance at it for longer than a mere moment. My eyes went to his hands, limp and lost at his sides, then to the muscled chest I knew lurked under his shirt, then away to the walls. If I wanted to stay sane, watching him wouldn't help.

'I wish I had something to say that wouldn't hurt more,' Leo whispered, barely loud enough for me to hear over the loud thrumming of my heart. My ears pounded with the rhythm and I wanted to scream.

'So, Orlando gave you this to give to me on Christmas Day?'

'Yeah,' he replied, his tone relieved, and he seemed glad I'd broken the awkward silence. 'He wanted you to have a gift from him you couldn't trace back to him yet. You know how he is with his mind games.'

'No,' I bit out. 'I don't. Because I didn't fucking know he existed! I want the truth, Leo. Even if it's shit and makes me hate you forever. I deserve it.'

He nodded. 'You do, but I don't even know where to start. There are some things I can't tell you, no matter how much I want to. How much I've always wanted to.'

'Start with something easy,' I replied, not wanting to give him an inch. 'How did you get wrapped up in Orlando's shit?'

He took a deep breath, and I expected him to fob me off again, but he went and surprised me by speaking.

'During the summer, we stay at the house on the grounds here. Have done for as long as I can remember. But the summer before you started here, Ollie and Griff went abroad with Henry and left me here with my parents and Winifred. And then my parents went away for their anniversary and for the first time it was me and my aunt alone.'

I nodded, following his words, not wanting to interrupt his flow.

'With my parents gone, Winnie sat me down at dinner and told me about a select group of people called *The Sanctum*. After dinner finished, she took me out into the woods to meet them. They were all there waiting for me. Them, and Orlando.'

Okay, I wasn't expecting that.

'*The Sanctum*?' My brain pounded in my skull. 'You know who they are?'

He shook his head. 'No. They all wore hoods and hid their faces, but I could take a guess.'

'And Winifred is what? In charge?'

'She was ...' he trailed off, a thoughtful expression on his face. 'But after her getting beat at the swim meeting, I'd say it's changed.'

'Then what happened?'

'They told me they were inducting me into *The Sanctum* as the newest Hawthorn member and I didn't have a choice, and as the newest member, I needed to do certain … tasks for them.'

'And those tasks included being Orlando's bitch boy?' I snapped, my anger simmering over.

Leo winced. 'Something like that, yeah.'

'Why didn't you tell me? Or Ollie? He had a right to know, yet you kept it from him, from all of us. Why?'

'They threatened the people I care about. My parents. Ollie. Griff. Red. You.' He sighed. 'I couldn't risk not helping them.'

'You could've told us something. Anything! We were all blindsided at the gala. He took Ollie captive for fuck's sake and you knew! You made me love you, knowing the truth.'

His hand reached out and grabbed mine.

'I am so sorry, Stutter. I know my words don't cut it, but I'm going to make shit up to you. I promise.'

'Quite a big promise to make,' I muttered, removing my hand from his grasp. 'I need you to leave.'

'I'll leave,' he said. 'I just want you to know nothing between us was fake, not in the end. I meant everything I said.'

My heart beat an unnatural rhythm, half of it wanting him to keep saying such sweet words, the other half ready to batter him.

'Stutter, I had to help them. Help him. You can see that, can't you?'

'What I can see is a coward. A liar. You had so many chances to tell me. To hint at something not being quite right. Everything you did caused me pain, and I'm not sure how long it'll take me to get over it. If I can get over it.'

I walked to the door, ready to open it and shove him through it, when a knock came.

Four

'SKYLAR!' Ollie's voice called through the door, interrupting the moment.

I flicked my gaze between the door and Leo, trying to decide what to do for the best, even though neither option was stellar.

'Skylar!' Ollie called again. 'Can we talk, please?'

Leo tilted his head, his eyes burning into my skin, and I shook my head. Not sure what I was saying no to, but it was something. I opened the door, narrowly avoiding Ollie's raised fist as he went to knock again. The relief on his face when he saw me woke up the butterflies in my stomach—it was rare to see such a genuine reaction on his face—but his relief soured when he spotted Leo standing behind me.

'I can see you've already got company.'

'Leo's leaving,' I said. 'Aren't you?'

'Apparently so,' Leo murmured, his eyes remaining on me. 'Let me know when we can talk again, Stutter.'

I nodded and said, 'I'll message you.'

He opened and closed his mouth, wanting to say more, but wouldn't with Ollie standing there. Things still needed to be said, and they were too intimate to have a witness.

Leo walked to the door, and with one last longing glance my way, he left the room, throwing a 'See you two later,' over his shoulder.

'Are you okay?' Ollie asked, closing the door behind him and stepping into my room. I gave a terse nod, letting out the breath I'd held in while waiting for Leo to leave. 'What did he want?'

'I asked him here,' I said, my eyes going back to the tiny bottle and note discarded on my bed. 'I needed to ask him a couple of questions about ... everything.'

'Did you get the answers you wanted?'

'Sort of.' I shrugged, deflated. The heaviness of the last hour hit me and I slumped down on my bed. 'What did you want to talk about?'

Ollie's eyes darted around the room. Maybe I'd caught him off guard. 'Huh?'

'You came here wanting to talk to me,' I pointed out. 'So, talk. The floor is yours. '

'I came to apologise. I acted like a prick at dinner and you don't deserve it. I've been all out of sorts since ... well, everything. I know it's not an excuse, but it's all I have.'

'It isn't all you have.'

His left eyebrow turned down as his right quirked up. Did I need to spell everything out for him?

'You came to apologise,' I said and sigh. 'But none of your sentences contained an apology.'

He had the decency to appear sheepish. 'Right. I should probably try again.'

I chuckled at the uncertainty on his face. 'Maybe.'

Not sure what it said about me, but I sort of loved it when Ollie acted out of sorts. All confused and uncertain and cute. It was one thing that made him seem human—more real—and those times weren't often enough, so I always grabbed them and held on with both hands.

'I'm sorry, Sky, for being such a dick about it all. If you need to talk to Orlando, then I'll have to sit down and accept it. It's hard for me, you know?'

'I know,' I hushed out, patting the empty spot on the bed next to me in invitation. 'I don't think there's a guidebook on what to do when you find out you've got a secret twin. Or what to do when your second boyfriend betrays you in the space of a year.'

'I should probably say sorry for that too, huh?'

'Pretty sure you already did.' I smiled at him. 'But you can again if you want. Can never hear the word sorry leave your lips too often.'

Ollie smiled too, and my eyes drifted to his lips. No, Skylar.

'I don't think I'll ever say it enough,' he admitted. 'I am sorry, though. For everything I did. It was shitty of me and even though I knew it, I just couldn't see it. Does that make sense?'

'Not at all, actually.'

We both laughed, and I lay back and examined the ceiling so I could talk without having to watch his reaction to my words. He followed me, lying beside me, our arms grazing each other, and the warmth settling in my arm from his was surprisingly nice.

'This whole Orlando thing has messed me up, Sky.' His whispered words were pained. 'I've always hated my dad and put my mum on such a pedestal, and to find out she lied to him about something so serious, I don't know how to handle every-thing. How to come to terms with it. And the worst part? I can't even ask her why she did what she did because she's dead.

Because she chose not to be here anymore. And that hurts. Like really fucking hurts.'

In my chest, my heart split in two for him. My relationship with my mum wasn't great or anything, but she'd never done something so ... shitty. Sure, she'd spent all my money and had married an absolute douche-canoe of a man, but she'd never hidden a secret sibling from me. Well, we'll ignore the whole keeping me in the dark about my father thing for the time being. Easier that way.

Ollie's fingertips lightly gripped mine, sending a tingle down my arm, and I let him. If he wanted to use me as his anchor, I'd allow it. Fuck, I'd allow him to do a whole lot more —which said a lot about me and my mindset. None of it good.

'Why do you think she did it?'

'What part?'

'Hid Orlando from everybody,' I clarified. 'Told nobody about him and gave him to her sister, of all people.'

'I don't know.' His voice broke. 'My dad left today, but I've asked him to come back next month so I can talk to him about it. Get to the truth. See if he really knew nothing or if he's a talented actor.'

'Do you think he would have acted so in the dark? Because when I saw him at the gala, the man looked crushed.'

Ollie went quiet before a rush of breath left him. 'I don't know. He'd never let Winifred, of all people, raise one of his kids, which is how I know Mum kept him in the dark. Especially not a son. An heir.'

'From what I know of your dad, it sounds unlikely. I always got the vibe that he hated her.'

'He *does* hate her. He's never been able to stand her and nobody has ever said why. Griff and I have tried to figure it out, but we've come up blank every time. I'd ask Leo about it but ...'

'But you're not talking to him right now,' I finished for him.

'Right. If the bastard could hide such important stuff from us, then he's not worthy of our conversation.'

'Don't judge him too harshly.'

Ollie turned to face me, but I stayed put, scanning the ceiling so I couldn't see the questioning look I'd no doubt find on his face. My words sounded suspiciously like I was sticking up for Leo Hawthorn, and after everything, I shouldn't be doing that. But I couldn't let Ollie fall out with one of his closest friends without hearing him out first.

'That's how it is, is it? One conversation with him and he's wrapped you around his finger again.' Ollie sat up abruptly. 'I'm out of here. Let me know when you're not kissing Leo's arse.'

I sat up too, watching him storm to the door, grasping the handle and flinging it open.

'You're being ridiculous.'

'I don't want to hear it.' The sound of the door slamming against the frame reverberated throughout my small room, lingering. Stupid of me to talk positively about Leo to Ollie really, especially after he'd found us in here together.

My insides jumbled. My thoughts thoroughly scrambled.

What was I meant to do? Nothing I could do, really. They'd have to mend the rift between them in their own time, and I needed to stay well out of it. And while I did that, I also needed to figure out my feelings towards them both. You know, simple stuff.

Ha!

They'd both lied to me. Betrayed me. Dragged me down to the lowest of the low.

Yet I cared about them still.

Well, fuck me.

Five

GRIFF'S RETURN to school came at exactly the right time.

With Ollie not talking to me and me not talking to Leo, chilling out in my room, or in the library, alone became super appealing. Not much else to do, really.

I spent the weekend thinking everything over: my feelings, the events of the past, and most importantly, what I could do to move forward. I'd drawn no conclusions as yet, but I was trying. Which was the most important thing, right?

Bouncing on my toes, I waited at the bottom of the steps outside the school's main entrance, waiting for the car with Griff inside to make its way up the hill and to my feet.

We texted daily, and I knew the boy was more than ready to get back to school and away from somewhere so boring and clinical, as he called it.

The wind whipped my violet hair in front of my face and I swatted it away, ready to get back inside to the comforting warmth—well, to a degree.

After an eternity but was probably in actuality ten minutes, a car crept its way up the hill, moving so slowly I could run the distance and back by the time it made its way to me, and I couldn't run for shit.

And then it pulled up in front of me, an ecstatic Griffin peeping at me through the open window. 'Clouds!'

'Hey, Griff,' I said, fighting back the tears swarming my vision. His entire aura had dimmed, but his wide smile was still affixed to his face like he hadn't just spent time in the hospital after being literally shot. 'Fancy seeing you here.'

'You missed me?' he asked, before opening the door with a flourish and slowly stepping out, tentative movements marring his usual buoyancy. Even with slower steps, his urgent energy bubbled up in the air. Infectious.

'Of course,' I said with ease. 'It's been no fun around here without you.'

'*Obviously.*' He nodded, and then together we rushed forward and launched into a big hug, melting my insides and making them mush. There was a warmth about Griff. Something innate nobody could steal, no matter how much they tried. 'The boys still giving you a hard time?'

'More like I've been giving them a hard time.' I laughed, locking my arm with his so the two of us could make our way to the dorms together. 'Things are ... tense.'

'Have you spoken to them? Properly?'

The hallway is empty, our footsteps echoing around us, as the rest of the school is busy with classes.

'Define properly.' Griff turned and narrowed his eyes. 'Okay, okay. I've spoken to Leo a little, and Ollie and I are getting there. I've not said two words to Orlando, and believe me, I want to, but I've not yet worked up the courage.'

'Want me to be there when you do?'

'Thanks for the offer, but I think it's something I need to do alone.'

Griff nodded, deep in thought, and I didn't interrupt. Sometimes it was nice to stay silent with those you love and care about.

Once the two of us made it back to my room, he broke the silence.

'Odd being in here without her, isn't it?'

Of course, he wanted to talk about Clover; her being his girlfriend and all. Or was she? The last time I'd asked Clo, they weren't putting a label on things, but things could've changed. It seemed insensitive to ask Griff, so I didn't.

'I keep expecting her to barge through the door, her face filled with thunder,' I admitted. 'Or blabbering away about something. Usually something to do with my actions and poor decisions.'

'She has a lot of opinions, doesn't she?' Griff's warm tone told me he missed her. We both did. 'She'll be back soon.'

'Did they let you go see her before you left?'

He nodded. 'Yep. She was asleep, so I spoke at her rather than to her, but the nurses told me she'd most likely be out within a week or so.'

'That's good news.' Mental note: message Clover. It wouldn't surprise me if she actively chose to 'be asleep' whenever Griff visited, because I'd had a few messages from her over the weekend, so I knew she was awake for a lot of the time. I'd planned to go visit her, but she'd told me not to bother—no point in both of us missing out on school work.

'Once she's back, things will be back to normal.'

'Not quite. We still need to figure out what Orlando's doing, who *The Sanctum* are, and what Leo's involvement in all this is.'

'What did he tell you?' Griff sat on the edge of Clo's bed

facing me, the sun shining through the window onto his red hair, turning it almost a burnt auburn colour.

'He knew about Orlando all along. He's met *The Sanctum*.' I counted each thing he'd told me off on my fingers. 'Oh, and they've initiated him, or plan to.'

The interested expression on Griff's face remained, but he said nothing, waiting for me to get my bearings and continue. Every time I remembered what Leo had told me, his face swam into my mind, and I couldn't focus on anything except for the fact everything between us had been a big fat lie.

'It makes no sense. Why wouldn't he have told me and Ollie?'

'Maybe he couldn't?' I'd been thinking about it all ever since Leo told me about *The Sanctum*'s initiation and how they expected him to go along with what they wanted. 'He said they threatened all our lives.'

'Nice to know he cares so much about us all.'

'Of course he does,' I said, without even having to think about it. 'The boy may be an arsehole ninety-nine per cent of the time, but the remaining one per cent gives a shit and you can bet it's the part of him that cares about us.'

'I'm sorry things with him haven't gone the way you thought they would.'

I shrugged, running my fingertips along the duvet, not wanting to focus on Griff's words, or in the sympathy I could hear lacing every word.

Ah, time for a subject change. 'Want to grab a pizza for dinner?'

Griff nodded his head like an enthusiastic pet. 'You bet!'

Six

WITH GRIFF BACK, school fell into a routine.

Either Ollie or Griff were never far away from my side, or worse, they sandwiched me between them both. In their eyes, Orlando posed a threat, as did Leo, and neither of them wanted me to get even more hurt than I already had been. Yes, it irritated me to have two shadows, but it also warmed my heart that they cared enough to do it at all.

But then an opportunity arose to be alone, and I jumped on it.

'Are you sure you'll be okay?' Ollie asked, pausing at the entrance to the changing rooms.

'Ollie,' I said, as if I hadn't already said it thirty times before. 'I'm gonna be sitting up in the stands watching you guys train while working on some homework. You'll be able to see me the whole time.'

'I know, but—'

'But nothing.' I put my foot down … metaphorically. 'If anything happens—which it won't—then you'll be able to hear me scream for your assistance.'

He took a step closer to me, and my breathing hitched involuntarily. 'You taking the piss out of my worrying?'

'N-no.'

'Your stutter gives you away, Skylar.'

I made a pfft noise. 'When doesn't it?'

'You'll still be sitting there when I finish, yeah?'

'Yep.'

'Then we can talk later?' The hope in his words made my head hurt. 'Really talk?'

'Sure. You go swim, then we can talk, but only if you do the whole practice and don't skip out early to make sure I'm okay!'

'If you're sure.'

'Oliver, if you don't fuck off in the next two seconds, I swear to you, I'm gonna beat your arse!'

He moved away from me and I laughed as the changing room door closed behind him before I made my way to the seating overlooking the swimming pool. I got comfortable—as comfortable as you could get in those plastic shitty chairs—and pulled out my History textbook and my notebook.

I'd planned to write an essay about Stalinist Russia, but I wrote a different heading across the top of my blank page. One that had nothing to do with education.

Ollie vs Orlando

The rhythmic tapping of my pen echoed, and my mind entered a trance. There were things I needed the answers to, and until I wrote them down, I wouldn't remember them. Any time they'd popped into my head over the last few weeks, I'd batted them away as quick as they'd arrived, worried they'd do me damage if I examined them. But I couldn't ignore shit. Not anymore.

My hand flew across the page, writing everything I could think of.

- *First time we spoke in the Hospital Wing (surely Ollie … right?)*
- *Closet make-out session during the first New Year's Gala (Ollie?)*
- *Who drugged me at the first ever party in the woods (Orlando?)*
- *Too many times in the library to count (must think of individual instances)*
- *Who set The Set on me? (Ollie?)*
- *Who killed Odette and Olivia? (Orlando?)*

Once I'd finished the list, I ripped the page out of my notebook and folded it into fours before placing it in the zipped pocket of my schoolbag. There were loads more times to add, but I could add them as they came to mind.

My eyes couldn't help being drawn to the boys in the pool, and a smile came to my lips. Fuck me, Ollie was hot.

Ollie always looked fucking hot whenever he swam.

The way his muscles rippled under the water's surface. The way his body glided through the water like a powerful machine making waves.

Since school had started back up, he had been swimming a lot. Apparently, having your secret twin brother nearly drown you in the exact pool you trained in didn't put you off something you truly loved. If anything, it made you work and train even harder.

Go figure.

I pulled out my phone, the thought of writing about Stalin out the window, and pulled up Hive. The moment the screen loaded, pictures of Ophelia and Oralie on either side of a smirking Orlando assaulted my eyes. I scoffed. Idiots.

Since the camp out, and everything that happened after it, I'd not had any issues with the girls at all. No, the three of us would never be friends, but we were acquaintances now, which was enough. Yet if they continued to hang out with Orlando, I might question their sanity more than I already had …

'Hey, Little One,' a voice said from behind me.

I jumped, my bum physically leaving the seat, startled. It landed back down with a thud.

Three guesses to who.

'H-hello,' I replied. I'd always turned into a stuttering mess around Orlando and I doubted that would change just because I now knew who he really was.

'What are you doing sitting here all alone? Watching my brother make a tit out of himself?' he said, a soft smile dancing on his lips.

I'd kissed those lips, hadn't I?

'Something like that.' I kept my gaze ahead to where Ollie and Griff were swimming laps. Leo's gaze locked with mine from where he stood next to the pool, and he raised his right eyebrow in question. I gave him a small shake of my head in response. 'I wondered when you'd seek me out.'

'You gonna pretend I haven't tried to get you alone already?' Orlando's eyes lit up. The bright blue of them shining even brighter in the pool house lighting. Like a picture-perfect model. Obviously. He was Ollie's identical twin, after all.

'No.' I shrugged. 'But I did wonder how long it'd take for you to make it happen regardless of the guys sticking by my side all the time,' I said in a hushed voice, not wanting it to carry down to the pool.

Ollie hadn't yet registered Orlando's arrival, and I wanted it to stay that way. He was too involved in his swimming to take notice of his surroundings, something he'd learned so he could win races and never get distracted by the competition. It also meant he blocked out a lot. He'd glanced up maybe once since we'd arrived.

Orlando laughed, but it lacked any joy. 'Those boys have you on a tight leash, don't they?'

'Those boys,' I emphasised, 'don't have me on any leash. I'm a grown girl and I can make my own decisions.'

'Sure, Little One. If it's so easy to break away from them and come talk to me, then why haven't you?'

'Could it be the fact you're a massive fucking liar? Or maybe because you're an imposter who's pretended to be his twin brother on more than one occasion?'

'Hm.' Orlando stared at Ollie, his eyes narrowed on the face disappearing and reappearing from under the waves. Ollie's forehead wrinkled and his eyebrows furrowed low, deep in concentration. 'Want to get out of here?'

'No!' It was a knee jerk reaction—one I hadn't fully thought through. I scanned around me and then down to Ollie to check he hadn't heard my shout. When he didn't call out, or stop swimming, I clocked the opportunity handed to me and came to my senses. 'Where would we even go?'

'The caretaker's closet?' He wagged his eyebrows, then chuckled after spotting my face, and said, 'I'm kidding. I thought we could go to the library.'

I mentally crossed off the line on my folded piece of paper that read, Closet make-out session during the first New Year's Gala (Ollie?) and then reversed it. I needed to be certain before crossing anything out. When I could, I'd alter it to say, Closet make-out session during the first New Year's Gala (Orlando?).

'The library?' I asked, sceptical.

He shrugged like it was a no-brainer. 'You feel most comfortable there. And you'll feel better knowing Flo is around and she takes no shit.'

'I have to warn you,' I said, smiling. 'I'm sort of her favourite. Flo won't let you mess me around.'

I smiled and then stopped myself. Was it fucked that my insides were warm and fuzzy because Orlando knew something like that about me because he'd paid enough attention to me while pretending to be his brother? He knew I loved the library above all else.

I didn't want to answer.

'I don't know ...' I trailed off. 'The guys may notice me missing.'

'Hate to break it to you, Little One, but they won't. There's another hour of practice, minimum.'

'You ask your little bitch Leo to make that the case, huh?'

He didn't dignify my sniping with a reply.

I weighed up my two options. Either I could sit and pretend to not write about Stalin for another hour, or I could go with Orlando and learn some truths. An opportunity like this to talk to Orlando with no witnesses wouldn't come around again.

'Fine. But I leave when I want to. No exceptions.'

'Of course,' he said, reaching out his hand for me to take a hold of. 'I'd never want to make you uncomfortable.'

I found *that* hard to believe.

Seven

BEING ALONE with Orlando didn't feel as wrong as I thought it would. If anything, it was comfortable—easy. Like we'd known each other for a long time. And I supposed we had, sort of.

Shit got harder to wrap my head around daily.

'So ...' I trailed off.

'So,' he replied, a wolfish grin melting me. 'How are you doing, Little One?'

'Honestly? I have no proper answer.' I chuckled. 'Things are fucked.'

'They are,' he agreed. 'And I suppose you've got a couple of questions for me.'

'You've supposed right.' I glanced around, making sure our conversation remained private. 'I'm not sure where to start.'

'How about I start the conversation for you? Hey, my name's Orlando. Skylar, right?' He held out his hand for me to shake, but I stared at him, keeping my hand to myself. 'I've waited a long time to introduce myself to you.'

'Is that so?' My eyebrows climbed on my forehead. 'Because you've had plenty of opportunities to introduce your-self, and funny enough, you've chosen not to every time.'

'I couldn't.'

'Of course you could. Don't lie. You *chose* not to.' I crossed my arms across my chest, staring him down, hoping to make him as uncomfortable as I could. 'Leo told me you recruited him into your shitty sanctum.'

'He did, huh?' Orlando's pointer finger rubbed at his jaw and a little shiver ran through me. He looked so much like his brother. It was uncanny. 'Did he tell you anything else?'

'You threatened my life if he didn't play ball.'

He stopped rubbing his jaw and narrowed his eyes into slits. 'Interesting.'

'Not how it happened?'

'It doesn't matter how it happened.' He waved his hand, brushing me off. 'What matters is you've been ignoring me, and now I've got you here alone, I don't want to waste our time together talking about that wanker. Somebody will come and break us up sooner rather than later.'

I didn't contradict him, because he was probably right. I doubted Ollie or Griff—or even Leo—were going to let me disappear with their sworn enemy for long without interfering. My fingers picked at a thread on my bottle green blazer, keeping busy, but my eyes locked on the imposter in front of me. There was something so familiar about him it hurt.

'So, what do you want to talk about if not your little lapdog?'

'I thought it was time we talked, Little One. I'm here to answer your questions, if I can. No ulterior motives.'

'Okay.' I nodded, mind made up. 'I've got a question for you, and if you don't answer, then I'm walking away right now and you won't get time alone with me like this again.'

'I'm sure I could convince you otherwise.'

I ignored his cocksure expression. Wanker.

'Before you arrived at the pool, I was writing a list.' Orlando remained quiet, waiting for me to continue. 'One weighing up what events were actually you and not your brother.'

'And did you come to any conclusions?'

'You killed Odette and Olivia.' As the words tumbled from my lips, I watched his face for any reaction, but he'd had a lot of practice at hiding his emotions to give me anything I could analyse. 'You drugged me at the first party in the woods.' His left eyelid twitched. 'You stabbed me after the fashion show.' His top lip quirked. I took a deep breath and finished with the one I thought would drag the strongest reaction from him. 'You pulled me into the caretaker's closet and fucked me.'

'A memory I replay in my head every night.'

My stomach twinged at the confirmation, but ever since I'd seen Orlando at the gala and realised who he was, I'd known that moment was all his. Ollie would never have risked showing his true feelings towards me, especially not as I flaunted a relationship with his best friend, and he pretended to be into an O girl.

'Of course you do, you sick bastard,' I spat, but it didn't hold anywhere near as much venom behind it as there should've been. The fucker had violated me, pretended to be somebody else, yet rage still didn't fill me the way everybody expected it to.

'But as for your other points … I didn't kill Olivia,' he told me, staring into my eyes.

An icy shiver fell over me, and I didn't believe a word he'd said.

'Trust me, Little One.'

'Trust you?' I scoffed. 'You expect me to trust you after you've admitted to something so heinous?'

'You trust Ollie, Griff, and Leo after everything they've done to you. How's it any different?'

'Because they've said sorry! They've never hurt me or tried to kill me, for starters. You know it isn't anywhere near the same.'

'Did those fuckers ever tell you how you ended up at Hawthorn? About how they made sure you were here to bully and destroy?'

'We've never spoken about it,' I said. What was his angle?

'They introduced the scholarship so you would come here and so Clover could return. Everything they've done is to hurt you both.'

So Clover could return? But she'd never been to Hawthorn before …

'That makes no sense,' I said. 'Clo never came here before the scholarship. She knew the Hawthorns from childhood. Something to do with her parents.'

It made sense the boys had introduced the scholarship to get us to the school. They'd hated us both in equal measure and you couldn't enact a revenge scheme on somebody without them being in front of you. Not an effective one, at least.

'You've always thought Clover was hiding something from you and knew a lot more about the school and the people here than she let on. Why's it hard to believe she came here before?'

'I—' I rattled my brain to remember something she'd told me. Anything to put an explanation in place, so I didn't have to believe Orlando's accusations. But he'd made a valid point. It had crossed my mind that maybe Clover held a few things back from me.

The moment her health improved, I'd have to ask her.

Orlando raised his eyebrows. 'I've got no reason to lie to you, Little One. Not anymore.'

'Okay, if you've not got anything to hide from me, then you'll answer a couple of questions I have.'

'I'll answer anything I can.'

'Right ...' I flicked through the filing cabinet of my brain, trying to find the correct thing to ask first. If I went in too hard, he may bolt. 'Why are *The Sanctum* after us?'

He raised an eyebrow, but I stood my ground. It needed answering, and I wouldn't let his quirked eyebrows stop me from asking.

'Isn't it obvious?' He shuffled in his seat. 'They want your dad to return.'

'Okay ...' I shuffled in my seat, getting a little closer to him. 'Then what's the reason for going after Ollie?'

'Oh.' Orlando laughed. 'I wanted to make my brother suffer for everything wrong. That fucker became the chosen one. The one our mother wanted to keep. The one she didn't cast away to her bitch of a sister.'

'But why did Millie give you away in the first place? And why did your dad not know about you before the gala?'

'That's a lot to answer in one brief conversation.' The smirk on his face wasn't as unaffected as usual. 'You know, Little One, I've often wondered why she gave me up. Did I seem evil from birth? Did I cry, and he didn't?' He shook his head, his anger snapping once more into place. 'I guess we'll never know.'

'I'm sorry,' I whispered, even though I had nothing to apologise for and as a rule, I hated it when people apologised for something they had no control over. 'People are pretty crappy.'

'Trust nobody. Not Leo. Not Griff and especially not Ollie. Not even me.'

I nodded, wanting to agree with him, but knowing my heart would find it hard to disregard my trust of Griff and Ollie —heck, even Leo I sort of trusted, and he'd betrayed me as of late. Bastard.

'Promise me.' His tone became urgent as his hand darted out to grip mine, a sharp shooting pain running up my arm from the tight squeeze he gave me. 'Promise you'll put yourself first, no matter what happens with all this.'

'I p-promise,' I stuttered, caught off guard by the intensity in his blue gaze.

His responding nod was firm. 'Good.'

Eight

OLLIE'S WRATH when he banged on my dorm door wasn't a surprise.

I should've returned to his practice at the pool, but when I left Orlando in the library, I couldn't bring myself to head back to the pool. I'd needed time to think about what he'd told me before I faced Ollie—or any of the boys.

'Skylar, open up!'

'I'm not opening this door until you calm the fuck down,' I called back. Sure, be pissed at me for putting myself in danger, but I wouldn't allow him to railroad me anymore. If he wanted to talk about it, then we could talk like calm, rational adults. Not petty children throwing their toys out of the pram.

'If I promise to calm down, will you let me in?'

I thought about it for a moment, knowing it'd make the boy on the other side of the door stew for a little longer. Riling Ollie up could be really fun sometimes.

I nodded, then remembered he couldn't see me through the door, so said, 'Sure.'

'You've sort of got to open the door for me to come in.'

'Oh, yeah.' I opened the door, and he came straight in, his

agitation still there, but I could tell he was doing his best to keep it in. 'So ...'

Ollie didn't wait long before he exploded.

'How dare you speak to him alone!'

'How dare you think you can talk to me like that! I let you in because you said you'd calm down. Not sounding too calm to me.' I shouted back. 'You were busy and the two of us went to the library and were in view of Flo the whole time.'

'Skylar, if he ever did anything to hurt you, I—'

'You'd what?' I growled. 'Because the last time I checked, you fucking hurt me worse than he ever has!'

'He tried to drown you.'

'You turned the entire school against me, made me believe you loved me, and then left me heartbroken.'

'He stabbed you!'

Okay, Ollie had a point there, but I wouldn't let him walk all over me. Not anymore. 'You may as well have done from the pain you caused.' I took a deep breath. 'Ollie, I don't want to fight about this. I spoke to him. It's already done. So please, can we talk about what he told me and figure out a way to stop more shit from going down?'

He nodded, reluctant to concede, but I knew he'd do it, anyway.

'He said little, but it's clear to me we need to be worried about *The Sanctum* and what they're capable of. They want my dad.'

'They do?'

'Yeah. Orlando told me.' I shrugged. 'He also said you made up the scholarship to get me here. By any chance, did it have something to do with my dad, too?'

'It's complicated.'

'I know.' My heart twinged in sympathy for the lost-looking boy in front of me. 'But for us to move forward, we need to clear the air.'

'Can we take a rain check? I need to get it all untangled in my mind, and the moment I do, I promise I'll explain everything.'

'Fine.'

His blue eyes locked with mine, a raging storm within them, and he pushed his hair back.

'I'm sorry for going off on you earlier. The thought of you getting hurt again drives me so angry mad. Skylar, I know with everything that's happened you won't believe me, but I love you and I want what's best for you, and if that means saying nothing when you decide something I'm unhappy with, then I need to accept that.'

My mind stuttered, his sentence disappearing in my brain after the three words I thought I'd never hear from him.

'Th-thank you.' I got more comfortable on top of my bed. 'You wanna hear a bit more about what I spoke to Orlando about?'

'If you want to tell me, sure.' He smiled. 'I'll always listen to you.'

I smiled back—I couldn't help myself when he said such cute things. 'I talked to Orlando about a list I've written. I want to figure out what events were actually him and not you.'

'Sky,' he whispered, rubbing his finger across mine. 'I want to figure shit out, too. Together.'

'Then you need to stop being so overprotective of me.'

'I worry about you.'

'I know.' I let out a small chuckle. 'And I'm not telling you to stop, because I kinda like it. But I need you to let me do my own thing.'

'Okay, I can try. So, what's on this list of yours?'

'Orlando answered one of my main ones.'

'What was it?'

'Turns out,' I said, trying for a joking tone, but not sure if it delivered. 'A couple of times I thought I hooked up with you … weren't you.'

The change in Ollie's face was instantaneous. 'I'll fucking kill him!'

'Ollie—'

'No, Sky!' He cut me off. 'The bastard raped you, and you expect me to ignore that?'

'No, but—'

'There's nothing you can say to justify it! You can't seriously be about to defend him?'

'Of course not. I don't even know how I feel about it all except violated. Mad. Confused. Do you know how hard it is to look upon memories I liked and see the reflection distorted? All shined with vomit or something and now I've got to clean it away to get to the bottom.'

'Such an imaginative way of putting it.'

I brushed Ollie off. 'Don't you dare be mad at me for not feeling or acting the way you expect me to, okay? Not when I don't even know how I feel.'

Ollie's face turned sombre. 'I'm here for you, Sky. Just know you can talk to me about any of this whenever you want and I'll try my best to keep a cool head. It's hard, though.'

'Yeah …' I trailed off, before laying back on my bed, facing up to the ceiling instead of at his perfect face. My stomach dipped around him and being alone in my room, talking about such vulnerable things, didn't help matters. 'All of this is hard, but we'll get through it. We've weathered worse storms, right?'

'I suppose.'

'Ollie,' I whispered, not wanting to startle him, but putting enough weight into his name, he knew whatever came next was serious. 'I've forgiven you for everything you've done and I'm laying here trying to stop myself from kissing you. If we can get past, well … the past, then we can get through all of this shit, too.'

'You're thinking about kissing me?' His whisper mixed with laughter. The bed beneath me jostled as he turned onto his side to face me. 'Of course, I've hoped …' he trailed off. I felt compelled to face him and turned onto my side so I could see the indecision flitting across his features. It always took me by surprise how attractive he was. How much I wanted him simply from looking at him; from seeing the little frown on his brow and knowing he was thinking deeply about something.

'You've hoped?'

'Hoped you'd reciprocate the feelings I have for you and one day you'd want me the way I've always wanted you.'

I scoffed. 'You haven't always wanted me.'

'Yes, I have. Even when I wanted to hate you, I couldn't help but want to get to know you better, to want to be in your company, and to want to be with you.'

I moved an inch.

Ollie moved an inch.

Until our noses were touching and his breath skated across my face.

'Is it okay if I kiss you?'

The butterflies in my stomach flew around in a frenzy, the question sending me over the edge. Had he ever asked before? I couldn't recall—doubted I could even remember my name— but the fact he had … Well, there was only one answer.

'Yes.' The word left me in a hushed breath. 'Kiss me, Ollie.'

Our lips clashed together in a passionate embrace, the instant spark of heat from our touching lips filling me with warmth, and I wanted him above all else. His hand came and grabbed the back of my neck, pulling me closer, and I moaned at the sensation of it all.

Fuck. The boy could kiss.

Hands wandered and our moaning increased, the two of us lost in the moment of finally giving in to our desires. Things were heating up—fast—and I knew things needed to slow down a little before the train went off the tracks.

After fuck knew how long, we broke apart, both needing to cool down. He pulled back and the smile he gave me made me want to pounce on him straight away, but I knew I shouldn't.

Our heavy breathing slowed, and the intensity in our locked gaze was almost too much for me to handle.

Once the atmosphere in my room had returned to normal, I took a deep breath and faced Ollie. 'So, what's our first plan of action?'

'We can discuss tomorrow,' he murmured, rubbing his thumb against my face. 'Is it okay if I stay here tonight? I'll sleep in Clo's bed. I need to be close to you, you know, just in case.'

My heart filled with an emotion I didn't want to inspect too closely, especially after our make-out session.

So, I said, 'Sure. You can stay in my bed though, if you'd like?'

Nine

WAKING up in Ollie's arms was like coming home.

And this time around? It felt real.

Things were so different from the last time we'd shared a bed together, and not only because I'd had a relationship with Leo in the in-between. Or maybe it was. Who the fuck knew?

Maybe I was a terrible human.

'Morning,' Ollie mumbled in my ear, pulling me from my darker thoughts. 'You sleep well?'

'Mmm.' I moved in the bed and turned to face him, so his hard dick no longer pressed into my back. Temptation like that before ten in the morning—unnecessarily cruel. Especially after the kissing session we'd had the night before.

Baby steps, Skylar.

He placed a kiss on my forehead, a gentle brush of the lips, and it once again awakened my body.

'I slept the best I've slept in a *long* time.' He blinked, a soft smile playing on his lips. 'I've missed falling asleep with you wrapped safe in my arms.'

'Mmm,' I repeated, noncommittal.

'Play it coy, Sky, but I know you well enough to see the light in your eyes and the smile you're trying to hide.'

My stomach tingled as he touched it, threatening to tickle me, but stopping before he did any damage. I always appreciated a teasing, playful Ollie, because I rarely witnessed it.

'Are we going to make a plan today?' I asked, wanting to change the subject away from anything banter-filled, so I didn't cave and launch myself on him.

'If that's what you want,' he said, his amusement laced in his tone. 'Suppose you want to get Griff in on it, too?'

I nodded. 'Well, yeah. Not gonna leave the boy out, am I? Oh! You've reminded me. Have you heard anything from the hospital about Clover?'

'No, but I can call them in a bit once we're up. Do you mind if I grab a shower?'

'Your room's close and has a much bigger bathroom,' I pointed out. 'You just want a reason to get semi-naked in front of me.'

'Maybe.' He smiled. 'But I'd rather see you semi-naked in front of me. Or naked. I'd never say no to that.'

A laugh left me. 'Of course you wouldn't.'

His face went serious.

'Sky, I'd never do anything you didn't want. If you never want to repeat last night, I'll understand. But also, if you do ever want more with me, then I'll be all over it with bells on.'

I chuckled.

Ollie reached his hand out and cupped my face. His blue eyes seared into mine.

'I want to be in your life, in any way you'll have me.'

Tears rushed to my eyes, but I blinked them away. Something about the moment seemed serious. Real. And if it was real, then my response mattered more than it ever had.

'I know.' I leaned forward and placed a soft kiss on his lips.

'And I don't want you to think I don't want you in my life, either. I'm just ...'

'Confused?'

'Sort of, yeah. I loved you, back before I knew the truth about everything, and it's hard for me to forget the betrayal, even if I have forgiven you for everything.'

'You've truly forgiven me. You mean it?'

'I've got no reason to lie to you,' I said. 'I forgave you a while ago. Truly.'

The blinding smile Ollie gave me in return made the vulnerability of telling the truth worth it. Because sure, I would never forget what he did to me, or the lies he told, but I also could forgive them. Since all those things happened, worse things had taken their place in my mind.

Ollie's betrayal was no longer the bigger fish.

I slipped out of bed and went to the bathroom to go to the toilet and brush my teeth. By the time I returned, Ollie sat upright in the bed, his phone in his hand as he scrolled mindlessly.

'There's an announcement on *The Hive*.' His eyes remained on his phone. 'Seems Orlando's decided as a Hawthorn legacy he's an automatic member of *The Sect*.'

'Seems like a bit of a reach, but go off.'

I made my way back to the bed and got under the covers once more, propping my back up against the headboard before resting my head against Ollie's shoulder.

'If he's going to be a member, then I won't be. I'll speak to the others, but if he wants some stupid fucking legacy, then he can have it. I want no part in it.'

'Are you sure?' I asked, needing to play devil's advocate even though I didn't give a shit. If you asked me, both *The Set* and *The Sect* could fuck right off.

'Yeah. It's a stupid tradition started no doubt about it by a grade-A arsehole.' Ollie put his phone down. 'You've helped me see the bullshit for what it really is.'

'Glad I could help.' My lips went to his shoulder without thinking. His warm and soft bare skin under my mouth had me wanting to continue trailing kisses down …

'You okay there?' He teased

'I'm good.' I sat back again, pretending some kind of lust demon hadn't taken over my senses. 'And very proud of you.'

'I could get used to you being proud of me if it means you touch me like that.'

LATER IN THE DAY, I found myself in Ollie's room with Griff and Ollie, and the three of us were discussing what we were all gonna do next.

The two of them were talking while I assessed them both, wondering when this had become my new normal. A family of sorts—one I'd found—making every day a little easier to exist in.

I wished Leo and Clover were with us, but it also made sense in a way they weren't. I had no idea how to proceed with Leo in the future, and Clover and Griff had their own stuff to sort out. As long as Clo got better and returned to school, I'd be happy.

' … then maybe we can find out what this bloody *Sanctum* wants with us and Leo.' Griff rubbed his hand through his auburn hair, pacing in front of the sofa where Ollie lounged. 'They've turned him against us, and there's no way there isn't a valid reason.'

'I agree,' Ollie said.

'Well, he told me they threatened all our lives,' I piped up, not wanting them to hate their cousin or doubt his loyalty. 'Surely a valid enough reason?'

'But he didn't know you.' Ollie leaned forward, his elbows going to his knees, deep in thought. 'And we were all pretty sure he hated you as much as we did back then.'

I shrugged. 'Maybe. He said he cared about Clo at first and I became more important later on.'

'Either way,' Griff said, 'I can understand it. I'd do the same if you or Clo were at risk. It's the reason I don't want to beat the dickhead for his actions.'

Ollie nodded. 'We've all made crappy choices over the last year.'

'Some more than others.' I laughed. It still felt odd to laugh all the pain and terror off, but I'd got to a point where I couldn't dwell on it any longer. 'But it's what we all choose to do now that matters.'

'And what do you think we should choose to do, Clouds?'

I'd been thinking about it and the best way to get closer to everything flashed in my mind like an obvious solution—one I hadn't wanted to touch but knew I had to.

I took a deep breath. My next sentence would go down as well as ... okay, I got nothing. It wouldn't go down well, basically.

'I think I need to get closer to Orlando,' I said.

'You'll do no such thing!' Ollie shouted.

'But it makes sense!' I shouted back. 'And you know I'm right. You don't want me hurt, and yes, I'm not thrilled either, BUT if it means we can get to the bottom of this crap before somebody else dies, then that's what needs to happen.'

'What are you saying?' Griff stopped his pacing.

'I'm saying I want to get a confession from him. Make sure he gets locked up forever. He's out on bail for shooting you, right? But we need to pile more charges on him if we want any of them to stick. He's got money to make this go away.'

'And what makes you think he'd confess to killing somebody to you?'

'He denied killing Olivia when I accused him, but he and I both know he stabbed me—and therefore stabbed and killed Odette. Maybe if I changed my statement with the police and told them I'd remembered the truth when he revealed himself at the gala?'

'They'll wonder why it's taken you so long to come forward. Assume you're doing it for an angle.' Ollie rubbed his jaw. 'But if you want to talk to them, I'll go with you.'

'I'd rather have a confession to take them than my hazy memories.' The boys nodded. 'And I think he'll talk to me, open up to me, if I give him the chance.'

'Ollie.' Griff started pacing again, his nervous energy needing an outlet. 'I think Clouds is right. We should at least give it a go. We can't rule it out.'

'There has to be something else we can do.'

'There probably is, sure.' I walked over to Ollie and sat down next to him, gripping his hand tight in mine. 'But I don't think it'll be anywhere near as effective, and I think we need to talk to Leo and let him know our plan. Maybe he can help us.'

'Send him a text.'

No need to tell me twice. I pulled out my phone and pulled up my conversation thread with Leo and tapped out a quick message.

Is there any way the three of us can meet with you?

Ollie glanced down at my phone, saw my message, then turned my chin to face him.

'While we wait for Leo to pull his head out of his arse, let's think about this, Sky. Really think about this. Do you think it's safe for you to be around my brother?'

'I know you don't want me to say yes, but I don't think he'll hurt me. Especially now he doesn't have to hide who he is from me. I kind of got the impression when I spoke to him he wanted me to get to know him and not the person he's been pretending to be.' And no, Orlando hadn't said those exact words to me or anything, but I'd got the sense he wanted to talk to me about something secretive but had held himself back.

My phone lit up in my hand.

Let's meet in actual private. Tonight. Midnight.

In actual private? What the fuck does that mean?

Ollie, once again eyeing my phone over my shoulder like a nosey bastard, said, 'I know where he means. Looks like you're being let in on one of our many family secrets.'

'I can't wait.'

Ten

AT TEN MINUTES TO MIDNIGHT, the three of us made our way from Ollie's room to the mysterious secret meeting place.

'So where are we heading?' I asked in a hushed whisper.

'The tunnels,' Ollie replied, his hand squeezing mine. 'When we were younger, it was how we referred to them in front of our parents and whoever else who might lurk and listen in on our conversations. "Actual private" became our code. Welcome to the club.'

I smiled, loving being included—like they were inviting me to join something exclusive.

Something the boys had shared between themselves and were now allowing me to be a part of.

'Do you think Leo will tell us anything important?' Griff asked the valid question, something we'd all wondered, I bet.

'I hope so, but I didn't give him any details about what we wanted to talk about.'

We stopped in the hospital wing and the boys ushered us over to a panel in the wall disguising a hidden door.

The panel blended in and looked no different from the

others on either side of it—no wonder I'd passed it multiple times since coming to Hawthorn without thinking of anything suspicious.

There was nobody around us, the corridor empty except for us three, but then again, we were in the hospital wing at midnight, so the quiet, eerie atmosphere made sense.

Bit suspicious the school needed an entire wing for a hospital, right?

'Why does this place have an entire wing for injured people?'

'They used it as a hospital during the war, Clouds. For once, the Hawthorns were useful for something other than lining their own pockets.'

Huh. Made sense.

I nodded, absorbing the information and drinking it in like a true history nerd. It was pretty fucking cool, actually.

Ollie, bored with waiting for me and Griff to stop talking, opened the door a fraction, wide enough for us to fit through. Griff went first, then me second, and I found myself in a dimly lit second hallway.

I voiced my thoughts out loud. 'This is so fucking weird.'

'You get used to it,' Ollie said, joining us in the hall and closing the door gently behind him. In the dimmer light, he looked even more handsome than usual. All dark, tall, and brooding. His face half hidden by shadows. 'We'll meet him just up ahead at the intersection. Now, we've got to be quiet while we're here.'

Ollie walked on, with me and Griff trailing along behind, actively trying to make as little noise as possible. The hall could lead anywhere, but I had faith the guys weren't leading me to my slaughter. There was no way to know whether somebody lurked on the other side of the wall, who could hear us, so walking on tiptoe and speaking in hushed tones couldn't be avoided.

I lived for the spy-movie-meets-secret-academy-novels vibes of it all.

On the outside, I tried to keep a cool head about me and hoped none of my excitement showed on my face.

'Hey,' Leo said from up ahead. 'You made it.'

'We asked to meet you, remember?' Ollie said, with no malice attached. A statement of facts.

'You're late,' Leo replied.

'We're like two minutes late. Calm your tits.' Griff laughed, before giving Leo a fist bump. Seeing a genuine smile on Griff's face aimed in Leo's direction of all people, well, it warmed me from head to toe.

'We don't have long. Orlando will wonder where I am in an hour's time.'

'How does it feel to be his little bitch?' Ollie taunted, a creep of malice reaching his tone now the initial pleasantries were out of the way. Other than at swim practice, the two of them didn't speak to each other much and if they had, I had no idea what they'd spoken about. 'Can't even disappear for longer than an hour before being checked up on.'

'Whatever,' Leo drawled. 'We've got more important things to be talking about and we don't have long. You gonna continue to waste the short time we have with shitty statements?'

'No.' Ollie's surly response meant I had to dampen the twitch in my lip, threatening to turn into a full-blown smile. *You can do it, Skylar.*

Leo nodded. 'Good. Shut your mouth and listen to me.'

Griff and I nodded, too. We all wanted to get the most out

of this conversation. I squeezed Ollie's waist from where I stood slightly behind him to get across my point. *Shut up and listen, Oliver.*

The boy struggled with that, but now wasn't the time for him to be his typical cantankerous self. Nobody had the time for that shit.

Leo rolled his eyes and ran his hand through his hair, the agitation dripping off him in waves—or maybe I noticed it because of how close we'd got not too long ago.

'Where do you want me to start?' Leo asked, looking at me for the first time since we'd arrived.

'What's Orlando's game?' Ollie asked, taking the lead.

'In what sense?' Leo replied, being difficult and awkward because he could.

'Well, he's decided he's a part of *The Sect* for starters,' I said, needing to guide the conversation somewhere. 'Is there an ulterior motive we should know about?'

'I don't know—'

'Plus,' I cut Leo off, 'he still needs you to do things for him, otherwise he wouldn't be watching you like a hawk.'

'To be honest.' Leo shuffled his weight from his left side to his right. 'I think he wants to cause havoc, Stutter.'

I let the words sink into my head and I could understand his point. Orlando had already caused enough havoc since revealing himself and becoming a student, and he didn't plan to stop. But he'd also caused enough havoc while hiding behind Ollie's persona, so what had made him reveal his identity?

Yes, now he could control the school, as himself, but he didn't seem to take the opportunity the way I'd expected him to.

'Okay ...' I took a step out from behind Ollie and moved to

stand beside him instead. 'But that's his personal agenda. What's his part with *The Sanctum?*'

'Isn't it obvious, Stutter? They're still hoping your dad will show up.'

'My dad? Anybody going to explain what he's got to do with their shit?'

'They think if you're in danger, he'll come here after all these years.'

I shook my head, not believing for a second we'd learned their true motive. 'I've been hurt plenty since coming here and he hasn't arrived so far, so it looks like they're tough out of luck.'

'*The Sanctum* doesn't tell me and Orlando everything, or anywhere near as much as I'd like. They're keeping their cards close to their chest.' Leo shrugged.

'So, Orlando's a piece on the chessboard the same as you?' Ollie asked, rubbing his jaw.

'A more important one, but yes,' Leo agreed.

'We can use it to our advantage,' Ollie said, and I hummed in agreement. He had a valid point. Not that I had any idea about what we could do, or how we could use it to our advantage.

'What does Orlando want with me?' I whispered, my gut churning. Orlando wanted me to play into his plot like putty, and I needed to make sure I didn't let that happen.

Ollie moved to stand behind me and rested his chin on my head, wrapping his arms around my waist.

Safe. Comfortable.

'At first, he wanted to hurt you. We all did. So, there's nothing new there. But now I think he wants you. As his girl.'

I coughed, almost choking on my breath, Ollie's squeeze on my hips keeping me grounded.

'He's hoping I'll be his girlfriend?' I said, thinking out loud. 'Do you think he's got so used to emulating his brother's life he wants to steal it?'

Nobody mentioned the fact Ollie and I were no longer together, but Leo shuffled his feet and turned his gaze to Ollie's hands placed on my hips.

The thought had struck me like lightning, and the moment it did, I understood. His endgame! He wanted his brother's life.

Maybe he fully believed Millie's choice took away his true childhood.

He'd said to me, "I've wondered why she gave me up. Did I seem evil from birth? Did I cry, and he didn't?"

Orlando felt wronged, and he thought by taking everything away from his brother, leaving him with nothing, he'd feel better about his lot in life.

I needed to convince him otherwise. He wouldn't feel better about it, and stealing shit from Ollie wouldn't be the solution he hoped it would be. If emptiness filled him now, it still would later down the road if he didn't come to terms with the why. Without forgiving those who had done him dirty, he'd remain in his miserable pit.

'I think so,' Leo said. 'And he won't listen to anybody telling him it won't work out the way he thinks it will.'

'Why would he listen to anybody?' Griff piped up. 'His mum gave him up and never mentioned him again to anybody. Can understand why the dick's sour.'

The four of us went silent. Griff had a fair point.

'I need to talk to him,' I said. 'Maybe I can help.'

Griff and Ollie stayed silent. I'd expected them to talk me out of it a little. Instead, they were learning to accept they wouldn't deter me with their protests.

'I'll set it up and message you.' Leo gave me a faint smile. 'Good luck, Stutter. You'll need it.'

Eleven

IT TOOK Leo a while to arrange for me to meet Orlando. Any time I messaged and asked about the holdup, he fobbed me off with some lame excuse.

Finally, something got sorted and Orlando agreed to meet me the next day and even though I shouldn't want to be alone with him, shouldn't smile at the thought of getting to see him in private, I couldn't help it.

Everything about my life was complicated, and my love life? Well, that was even more fucking complicated.

I'd loved Ollie, and he'd betrayed me.

I'd fallen for Leo, and he betrayed me too …

Orlando had betrayed me too by lying about everything, and yes, I was aware how fucked up it all was, because not only had he assaulted me, but he also sure as hell put a knife into my stomach. Who knew what else he'd done in his pursuit of stealing his brother's life?

'Are you sure about this, Clouds?' Griff's gentle and kind face held no judgement. 'I can come along if you'd like, as moral support.'

'I don't think he'll talk to me with you there.' I gave him a half smile. 'And I promise you, no matter what he tells me, I'll pass it along to you straight after.'

'I know you're right.' His fingers played mindlessly with his pen. 'It sucks we have to do all this on his terms, you know? I get he's had a hard life, but fuck, Clouds, haven't we all?'

I nodded; my tongue weighed down in my mouth. We all had things happen we'd rather forget. Griff's parents had died when he was young. Ollie's mum had ended her own life. Clover, well, I didn't know what happened to her, but the way she and Leo acted around one another, something had definitely taken place to scar them both.

'He feels like he lost out on family. On a life. No matter how much we understand, and have similar skeletons in our closets, he will still see himself as the victim. He will never see it any other way.'

'What makes you so certain?'

'I don't know.' My mind swam with the words Orlando had already spoken to me on the subject. 'I know him somehow. Understand his thinking.'

'If you say so.' Griff stopped playing with his pen and glimpsed up at the board, some ethical problem plastered on it. 'Is it weird I hate the bastard, but also want to forgive him and see if we can sort it out? He resembles Ollie so much it's a mindfuck.'

'And he's your family, too,' I pointed out. 'It makes sense you want to help him, the way you've helped me.'

'I've not really done much for you, Clouds.' He wrote whatever we needed to know down, thank fuck, because I hadn't paid attention to any words leaving our teacher's mouth. 'I wish I could do more. Give you your own money. Help pay your way through university. Make it so you don't have to rely on anybody ever again.'

'I don't expect you to do that.' I batted his shoulder with the palm of my hand, my heart happy to hear his love for me. 'And besides, I'm happy with making my way in this world by myself. Not like I even know my dad. Would seem wrong to use his name and status to get ahead.'

'I suppose.' Griff didn't sound sure. 'Just sucks how the uncle I remember doesn't match up with the one who's screwed you over.'

'I forget you remember my dad, even a little.'

Even though I'd come to terms with the fact Griff and I were cousins, it still didn't compute he knew somebody I shared blood and DNA with better than I did.

'My memory is a little fuzzy.' He winced. 'And a lot of the memories I have of him include my parents, so they're from a long time ago.'

'Anything stick out in your mind?' I asked, starved for even the slightest mention of something to show me my dad wasn't a complete waste of space.

A smile came to Griff's face. 'Uncle Jacob helped me when I got stung by a bee one time. I was outside in the garden alone, playing on the red slide set I had out there, and I got stung on my arm by a very large, super angry bee.' He laughed, lost in the past. 'I was terrified, and it hurt so bad, and I screamed, unable to see anybody who could help me. But then Uncle Jacob arrived in a flash. He helped me down from the slide and rushed me into the house, put cream on it, and made me laugh so I'd forget the stinging pain.'

I smiled at his cute story. But it hurt me as much as it warmed me. Not that I'd had a red slide in my garden, or a bee sting as a kid, but it still bothered me knowing I would never have those memories with my dad the way Griff had.

'Sounds like he cared about you,' I said, trying to blink away my depressing thoughts.

'He'd care about you too if he was here.'

'We don't know for definite, Griff.' It didn't help to think about it. Not if I wanted to stay sane.

'How do we know he knows about you?' Griff nudged my ribs. 'He might not even know you exist!'

'You think Cora kept her gigantic trap shut about my existence?' I laughed at the thought. My mum would've run her mouth the moment she found out about me. No way would she have ignored the potential payout me having a rich father would bring her. 'That woman can't even keep her mouth shut about the fact she thinks both Leo and Ollie are attractive. Plus, *The Sanctum* assumes he knows about me, otherwise their plan wouldn't be to hurt me to get to him.'

'Cora does like the sound of her own voice,' Griff agreed. 'But without asking her, we don't know.'

'I'll add it to my list of things I need to find out about.' A list growing longer by the day.

'We'll get to the bottom of all this, Clouds. I promise you.'

I MET Orlando at the time he'd chosen, in the spot he'd picked, and found him already there, pacing, waiting for me.

He stopped when he saw me walking towards him, and his eyebrows relaxed.

'You came.'

'Of course I came.' I shrugged, confused by his surprise. 'I wanted this arranged.'

'I thought it might be a trick.' He came to stand in front of me. 'When Leo told me you wanted to meet me, I thought maybe my bigheaded brother would come instead.'

'Well, it isn't a trick.' I swung my arms around. 'Here I am.'

'Where did you want to go?' he asked, reaching out his hand for mine. 'To the library?'

I placed my hand in his. 'No. I thought we could go back to my room? Nobody will overhear us there.'

'Your room?' He faltered, missing a step, but correcting it before I could comment. 'I've never been in your room.'

'There's a first time for everything.' I walked away from him and he followed, our hands still locked together. 'If we stay out in public, then anybody could listen in.'

'And my brother knows about this?' Orlando's tone was sceptical, and rightfully so.

'He does.' I nodded.

Sort of.

'Okay then. Let's go to your room.'

The two of us walked in silence, drawing the eye of every student and teacher we passed on our way. People were staring at me walking down the hallways hand in hand with my ex-boyfriend's biggest enemy—not to forget the guy who stabbed me.

Thankfully, we arrived at my door sharpish.

'I'm surprised Ollie or Griff aren't standing outside acting as your bodyguards.'

'I'm my own person,' I said in a tone more sullen than I'd have liked. His words had hit a nerve. 'I don't need a bodyguard.'

'But they hover around you, anyway.'

'Because they care about me.'

'I care about you.'

'It's not the same.' I opened my door, unable to look at him.

He may believe he cares about me, but he doesn't. Not really. 'Welcome to my humble abode.'

'It's about the same size as mine.' He laughed, entering the room behind me and closing the door.

He'd handed me the perfect opportunity to ask something I'd been thinking about ever since he revealed himself.

'I've been wondering, actually ... Where do you live? Where's your room?'

He laughed, bitter. 'In the house on the grounds with my mum.' He spat the word. 'Hidden and locked away in the attic like a proper British ghost.'

'Ah, yes. Rich British families are very adept at hiding their secrets away in a place rarely seen by society.'

Orlando grunted and took a step closer to the bed before pausing. 'Er, do you mind if I sit on the edge of the bed?'

I blinked, surprised he'd asked, and nodded my head.

He sat down and continued, 'My mum always told me she'd announce my existence one day, but that she had to wait for the right time, and at seven, I believed her. But then more and more time passed, and I remained hidden away, unable to socialise or make friends. Unable to create a bond with my brother and cousins.'

'Sounds shit. I'm sorry.'

'Nothing for you to be sorry about.' He shrugged. 'Not like you told the witch Hawthorn to lock me away with the bats.'

'There were bats up there with you?'

Orlando's grim nod told me all I needed. 'The entire room reeked of misery. When I turned fourteen, Mum announced I was going to join *The Sanctum*.'

'Rather young, isn't it?' I went and sat on the edge of Clover's bed so I could look across at him. Catch every expression on his face. Analyse every movement. Every tick.

'They made an exception for me and thank fuck they did. They were the people who knew about me, and it was nice to be included and be a part of something bigger. I'm sure you can understand? Being an only child and friendless before coming here and all.'

'Nice to know you've worked on your tact,' I teased. Orlando grimaced, and I couldn't help but laugh at him. 'I'm joking with you.' I crossed my legs underneath my body and got comfortable. 'And you're right, I can understand that. Before I came to Hawthorn and made friends with Griff and Clo, I'd been an outsider back at my old school—at least in my perception—and it seemed to me like I didn't belong. And now I've got a proper family. One who has my back and supports me through everything.'

'Nice for some.'

'You could have one, too,' I pointed out, not accepting even one ounce of his surliness. If the boy wanted to behave like a child, then so be it, but coddling him wouldn't solve anything. 'You know, if you hadn't chosen a life of crime and murder.'

'I didn't choose it. It chose me. Literally. When *The Sanctum* decides you're one of them, there's not much you can do. You either join up or someone you love dies.'

'What if you don't have anybody you love?'

'Everybody loves something or someone, Little One.'

Twelve

'I DIDN'T LEARN MUCH,' I said, finishing my story.

My words were the only sound in the quiet hospital room alongside Clover's soft snoring.

I studied my best friend and sighed. When I'd arrived, she was bright-eyed and ready to hear about everything she'd missed out on, but after an hour, her eyelids fluttered shut and I didn't want to wake her.

Anytime Griff came to visit, she pretended to be asleep, and I wouldn't let that shit fly much longer. It was getting pretty ridiculous. If she didn't want to be with Griff, then she needed to have an honest conversation with him and tell the truth. Let the chips fall where they may.

The doctor had said Clo could return to school in two weeks' time and we were all more than ready to have her back. Visiting her in the hospital couldn't compete with having her beside me in our tiny box of a room all the time.

Clo's sheets rustled, and her eyes opened. 'Sky?'

'I'm still here,' I replied.

'Sorry I fell asleep.' She brushed the tiny glob of spit from her bottom lip. 'I've been finding it so hard to stay awake with the medication they keep plying me with.'

She'd given me the perfect opening.

'Ah … So, is that why Griff keeps reporting you as asleep every time he returns?'

The blush travelled from her forehead down to her chin.

'Got anything to say?' I shuffled my chair closer to the side of her bed. 'Because I'm struggling to keep a straight face whenever he asks me if you've been awake when I've visited.'

'It's complicated.'

'Well, make it less complicated.' I snapped. 'Because if you don't want to be with him, then you need to tell him. He'll be upset, sure, but isn't stringing him along so much worse?'

'I don't know if I want to dump him.'

'Thought you hadn't put a label on things?'

She made a throwaway gesture with her hand. 'We haven't. I don't know how I feel, okay? Not like anything around here has been easy for any of us the last couple of years.'

'Talking about the last couple of years …' I trailed off, unsure how to breach the subject of Clo's history at Hawthorn. Orlando had told me of her attending the school before, but it hadn't come up in conversation with the boys yet, and I guess a large part of me was putting it off, because if true, it was yet another lie they'd all kept from me.

'Yes?'

'Orlando mentioned something interesting a couple of weeks back.'

'He did?' Clover pushed herself higher, rearranging her pillows. 'What?'

'He told me you were a student at Hawthorn, and they used the scholarship to bring you back.' I watched to see if her expression changed. 'Anything you want to tell me?'

She swallowed hard. 'Sky, I promise I've wanted to tell you for the longest time, but I haven't known how to.'

That didn't sound good, but I bit my tongue from retorting too quickly.

'Yeah, I started Hawthorn in year seven and left before the end of year nine. The Hawthorns covered my costs here for those years, but not as a scholarship or anything. My parents worked for the Hawthorns and our family lived in the house at the back of their estate since I was like three or something stupid. I can't remember a time before the Hawthorns.' Clo's hands rinsed together in her lap, her gaze studying the movement, unable to make eye contact. 'But when we were in year nine, everything changed.'

She went silent, lost in the past.

After a moment, I shattered the silence. 'What happened?'

'Things went missing around the estate. Small things at first, you know, like the odd vase here and the odd plate there. But then bigger pieces disappeared overnight. And Edward or Lottie weren't the ones getting rid of these items. Some of them were family heirlooms and had been in the home for generations.

'After three months of this happening, Edward accused my parents of stealing the items from them to sell and turn a profit. And from there, everything turned sour real fucking fast.'

The story surprised me. Yes, I'd expected something of the sort, but the way Edward and Charlotte treated Clo at school events told me they didn't hold a grudge towards her.

'Edward and Lottie stopped paying for your schooling?'

Clo shook her head. 'I turned them down.'

A conversation I'd overheard between Clo and Griff floated into my mind.

"Bit rich, babe, when you stick by your parents."

'I remember Griff saying you sided with your parents,' I said, wanting the conversation to continue flowing. 'Is that what made you leave Hawthorn?'

Clo gulped some water from the cup on her bedside table. It seemed silly to point out it had been sitting there since before I'd arrived. 'Yeah, among other things. I suppose you've guessed the history between me and Leo?'

I fake gasped. 'You and Leo have a history?'

'Oh, shut up!' Clo leaned over and smacked the part of my body she could reach. 'Okay, so maybe I've been nowhere near as subtle as I thought.'

'Neither of you is subtle around the other.'

That got a deep laugh out of Clo. 'No, I suppose you're right. I can't explain it, Sky. Leo Hawthorn brings out the worst in me. It's like I see him, and hear him, and want to stab the bastard in the eye.'

I laughed, ignoring the twinge in my stomach. With Leo, I struggled to analyse anything. Everything seemed too fresh to go over.

'Anyway, Leo and I fractured big time once I took my parents' side and moved with them out of the area.'

'What made you return when the scholarship letter arrived?'

She fidgeted in her bed. 'Truth?'

I nodded.

'I missed them all. I thought everything would be okay and when I returned, the four of us would pick up the way we had been before. We both know that's not what happened.

'And then when you joined, I knew they planned to make your life hell the way they had mine. I didn't tell you the truth, because yes, I felt embarrassed. And it really was nice to have one person not know what went down. But also, I wanted you to listen to my fears about their actions without thinking I had an ulterior motive, all because I hated them for what they did to me.'

'I get it, I do.' I shook my head, letting the information settle in my membrane. 'Even if I wish you'd told me it all a lot sooner.'

'Can you forgive me?'

'Don't ask such a stupid question.' I flicked her hand. 'You're my best friend. And sure, I'm pissed at you hiding things, but you almost dying sort of puts it all into perspective for me, ya know?'

'Well, now you know how it feels!' Clo laughed. 'Between you being stabbed and drowned and drugged, I've barely been able to keep myself sane.'

'I apologise if someone's attempted murders have inconvenienced you.'

'You mean Orlando's attempted murders, right?'

'We don't have confirmation,' I said, tasting the lie as it left my lips. Did I need confirmation when my own memories told me the truth?

'Okay, Skylar. Live in denial alongside me a little longer.'

'How was she?' Griff asked the moment my foot left the car and touched the grounds of Hawthorn Academy.

'Fine,' I said, brushing down my skirt. 'They reckon she'll be back within the month.'

'Good.' He nodded, then stepped forward to place his arm in mine. 'It's not right being here without her.'

'No, it isn't.' I agreed. 'She told me about her parents.'

'She did?'

'Yeah. Orlando mentioned she was a student here back in the day and she said something that gave me the perfect opportunity to ask her about it.'

'I'm glad she told you. It sucked keeping it to myself.'

'I get you were honouring her wishes, but it makes me sad, ya know? I get it wasn't your place to say anything, the same way it wasn't hers to tell me about your parents.'

'Right.'

The two of us made our way into the quiet main building. I'd come back during dinner time so barely anybody floated about, all of them occupied with eating or something else mundane.

'Where's Ollie?' I asked.

'In the dining room. I said we'd meet him there the moment you got back.'

'Wonderful! I'm starved. The hospital may cost a few bob, but the options for visitors aren't stellar.'

The two of us found Ollie sitting at our usual table alone, his face dark, his gaze locked on Orlando sitting at a table with *The Set*. Orlando was in the middle of telling a story the girls found hilarious if their laughter and red faces were any indication. Ophelia threw her head back, her mouth so wide it resembled a black hole.

'How dare he sit over there like none of this is fucked up?' Ollie grumbled the moment we took our seats beside him. No greeting needed. There were already plates for me and Griff— Ollie must have ordered for us—and at the sight of the pizza, my mouth watered.

'I think he's aware it's fucked up, mate,' Griff said around a large bite of his steak. 'Has to act like it doesn't bother him, though, right?'

'What do you mean?' I asked. Neither me nor Ollie acknowledged the moment he placed his hand on my thigh under the table.

'Well, he has to act like none of this has bothered him. It wouldn't look good for him to appear from the shadows and crumble. It would show up his mum, *The Sanctum*, among others. But honestly, it wouldn't surprise me if he thought this was even more fucked up than you do, Ollie.'

'What's that supposed to mean?' Ollie snapped, turning his pissed off face in Griff's direction. It irked him—rightfully so—whenever anybody said something even remotely positive about his twin. 'The guy's a dick, and a murderer, Griff. He shouldn't be here.'

'Never said he should. Just saying I'm sure he knows how fucked up this all is, that's all.' Griff shrugged and went back to cutting up his dinner.

'And nobody has proved he murdered anybody,' I whispered. 'All we have are my memories and I didn't see him stab Odette or anything.'

'No,' Ollie agreed. 'But he did stab you, so if he can do that, then stabbing Odette isn't outside of his wheelhouse, is it?'

'Why don't you ask him?'

'I don't want to talk to the prick. Ever.'

'He's your twin. You don't have to like it, but you have to accept it.' Reasoning with him, or at least attempting to. 'Aren't you even a little intrigued?'

Ollie's hand on my thigh tightened, squeezing me to the point of pain.

'No,' he bit out. 'I don't want to have anything to do with him until I speak to my dad.'

'Understandable, mate,' Griff said, and I nodded in agreement.

'Is he still coming this weekend?' I asked, trying to visualise the calendar in my head and failing miserably. Who even knew the fucking day of the week anymore? Not me.

'Clouds, it is the weekend.' Griff reached over and put his hand on my forehead.

'Right.' I'd have hit my head with the palm of my hand if it didn't mean hitting Griff. 'Duh! Silly me.'

'He's said we can discuss it all tomorrow. Winifred and Orlando are going off grounds for the day and we'll have the house all to ourselves.'

'Want me to be there for support?' I didn't particularly want to be there, but if Ollie said yes, then I would.

'Thanks, Sky.' The palm on my leg loosened. 'But this is something I need to do alone.'

Thirteen

OLLIE

'I'LL BE LEAVING AGAIN TOMORROW.' Dad shuffled in his dark green wing back armchair. 'I can't take any more time off from the company, and I'm not gaining much by staying here.'

I nodded in understanding, even if I didn't understand a bit.

Yes, I could grasp the fact my dad needed to get back to work. Couldn't stop making the Brandon millions even after learning you've had a son you didn't know shit about for eighteen years.

But that was Henry Brandon for you. The man didn't care about much aside from himself.

The table between us had empty glasses and a bottle of whiskey on, yet neither of us had reached to touch them. The conversation we were about to embark on needed to be done completely sober.

'And I guess I need to address the elephant in the room,' Dad continued, examining the lit fireplace, the flames dancing on his face. 'It would seem your mother hid something important from us both.'

Fuck having this conversation sober.

The decanter was in my hand; the stopper pulled out, and the whiskey poured into the glasses within seconds. I handed one to my dad, who took it with a nod of thanks, then sat back and took a large sip of mine.

The liquid burned on its way down my throat.

'So, you didn't know?'

'No,' Dad whispered. 'I didn't. I thought he died.'

'How?'

No matter how many times I tried to wrap my head around it, I couldn't come to a place where it made sense my dad hadn't known.

If I didn't look exactly like Orlando, I'd question whether we were related, or whether it was all a ploy of Winifred's so she could gain the upper hand and take control of the Hawthorn and Brandon fortunes.

She wanted nothing more than all the money under her command. We all knew it.

But Orlando had my face; had my DNA running through his veins and I couldn't deny it, no matter how much we all may have wanted to.

Dad shook his head. 'I'd known your mum was pregnant with twins, but I wasn't in the delivery room when you came along. I'd been working up north and came as soon as I heard she'd gone into labour.'

He took a long draw of his whiskey, his eyes lost in the past.

'By the time I arrived, you were here. Blue-eyed and strong-jawed. You were everything we'd dreamed of. Then I asked after your brother ...' He rubbed his stubbled jaw. 'They told me he didn't make it because of a complication.'

'And you never thought to tell me?' Everything in my mind

jumbled together. Scrambled and shitty. If my dad was telling the truth—and I couldn't see a good enough reason for him to lie—then why hadn't anybody told me I had a twin, even one who hadn't survived?

'Your mum and I decided not to. We thought it for the best, Oliver.' Tears welled in his eyes. 'We didn't want you to live with the burden of the truth.'

'Learning I'm a twin wouldn't have been a burden.'

'No, you're right.' Dad nodded. 'But learning you were the reason your twin didn't live would have been.'

'She told you I killed him?' I blinked, this new reality of mine blurring before me. 'How?'

'He became tangled in your umbilical cord.' Dad laughed, the sound sour. 'Well, we both know it for the lie it is now, but at the time, keeping you in the dark benefitted us.'

I stayed silent, letting his words enter my bloodstream and sit there. My mum lied to us both. She knew the whole time Orlando was alive and breathing and living with her sister, of all people. The sister she hated. The sister she'd hated her whole life.

'Have you spoken to him?'

'Who? Orlando?' I shook my head. 'I'd rather not, thanks.'

'Your aunt won't let me see him.' The tears in Dad's eyes became thicker and fuck me. I couldn't handle it if the man started crying. I'd probably break out into a run and leave the house pronto. 'Says he doesn't want to talk to me. That I should respect his wishes.'

At a loss, I shrugged.

Dad sensed I didn't want to talk about Orlando anymore. Or maybe he had no words left, either.

'Oliver, there's something I need to tell you and I know it'll be hard for you to hear. But the last year, before your mum died

...' He trailed off, his eyes still fixed on the glow from the flames. 'The last year was hell.'

He turned his gaze to me, his eyes boring into mine, and I could see the red veins in his eyes. Could see how exhausted and messed up the big revelation had made him.

An anger burned in them, too.

'Hell?' I sputtered, my memory not lining up with the use of that word. 'For Mum, you mean.'

'Yes.' Dad's tone sent a chill up my spine. 'Your mother lived in a state of hell, Oliver. The world always seemed too much for her. There were times your mother could be vindictive, mean, and downright nasty.'

I couldn't let him speak badly about her. Not without butting in. 'That's not—'

'Oliver.' He cut me off. 'You were too young to see the truth of the situation. We both tried to keep the other side of her from you.'

I scoffed. Deep down, I'd known he would discredit my mother's memory. He'd always found any opportunity he could to do so ever since I could remember.

'I was ten!' I slammed the now-empty glass down. 'Ten isn't too young to see how you acted. How you treated her.'

'You're remembering the past wearing rose-coloured glasses, Oliver,' Dad growled, his anger rising to match mine. 'Your mother was unwell. She searched for every escape she could find. Wanted a different life for herself but knew it to be impossible.'

'It was impossible because you wouldn't set her free!'

Dad slammed his empty tumbler down, matching my ire. 'I did no such thing. All I ever did was try to save her from herself. Both when we were younger, right until her passing.'

'Even if any of that bullshit's true, the last year of her life being hell doesn't explain why she'd hide a second son from you or why she'd let Winifred raise him.'

'I wish I knew the answer. But your mum ... she did what she wanted. No matter who got hurt in the crossfire.'

'What does that even mean?' I shouted, so close to jumping out of my chair and punching my father square in the jaw.

'As you know, when you were five, your aunt Eliza died.'

I nodded, biting my tongue. The taste of copper filled my mouth, and I laughed darkly, keeping my mouth closed so the blood wouldn't leak down my chin.

'Well, Aunt Eliza and Uncle Damien didn't die unprovoked.'

I opened my blood-filled mouth to ask a question, but another shout got there before I could.

'What do you mean?' Griff roared from the doorway. Leo close on his heels.

Dad grimaced at Griff's appearance and shuffled in his chair, straightening up.

The two of them came to stand beside the fireplace. 'Tell me. What do you mean?' Griff repeated.

'I can't tell you. Nothing concrete, anyway.' Dad shook his head, troubled. 'But what I can tell you is your mother didn't handle it well at all, Oliver. She went off with Jacob Cooper and started an affair. Disregarded her commitments to you. To me.'

Leo and Griff took the remaining empty seats in silence.

'Her health declined more each year, and throughout every battle she fought, I stayed by her side. Ready to pick up the pieces. Yet every time she ran back to him.'

He took a deep breath.

'Son. You have no idea what I have done for you. What I continue to do for you.'

I stayed silent, still biting my tongue, but for a different reason. If I opened my mouth, I would spit out all the hatred sitting on my heart—but not hatred aimed at my dad. Oh, no. Hatred aimed at Jacob fucking Cooper.

'Your precious Millie,' Dad said, his face contorted as he stood from his chair, 'was a bitch. She did everything in her power to get out of this life. To get out of being here for you, and for me. She'd never wanted to marry me, but I thought we'd make each other happy, arranged marriage or not. I've never been more wrong in my life.'

Maybe I spoke too soon. Seemed I could still find a lot of hatred for my dad, too.

My entire childhood, I'd seen how Henry treated Millie. Had seen how he railroaded her. Had made her feel small, as if she weren't any better than shit on his shoe. No wonder she'd run into Jacob Cooper's arms.

I'd never blamed her for seeking the attention she deserved from elsewhere.

No.

I blamed Jacob Cooper.

I blamed him for leaving her and causing her to see no other way but to do what she did.

His actions had led us all here. And, yes, I may slowly be coming to terms with the fact he was the father of the girl I love, but I couldn't deny that bringing Skylar into this world was the one good thing the fucker had done in his rotten life.

I could no longer bite my tongue—both metaphorically and physically.

'You made her miserable,' I spat, looking up at my father. 'You caused her to seek out Jacob Cooper, and you're the reason she's dead. You're the reason she can't be here right now and defend her actions.'

'Now, look here, son,' Dad said, and I leapt out of my chair so the two of us were standing chest to chest.

Leo jumped up, too, ready to step in if anything turned physical. I'd deal with that prick later.

'You look here,' I said, my voice raised louder so my dad couldn't interrupt me. 'There's a reason she never told you about Orlando. There's a reason she chose to leave this earth rather than spend another day with you. I hope you're happy with yourself.'

I took one last glance at my dad and left the room. It wasn't safe for me to be around any of them any longer. Listening to my father's vile lies had pushed me to the edge.

Millie may have been a lot of things, sure, but a bitch? No, I couldn't accept that bullshit, and I planned to do everything in my power to prove it.

I needed to find Sky. Seek solace in the one person at this school who had never lied to me.

She would understand my need to know more about Mum's past, and she'd help me find it. The girl loved a challenge, and learning all she could about Hawthorn shit was already high on her to-do list.

'Ollie, wait up!'

A growl left my throat unbidden at my cousin's shout.

I'd wait all right.

I waited until Leo got close enough, pulled my hand into a fist, and then I landed a punch dead centre of his face.

Fourteen

VALENTINE'S DAY.

How the fuck were we already living through another Valentine's Day?

From the moment I woke up, everything seemed different to last year, for many reasons, and I didn't know how to spend my day. I hoped the couples of the school didn't walk around shoving their love in everybody's faces. Nobody liked a PDA: public display of affection.

Why did the day feel so different?

For starters, I didn't wake up Clover and get punched in the face. A nicer start, but I'd have preferred a bloody nose if it meant she'd woken up in the bed parallel to mine.

Secondly, I didn't have a boyfriend this year—and yes, I classed Ollie as an ex-boyfriend. It may not have been real for him, but it was for me, which mattered most. Full stop. End of story.

And lastly, a mere month and a half ago, I'd envisioned this day with a different guy by my side.

A guy who still did nothing more than glance at me across campus and frown when he caught me glimpsing back.

'Little One.'

The hairs on my arms stood on end at the smooth, sultry tone of Orlando. He sounded the same as his brother, and every single time, it disconcerted me.

'Orlando,' I replied, turning on the spot to face him. 'What do I owe the pleasure?'

'No need to be like that. I thought after our little talk in your room, you'd be more open to being seen with me.'

'I have no issue being seen with you. Most people will assume you're Ollie, the way they always have.'

'Low blow, Little One, but factual, so I'll let you off.'

I sighed, weary in my bones. 'What do you want? Your brother's gonna show up in a moment and I can't be arsed to watch you clones fight one another.'

'Why do you assume we'd fight?'

'Because I know your brother. He's got a lot of pent-up anger towards you, towards the world, and he'd love an outlet for it. Don't walk into his fists for no reason.'

'I have no intention of walking into Oliver's fists. Besides, Leo's already done that, and I don't want a pretty shiner like he's got. It'd ruin this gorgeous face.' Orlando stopped moving from side to side and waved his hand in front of his—admittedly gorgeous—face. It didn't help that he had the same face as Oliver, and at a glance, they blurred into one person.

Leo had run into Ollie's fists? News to me.

When I talked to Ollie last night after his talk with his dad, he hadn't mentioned Leo being there, or really much of what they all said. He told me he'd fill me in once he wrapped his head around it and I didn't want to push him before he was ready, so I'd left it.

Orlando's talking made my mind centre back into the here and now. 'I hoped maybe we could meet later.'

'Where?'

He ignored my question. 'I've got a gift I want to give you.'

'A gift?'

'It is Valentine's Day, Little One. Or have you forgotten?'

'How could I forget?' I asked, gesturing towards the younger years over by the treeline passing around large red heart cards to one another. 'I don't understand why you'd give me a gift.'

'It's the first time I can give you one without hiding behind somebody else. I'm gonna jump on the chance.'

'And what makes you think I want a gift from you?'

'Trust me, Little One. You'll want this one.'

'You can't meet him alone, Sky.'

I rolled my eyes to the heavens and bit down the angry retort sitting on my tongue.

'Oliver, you're a little overbearing, did you know?'

'I'd rather you think I'm overbearing than have you wind up dead on the pool house steps.'

'Orlando won't kill me if I meet up with him. Is there any reason you don't want me to go aside from the fact you think I'm weak and can't fight for myself?'

'Now you're putting words into my mouth.' Ollie shook his head. 'If you must know, I hoped we could grab dinner together tonight.'

A lot of hoping coming my way from the Brandon twins today.

'We always grab dinner together.'

He let out an exasperated sigh. 'I mean *together* together.'

'Oliver Brandon,' I said, a smile playing on my lips. 'Is this your neanderthal way of asking me out on a date?'

'Maybe.' It came out mumbled.

I waited, stifling the laugh I purposefully held in. It was yet another one of those instances where Ollie looked cute, all out of sorts. He needed to stop doing that, otherwise I might get some stupid idea in my head and think he likes me for real.

He took a deep breath. 'Skylar, would you like to have dinner tonight? As a date.'

The laugh I'd held back came out. 'Well ...'

Ollie shifted his weight and raised an eyebrow in my direction. 'Are you going to make a man beg, Sky?'

'If I thought you'd actually beg then, yeah, I'd totally be game to see that.' I laughed. Ollie wouldn't beg me for anything, even if hell froze over.

But to my surprise, and shock, and also kind of embarrassment, Ollie got down in front of me on his knees, his hands gripped together in front of his chest.

'Skylar Crescent. Please, I beg of you, have dinner with me tonight, as a date. I promise I won't fuck it up. Fuck, I won't even complain when you meet Orlando alone afterwards.'

My cheeks burned. Jeez, who knew having somebody beg in front of you in public was so discomforting?

'Get up, you stupid bastard.' I nudged his shoulder with my hand, but he didn't move an inch. 'Ollie, seriously, get up.' He still didn't move, a glint of menace shining in his blue eyes. 'Yes! Yes, I'll have a dinner date with you tonight if you please, please, get up off the grass right this instant.'

The smirk on his face as he stood up filled me with violence. Violence I would never act upon, but he had a face you wanted to hit now and then.

'Trust you to act like an idiot,' I said, breaking the tension. 'I'm sure you're all smug now you got what you wanted.'

'Sky, haven't you figured it out yet?' He placed his hands around my lower arms, the most earnest expression in his eyes when our gazes locked. 'Spending time with you is all I want. Everything else is a bonus.'

'TELL ME THE TRUTH,' Ollie said, grabbing my hand so our arms would swing between us as we walked. 'You're thrilled you said yes.'

I laughed, not wanting to confirm or deny.

I'd spent a lot longer than usual getting myself ready for dinner and let's be honest, I knew what it meant deep down even if I didn't want to analyse it.

Ollie showed up to my room looking absolutely bloody gorgeous in a grey suit and I struggled hard to step out into the hall and close the door behind me, rather than staying put and asking him to join me inside.

What was it about the boy that made me melt?

Like he could make me do anything he wanted, from a mere touch or glimpse or sentence or ... well, anything.

'Did I mention you look amazing?' The words covered me from top to toe in a glow. Compliments were always welcome, but ones from Ollie were the icing on top of the cake.

Get a grip, girl.

'Thank you,' I said. 'I'd be a liar if I said you looked anything but amazing yourself.'

'Sky, I ...' The tone of his voice alarmed me. Okay, maybe not that dramatic, but it settled in my stomach in a way that made me think he may be about to get gushy, or say something to ruin the peace between us.

'If the next thing out of your mouth is gonna be deep, wait until we've got some food in front of us, okay?' At least then I could move food around my plate with my fork and not look at him as I did so.

'Ay, ay, captain.'

'Seriously?' I laughed. 'You're such a dork, Oliver.'

'Coming from the girl who spends most of her days reading or learning about events which took place absolute donkeys ago.'

'Hmm.'

The two of us kept walking, but before we came upon the dining room, Ollie diverted us to the left, away from both the school exit and the dining hall.

'Where are we eating?' Nobody else seemed to be around and I didn't recognise where we headed. 'Where else on campus is there?'

He smiled, the corners of his lips curling up in the way they did when something highly amused him. 'You'll see.'

'Okay ...' I trailed off, letting him guide me in whichever way he chose by our grasped hands. 'Did I tell you Orlando said he had a gift for me?'

Ollie hummed noncommittally.

'Well, do you think I should find out what it is?'

'You should do whatever you think is best,' Ollie said, and his diplomatic act surprised me. Then he opened his mouth and dashed it all away. 'I think you'd be stupid to encourage him further, but what do I know?'

'How to be a dick,' I muttered, but his face didn't change, so who knew if he heard me or not.

Ollie stopped in front of a door I'd never needed to enter before, hidden off to the side. 'Here we are.'

'And here is ...'

'The private dining room, mainly used for visitors to the school or small meetings when parents come.'

He opened the door, a grand gesture of sorts, and waited for me to walk inside first.

At first glance, the room appeared the same as the main dining hall, but a fraction of the size.

A table was set up for the two of us in the centre of the room, but before I headed to my seat, something caught my eye on the wall opposite the entrance.

What the?

I screamed.

My eyes, my brain, unable to comprehend the view.

Because there, dangling from a wooden beam running down from the ceiling like some sick marionette puppet, hung the rotting, decaying corpse of Mr Hawkins.

Fifteen

'GUESS WE DON'T NEED to ask Orlando about the gift anymore,' Ollie said, his tone deadpan.

But me? The shockwaves running through my body prevented me from speaking.

Of course, Ollie could joke at a time like this.

The moment I'd realised the sight before me, I'd turned away. I didn't need the vision of him haunting my dreams more than he already managed to, and I stayed back, not wanting to get a closer look.

One thing that didn't surprise me? The fact Orlando gave me a dead body and believed it to be a reasonable Valentine's day present. What says love more than a rotting corpse of the man who assaulted you not so long ago? Wait … Why did my stomach drop in a nervous yet excited way at the thought?

Fuck, Sky.

Do not go getting a thrill at the fact Orlando took matters into his own hands and delivered the only proper punishment he could.

A waiter entered, saw the body, paled, and turned to walk straight out again.

'Oh no you don't,' Ollie said, stopping the man mid-step.

'What can I do for you, Master Brandon?' the waiter asked, timid as fuck.

'You can call the police for a start. Then I suggest you go get my good-for-nothing aunt and tell her about this mess.' He waved his hand toward Mr Hawkins, encompassing the *mess* he wanted sorted. 'Then you can find us somewhere else to eat where the stench of death isn't lingering over the table.'

'Y-yes, S-sir.'

The waiter rushed off, and I swallowed down a giggle threatening to burst out of me. 'Wow. Nice to know you can reduce others into a stuttering fool.'

'Nice to know you haven't lost your sense of humour,' he said. I took two steps towards him and he reached me in the middle, holding the lower part of my arms in place, grounding me. 'Are you okay?'

I let out a gust of air. 'I'm not sure.'

The steadiness and warmth of his hands on my skin soothed me. Things may be awkward and unsure with Ollie, but with each day, he proved he cared about me.

'That's understandable. Shit, Sky. I hated the man, and wanted to see him dead, so can't imagine how you feel, but this? It's grotesque.'

Grotesque. Twisted. Monstrous. *Disturbed.*

It was all of those and more.

Yet ...

The two of us remained in our bubble, silent, while we waited for the masses to arrive, because of course they would. There were no secrets at Hawthorn—no way to hide what went on behind closed doors, no matter how much you may want to.

Students hovered outside the door, seemingly too afraid to

cross the threshold. The buzz of their whispers, the hushed excitement, all of it created a symphony of sorts.

I leaned in closer to Ollie, placing my lips against his ear. To onlookers, we'd appear to be in a close embrace. 'This doesn't look good for either of us.'

'You don't say?' he joked, but then his face turned serious. 'It looks worse for me. Nobody's gonna think you're capable of murdering a man, let alone having the strength to truss him up like a dead pig in a butcher's window.'

'The police already hate me and think I killed Olivia.' My frustration at the police's stupidity had me shaking my head. Those wankers. Detectives Smith and Saunders would have a bloody field day with this. 'Maybe they'll think I put you up to this or something.'

'You'd have no reason to stage it like this. Me? I arranged the room, the dinner ... God, Sky, everybody saw me on my knees on the grounds earlier today *begging* you to come on this date.' His eyes glazed over, seeing something I couldn't see. 'This must be his game.'

'Who? Orlando?'

Ollie nodded, his dark hair brushing against the side of my face. 'Leo said he wants to take over my life. Steal it. Well, what better way than to have me locked up forever more?'

'We won't let it happen.'

'I'm not sure we're gonna have much say in it.'

With such an ominous statement out there, Ollie turned quiet again. We said nothing more, not even after the police arrived and questioned us both about why we were there and who'd known about it and so on.

We still hadn't said another word to each other when the police asked—albeit in a way evident to all it wasn't a request and more of a demand—Ollie to return to the station with them so they could talk to him further.

Our eyes locked as he followed the detectives out of the room.

His said: *Fuck.*

Mine said: *I think I love you.*

But lucky for me, he couldn't understand eyes.

I PACED my room for hours.

After Ollie followed the police, I'd spoken to Ms Hawthorn, who seemed uninterested in the whole thing.

Of course she did the bitch. She knew the truth of it all. I could see it plain on her face the moment she surveyed the room and saw Orlando's handiwork.

Suppose having a murderous son didn't shock her too much, seeing as he'd already killed before and most likely would kill again.

The thought sobered me.

Ollie's text came at a quarter to twelve.

I'M BACK. SHALL I HEAD TO YOU, OR WOULD YOU PREFER TO COME TO ME?

I didn't even need to think about it.

I'M ON MY WAY.

Within moments, I grabbed my phone, dorm key, and slipped on some shoes.

I made it to his room in record time.

'Hey,' he said when he opened the door. The redness under his eyes and the upright status of his hair told me he'd rubbed his tired eyes and pulled his hand through his hair more times than he could count. I hated to see him so dishevelled.

Ollie and dishevelled were two words I would never expect to see together.

'Hey.' I moved into his room, kicking off my slippers as I did so, before pulling him into the biggest, hardest hug. 'Are you okay?'

'I'm fine.' His arms squeezed me, relaxing once the hug had gone on a little too long to stay platonic. 'Those wankers think I did it.'

'It makes me wonder if the two of them ever solve any crimes or if they bumble around in life hoping for the best.'

Ollie laughed. 'Well, this time around, they have a couple of things to fuel their fire.'

'Like?'

'Like the fact Orlando and I share literal DNA.' He ran his hand through his hair, walking over to sit on the edge of his bed. I, like a well-trained puppy, followed him and did the same. 'And I'm not even being facetious. The one thing setting us apart is our fingerprints.'

'And I assume Orlando would never be stupid enough to leave prints anywhere.'

'Wouldn't surprise me if he'd left hair, or saliva, or something on the body so they could point it at me, too. They said they'll be questioning him later on, but I'm sure Winifred will make it hard for them.'

'He's already on bail, though,' I said, fiddling with the hem of my pyjama top for something to do. 'Surely they'll investigate him more in depth because of it.'

'Money talks, Sky. It always has and it always will.'

Shitting hell, what a depressing thought.

Yet one I couldn't deny.

'So, what do we do about it?'

'Hope the bastard left his prints on the guy. Or that the police see this for what it is.'

'And if neither of those come to pass?'

'Fuck, I don't know. Guess we could always run away.'

I laughed. 'Be serious.'

'I'm trying.' He flopped down onto the bed, pulling me down with him. 'I wonder when this will all end, you know? We've got demons at every exit.'

'Not just when, but also how,' I said. 'I don't see Orlando giving up.'

'Me either.'

'But he is on bail for a serious crime, and as much as I've seen the corrupt way they deal with things here, I'm still a little hopeful. Only a tad, sure, but enough. I came to Hawthorn to get good grades and go to a good university and live a good life and fuck, I'm gonna do those things.'

The words rushed from my lips

Bottled up, now bubbled over.

Ollie turned to his side to face me. 'I believe in you, Skylar.' His fingers grazed the side of my face, his gaze one of awe. 'What I can't believe is that you're here, with me, letting me touch you, be near you.' His breath fluttered my eyelashes. 'You're beautiful, funny, kind, understanding, and all the things I'm not.'

'Not true,' I said, a playful smile on my lips. 'You are pretty funny.'

His chuckle reverberated through the room.

'Thanks,' he said. 'We need to get the gang together, don't we? Make a plan of action.'

'I thought we'd decided I was gonna get closer to Orlando?'

He sat, abrupt. 'You still wanna go through with it?'

'Why wouldn't I?'

'Skylar.' He said my name as if I were a child to be scolded. 'His idea of a gift today has got me in a lot of shit. He killed a man for you, and wants you to know it.'

I shrugged, staring up at Ollie. 'Even more reason to get close to him, no? He's trying to grab my attention, and fucking hell, he's got it.'

'I don't want you to get hurt.'

'And I appreciate you for that.' His warm skin under my fingers made me shiver. 'But we need to be smart about this. Maybe he'll slip up.'

'Maybe,' Ollie agreed. 'Or maybe he'll get bored and murder you, too.'

Sixteen

CLOVER'S RETURN came at the best time.

A couple of weeks had passed since the whole dead body in the dining room thing and no matter how hard I tried to pin him down, Orlando avoided me like the plague. The bastard.

He knew my game; what I wanted.

And he was playing one right back.

Ollie had gone into the police station a second time to answer more questions, but they had nothing and he returned the same day.

Weirdly, life went on.

Lessons took place, food got eaten, and I spent time with all the boys except Leo.

And absolutely nothing built any momentum.

'I am so happy you're back! I don't even think you *know* how much I've missed you.'

'Ditto.' Clo laughed. She'd returned an hour ago and started reorganising her clothes the moment she got into our room. It calmed her, or so she said. I thought she needed something to do with her hands while we spoke—something to do to prevent her from having to face my direction and see my disapproval about her not having ended things with Griff yet.

'I never thought I'd say this, but I'd much rather be here at Hawthorn than at the hospital another minute.'

'Wow, Clover Luck admitting she'd rather be at Hawthorn? I've heard everything now.'

'Oh, shut up. You've stayed there. You know the tedium.'

I nodded, able to sympathise. My time in the hospital after getting stabbed was the worst. Well, aside from getting stabbed. That really sucked.

'I also know I've got a lot to fill you in on, but also somehow nothing to tell.'

I'd texted most of it to her, and we'd face timed too so I didn't have too much to add. The joys of technology, making conversations in person pointless ninety-nine per cent of the time.

Jesus, when did I get so old?

Clo nodded sagely. 'Feel that.'

'It's all fucked, isn't it?' I watched her as she methodically took out all her tops from the top drawer of the chest of drawers, placed them on her bed, and then folded them one by one, before placing them back in the drawer. Quite soothing, actually. The monotony of it.

'Tis ...' She paused in her folding, her tension-filled stiff back facing me. 'Have you heard from Leo?'

'Nope.' I laughed. 'Since we met him in the walls, he's stayed silent, to us at least. He talks to Orlando instead.'

'How are you doing, really?' Clo turned to me reluctantly. 'I know I've been a bit of a cow about him and you and blah blah.' She waved her hand to encapsulate everything, and I understood the unspoken words. 'But I know his betrayal did a number on you.'

Understatement of the century.

'Yeah …' It was my turn to turn away from her. 'I wouldn't say I'm over it or anything, but it's not in the front of my mind.'

'Really?' Pretty sure if I were to glance at her I'd see a cocked head and a raised brow, but out of principle, I kept my gaze averted. So who knew?

'Really.' *Good, it sounded convincing.* 'There's more important shit to face. And yeah, okay, I'd like an actual explanation from him or an apology or *something,* but I can wait. It'll come in time.'

'You think he's gonna say sorry?'

Suppose I needed to stop averting my gaze. I turned toward her, and sure enough, her cocked head and raised brow greeted me.

'I think so, yeah. I know you and him …' I trailed off, not wanting to get into it again. 'But we were real, and it meant something, and even though he made some poor decisions, he's not bad or evil at the heart of it all. More like a messed up rich kid who got dragged into a secret society who threatened to murder all those he loves.'

'So normal every day shit?'

'Around here, yeah.' We laughed, the sound freeing. 'Imagine if we were at a normal school? Life would be so boring.'

'Boring, yet safe.'

'True.'

Clover went back to her folding, and I went back to staring at her back. 'What's our plan?'

'I've been thinking about searching Hawthorn House,' I said. The idea had come to me a week ago, but I'd waited for her to return before putting it into action. I liked having the boys around, but you couldn't beat spending time plotting and scheming with your best friend. 'Wanna join me?'

'Assume the boys will join us?'

I nodded. 'I haven't asked them yet, but Ollie and Griff, yeah. No Leo. He'd tell Orlando which we don't need.'

'I'm in. When you thinking?'

'Not sure yet. Got to wait for Orlando and Winifred to disappear for long enough to do it without their eyes on us the whole time.'

'Do they ever leave?'

I thought about it for a moment. 'Eurgh, maybe I do have to include Leo.'

'Why?'

'Because he'll know when they're off to a *Sanctum* meeting and can give us the heads up.'

A growl came from low in Clo's throat. 'I do hate it when the bastard has a use.'

'It is mighty frustrating, but at this stage, I think it's unavoidable.' Leo always seemed to know everything and if he knew we were searching the house, he may even keep them out longer, so we're not discovered.

Clover's grave nod made me smile. 'Like Leo himself. Every time I think I'm free of him, there he is.'

'I'll message the guys. Are you ready to see Griff?' A thought hit. 'He knows you're back today, right?'

'He does.' She let out a deep sigh. 'I should talk to him, shouldn't I?'

'About?' I asked, but she didn't need to answer. I'd put the question out into the universe to feign ignorance. Or maybe so I didn't have to say something rude like, *you think?*

'About how I'm feeling.'

'And how are you feeling?' I sat up a little straighter, resting my back against the cold wall.

'I still haven't decided whether I want to end it,' Clo said, sitting down on her bed so she could look over at me opposite her. 'But he should know I'm not certain about us. He deserves to.'

'He does,' I agreed. 'Remember, if he responds poorly, to stand your ground. I love Griff like a brother, but he has a tendency to be a little too happy-go-lucky about everything. To live in a certain level of denial.'

'I'll ask to go back to his place with him tonight after we've spoken about Hawthorn House.' The glint in Clover's green eyes showed her resolve. 'Talk to him then and see how it goes.'

'Sounds like a plan,' I said. I messaged the guys in our group chat. 'Knowing them, they'll be here within five minutes.'

Clover laughed. 'They are pretty desperate.'

'Quite endearing though.' I laughed. 'Let's hope they'll be agreeable to the plan without too much coaxing.'

Clover replied in an ominous tone. 'Let's hope we don't find any more secret Hawthorns lurking in the walls.'

' ... he'll keep them occupied, I'm sure of it,' I concluded.

Ollie and Griff were sitting on my bed, and Clo sat on hers. It created a much-needed divide between us all.

My heart almost broke at seeing the relief on Griff's face when he spotted Clo looking well and restored. *Hm.* How many messages and calls of his had she missed or ignored while feigning illness or sleep? I probably should have dug a little deeper when he came up in our earlier conversation, but I didn't want to push her. Clover didn't do well when pushed—

she lashed out and made you hurt as much as she hurt. Not one of her better qualities, and I couldn't say I liked that side of her, but I doubted she took pride in it.

'What if Leo doesn't uphold his end of the deal and caves and Orlando about it?'

'Then we say you were searching for something for your dad,' I said, having thought it all through. 'He stayed there after the gala for a while, right?'

'He did,' Ollie said, assessing me. 'How long have you been cooking this up?'

I laughed. 'A week or so. If the parents left anything behind, it'd be there.'

'It'd also be the first place she'd put things if Winifred had anything of our parents' she wanted to hide.' Griff rubbed his jaw. 'I'd love to find something of my mum or dad's. I know I have the estate and everything in it, but something from their time here would be pretty cool. It's like they'd wiped their time at the academy from their life after they left.'

'It's odd,' I said. 'What happened for them to all … disintegrate?'

'We'll figure it out,' Ollie said, a certainty to his tone I found rather attractive. 'We always do.'

'Here, here!' Griff raised his non-existent glass in the air.

The four of us back together, laughing and joking around, made me happy in a way not much else did. Without being able to see the future, I had no way of knowing whether these times would last past Hawthorn—or even the next few months—but I did know at that moment I loved them all and wanted them to be in my life forever.

Here's to hoping I survived long enough for it to happen.

Seventeen

LEO HAD DELIVERED the goods with little prompting.

Orlando and Ms Hawthorn were off campus doing *Sanctum* business and we were snooping around Hawthorn House and had at least three hours until they returned.

Happy days all around!

'Do you think we'll find something?' Griff asked, a cloth of fabric pinched in between his fingers held at least three inches away from his unusually disgusted face. 'This place has always given me the heebies.'

'Oh yeah?' The boys had spent all their holidays here over the years and I expected them to at least *like* being here. Guess none of those holidays were their choices, though.

Does anybody truly like doing something they're forced into?

'It's always been so ...' Griff waved his hand, the red fabric fluttering. 'Lifeless.'

I looked around the room, trying to see it through his eyes, but the bare walls were all I could take in. 'I get what you mean. Like for you guys, this place was temporary, but for Winifred, this is home.'

'Right!' Griff put down the fabric and went to inspect a cabinet next to the enormous four poster bed in the centre of the room. 'This is her home—Orlando's home too, come to think of it—and it's as if nobody ever enters.'

'Orlando never got to have one of these rooms,' I said, fingers grazing along the spines of the books living on a shelf. I noted none of them seemed like appealing reads. Understandable, I supposed, if they were all merely for show. 'He told me he stayed up in the attic, or at least I think he did. Between me and you, I find it hard to take in what he says.'

Griff paused his perusing. 'Why?'

'For starters, he looks so much like Ollie. It fucks with my head a little.' Griff nodded. 'And then there's the whole *I've kissed him and more while thinking he was somebody else* thing. Probably the thing putting a spanner in the works the most.'

'Makes sense,' Griff said.

'Yeah, but that doesn't mean I like it. Everything's so fucked and every time I move forward or come to terms with what happened to me ...' I shook my head, struggling to articulate what I meant in a way Griff would understand. 'I don't know. It's all so hard.'

'It'll get easier, Clouds.' Griff moved across the room and brought me into the biggest bear hug. His lips placed a gentle kiss on my head, and I leaned into his warmth. 'We'll get to the bottom of who wants you dead and why, and then we can be free of this shithole.'

I nodded against his chest, my words muffled. 'If you say so.'

'I do say so, and I know all.'

We moved apart. 'Ah, Griffin Cooper, the omniscient.' I bowed low. 'I am blessed to be in your presence.'

He barked a laugh. 'Good one.'

The two of us went back to searching the room, neither of us knowing what to look out for, when somebody else entered the room with a heavy tread. I turned, expecting to see Ollie in the doorway, but my heart jolted at the sight of Leo there instead.

'Hey,' he said.

'Hey.' I turned my head to Griff, who had turned to stare at Leo, suspicion in his gaze. 'What are you doing here?'

'I thought I could come help,' Leo said. It always knocked me off guard to see him so ... awkward. Uncomfortable in his own skin. It didn't fit my idea of him, of the Leo I think about a lot more than I probably should. Scratch that. There's no probably about it.

'Err ... sure,' I said, sending a tentative smile his way. 'We're nearly done in here, but you can help with the next room if you want?'

Griff shuffled towards the door. 'I'll go find Clover and help her.'

Coward.

Neither me nor Leo stopped him from leaving. If Ollie caught wind about me and Leo being alone together, he'd appear, so anything the two of us needed or wanted to say to each other had to happen pronto.

Once Griff got far enough away he wouldn't hear, I said, 'What are you doing here?'

'No ulterior motive, Stutter. I'm here to help.'

My gaze narrowed on his too-perfect features, trying to find a fault and only getting salty when finding none, and assessed him.

'Okay, well ...' I looked around the room. We'd already

searched most places. 'How about you help me go through these books and then we can move on?'

Leo came over to the bookcase and started on the top row while I crouched down to begin at the bottom.

'Sky,' he said after a few minutes, jolting me from my thoughts. It unnerved me any time he used my name.

'Yes?'

'I'm sorry.'

Should I stand up and let him tell me to my face? Staying put and remaining at knee height seemed the best plan of action.

No.

Don't be so silly, Skylar.

I stood up, tilting my head to look him in the eye. 'What for now?'

He sighed, running his hand through his hair. 'I don't think the word "everything" suffices, but it's all I can think of.'

'Everything is a cop-out.' I scoffed. 'Maybe get a little more specific.'

His lips lifted at the corners by a fraction.

'I can do that.'

I waited. If he had something to say to me, then he needed no more prompting.

'Skylar, I am so sorry for betraying you and not telling you about him. Everything got so out of hand and I acted like a total prick towards you. At first, when I suggested we fake date I wanted to spite everyone. Except maybe Griff.

'But then I realised how much I loved hanging out with you and enjoyed your company, and I wanted to spend more and more time with you. The line got blurred pretty fucking fast and every time I opened my mouth to tell you the truth, something stopped me or something more important happened and stole our focus.'

'Why didn't you give me a heads up before the gala? You let him steal me away in a dance and reveal it all and did nothing to tell me or to stop it. You knew he'd taken Ollie's place. Fuck, you helped him to take Ollie's place multiple times. You helped him *fool* me. Knowing all he did and his true identity.'

'I know, and I accept if you can't ever forgive me. I can barely forgive myself.'

I made a noise, a *pshh,* 'I find that hard to believe. You're Leo Hawthorn. You'll get over it soon enough and go back to your surly, slightly amused ways.'

'You don't think much of me, do you?'

'Leo,' I said, blinking at the beautiful yet ugly sight of him before me, wanting to make sense of my emotions but not having the time or the strength to do so right then. 'I try not to think of you at all.'

I LEFT Leo to search the next room alone and headed up to the attic by myself so I could get some peace. Or attempt to, at least.

My mind whirled.

Apologies. Betrayals. Murder attempts. Heartbreak.

Just another day at Hawthorn Academy.

One room took up the entire attic, and the moment I entered, I knew I stood in Orlando's room. His lair. The place he withered and hid and plotted and schemed.

Really, the place looked fucking miserable. All dank and dark and barely lived in, yet at the same time, you could tell he'd tried to make it cosy. A collage of pictures adorned the walls; ones taken from a distance he'd spied to get, ones with me or Winifred or of him alone, taken by somebody else.

A half-life. Lived by somebody unable to act freely.

Do not feel sorry for the bastard. I chastised myself. *Don't go getting all sentimental.*

Easier said than done. Not with the truth of his existence laid out before me in such disrepair and decay.

The room had a single bed placed in the left-hand corner. All thin metal railings and a thread-bare mattress which had seen better days.

Against my will, my heart hurt for the little boy subjected to this, and to the teenager that boy had become.

Seeing pictures of myself staring down at me from the walls unsettled me in a way I couldn't explain. Some of them were ones I'd posed for with him, and were actually of Orlando, but others ... they were of me from afar. Taken through gaps in a door, or maybe even from inside those secret tunnels. Who the fuck knew except Orlando? Asking him for clarification didn't make the top of my to-do list funny enough.

Oh, by the way, I stumbled across your room and ever since, I've wondered where and how you took those candid shots of me. Do tell.

Yeah, not happening.

A box in the right-hand corner of the room drew my eye. Most likely because there was fuck-all else for me to peek at, excluding a bedside cabinet and a chest of drawers and wardrobe combo.

A large, ornate, old trunk chest.

And my hand twitched to open it and delve into all its secrets.

So I did.

Books and newspapers filled the chest to the brim and

what at first glance appeared to be junk, but I reckoned had a purpose if Orlando had deigned to keep it. Especially as it seemed he kept little else.

I picked up the sheet of paper from the top, sat down on the dusty wooden floor cross-legged, and read.

The truth about Hawthorn Academy and what really goes on behind closed doors at the elite establishment.

Whistleblowers have caused a great deal of upset for those who run Hawthorn Academy in the past few weeks. The story is still unfolding, but we secured the latest scoop.

Both former and current students of the elite establishment Hawthorn Academy, located in Beurre, have started a petition and investigation into the goings on and malpractices of both faculty and students.

Hazing is rife at boarding schools, and it would seem Hawthorn Academy is no different when it comes to this age-old tradition.

Insiders, who wish to remain anonymous, have told all to our reporters, including a previously unknown story of a girl dying during an initiation ...

Story continues on page 12

SANDY PARKS DEAD, FOUND IN SCHOOL BATHROOM

The students who found her are staying quiet, but we know the truth.

On Friday 2nd February, Sandy Parks entered the girls' bathroom on the second floor of the English building ... and never walked out.

Her death has been deemed an apparent suicide by the police, but we all know they can be bought, don't we?

What The Set and The Sect don't want you to know:

The Set (most importantly Millie and Eliza Hawthorn), and *The Sect* (Damien and Jacob Cooper, Edward Hawthorn and Henry Brandon) were all present either before or after Sandy entered said bathroom, lurking around. What are they hiding? Well, wouldn't you like to know?

And don't worry, because we've got you.

Everybody knows the two groups have rules which students must adhere to at all times, and if you knew anything about Sandy Parks, you'd know she didn't abide by those rules.

She was an outlier.

An anomaly.

And the Hawthorn twins did *not* like that!

And they wanted her to pay for her crimes.

Are they capable of murder? Only they know the answer, but us students here at the Hawthorn Herald believe they're capable and more ...

My dearest, Jacob,

How I long to see you, be near you, touch you.

I understand why these things cannot yet come to pass, but I want you to know I miss you and wish you were here by my side every single day of my life.

Baby Oliver is doing well, even if he cries a lot for a toddler. At times, I wonder if he's crying because he senses the truth, but then I remember it's most likely wind and my day continues.

As for your daughter, Cora named her Skylar Crescent, which tells you everything you need to know about the upbringing she's about to receive. Maybe one day you'll get to meet her.

I'd love to hold her, but I can't be seen visiting anybody on the other side of The Divide. I hope you understand and won't judge me too harshly for it.

You never were one to judge me for my life's decisions, as poor as they may be.

Sometimes, I wish we were still at Hawthorn together, happy, and unburdened by the events of the past. Yet I know it's a dream. One I wake up from every morning and put into my mind at the start of every night.

Your brother and my sister are still sickeningly happy and are in love in every way. Being around them, I see what we could've been, if circumstances had allowed.

Their boy, Griffin, is the spitting image of you as a child. To look at him is hard, as I see how a child of ours would be, and it hurts.

Please come back to Beurre one day and take me away from this sorrow, this misery I call life.

Love you with all my heart,

Millie

P.S. I know you are already aware of this, but I feel the need to reiterate it. Henry can never learn the truth of what we did. If he does and I die, know his blood-soaked hands are the culprit, and seek my justice.

COOPER COUPLE KILLED IN CAR CRASH, FIVE-YEAR-OLD SON SURVIVES

Eighteen

ONCE I FINISHED READING, I called the guys up to me so they could see it all for themselves.

I took pictures while I waited so we could view them later, away from the darkness of the place.

The letter from Millie to my father proved he knew of my existence, but then again, the letter had never been sent, otherwise Orlando wouldn't have an original copy of it.

Did Winifred stop the correspondence between them? Infiltrate the system somewhere along the way and ensure it never reached its destination?

The day had brought up as many questions as it had answers, and I was so, so very tired of it all.

The four of us had returned to Ollie's room, sans Leo, and were sitting around on the floor, uneaten pizza going cold on the coffee table in front of us. Which, if you know anything about me and/or our group, you'd know that was fucking unusual.

Ollie's hand rested on my knee like it belonged there.

Maybe it was time to stop fooling myself and accept it did ... belong there, I mean.

'So,' Clover said, breaking the fraught silence. 'What do we do?'

'What do we do?' I repeated, broken. Little we could do at present. 'What do you mean?'

'Well.' Her tentative tone matched the tentative look in her jade-green eyes. 'We set out to find something, and we did, even if we found something completely different from what we expected.'

'Right ...'

Griff and Ollie remained quiet. Griff wringing his hands together in his lap while Ollie drew circles on my knee, attempting to distract himself. One of his more loveable quirks, by far. Whenever he got lost in thought, happy or sad, he circled patterns on my body.

'So,' Clo continued, 'we've got something to work with now. We can flick through the yearbooks and see if there are any mentions of Sandy Parks. We can talk to Leo and ask him when *The Sanctum* meets next and see if there's a way for us to spy, which will prove to us once and for all whether he's on our side. Plus, Mother's Day is coming up.'

'Nobody else has a mother coming,' I pointed out. I'd already accepted Cora would show her brash self even if I didn't invite her, so once again, I'd sent her an invitation to get ahead of the curve. Lottie, Leo's mum, had even been kind enough to offer Cora a lift, so they'd arrive and leave together.

Lottie truly was my idea of a modern-day saint.

Yes, she'd offered when Leo and I were still together, but she hadn't redacted it even after everything went down at the start of the year.

'Not true. Leo will be with you.'

'Yeah, I suppose.' I placed my hand on top of Ollie's, silently supporting him and to imply my feelings about spending the day working with Leo, all without saying a word. I hoped he got my meaning, but maybe I needed to speak to him about it later, once Griff and Clo left. 'I'll talk to him.'

Clover nodded, accepting it without saying something stupid like *I can talk to him.*

'Maybe Cora will tell me more about my dad,' I said. 'I don't like to encourage her drinking, but it seems this situation might call for it.'

'Not gonna lie, Clouds. Your mum is pretty hilarious after a couple of drinks.'

I bit my tongue. My snap response didn't seem appropriate.

There was a reason Orlando had a printout of the heading of the article talking about Griff's parents' accident. One none of us wanted to talk about.

'You wanna come sit with her, then?' I said instead. Griff's cheeky grin, not seen on his face as often recently, sprung to his face.

'As tempting as that is … no.'

The three of us laughed. Ollie didn't. It was as if he wasn't in the room with us, so lost in his own demons.

I couldn't draw him out of his head with these two here.

'Why don't we call it a night? We can sleep on all we've learned and talk about it tomorrow. I'll message Leo and get the ball rolling about talking to Lottie and Cora together on Mother's Day,' I said.

Griff and Clover mumbled their agreement.

'You're the best, Clouds.'

Hawthorn Academy always fell still in the middle of the night.

Barely any noise, barely any movement, or at least not any I could hear from Ollie's room at the end of the hall.

He feigned sleep beside me, his back to my chest being the little spoon.

I hadn't yet called him out on it, as I'd tried to fall asleep myself and leave him to his thoughts, but how much longer I could leave it for was up in the air.

'I know you're awake,' he murmured. 'I'm sorry for shutting you out.'

'That's okay.' My arm was slung across his side, my hand resting on his hip. There was something so intimate about being with him in his most unguarded moments I hadn't got used to yet. Skylar of old would squeal at her current reality. How close the two of us had become, an intimacy built from sharing secrets and thoughts and our minds.

Even I'm sick of how sick I sound.

But I couldn't help it. Ollie made me feel all the things all at once.

'Seeing her handwriting shit me up.'

'I get it. You don't have to explain yourself to me.'

He turned to face me, my arm remaining draped across his body. 'I don't have to, no, but I want to. I like talking to you.'

'I like talking to you, too,' I whispered, my breath causing his eyelashes to flutter. 'But it can wait. We don't have to do this tonight.'

'If I don't talk it over, I'm never gonna get any sleep.'

I brushed my lips against his in the barest hint of a kiss. 'Okay. Talk away.'

He inhaled through his nose, exhaled through his mouth.

My eyes transfixed on his lips, watched and waited.

Fuck, he's beautiful.

'It was so weird to see her writing, see her basically admit to doing what she did, and show no remorse for it. Or maybe she had remorse. I don't know. And that's what fucking sucks the most and will forever suck. I will never know what went through her head because she left me and never shared her secrets.

'And the fact your dad could show up, as much as I've always hated him and wanted him dead, fills me with a sense of excitement I can't explain even if I tried. Because maybe, just maybe, he'll have some knowledge we don't have. Can answer the questions burning the back of my brain.'

His words washed over me. It was my turn to draw circles on his skin.

'Every time I have a moment to myself, a moment of peace, my mind wanders to her, to him, to my aunt, to you and your dad, and I'm struggling to keep it together.'

Heart officially broken. The pain in his voice gutted me the way not much could. If I hadn't forgiven him for all the crap he put me through, I would now.

Ollie had changed so much in the past year, and he most definitely wasn't the same person I met on my first day at the academy.

My eyes met his, and the tears lingering at the corners of his eyes caught me off guard.

Ollie upset or Ollie in tears—well, it was never easy to see.

'All of this is a mess,' I whispered. 'And I know you feel you have to keep it together in front of everybody else, but you never have to with me. I'm here for you, O.'

'I'm so thankful you've forgiven me, Sky. I don't know what I'd do without you.'

'You'd survive the way you always have.'

'Yeah, maybe,' he said. 'But I'm glad I don't have to.'

Our conversation got derailed by kisses. Man, kissing Ollie again had the butterflies living in my stomach in overdrive. They didn't know what to do with themselves.

A little—okay, a long—time later, we paused the kisses and gazed at each other.

'I wonder what Lottie and Cora will say,' Ollie said, his lips resting on my forehead, grounding me.

'Guess we're going to have to wait until Mother's Day,' I replied.

My favourite day of the year. *Not.*

Nineteen

'LITTLE ONE, WAIT UP!'

Orlando's voice travelled down the empty corridor and my feet stopped of their own volition.

'Oh, I'm good enough to talk to now, am I?' I scoffed, tapping my right foot on the floor—my frustration towards him in physical form.

His top lip curved up. 'Upset I've ignored you?'

A sound came from the back of my throat. 'Not upset.'

'What then?'

'Pissed. Livid. Fuming. Take your pick.' I continued walking, and the boy followed, his steps matching mine. 'Only you would think it okay to leave me a dead body as a gift, then refuse to talk to me afterwards.'

He laughed. 'So you didn't like your present?'

My stomach roiled, the image of Mr Hawkins's body strung up flashing in my mind. It featured frequently in my nightmares, but I tried to never think of it while awake.

'You're sick,' I said. 'I know shit's happened to you, but fucking hell, you're twisted, Orlando.'

'And you'd rather me be vanilla and boring like my brother?'

'Least your brother understands right from wrong.'

'Does he? Because if I remember right, he bullied you and convinced the entire school to do the same.'

'Bullying and group coercion are a tad different to *murder*.' The library came into view and I let out a deep breath. *My happy place.*

'You make it sound so black and white, Little One.'

'Because it is.'

My blood boiled. He always acted so arrogant, so important, so *right*. To the point where it made me question myself and my values. My beliefs.

'It isn't.' He shook his head and his disappointment bothered me. How bloody ridiculous of me! Why should I care how he feels?

'Whatever. What do you want, anyway?'

'To see you,' he said. The answer, so simple, it should've been obvious. 'We've not spent time together recently.'

'Once again, because you've *avoided* me.'

'Well, I'm here now. Can I sit with you?' He gestured to the back toward my usual table, and I nodded without enthusiasm.

The two of us sat down, and I ignored him, getting my things out of my bag and setting them up on the table, ready to tackle my homework.

Orlando, who I could see in my peripheral vision, seemed amused at my attempt to ignore him. *Bastard.*

'So ...' He prodded my elbow. 'Did you enjoy poking around?'

I raised my eyebrows his way. 'Huh?'

Orlando laughed. 'Oh, come on, Little One. I'm well aware you and the rest of the Scooby Gang played detective on the weekend.'

What would be best? To hold my tongue or find out who told him?

'I don't know what you're talking about.'

'Lying doesn't suit you. And no, before you ask, nobody told me anything. Not even Leo the arse-kisser.'

'Then what makes you so sure we were there?' I raised my eyebrows. He always seemed so cocky. So sure of himself. It made me burn inside, the way he went through life acting as if his past more than made up for him being an arsehole in the present.

It didn't.

Not entirely, anyway.

'You think I don't have cameras set up?' He scoffed. 'I thought you knew me better, Little One.'

It was my turn to scoff. 'I barely know you.'

'Not true.'

'Orlando.' I hoped my use of his first name had him real-ising my seriousness. 'All I know of you is you lied to me while masquerading as your brother, and you assaulted me, stabbed me, and attempted to drown me. None of those put you in a favourable light.'

'My brother isn't a saint.'

'He's never pretended to be.'

'Oh, which makes him better than me, does it?' Orlando spat.

'Why are you picking a fight with me?' I asked, putting down my pen and giving him my full attention. 'I'm not the one you're angry with.'

'Not like I can take it out on *her*.' He rubbed his jaw, and I watched the path his finger made, afraid to find anger or anguish in his eyes. 'She's not around.'

'She gave you away before she died, though.' It seemed silly to point it out and add to his ire, but I couldn't help myself. *Keep poking the bear, Skylar.*

'And what do you mean?'

'So, there was an overlap in time where she could have made an effort to see you, or spend time with you.' Maybe I should think through what I wanted to say before saying it, but it seemed my mouth liked to run away from me before I could catch up. 'Did you ever spend any time with her?'

'Once. For a grand total of two hours.'

'I want to say sorry, but that's bullshit because I've got nothing to be sorry for. Millie's the one who should be sorry. Maybe she had a reason to do what she did?'

'No reason would be enough for me. A reason is an excuse, no matter which way you turn it.'

I didn't agree. Not fully. Sometimes a reason is just that—a reasonable explanation—and not an excuse.

Orlando had made up his mind, though. All his life he'd thought about it and come to his conclusion, probably a long time ago.

'I suppose,' I mumbled. Blinked.

How long would it take for me to not see Ollie when I looked at him? The mind fuck of it all kept fucking me up more, the two of them blurring into one.

Orlando's fingers grazed the back of my hand. 'Penny for your thoughts?'

'It'd cost you more than a penny,' I joked. 'Half the time I've got no bloody clue what's going on up there.' I pointed to my head. 'It's a minefield.'

'I'm sure mine could give yours a run for its money.'

'I'm not gonna fight you. Rarely do I enter into battles, knowing I won't win.'

'Can't say I've seen you enter many battles,' he said, taking my words seriously. 'And no, your run-ins with *The Set* don't count.'

'How are you finding hanging out with them? Is being a member, or should I say the *only* member, of *The Sect* everything you thought it'd be?'

'You think I'm silly for caring.'

'I never said that.'

His lips turned up at the corners. 'You didn't have to. Your face gives you away.'

'Talk to me then. Explain.' I placed my hand on his where it rested on top of the table. I'd told the boys I could get close to Orlando and use it to my advantage, but in reality, I'd been doing a pretty piss-poor job of it. 'I want to understand.'

'All my life I didn't fit in,' Orlando said. His bottom lip wobbled from keeping his emotions under wraps. 'Wasn't given the same opportunities as my brother or my cousins.' His bright blue eyes accosted mine, trapping me. 'And now I can have those things. They're mine for the taking.'

'By brute force, you mean,' I said, unable to bite my tongue.

'Nothing brute about it. I declared myself to be a member of *The Sect,* sure, but there was no violence involved. Oliver and the others stood down and left me to it.'

'You can't blame them.'

'I blame them for a lot of things.'

'Them and everyone else, yeah.' I squeezed his fingers to seem kind or approachable or who the fuck knew what, really. Orlando may be fucked up, and he may be a violent prick who deserved to rot behind bars for the rest of his life, but I couldn't bring myself to act too harshly toward him. It would be like kicking a puppy or knocking a vulnerable person over. Unnecessary and mean.

'Wouldn't you?' He bit out. 'You have as much reason as I

do to hate them all, Sky, yet you don't. You've let them worm their way into your brain.'

'Maybe so. Or maybe I'm my own person and I've realised shit on my own. You seem to think I'm incapable of thinking for myself.'

I snatched my hand back.

He blew out a breath through gritted teeth. 'I don't think you're incapable of thinking for yourself.'

'Then what do you think?'

'You're being manipulated and you can't even see it.'

God, that made me laugh! '*Someone* is trying to manipulate me, yes, but I don't think it's Oliver.'

'That's how it is, then. You think so poorly of me?'

'Orlando, you've not given me much else to go on. You're lucky I'm even sitting here talking to you!'

'Little One, I—'

I cut him off. 'No. No excuses. Own your shit or I'm leaving.'

'Own my shit?'

I nodded. 'Think it's time, don't you?'

'Can we go somewhere more private?'

'Where's more private than an empty library hidden at the back?' I asked, darting my gaze around to find nobody else within earshot. Orlando opened his mouth to answer. 'The question was rhetorical.'

'Fine.' He bit out. 'I'm sorry for everything.'

'And by everything you mean ...'

The contempt on his face would've made me laugh in any other circumstance, but I made sure my face stayed unmoved. Why was I even giving him a chance to fess up and tell the truth? Not like he'd taken the opportunity in the past whenever it presented itself.

'Fine!' he snapped when I remained quiet. 'So, you asked me about a list back when I joined, remember?'

I nodded. I remembered the list. I reached into the inside pocket of my blazer and pulled out the well-worn piece of paper I carried around at all times.

Ollie v Orlando

- First time we spoke in the Hospital Wing (surely Ollie ... right?)

- ~~Closet make-out session during the first New Year's Gala (Orlando?)~~ Orlando

- ~~Who drugged me at the first ever party in the woods (Orlando?)~~ Orlando

- Too many times in the library to count (must think of individual instances)

- Who set The Set on me? (Ollie?)

- ~~Who killed Odette and Olivia? (Orlando?)~~ Orlando - Odette

'Can I see?' Orlando asked, his hand open, waiting for me to hand it over. I gave a slight nod of my head and handed it over. 'If I answer these, does that count toward owning my shit?'

'Yeah, I'd say it does.'

'Okay. The top one, about the hospital wing? Me.'

I failed to hide the incredulousness from my tone. '*You?*'

'Yep.' He popped the p, no doubt to irritate me. 'The real Ollie knocked on your door, but you'd passed out, so after he helped Leo get you to the hospital wing, he bolted. Decided it would be best to introduce himself to you at assembly the next morning.'

'And you know this because ...'

'Because Leo messaged me the moment Ollie left and told me to get my arse down to the hospital wing pronto if I wanted to meet you face-to-face. So I did.'

The first conversation between me and Ollie, wait, between me and *Orlando,* was hard to recall. Everything about my first evening at Hawthorn was fuzzy. Passing out does that to a girl.

'And then you called me beautiful,' Orlando continued, unable to see the turmoil in my eyes. His words sparked something in my brain.

'Right, and then you told me you were glad I noticed you.'

Another snippet of his words came back to me from our first meeting.

'Maybe you should remember that fear is good. Being scared can ensure you live. That you don't make life-threatening mistakes. Ever considered that, Little One?'

I blinked at Orlando in front of me. 'You called me Little One.'

'I did. I wanted a name for you nobody else would use. So when you learned the truth, you'd know things that were me and those that weren't.'

I felt like a fool. A big fucking fool who couldn't see the world correctly. How had I missed so much? It never even entered my mind to question the times Ollie used a nickname for me and those he didn't.

Was anything on my list even Ollie?

I repeated the thought to Orlando.

'Technically, he set *The Set* on you. Kind of. It's complicated.'

'Uncomplicate it,' I said through gritted teeth, having thoroughly lost my patience. 'Explain what you mean.'

'Back when Ollie first came up with his bullying plot, he had the O girls wrapped around his little finger. He could do no wrong in their eyes and they'd do everything he asked of them. But once you came here, and he met you, well, he had doubts about how far his conscience would allow him to go.'

'Right ...'

'He told the girls to back off a bit; to not go as far as before. The day they beat you up in the toilets, he was livid.' A sick and twisted smile came to Orlando's lips. 'But what my dear brother didn't realise? Any time he told the girls to cool down, I went behind his back and met with them and contradicted him.'

My heart stuttered. 'You're the reason they escalated?'

He shrugged, as if his answer wouldn't cut me in two. 'Partially. I can't take any credit for the charity fashion show, even if I'd like to.'

'Thanks for telling me,' I said, my thanks feeling dirty and like a betrayal to myself. 'I've got some homework to do now.'

He put his hands up in a placating gesture. 'I'll leave you to it.'

The chair dragged along the wooden floor when he pushed back and the noise of it went straight through me. I hated those types of noises. You know, like nails on a chalkboard or the scrape of a knife and fork when they clashed? *Eurgh.* I shivered just thinking about it.

Orlando's finger pressed against my chin. He turned my head, and I blinked, finding his across from mine within touching distance. 'I am sorry, Little One. Even if you never believe me.'

Before I could put a stop to it, Orlando's lips touched mine. A soft, gentle kiss. A goodbye kiss, of sorts.

And for a split second, my lips moved with his. I joined the kiss as an active participant for a moment.

Fuck.

Twenty

MOTHER'S DAY CAME AROUND, and even though we'd all been building it up in our minds for the last two weeks, it came without much fanfare.

Unlike my mother.

Who arrived with fanfare and so much more.

'Skylar, my darling, how I've missed you!' Mum flew at me, wrapping me up in her bony arms, a hug for the ages. 'You are so beautiful. Truly stunnin'!'

'Thanks Mum,' I mumbled. I took her in from head to toe and cringed, per usual. Today's ensemble was, well, it was a *look,* that was for sure.

A bright dress, in a pattern yet to be determined, and leggings underneath. Strappy stiletto heels on her feet, her tattoo of a rosary necklace on show. She'd got said tattoo because she'd seen it on a celebrity and loved it, so wanted to get it herself and not because the woman had a religious bone in her body.

The trend, not the meaning, mattered most to her.

'Skylar, dear, you do look rather wonderful,' Lottie said. Her bright smile lit up every room she entered, and it instantly made me happier. If you got close enough, you could see the tension lines forming at the creases of her eyes. Trust a short car ride sitting next to my mum to break somebody's Botox.

'Thank you, Lottie. You look amazing yourself, as always.'

She waved me off. 'In this old thing?' She laughed. 'Now where is my son?'

'He's on his way.' I stood on tiptoes, trying to spot Leo's head above the crowd.

'Unlike him to be late,' Lottie said.

'He had something he couldn't get out of,' I replied, not mentioning how the *something* was acting as an errand boy for Orlando. When I first asked Leo to confront the mums with me, he seemed uncertain, but a couple of days later he texted to say he'd do it.

I hated how we were no longer on talking terms in the way we used to be. I wished he'd open up to me so we could talk it all over, but until I forgave him or at the least accepted his apology, it seemed like a far-off day.

Huh. Sounds like a me problem, actually.

'Thank you both for coming,' I said, filling the time until Leo arrived. 'Been up to anything exciting since I saw you last?'

'Oh, you know me!' Mum said, knocking my shoulder with her thin, veiny hand. 'Bit o'this and a bit o'that.'

I nodded, because yes, her response made sense to me. What else did her life consist of other than visiting the market, lounging around beside her shitty husband, and gossiping away with Leslie?

'Sounds lovely,' Lottie said, her smile saying the opposite. 'Can't say I've got anything to report. Edward's been busy with ...' she trailed off, unsure how to finish. 'Everything.'

Maybe that was her way of referring to the fact Edward held a literal gun at Orlando during the shit show of a gala.

Pretty sure he never fired it ...

'I'm so sorry I'm late.' Leo's voice came from behind me. He placed a kiss on his mother's cheek before doing the same on Cora's. Smooth bastard.

No lingering glint in his eyes told me he felt awkward about being there with me and our mums. Nothing to hint at how he felt about the events of the past year.

Last Mother's Day, the four of us spent it together, but Leo and I were barely friends back then.

It also was the day Jacob Cooper, my father, first got mentioned.

And I still knew as little now as I did then.

'That's alright, darling!' Mum's lipstick covered teeth beamed at him. In her eyes, Leo could do no wrong. 'You're looking rather dashing today, young man. I hope you're treating my Skylar well.'

'Mum,' I mumbled, not wanting to draw attention to us more than her loud, booming voice already did. 'Me and Leo aren't together anymore.'

'A mother can dream for that to change, can't she?' She nudged Lottie's arm. 'We'd both love to see you two happy.'

'Thank you, Cora,' Leo said, his tone one he often used with my mum. Placating and friendly, mixed alongside a twinge of distaste. My favourite. 'But Skylar's done the right thing. You should be proud of the daughter you've raised.' *Pfft*, like she had much to do with how I turned out. 'I don't deserve her.'

'Poppycock! You're doing the thing all men do, down-playing your many, many wonderful qualities.'

I rolled my eyes, unable to stop myself any longer. The woman, alongside being rather delusional, didn't know when to quit. Or maybe she did, and she ignored the red flashing lights in her head on purpose.

'I assure you,' I said tersely, 'he isn't.' I put my arm through

Mum's, ready to sweep her away if she didn't shut her mouth. 'Shall we head through into the hall?'

'We must stop at the bar on the way! I'm absolutely parched!'

'Leave the bottle!' Mum told the waiter. 'No need for you to keep coming over and topping us up.'

God, was it possible for the woman to make me cringe more?

Mum burped. 'Oof! Soz about that everybody. Wine on an empty stomach makes a mess of the best of us.'

Ah, as always, the answer was a big fat resounding yes.

The ground could open and swallow me and it still wouldn't be enough.

Nothing could save me from my reality, no matter how many times I'd wished for a different mum—a different family.

'Mum,' Leo said, after the waiters took away the first course. 'Sky and I have got a few questions for you about the past.' He sat back in his chair. 'You too, Cora.'

Leo, ever the cool, calm, and collected one of the two of us. *Bastard.*

'I can't say I didn't see this day coming.' Lottie sighed, indicating a whole weight lived on her shoulders. 'But remember you two, I don't know as much as Edward or Henry.'

'Of course,' I said, fiddling with the fork next to my main plate. When I first joined Hawthorn, the cutlery of a fancy meal scared the shit out of me, like knowing what to use and when, but now? Now I was a pro.

A lot could change in eighteen months.

'What happened back when you all went here?' Leo asked,

his hand touching Lottie's on top of the table. I'd always loved their relationship, how sweet and genuine it seemed, and my heart panged.

'A lot happened, Leo,' Lottie chuckled. 'You'll have to get a little more specific.'

'A girl died, Mum,' Leo said, getting to the point. 'And a lot seems to imply Dad and his friends had something to do with it.'

'How'd you find out? All the records are sealed and a lot of money was thrown at the problem to make it go away.' Lottie took her hand from Leo's and fiddled with the napkin on her lap. 'Winnie did a lot to help them all back then. Maybe you should talk to her.'

'Talk to the woman who hid a kid from the entire family for years?' Leo raised a sardonic eyebrow towards his mum. 'Funny enough, Mum, I don't think she'd tell us much.'

'I can't tell you much either,' Lottie said. 'I'm a few years younger and didn't know any of them then. I know what your dad's told me since, and the whispers I heard at the time.'

'Anything would help us, Lottie,' I said. 'Please.'

'All I know is the girl's family accepted payment and the matter never went any further. Winifred hushed a lot up as she'd joined the faculty the same year, so was in a better position to make it all go away. No matter how much the Hawthorns seemed to dislike one another, they always had each other's backs, no matter what. Millie and Eliza made a mistake, and Edward and Winifred did all they could to make sure nobody ever learned of it.'

'So, the girl died because of Millie and Eliza?' I asked, frowning.

'I never said that.' Lottie pursed her lips. 'But I have my suspicions, yes.'

'Thank you,' I said. I could tell from the sad expression on her face she wished she had more to tell us. If Lottie knew more, then we'd know it too. 'We appreciate you telling us.'

Leo nodded, assessing his mum. 'And Cora,' he said, turning to my mum, who had stayed quiet. No doubt drinking the bottle of wine she'd made the waiter leave. 'I know you may not want to talk about this, but we have to ask.'

'And if you know nothing, that's cool, too,' I added. I didn't want her to think we were putting her under an inquisition or anything. Mum didn't handle getting called out well.

Mum glanced between the three of us, a shrewd expression on her face, the fog of alcohol lingering but not as thick as a moment ago. 'If this is about your dad, Skylar, then no fear.' Mum's words slurred, so it sounded more like *iz-zis-bout-dad-sssskylar-n-fear.*

Lottie squinted in her direction, and I shrank down in my chair a fraction. Every time she spoke, my embarrassment levels climbed a notch, but for the first time it hit me that maybe that was a part of the problem?

Mum, even if a total mess, never acted ashamed of her actions or like she regretted the fact she wasn't the best human. If anything, she embraced it in a way I could only dream of embracing my own issues. Maybe a lesson lurked in there somewhere. Something about being unabashed and unashamed to be yourself. Maybe ...

' ... coming here.'

Leo and Lottie's gasps at whatever Mum said while my mind disappeared into itself forced me to pay attention.

'You've done what?' Lottie asked, her shock palpable.

'So the last time we all got together,' Mum said, as if we'd all decided to hang out because we liked each other, 'got me thinking about Jacob.

'Which had my mind going back to a letter I got from him a while back now. It told me what to do if I ever needed to contact him for whatever reason. So, I thought, well why not reach out and fill him in on the goings on here? Tell him his daughter faced potential assault and murder at every corner and see what he had to say for himself. And like I knew he would, he said he'd come back.'

My stomach filled with nerves, and sickness swirled.

'You ... reached out to my dad?' I couldn't believe it. At no point in my life had she thought to reach out to him, yet all of sudden, she had. Why?

My eyes narrowed on her bloodshot ones.

'Mum, is everything okay?' I asked. 'You've always told me we're better off without him.'

'And we are.' She gave a decisive nod. 'But we both know I'm not the best mum at the best of times, Skylar, and I wanted to help you. He is rather rich, you know?'

Ah, and there it is.

If my dad appeared and gave me money, then by proxy, Cora would come into money—or so she assumed.

'It's exciting, isn't it?' Cora laughed, raising her glass to cheer us, oblivious to the tension at the table. 'Let's drink to me, for solving all our problems!'

Twenty-One

THE REST of the day passed so fucking slowly I almost gauged my eyes out with the dessert spoon, waiting for it all to be over.

Leo seemed to be suffering as much as me.

A lingered look and a shared smile spoke volumes.

'Oh, darling, hasn't today been the most marvellous!' The powerful stench of Mum's perfume itched my nostrils. How on earth did it still smell so strong after so many hours? Cause I could guarantee it was a cheap knock-off found at the local market. 'I do love seeing you here, making friends in all the right places.'

Translation: *wealthy places.*

'Thanks, Mum,' I said, returning her hug half-heartedly. 'Get home safe.'

'I'll make sure she does,' Lottie said, her smile tight. 'It's so lovely to see you again, Skylar. Wish Clover a happy birthday tomorrow for me, please?'

I nodded. 'Of course.'

Lottie remembering Clo's birthday after everything between the two families went through showed her sweet and genuine nature.

Leo and Lottie said their goodbyes, but I didn't listen in. No, instead I watched as Cora stumbled to the top of the steps outside the main entrance. Bless her. Maybe I needed to cut her more slack. She tried her best ... even if her best had never been good enough by my standards.

I watched as Lottie took Mum's arm and placed it into the crook of her elbow and guided her down to the car safely.

Leo and I remained at the top and waited for them to depart, waving as they did so.

'So ...' Leo said once the car disappeared from sight. 'Didn't learn much, did we?'

'Nope,' I said, then laughed. 'Except for the fact my dad's about to arrive and give *The Sanctum* everything they've wanted this whole time. Not to mention piss Ollie off.'

'God, Cora's a hoot. As if she's had this in her back pocket the whole time.'

I shook my head. 'I've stopped trying to understand her. I've never managed to in the past and it ends up giving me a headache.'

'That's fair, Stutter.' He turned to face me, and I couldn't place his expression, which was odd because I thought I knew all his facial movements. 'Orlando won't hear about the impending arrival from me.'

'In theory then, he shouldn't hear about it at all, because I sure as fuck ain't gonna tell him.'

I rubbed my arms to keep warm, the chill of the March air settling in. It'd make sense to go back inside, but inside meant telling Ollie—and Clo and Griff—what we'd learned and I wanted to put it off for a little longer.

'He has his ways,' Leo said. 'Hopefully nobody at the next table listened in, or one of the wait staff.'

'They all seemed pretty occupied. Didn't you see the incident between Celia and Cordelia's parents? Think most eyes and ears saw and heard the display, lucky for us.'

Leo nodded, his lips pursed, and somehow became the spitting image of his mum. I blinked.

'You know the worst part of all this?' I asked, hugging myself. 'Mum doesn't even realise she's done something wrong. Or at least something that could fuck up a lot of people's lives, including mine. Probably thinking about the potential payout she could get out of him.'

'You don't think highly of her, do you?' He sounded both bemused and a little critical.

I frowned at him. He'd spent enough time with her, and me, and us together to know the answer. Why did his tone bother me?

Leo's opinion should mean shit to me. Not like he was the walking epitome of a person walking the straight and narrow.

'I just ...' I said, reluctant to put my thoughts out into the universe. 'I can't explain it. It's like I can't overlook her faults, no matter how hard I try. She's flawed, aren't we all? But hers flash at me anytime I'm around her, or converse with her, or even think about her.'

A stone sunk to the bottom of my stomach. Acknowledging my flaws was hard.

'Surprised you don't feel strongly about my flaws,' Leo said. His lips curved into a small smile. 'Because there's a lot of them.'

'Understatement of the century.' Others were flooding the stairs and the school grounds, saying goodbye to their mums or meeting up with friends. We were no longer alone, but neither of us moved. 'I've had a lot of years to think about Cora.

Give me another ten years and then maybe your issues will be as bright.'

'Sky—' he started, but I cut him off.

'If you're about to apologise again, I might hit you.'

He chuckled. 'I mean it, though.'

'I know.'

'So GLAD YOU didn't have to be there,' I said, blinking at Ollie's face, having a hard time coming to terms with the fact the two of us had fallen into a pattern of sorts without defining what *this* was.

Then my sentence repeated in my head. *Fuck.*

'I didn't mean it like that,' I blurted out. 'I wish you could be there because your mum was there.' I figuratively hit my forehead with the palm of my hand. 'I meant ...'

Ollie smirked, running his fingers down my bare shoulder to my elbow. 'Sky, it's fine. I get what you mean. Don't have a conniption about it, okay?'

'Okay,' I whispered.

The TV lit up his face, whatever was playing on the screen playing out across his features in a light show, and a sense of calm covered me.

'Ollie, how the fuck am I meant to deal with my dad arriving?'

'What d'you mean?'

'That'—I shuffled up his bed, putting my arm under the pillow and pulling it towards me—'it's all a bit fucking weird. He isn't real to me. Never has been. But since learning I'm actually going to meet him? It's all a bit much.'

'I'll be there by your side the whole time.'

'But we don't even know when he's showing up!' I rubbed my eye, pressing in, wanting it to alleviate the pressure building there. 'What if you're not there?'

'Then you message me straight away and I'll come running. Sky, we're in this together.'

'Are you sure? Because I don't want you to see him if it's gonna bring everything up for you. He's not worth it.'

'You mean more to me than my hatred towards him ever could.'

'Promise?'

'Sky,' he whispered, softly touching my cheek, 'I don't think you get how much I feel for you.'

My chest hurt, both good and bad fighting one another in equal measure. Getting my hopes up, or jumping to conclusions, hadn't done me much good in the past. Best not start again now.

'I ...'

He stopped me. 'You don't have to say anything.'

'I know, but I want to.' I took a deep breath. 'I guess I'm waiting for the other shoe to drop, as they say. Things are so different between us now, sure, but there's still a little nagging voice in the back of my brain who tells me you can't possibly like me for real and I'm being fooled again.'

'It's my fault the doubt's there. Fuck, I put it there.'

I couldn't deny it. Leo had added to it, but Ollie was the instigator of the original betrayal.

'And I don't know if a promise will even hold the weight it should because of all my previous bullshit, but I promise you, this isn't anything like the past.'

I nodded, tongue too tied to speak.

Ollie leaned forward to graze his lips across mine in a gentle, soothing kiss.

Our eyes locked when he leaned back to look me over.

'You mean more to me than anything, and I'm going to spend every day of my life proving it to you.'

Twenty-Two

THE FOUR OF us were on the campus grounds, taking in the warmer weather.

Orlando and *The Set* were nearby, laughing and joking and acting like twats to grab my attention, no doubt. It hurt, but I needed to ignore him. To get close to him, he needed to come to me next time. I'd done enough chasing.

He'd see through me if I acted too desperate and forgiving.

The five of them had reinforced the rules listed on *The Hive* app and had added some new ones as well. We seemed to be immune to them, but the other students weren't so lucky.

Ophelia acted like the Queen, fully in her element, alongside Orlando as her King.

Pathetic.

'Look at them over there,' Ollie said, his eyes drawn to the same spot as mine. 'How have we ended up in such a fucked up parallel universe?'

'Beats me,' Griff said. 'I don't know how everybody else here isn't in an uproar.'

I scoffed. 'Why would they be? The new rules mean they'll get beaten up or bullied for saying anything against Orlando or the girls. I'm surprised the parents haven't stepped in, but who knows what Winnie has on them all? She seems the type to keep information against everyone for blackmail purposes.'

'You've sussed our aunt out well, Clouds.' Griff's gaze moved away from the group. 'I, for one, am glad we don't have to pretend about any of the bullshit anymore.'

'You mean *The Sect*?' I asked. Griff rarely spoke about any of that kind of thing with me, so I didn't realise how much he didn't care about it all.

He nodded. 'I never did care.' He shrugged. 'I went along with Ollie and Leo because it was easier for everyone.'

Ollie narrowed his eyes at Griff, but stayed quiet. He had his thinking stance in place, and I'd learned to leave him to it when he got into that head space.

'God, you're so full of shit.' Clover said it so scornfully it nearly knocked me back. She stared at Griff as if seeing him for the first time. 'You bloody loved it. You always have loved attention and being a part of the tradition gave you what you needed and some. Don't downplay it because you've realised how pathetic you were from observing and judging Orlando.'

Griff opened his mouth. Closed it again. The wind ruffled his red hair, the colour brighter in the soft sunlight.

'Sorry?' he sputtered.

'You heard me.' Clo crossed her arms over her chest, her stance one of a woman willing to fight. *Oh, great.* She should have spoken to him back when she returned from the hospital, but nope, she'd wanted to live in denial for a little longer. Now it was all about to spill up and over in the middle of campus. Ollie and I were a part of the collateral damage by standing close to them. 'You act like you're so smooth, so casual, so cool … We all know the real you.'

'Clo,' he said, taking a step toward her, an outstretched hand she avoided by stepping back herself. 'Let's go back to your room and we can talk about whatever this is, yeah?'

'No.' She shook her head. 'I don't want to, okay? I ...' She blew out some breath. 'If we go somewhere alone, then this won't go the way I want it to. The way it *needs* to.'

'Okay,' Griff said, his tone placating her. God, my heart broke for him, but I froze in place, unable to do anything to stop the implosion happening before my eyes.

'I'm sorry,' Clo said. 'For a lot of things, really. Griff, you mean a lot to me.' She took his hand in hers. 'But this isn't working and I think it's best if we end it here.'

'Clo, if you'll give me ... us ... the time to talk in private,' Griff said, but she cut him off.

'I can't. I'm sorry. Maybe it's best we have some time apart.'

Ollie and I stood shocked at everything unfolding in front of us, knowing not to get involved but also unable to walk away from the display. Devastation played out on Griff's face.

Griff's bottom lip wobbled. 'B-but—'

'Please don't make this harder.' Clo let his hand go and took a step back. 'I'm gonna go back to my room. I'll see you all later, okay?'

I nodded. Ollie shrugged his shoulders and Griff stared at her, shell-shocked.

Clover sent a half-smile in my direction, then left in the direction of our room. As if she hadn't dropped a bomb. As if the shockwaves of her words weren't still reverberating through our small group.

I moved from my spot beside Ollie to Griff's side, pulling him into an embrace. 'Wanna ditch Ethics?'

He nodded against my shoulder. 'Please.'

'We'll go to your room.' I looked over at Ollie. 'You coming?'

IN THE EVENING, I left Griff and Ollie and went back to my room, unsure what mood I'd find Clover in.

She hadn't come to dinner, and I hadn't seen her in the halls on her way to and from classes, so chances were she stayed up in our room all day, wallowing in her misery.

I gave a timid knock on the door before letting myself in. 'Clo, it's me.'

She sniffled, her body buried under the duvet.

'Do you want me to leave?'

Another sniffle. Some movement. A muffled, 'No.'

I took it as an invitation to stay. Doubt I'd get much more out of her until she was ready.

It sounded odd, but I needed reassurance from her that now she and Griff were over, things wouldn't change between us. That I wouldn't get put in the middle of the two of them if everything remained tense.

I got comfortable on top of my bed. Who knew how long it'd be before Clover uttered a word to me? Either way, I would be there when she did.

My mind wandered, as minds were known to do.

Everything had turned to shit at a faster pace than usual.

My anxiety spiked at a ridiculous rate, my relationships unravelling before me, an empty spool beside tangled threads, all mixed up and knotted.

Mum's words, said so casually on Mother's Day, kept coming back to me. *'Like I knew he would, he said he'd come back.'*

But when would he come back? In a few days, a week, or a month? Or worse, longer?

The unknown killed me. The fact he could arrive, disrupt my life, and make himself a target for *The Sanctum*, was enough to have me praying he wouldn't show his face—and believe me, I never prayed for shit. It seemed wrong to pray to a being I didn't believe in, but on the off chance it worked as some sort of manifestation, I couldn't pass up the opportunity.

Jacob Cooper, the ever elusive father of mine, would become a lot more real if he came to Hawthorn, and I was unprepared.

His impending arrival had the ability to make things a fuck ton worse.

There was also a slight chance things could improve.

Wouldn't mind a future-telling crystal ball right about now.

'Sky,' Clo said, her voice clearer. Her head popped out from under the duvet, while the rest of her body stayed hidden. She resembled a slug with a human head. Or a caterpillar wrapping itself into its chrysalis. Or some kind of monster from an episode of *Doctor Who*. One of the three, at least.

'Yeah?'

'Do you think I did the right thing?'

I pondered her question. 'Well, I guess it depends what you're asking. You did the right thing in ending it, but did you do the right thing by dumping him in front of me and Ollie in the middle of campus? Er, maybe not.'

She sighed. 'It was shitty, but I meant what I said. If I didn't do it right then and there, I'd have made excuses *again* and let it go on for even longer.'

'I get it. Whatever you did would have upset him.'

'I know.' She sniffled, wiping a stray tear under her right eye. 'I'm such a cow.'

'You're not,' I said. A gut reaction of sorts. You know how the expected answer comes out unbidden before you could think it through? Well, it happened to the best of us.

Because Clover acted like a cow at times. *Fuck, doesn't everybody?*

'He'll forgive me, won't he?'

'He will. This is Griff we're talking about. I reckon it'll take time, but he's the best person out of all of us.'

'Not hard that, is it?' Clover laughed. 'We've all got our faults.'

'Wouldn't be human without them.' I went over to her bed and sat down on the edge. 'Want a hug?'

'Skylar Crescent is offering me a hug?'

'Oh, shut up. You make me sound like an ice queen.'

'You're not, Sky.' Her tone was earnest. 'If Griff is the best of us, then you're a close runner-up.'

'I find that hard to believe.'

'Well, you are. You're the one who wants to give Orlando a chance to prove who he is. The rest of us would leave him to the rats if the opportunity arose.'

'His life hasn't been easy,' I said, hearing the excuse clear as day.

'Neither has yours, but don't see you killing anybody and stringing them up like a set of Christmas lights.'

The image of Mr Hawkins's body flashed in my head, the same way it had in my nightmares ever since I saw it.

I'd yet to speak to Orlando about it. I may be the one willing to get close to him and see if he had anything worth saving lurking deep down, but it didn't mean I wanted to get *too* close and get blinded by him. The way he resembled Ollie confused me a lot more than it should.

'We're not talking about me right now.' I shuffled back on the bed to rest my back against the wall, stretching my arm out for Clo to hug me if she wanted. 'I'm proud of you, by the way.'

'You are? What for?'

'For doing the hard thing.'

Twenty-Three

GRIFFIN NEEDED CHEERING UP.

The split a week ago had thrown him off a lot more than I thought possible. Yes, I expected him to get sad and morose, to be down in the dumps for a little minute, but this was worse than even that. His actions were that of a completely different person. One who didn't smile; didn't laugh or joke.

I hated every single second of it, and determined to do something about it, I got permission to take him off campus for the day to the cafe we all loved in town. A change of scenery would do him good.

'Clouds, you don't have to waste your weekend spending time with me,' Griff said when he opened the door to my smiling face. 'I'll make you miserable, and it won't do to have us both sad.'

'You could never make me sad, Griff.'

'I did last year,' he pointed out, a glimmer of his smile appearing before leaving as fast as it arrived. 'You know how sorry I am, right?'

I shoved his shoulder lightly. 'We're well past whatever it is you're referring to, so stop making excuses and come into town with me.'

'I suppose I could eat some cheesy chips.'

I nodded. 'Of course you could. Now let's go, we're wasting daylight.'

THE BOTTLE of ketchup made a noise as I squeezed it, making both me and Griff laugh like the children we were at heart.

'Thanks for this, Clouds.'

'No need to thank me. You'd do the same for me. Shit, you have done the same for me two times over already.'

He winced. 'You spoken to Leo?'

'Yeah, we've talked. He apologised a bit, and I think I'm gonna accept it pretty soon. I'll never forget what he did, or the way he toyed with me to begin with, but ... I don't know. The whole reason we "got together" in the first place was to piss off Ollie and Clover. Not like I can hold too much against him.'

'You can hold the whole knowing about Orlando's existence thing against him, though.'

'Well, yeah.' I took a bite of my chips, so I didn't have to say anything more yet. My anger at Leo had left me. As had—most —of my feelings towards him.

'I don't judge you for any of it,' Griff said, swallowing his own mouthful of chips. 'And I won't judge you for anything you do in the future, either.'

I took a swig of my water. 'The same goes for you, of course.'

'Of course.' Griff smiled across the table. 'We're Griff and Sky, and together, we're unstoppable.'

'I brought you here to cheer you up,' I said. 'Not so you'd work your magic on me and make me smile.'

'I love you, Sky.'

'I love you, Griff. Forever and always.'

'Do you think you'd rather be a bear with a human head, or a human with a bear's head?'

I thought through my answer carefully.

'If I'm a human with a bear's head, is the head proportionate to my body, or is it abnormally large?'

Griff rubbed his chin, taking it as serious as I hoped he would.

'I guess it would have to be proportionate, wouldn't it? Otherwise, your neck wouldn't be able to hold it up. You'd end up in hospital, or worse.'

'Okay, well, as long as my bear's head isn't too large, I'll choose that one,' I said, happy with my decision. 'What about you?'

'We can be a pair of bear headed humans together. Right pair we'd make at family gatherings.'

'Not like our family gatherings would have anybody but us two.'

'Oh, yeah,' Griff said. 'Suppose so. Unless your dad shows.'

'Don't remind me.' I placed my arm into the crook of Griff's elbow, ready to walk up the stairs into the main building. 'Do you reckon he'll show?'

'Jacob? Cora seemed certain he would.'

'Cora's always certain she'll win the lottery, but that's never happened either.'

'Your mum is something else.' Griff chuckled. 'She's a force, like you.'

'Are you comparing me to my mum?' I couldn't decide if his words were what mattered most or if it was offensive that he thought even a little of me was like her.

'I guess,' he said, not sensing the danger. 'I know you don't get along, and she's treated you poorly all your life, but well, it doesn't mean you aren't similar in some ways.'

'Tread carefully, Griffin Cooper.'

'Full-naming me?' He chuckled harder. 'Okay, I'll leave it out. We going in?'

'Yeah, I need to stop by the office to sign us back in.' I smiled up at the gargoyles. When did Hawthorn become more like home than my mum's place? 'You wanna watch a film together or shall I leave you alone?'

'You can come to my room. I've been saving a TV series for us to watch together. Some kind of musical thing.'

'Sounds right up my alley.' I pushed open the heavy door at the entrance using my shoulder, putting my full weight into it. The doors may very well be beautiful and ornate, but shitting hell, they weren't easy to open.

I stumbled inside, Griff's laughter ringing through the large entrance hall. My arse landed on the floor, the thud audible to all. 'Shit.'

Griff stopped laughing. He stopped everything.

I took in his shocked expression, his jaw hanging wide open.

'D-dad?' he stuttered, blinking fast.

Dad?

Once I got myself up, I turned to face whatever had shocked Griff so much.

A man stood in the hall, tall, with light brown hair, and an expensive suit on.

I put it together rather fast. It wasn't Griff's dad standing at the entrance of Hawthorn Academy like he owned the place.

No.

It was mine.

Twenty-Four

'I CAN'T BELIEVE Jacob's here.'

'And what? He was waiting in the main building alone?' Ollie brushed a strand of hair back, which had wriggled loose from my ponytail behind my ear.

'Yeah. Griff thought he'd seen his dad at first. His face went sheet-white, and I expected him to keel over.'

'What happened next?'

'I froze, then when I realised, I bolted out of there as fast as my legs would carry me. I want to talk to him, but not until I'm ready.'

'According to Leo, he's staying over at Hawthorn House.'

'When did he tell you?' I asked, narrowing my eyes at him. 'I didn't think you and Leo were on talking terms.'

'We're not.' I waited. It didn't take long for Ollie to cave. 'He texts me from time to time.'

'Kept that quiet, haven't you?'

'I haven't kept it from you on purpose,' he said. 'More like I haven't found the right time to bring it up. Wasn't sure where you stood with him right now.'

'He's apologised,' I said.

'Have you forgiven him?'

'Don't think I'll ever forgive him, but maybe one day we can be friends again.'

No matter what went down with Leo, I missed him. Even before things became ... difficult ... between us, we'd found a sort of friendship together—a kinship of sorts.

'How do you feel about it all?'

'We'll never go back to the ways things were,' Ollie said, 'but I don't want to ice him out my whole life.'

'He has helped us recently.'

'He has, but he also caused a lot of the problems so ...'

My fingers trailed up his arm, loving the smoothness of his bare skin underneath my fingertips.

'Enough about Leo,' Ollie said. 'Let's talk about your birthday.'

I groaned. 'Do we have to?'

'What you got against your birthday?'

I gave him the evil eye. 'Nothing. I don't wanna celebrate it.'

'But you're gonna be eighteen! We can't ignore it because a few knob heads are trying to ruin our fun.'

'Trying to ruin our fun? Ollie, they're trying to kill me.' I scoffed. Talk about an understatement.

He laughed. 'Either way, it's your birthday and we're gonna do something.'

'What you got in mind?'

'A party in the woods for everyone.'

'I'm pretty sure it's like the worst idea ever.'

'Maybe, but I miss letting loose with no worries.'

'We've never been able to.' I pointed out.

'Believe it or not, a time existed where parties at this place weren't a total disaster.'

'I find that rather hard to believe.'

'Okay, so maybe not a *total* disaster and a mere *minor* disaster instead.'

We cracked up, laughing at what we both knew to be true. No party at Hawthorn went well.

'Fine, but if the party goes tits up, then don't come complaining to me, you hear?'

Ollie laughed and kissed my cheek. 'I hear.'

I still hadn't told him about the kiss Orlando planted on me. It meant nothing to me. A blip in time, where I acted poorly, but not one I wanted to repeat.

Things were weird between Ollie and me. We weren't a couple, as far as I knew, but we spent every waking moment together. Either we slept in my room or his, and we ate all meals together. Recently he'd been more free with his physical touch and affection too, giving gentle touches and placing soft kisses on my cheek or my forehead or hand.

If he was showing me he could be a gentleman, it was working.

'While on the topic of your birthday, I've got something I want to ask you.'

'Go for it,' I said. God, I could fall into his bright blue eyes and swim around for days and never get bored.

'Sky, would you like to come away with me this weekend?'

Come away? I blinked at him, repeating his words in my head to decipher them. 'Away? Like to a hotel or s-something?'

'Yeah.' He gulped, his nerves on show for me to see. 'In London.'

I wanted to, but the memory from the last time we stayed in a hotel together still smarted. Back then, he was using my heart as a tennis ball while denying his own in the process.

Maybe he wanted a re-do.

Maybe I also wanted a re-do.

'Okay,' I whispered. 'I'd like that.'

'Yeah?' The relief on his face made me smile. Seeing Ollie unsettled would never get old. It reminded me of his humanity.

'Yeah. Thank you.'

WE RARELY ATE dinner together in the dining room these days. With Griff and Clo having entered a stalemate of sorts, when we were all in the same place, things were still a little awkward.

'Are you sure you're up to it?' I asked Clo in our room before we went down to meet the boys for dinner. 'We don't have to if you don't wanna.'

'I want me and Griff to remain friends and splitting the group up isn't the answer to making it happen.'

'No, I agree.' But how to put it delicately? 'The split might have hurt Griff more than you, though.'

Not sure if my sentence held the tact I aimed for.

'Has he said something to you about it?' Clover frowned, fiddling with the hem of her skirt. 'Should I stay up here and you go alone?'

'Don't be silly! I didn't mean that.' I shook my head, tongue-tied. In my head, what I wanted to get across made sense, but the words weren't coming out right. 'Ignore me.'

'If it gets awkward at any point, I'll come back up here and you can sneak me up a plate of chips. How's that sound?'

'It's a deal.' I smiled. 'Now come on. I'm starving!'

We went down to the hall without talking, both of us lost in our own heads.

Ollie waited outside the dining room, Griff at his side, shuffling his feet, his eyes locked on the ground. Griff always acted so confidently. I never knew how to approach him when he acted so differently than usual.

'Hey guys,' I said on arrival. 'What's going on?'

'Not much. Been waiting for you,' Ollie said. He placed a kiss on my cheek and I smiled. Recently, he'd become a lot more touchy-feely, taking pleasure in touching me freely or placing kisses on my cheek or head. When we slept beside one another each night, other than spooning me or grazing his fingertips along my arm, he kept to himself. A perfect gentleman.

A large part of me wanted him to shake off the persona of being a gentleman and act on the inevitable.

Because at this point, I could accept we were inevitable.

Both my heart and my head told me we were, which was good enough for me. I hoped Ollie felt the same way, but time would tell. He'd spent his whole life covering up his true feelings, and it was a mechanism of sorts he hid behind when necessary.

'Shall we get in there?' Clover asked, rubbing her stomach. 'I'm starved.'

I narrowed my eyes her way. 'Starved?' I laughed. 'You baked a dozen brownies today.'

'Your point?' She tapped her foot on the ground and crossed her arms across her chest, which made me laugh harder.

'And you ate half!' I said.

'I did.' A decisive nod of her head drove her point home. 'But it doesn't mean I'm not hungry now. Girl's gotta eat to survive, Skylar.'

'Then let's go eat and shut you up.' I headed into the hall, the three of them following in step behind me, and a gasp rang out through the room. I turned my head to look back at the others and whispered out of the side of my mouth, 'Is it me, or is everyone staring our way?'

'They're looking at us alright,' Griff whispered back, his eyes locked ahead to where *The Set* were sitting with Orlando. 'Wonder what dick features said to them all?'

'What makes you think it's him?' I asked, ignoring the stares as I took a seat at our regular circular table.

'The smug, smirking smile on his face, for starters,' Griff said, sitting in the seat next to me. 'He's basically the cat who got everything he ever wanted.'

Clover sat down next to Ollie, who had already taken his spot next to me, and the four of us continued small talk, all while pretending we were oblivious to the tension in the air. If we ignored it, maybe it'd go away.

Yeah right.

Things never went away at Hawthorn. They stayed in the background, or under the surface, biding their time until you least expected it.

What was worse? Waiting for something bad to happen, or having it happen straight away? Either way, you remained on edge.

The waiter came to our table and took our order, disappearing as silent as he arrived.

Griff, who hadn't stopped fidgeting in his seat since we sat, leaned in to whisper in my ear. 'Orlando's standing up. Think he's heading over here.'

'Wonderful,' I mumbled. 'Just what we need.'

My eyes found Orlando as he moved through the room, stepping out of waiters' way and avoiding collisions with any students leaving towards us.

Ollie's hand gripped my knee under the table, either to send support to me or to keep himself in check. I welcomed his touch, no matter the reason.

'Well, well, well.' Orlando's voice trickled through me like honey. *Smooth bastard.* It bloody irked me the way he sent my emotions on such a rollercoaster. 'If it isn't the person I've been waiting to see.'

He meant me, right?

'Oliver.' Orlando turned to him. 'You've been avoiding me.'

Okay ... maybe he didn't mean me. My heart stuttered at the insult, the wrongness of that not lost on me, but stutter away it did.

Ollie, rather unimpressed his brother had come over in the first place, let alone had the audacity to talk to him, didn't respond.

'Okay, I can play your game. Little One, you okay?'

I rolled my eyes at his obvious attempt to piss off Ollie. Sadly, it worked.

'Don't you dare talk to her,' Ollie growled and sat up straighter in his chair. 'You've got my attention. Now, what do you want?'

'Oh, nothing in particular.' Orlando's smirk grew. 'Did Skylar tell you about our talk?'

'What talk?' Ollie voiced the same question I had, because as far as I could remember, we hadn't spoken alone in a while. Not since before Mother's Day ...

Shit.

He meant the kiss.

I squirmed in my chair, hoping nobody could see my face as the realisation hit of what Orlando intended to do. If I was being honest with myself, I had myself to blame. Telling Ollie should've been at the top of my priority list, even if it meant nothing and we weren't technically a couple.

Orlando rubbed his chin, pretending he had to think about it, when the bastard already knew *exactly* the talk he referred to. 'Must've been a while back, come to think of it. In the library.'

Ollie and Griff both swung their heads in my direction, while Clo's gaze narrowed on my face from opposite me.

'It can't have been important, because Sky's never mentioned anything about it,' Ollie said. Oh, how I admired his confidence.

Griff and Clo glanced at each other and shared a tentative smile. If this was the thing to make them comfortable being together again, then fuck, I had to run with it and allow it to play out in whatever way Orlando wanted. He'd orchestrated us all into this scenario, after all.

'Or maybe it was *too* important, and that's why she never mentioned a thing about it to you.' Orlando took the empty seat between Clo and Griff, and banged his palms down on the table. 'Assuming she never told you about our kiss, either.'

Orlando took the pin out of the grenade he held and threw it down.

The resulting explosion went the way you'd expect it to.

Ollie removed his hand from my leg, his chair screeching as he pushed it away from the table—from me—and stood up. 'What did you say?'

'I thought you and Sky were closer now.' Orlando shook his head. 'Sorry if I dropped a bomb.'

Nobody believed his insincere words.

Ollie turned to face me, not giving his brother the satisfaction. 'Is this true?'

'He kissed me, yeah.' No point in denying it. 'And it's slipped my mind ever since because it meant *nothing*.'

'Oh, don't be like that, Little One. No need to hide from me.'

'I'm not.' I shrugged. 'I'm being honest.'

'You're lying because Ollie's staring at you!' Orlando stood from his chair. My laugh came out awkward and barking, but I couldn't help it. The two of them were twins when angry— which, yeah, duh—and even their actions were mirrored. Both of them were rubbing their jaws and staring daggers at me. Kinda nice to have something unite them—even if it was through their displeasure at me.

'I think you should leave, Orlando,' Clover said, finding her voice in the chaos. 'I'm sure Skylar will seek you out if she wishes.'

Orlando hadn't taken his eyes from me. The black of his pupil overtook his eye. Evil through and through.

'You'll pay for this, Little One.'

Twenty-Five

RETURNING to the hotel in London with Ollie had apprehension running through me.

A crime scene from Skylar past. It held a lot of memories—tainted ones from a time where Ollie lied to me as often as he breathed. Glad to know he'd worked on that.

'I thought I'd leave the evening up to you,' he said once we made it up to the room. From the moment we entered, my body gravitated towards the ceiling to floor window. Viewing the city in this way always filled me with such warmth. 'Didn't want you to think I didn't care about you.'

'Thanks,' I mumbled. The only word I could think of to describe my emotional state: overwhelmed. I always found it odd whenever Ollie tried to show me how much he'd changed. Like if I believed him, he'd pull the rug out from under me, and everything would twist and once more I'd be the punchline of a joke. 'Do we have to go out?'

'Not if you don't want to.' He stood in the centre of the room, surveying everything around him. 'We could spend the night watching the sun go down over the skyline if you like?'

I smiled. He knew how much I loved this view of London. 'The view from here is beautiful,' I said.

'My view's always beautiful when I'm looking at you.'

'Smooth.' I laughed to hide my uneasiness.

His eyes locked with mine, but he stayed still. 'I mean it.'

I waved him away, afraid to fall too heavy for his suave words, but knowing in my heart I'd fallen already. Something about him sang to my heart. A chemistry existed between us that I couldn't deny.

'Sky,' Ollie said, taking a step towards where I stood frozen by the window. Whenever he moved, I sensed it deep in my bones. 'I wanted to take this time to talk to you, and I planned to wait until dinner, but honestly, I think I'll explode if I don't come out with it now.'

'Okay ...'

What did he want to talk about? Did he want to end things between us even though technically there wasn't even an "us" to end? *No, don't be so fucking silly, Skylar.* Why would he have bothered to arrange a weekend stay away? He wouldn't have. Not if he planned to tell me he wanted nothing to do with me anymore.

After Orlando had crashed dinner to reveal our kiss, I thought things would get even more tense between us, but nothing changed. Ollie asked for my version of events once we were back in his room, and after I'd told him, he was more than happy to forget it ever happened.

"My brother orchestrated it so he had something to hold over you, babe, and unlucky for him, it didn't work."

We hadn't spoken of it since, but now, in an empty hotel room watching Ollie pace in front of me, my mind couldn't help but jump to conclusions. All of them horrible.

' ... forward.' Ollie stopped talking, his right eyebrow raised in question. 'Everything alright?'

'Yeah, yeah. Sorry about that. Got lost in my head for a second there. What were you saying?'

His entire body moved from the force of the breath he exhaled. 'I've forgotten what I said.' He laughed, rubbing his jaw. 'Okay, let's try this again.' He took a step closer. 'Skylar, I know a lot of shit's happened and I'm at fault for most of it, but I feel like we're in a better place again. After everything I did, I don't deserve your forgiveness, but I'm so glad you gave it, and now I've got it, I never want to do anything to make it go.'

I tried to process his sentences to make sense of where his mental path headed, but I also didn't want to get my hopes up in case he threw me a curve ball.

'Skylar, it would make the happiest person alive if I could once again call you my girlfriend.'

'G-girlfriend?' I stuttered, my nerves on show, but not at the idea of being his girlfriend. It hadn't occurred to me how much I wanted to be a couple again until he said the words. No, my nerves were for something else entirely. My worry stemmed from the thought of Orlando's reaction. He wanted to steal Ollie's life, and if I became his girlfriend, would he become even more determined to make me his?

'Sky?' Ollie said after I remained silent for a fraction too long. 'There's no pressure here, I promise. I'm sorry. I shouldn't have assumed because you agreed to come stay away—'

I found his rambling pretty fucking adorable, and it made me smile, all teeth and gums, so I cut him off. 'Stop talking for a second.' My laugh softened the harshness of the words. 'I'd love to be your girlfriend.'

'You would?' The shock on his face made me laugh harder. Gosh, he was so dang cute.

'Of course I would!' I closed the distance between us and

wrapped my arms around his shoulder, clasping my hands together at the nape of his neck. 'Lately we've acted like a couple, but without the label.'

'True. So you're good with this?'

'Ollie, I'm *more* than good with this.'

Our lips gravitated together, the magnet strong at work once more, and what started as a gentle kiss became something a little less so.

We kissed for hours, and every moment, I fell further.

'BABY, COME TO BED.'

My voice carried across the room.

Ollie sat in the armchair, his black jogging bottoms sitting low on his waist, staring out of the hotel window made of floor to ceiling glass.

Ollie had carried his issues and worries to London, and it killed me to see him so out of sorts.

'In a moment,' he said. 'Go to sleep, Skylar.'

I got out of bed and wrapped a sheet around myself to keep my dignity. We were on a high enough floor and nobody could see in, but I still didn't want to walk around in the nude. I went and joined him, draping myself and the sheet over him. He opened his arms, and I straddled him, as I wrapped my arms around his neck and linked them so he couldn't move me.

'Come sleep with me,' I whispered in his ear. 'We have to go back to school tomorrow, and I want to make the most of our time away from the Hawthorn bullshit.'

'I don't want to make you feel shitty,' he mumbled, gripping me tighter. 'And I'm too in my head.'

'You know you can talk to me.'

'I don't know if I can,' he said, sounding vulnerable. 'It's so hard to form the words. My mind is clouded, Sky. I'm so fucked up about all of this.'

'I know, baby.' I kissed his cheek and moved one of my hands to ruffle his hair. These intimate moments, when the world was silent, were some of the best. It helped me forget we were two teenagers trying to survive adult bullshit we hadn't asked for. 'Are you thinking about Millie again?'

He nodded slightly.

I struggled to connect with him about it all in a meaningful way, and not just a way that came across false. I didn't have a great relationship with mine, and even though she hadn't been too bad during the Mother's Day festivities, Cora and I still had a long way to go until we were in a good place. The actual test in my eyes would be my birthday. If she texted me, I'd maybe be able to forgive her a little.

Ollie didn't have the option.

He had secrets, lies, and pain. Not to mention a secret twin.

In my quiet moments, when I watched him struggle, I disliked Millie more and more. Maybe it was shitty of me to feel so strongly about a woman I would never meet, but I couldn't help it. My heart connected with Ollie's in a way I couldn't describe, and knowing the pain she caused him meant she'd pained me, too.

'What's going through your tortured mind?' I asked, trying to get him to open up. Wanting to climb inside of his head and swim around in his brain matter.

Bit fucking dark, Skylar.

'Why would she give him up?' The tone of his voice made my heart melt and caused tears to well in my eyes, glad I'd buried my head in his chest so he couldn't see them.

Ollie was proud, and not the kind of person to confront his issues head on.

He also sounded sad about Orlando for the first time. I often wondered if he wished he could get to know his brother, but his pride and anger were both getting in the way.

'Why would she abandon me?'

It took me a moment to follow his change of subject. 'I wish I could answer, O.' His inner child lurked in his eyes, sad and hopeful at the same time. 'But your mum's illness ruled her.'

'That's no excuse!' he spat. 'She could have tried harder. Tried to get better, for me.' His voice cracked, and I kissed his cheek again, hoping my love for him would show in the action.

'Maybe.' I sighed. The moonlight and city lights left him half in the shadows. 'We can't rewrite the past.'

'I know,' Ollie said, his eyes haunted. 'But it doesn't mean I can't be angry about her choices, because I am Sky. I'm pissed. I've always looked up to Mum and wished she was still around. I always thought of her as everything good and pure in this world; somebody who got hurt by life and circumstance.'

I continued to run my fingers through his hair to soothe him. I stayed silent, knowing he didn't need my words right now.

'They killed her sister,' he whispered. 'Whoever they are. They did this to her. If Eliza hadn't died, Mum may have made a different decision. Things wouldn't be the way they are.'

'And I wouldn't be here,' I murmured, an involuntary slip of the tongue. If the past didn't unfold the way it had, then the present wouldn't be how it is, and I firmly believed that. Everything happened the way it did, for good or bad.

I placed my cheek up against his chest. The thrumming of

his heart kept me grounded, stopping me from focusing on the slither of anger inside.

'Right,' he said. 'But I'd still have my mum.'

The hurt at his sentence pierced my heart, like a harpoon making a clear wound, entering and exiting in one swift motion.

I wanted to move off him, go back to bed and curl up in the foetal position and breathe.

'Right,' I agreed through gritted teeth.

'I'm a dick,' he said after a beat. I nodded against his chest, not wanting to raise my head and make eye contact. He sounded so defeated. So knocked down by life and I couldn't help. Couldn't reach him.

And the idea scared me.

'Maybe it would've been better if she'd given me up,' he said, resigned.

I moved so fast it surprised me I didn't give myself whiplash. Listening to him talk crap about himself made me mad, and I wouldn't listen in silence anymore.

'Don't say that.' I gripped his chin in between my thumb and forefinger, locking him in place so we were staring into one another's eyes. My baby blues met his equally blue ones.

God, imagine the blue eyes of our children.

Wait. Woah. Where the fuck had that thought come from?

I shook it off and focused back on the beautiful, broken boy.

'You do not get to think of yourself that way.' My tone brooked no argument. If he wanted to talk shit about himself, he wouldn't get to do it without repercussions from me. 'Only I get to think shit about you, you understand me?'

He chuckled darkly, but I saw his eyes lighten a little.

'You must have thought a lot of shit in the last eighteen months.' He gave a small smile.

'Oh, you bet your arse I have,' I agreed. No way would I beat around the bush. I respected him more than that. 'But, I've also thought a lot of good thoughts, too. Mainly ones about your chest, your face ... your dick.'

His whole body shook with his laughter, and I smiled. I'd shocked him.

'You like my dick, Miss Crescent?' he asked, one eyebrow raised. His grin turned devilish, full of dark thoughts and some not so dark thoughts.

'I do, Mr Brandon,' I said, 'but I'd like you without it.'

'Is that a promise?' He moved me so I straddled him, my knees on either side of his thighs. His hardness underneath me pressed against the spot I wanted it most.

'Hmm,' I mused. 'Now I'm not so sure.'

Ollie squeezed my ribs, and I let out a little laugh. I wasn't ticklish per se, but I also got a little squeamish when somebody tried. Bastard knew it, too.

His dick twitched underneath me, and I smiled.

'Let's go to bed,' I whispered in his ear.

'Or,' he whispered back, 'we could stay right here.'

'Oh, yeah?'

'Yep,' he said, squeezing my waist now tighter than before. 'We're in the perfect spot in front of the city. Live a little.'

'If you insist.'

Twenty-Six

MY EIGHTEENTH BIRTHDAY, one I was lucky enough to be alive to see, arrived and celebrating it fell very far down on the priority list.

Not now Jacob Cooper had shown his face.

When Griff and I had found him in the school hall, waiting for us to get back, something overtook me and I legged it out of there as fast as my legs would carry me.

Hadn't seen or spoken to the man since.

Griff told me Winifred had invited him to stay at Hawthorn House as her guest, and as much as I felt sorry for the man's predicament, I didn't plan to storm over there and demand answers from him without thinking it through.

No. He could sit and stew for a bit longer.

I'd go to him when ready and not a moment before.

'... this top?'

I blinked over at Clo, standing in front of the wardrobe, hands on her hips, an expectant expression searing through me.

'Sorry?'

'Have you listened to a word I've said?' Clo's tone told me

she was getting bored with me tuning her out and living in my head.

'Clo,' I said, ignoring her question. 'Do you think a party tonight is a good idea?'

Griff and Ollie had arranged a party, and it had to be the worst idea they'd had in a long time. Yet because they were doing it for me, I couldn't get mad.

The other students at school would benefit more than me, but in a way, it meant I was doing my bit by giving everyone something fun to make them forget people were being assaulted and/or murdered.

Even five months later, it sounded ridiculous to me.

Orlando still being a student here was laughable.

'What do you mean?' she asked.

'I mean what I said. Do you think a party in the woods tonight is a good idea?'

'When are they ever a good idea?' Clo laughed, pulling a top off its hanger and putting it on. 'I can't say this one is more ill-advised than any of the others.'

'Now, see, usually I'd agree with you, but this time I'm not so sure. My dad's here, which means *The Sanctum* is gonna make a move on him soon, right?'

Clo shrugged. 'One more night before you talk to him won't make much difference.'

'I suppose.' I couldn't explain why, but my stomach told me I didn't like any of this. 'I've got a bad feeling, tis all.'

'You've always got a bad feeling,' Clo said, but not unkindly. More a statement of fact than a mean observation.

'It's been warranted in the past.'

'Except for the times it would've saved you from nearly dying.'

Okay, the girl has a point there.

'Whatever,' I said. 'Maybe I should forget my worries for the night.'

'Sensible of you.' Clo nudged her head to the two plastic cups filled to the brim with vodka and coke. 'Now drink up, otherwise you'll worry more.'

'Oh, ha, ha.'

'Sky, come on. Let's forget everything for the night and enjoy ourselves. We don't have long left here together.'

'We've got three months,' I deadpanned.

'Which is nothing in the grand scheme of life.' She pointed at me. 'Get dressed. Now.'

HIDING from the party became more and more appealing with each passing second.

I understood why Ollie and Griff had wanted to make this happen, had wanted to make me forget all the other birthdays in life my mum or others had forgotten or ignored on purpose, but I'd have much preferred to stay in with the people who mattered most to me.

'You okay, baby?' Ollie asked, handing me a glass of violet gin and lemonade that glowed under the twinkle lights placed on the trees.

'I'm good.' I took a large gulp of the liquid.

'Are you sure?' he asked, pulling me closer to him and turning me around to place my back up against his front, his muscled arms gripping me in place.

'Yeah, just thinking.' I pushed myself further back into his arms, the safety of them filling me with an emotion I wanted to bottle up and take out on rainy days.

Ollie kissed the top of my head, and I squirmed a little—in a good way.

We may not be a couple again, but standing under these trees, the connection between us thrummed loud. A genuine connection. One that thrummed underneath every interaction, every bad time and every good time.

'Sky, I want to make you happy no matter what. You know that, right?' he asked, his gaze seared into mine.

'Sometimes,' I whispered. 'But sometimes I have no clue.'

'Well, I need to do a better job then, don't I?' he whispered back. The moment was intimate, and like all intimate moments between me and Ollie, it came to an abrupt end.

A hard body jostled into me, knocking me to the side as they went by, not stopping to glance back at who they'd accosted.

'Fuck,' I said, my dress now covered in the sickly sweet smell of violet. 'Wanker!'

I stepped out of Ollie's embrace and brushed off the liquid, but as per usual, my actions did nothing to aid the mess.

'Who was it?' he asked, his tone low.

'Nobody important,' I said. I grabbed his arm to stop him from heading off like a bull in a china shop and pulled him back to face me.

'Are you hurt?'

'Nope, just wet,' I said, then laughed. Wet, but not the birthday wet I wanted to be, that was for damn sure.

How much alcohol have I had?

The thought of having sex with Ollie occupied my thoughts often, especially after the events of last weekend.

Instead of spending the evening with wankstains I

disliked, Ollie and I could have been enjoying our own private celebration—alone.

And I know we did last weekend at the hotel, but I'd happily do it all over again.

'Why are we around people again?' I asked.

'Huh?' he growled, distracted, still fixated on whether they hurt me.

'Why aren't we celebrating alone?' I waggled my eyebrows.

'We can do *that* anytime.'

So, yeah, true, we could have sex whenever we wanted now we were an official couple, for real this time, and spent every night together, but I also hated the way he said it. The implication of it.

Like I was a sure thing. *Easy.*

I peeled myself out of his grip.

'Skylar!' Griff hollered from somewhere nearby and I turned around, searching all over to see if I could find his shock of red hair hiding amongst the other people.

'Yeah?' I called back, unable to see him. I moved away from Ollie and searched the surrounding crowd.

'Clouds!' Griff called again.

'Oof!' I said as air left my lungs in a rush, our bodies colliding. He barrelled into the side of me, causing the two of us to fall flat on the floor. 'What did you do that for?' I snapped.

Griff laughed, a cheeky chuckle in my ear, getting a kick out of this. It was nice to hear him giggle, so I couldn't be too mad.

'Ah, come off it, Clouds. It didn't hurt.' He moved back off of me and assessed me from head to toe.

'How d'you know?' I asked, raising my eyebrow. I mean, I wasn't hurt, but not like he could tell from briefly glimpsing at me.

'Can just tell.' He shrugged. 'I know you, Clouds. I've seen you hurt more than enough times now.'

His last words were darker, his tone hushed, and a tug came on my heart strings for him. I never stopped to consider how my constant beatings were affecting him. Griff always came across so happy-go-lucky I assumed those instances had run off of him like water down a duck's back.

'Griff,' I whispered, reaching out to grasp his hands in mine. 'I'm sorry.'

'What are you sorry for?' he asked, squeezing my hands. 'Sky, you have nothing to apologise for. You can't help that people wanna hurt you.'

'I feel bad. Like everything these past eighteen months or whatever is my fault.'

'That's bullshit, and you know it. There was no way you could've known coming here would go the way it did. I mean, fuck, Clouds, you didn't know about your father before you came here. How could you know they'd rigged the scholarship all along?'

'I-I—' I stuttered, unsure of what to say.

'Sky, none of this is your fault, so don't you ever apologise to me again unless it's for some shit you did do like eating the last slice of pizza without asking the room if they wanted it,' he said, the accusatory look on his face making me smile.

'That was one time! *And*,' I stressed, 'I thought the pizza was mine. So why would I have needed to ask?'

'Yeah, yeah. Tell it to the judge,' he said, beating his fist into his chest.

My hand made contact with his shoulder, and I pushed him further onto the dirty ground. 'You kill me, kid.'

I moved and pushed myself up from the floor, so I sat upright once again. Griff reached out his hand so I could pull him up. I had to use all my strength. Fuck, the boy had muscles.

'Are you enjoying yourself?' he asked.

I took in the hoards of students milling around us, dotted around the clearing.

'I ...' My eyes met his.. 'Honestly, Griff, I don't know.'

'Me and Ollie meant well.'

'I know,' I said and hauled myself back to standing. I put my hand out for him to grasp, then pulled him up, too. Griff smiled at me.

'I love you, Sky.' His eyes met mine, the green and blue ocean hue of them glowing in the dark of the woods.

'I love you, too.'

'LITTLE ONE,' a growl in my ear stopped me in my movement.

I'd headed away from the party, wanting to get away. The loud music hurt my head, and I wanted to think without being the centre of attention.

Before coming to Hawthorn, barely anybody knew my name, let alone looked at me and cared about what I did or who I spent time with.

'Orlando,' I said, knowing it was him without having to turn. Who else would call me Little One?

'What's the birthday girl doing out here all alone?' he drawled, and a chill filled me.

'Nothing much,' I replied casually. 'I wanted to be alone for a moment.'

'Hope you don't mind me gatecrashing?' he asked. The question was a loaded one filled with double meaning. Not only had he gatecrashed the party, but also my moment of solitude. I knew Ollie and Griff had specifically not invited him, even though they announced said party to the entire dining room, so couldn't dictate shit.

Neither of them wanted him anywhere near me—especially not out in the woods in the dark of night.

'I don't, but I'm sure your brother will have something to say about it when he sees us.'

'He always seems to have something to say when it comes to you, Little One. Don't you see you're trapped?'

'T-trapped?'

Orlando walked towards me. With each step, my heart rate climbed, getting faster and faster to where I thought it would leap out of my chest.

'You know. The way Oliver doesn't allow you out of his sight? Doesn't allow others to spend time with you without him knowing who you're with and where you are? Sounds pretty stifling to me.' His lips grazed up against my ear.

'It's n-not.' I stuttered. Why did Orlando make me revert to my shy, stuttering self? 'Me and Ollie are happy together.'

'Of course you are,' he mocked, putting his hands up in a placating gesture. I'd spent enough time with him, both in disguise and not, to know he was laughing at something on the inside.

'We are.' I grit out, more forcefully than before.

'No need to lie to me,' he said, his tongue snaking out of his mouth to touch my neck in the softest of grazes, but hard enough to make me shiver. My nipples peaked under my dress, and this time, I couldn't blame the weather.

It didn't help that he looked like a carbon copy of my boyfriend—looked like the spitting image of the boy I loved.

Sounded like him, too.

'I'm not lying.' I needed to head back. At least within the party's safety, people would be witness to whatever came next.

Orlando reached out for me.

'I am, am I?' he growled, grabbing my wrist to hold me in place.

'Please Orlando,' I whispered. 'Let me go.'

Twenty-Seven

ORLANDO

'I CAN'T DO THIS,' Sky whispered, her gaze pleading.

Her beautiful blue eyes were wide and red-rimmed, tears glistening in the corners, threatening to break free and run down her face.

A face that made me feel more than any single thing ever had before.

'Can't do what?' The words came out clipped. Angry. Did she mean she couldn't talk to me? Couldn't be near me?

My thoughts raced ahead, and the anger crept further in. My vision turned red at the edges; a slow fog, a haze clouding my vision. My judgement. *Everything.*

I pushed her, my hand still gripped around her wrist, until we came to a tree and I used my force to press her up against it.

Her pulse rapid under my thumb, her heartbeat increasing.

It all gave me a sick thrill. A bolt of lightning through my body, sending every nerve ending into overdrive.

I wanted to *destroy her.*

Wanted to plunge my dick so far inside of her she'd split clean in two.

Wanted her to gag and cry and scream in despair.

What would she look like if I ruined her? Cut her pretty cheeks and slashed her throat? Watched as the blood spurted, then trickled down her pale neck.

'Orlando,' she said in a croak, drawing me out of the depraved images in my head. Her tears were flowing fast, and I wanted to lick away each one.

'What?'

'You're hurting me.'

Those words should have had me backing off, stepping away, but instead, I moved closer. Our bodies were as close as they could be without me climbing inside of her chest cavity. Would it be warm there, nestled between her rib cage and her heart?

'Stay still!' Spit flew from my mouth and landed on her face. She winced, and I could see myself in her eyes—could see her reaction to me. And I wanted to stop, but I didn't know how.

I'd never had to stop the beast before. Had never wanted to, even.

Without my brain and heart aligned, I needed to take a step back. Take a breath. Truly think before I fucked things up with her more. Everybody believed I didn't care about my little one. They thought I wanted Ollie's life—which, yes—and therefore wanted Skylar because he had her. Because she belonged to *him*.

It may have started that way, but time changed everything.

I removed my hand from her wrist and brought it up to cup her chin. My lips placed a soft kiss on her cheek.

My other hand, seemingly with a mind of its own, trailed down her body. Breached the top of her trousers. My fingertips played with the lace band at the top of her underwear.

Fuck.

I had to get out of here.

Before I touched her. Before I let the voices in my head corrupt her—and me.

'Little One,' I whispered.

Her tear-stained, mascara-streaked face glanced up at me. Her eyes pained. This hurt her. *I* hurt her.

'Orlando.'

'I'm sorry,' I whispered, my tone harsh, before pulling myself away from her.

I turned and fled.

Running out of the trees and away to another clearing. A place where I could get away from her. Get away from the urges I had. Get away from the monster within.

THE EMPTY CLEARING I found myself in was far away from the party.

So far away, in fact, I could no longer hear the thumping bass of the music. I could no longer hear anything once I stopped and took it all in.

Until ...

'Orlando!' Ophelia called, her voice getting louder as she got closer. 'Baby!'

It came out as a whine, her nasal voice sending goosebumps up my arms. I stayed facing away from the direction I could hear her stumbling, hoping she'd get the hint when I didn't answer or turn to face her.

Ophelia spent the whole of last year not being able to tell

me apart from my brother, yet nowadays, she knew within a second.

Explain that one.

'There you are!' Her voice was at my back now. Close enough for her to reach out and touch.

'What do you want?' I asked after a couple of minutes. My silence not giving her the hint I hoped it would.

No, instead of leaving, the stupid bitch came closer.

'I've been trying to find you for the last hour,' she said, her words slow and drawn out as if she were talking to a toddler. She'd been drinking all night, and the vodka had finally gone to her head and made itself at home. 'Somebody said they saw you slink off with Skylar the slut.'

The entire sentence ran into one another, her words slurring together, and I laughed at her, all sinister and devoid of actual joy. Not that Ophelia could tell.

'Skylar isn't a slut,' I growled. 'Don't let me hear you say shit about her again.'

Ophelia came into view, her crop top barely covering the girls.

'Oh, shhhhh.' Her pointer finger covered my lips. 'I don't want to talk about her.'

I grabbed her finger, bent it back, and moved it away from me. Her face twisted in discomfort, but she didn't make any noise.

'Why? Because she's more of a woman than you'll ever be?' I asked, wanting to antagonise her. Wanting to piss her off and bring out her claws. I needed a fight, and she'd walked straight into my cage.

My headspace remained fucked, and I was out for blood. Any blood.

'Skylar Crescent is a nobody and doesn't deserve your attention. Let your loser brother have her.'

'You didn't call my brother a loser last summer when you were hanging off him.' My words poked at her. I may not have been there to watch it unfold firsthand, but Leo told me enough about how Ollie acted last summer.

'Well, I've seen the light,' she tittered, 'and I want the sunshine state.'

God, this girl.

'That's Florida itself.'

'Same thing,' she said, brushing my bicep up and down. I rolled my eyes at her flirtatious tactics—ones I wouldn't allow to work on me.

'Either way,' I told her, 'I don't want you.'

'Because of her,' she spat. 'She doesn't want you.'

'I thought you didn't want to talk about her?' I asked, needling her further.

Come on, Ophelia.

Give me what I want.

'All anybody at this fucking school has done since *she* started here is talk about her! She's been the focus of every single fucking person, and I'm sick of it! Sick of her! Things would be a lot easier if she died when you stabbed her. But even that you fucked up.'

The end of her sentence blurred together in my mind, and I fixated on the fact Ophelia believed the world might be better off without Skylar in it.

A lot easier if she died.

I saw red.

My rage hit me in a flash. Every vile thought, every slur she'd said about Skylar, hit me full force until I couldn't hear anything else. Like a loop, her words played over and over. She was still talking, her mouth moving a mile a minute, but I could no longer understand any of the words she spoke.

An animal made a sound in the distance, scuttering through the brush, which caused her to stop talking for a moment. I watched, as if in slow motion, Ophelia turned in the noise's direction, searching for the animal who made it.

I took advantage of her distraction.

Picked up a large branch and swung.

The branch connected with her skull, and a crunch reverberated throughout the area. Ophelia made no sound; the blow knocked her out cold.

Her body slumped down to the ground, thudding as she landed. A sick thrill filled me. A jolt of pleasure that brought a wide smile to my face. I dropped the stick and came to my senses.

I needed to leave. Go to bed and forget this terrible night had even happened.

As I walked away, I glanced back to Ophelia, laying in the centre of the clearing, all peaceful.

Stupid fucking cunt.

She deserved to suffer the way Odette had. The way Olivia had.

Maybe Oralie needed to watch out, being the last one left and all …

Twenty-Eight

WHAT THE FUCK JUST HAPPENED?

My thoughts swirled around in my head. Twisted and entwined with others until they were no longer decipherable; until I couldn't tell them apart anymore. Couldn't separate the truth from my nightmares and fears.

I stayed rooted to the spot in the clearing, unsure of what I should do, where I should go.

If he hadn't got a grip on himself, would he have gone further? Would he have given in to whatever dark and depraved thoughts swirled in his head?

I'd always let Orlando off—more than I should—but I couldn't deny his actions this time. No writing them off and pretending they weren't heinous.

He assaulted me.

Or at least attempted to. *No*, scratch that, because calling it an *attempt* made it sound as if he were unsuccessful. As if it could only be called assault if some form of penetration or pain took place, which is utter and total bullshit. Anything unwanted, anything that crossed boundaries or went against your consent, equalled assault, plain and simple.

I adjusted my clothing, putting myself to rights again. At least in appearance.

Breathe, Skylar.

Orlando was nowhere to be seen. He'd departed like a man possessed. Maybe he was, which would explain why he'd acted so out of character. But then again, it wasn't out of character, was it? The boy had an anger problem, one I'd seen the brunt of on more than one occasion.

The fucker stabbed you, Skylar, and you're still making excuses for him!

All I could do was stay put and wait for somebody to find me, because somebody *would* find me. Clo, or Griff, or Ollie, or fuck, even Leo, would search for me. I'd been gone long enough. Surely at least one of them would notice.

What the fuck was I going to tell Ollie?

I couldn't keep this from him—didn't want to keep this from him. After everything the two of us had been through these last months, I didn't want to have to hide anything from him, or to feel like I had to.

Especially after I hid *that* kiss. Look how that had turned out.

How long have I stood here, alone, stuck in my mind?

Time blurred in a haze—probably due to all the alcohol. Would things have gone differently had I drunk less? Did my actions cause people to feel entitled? Ollie, Hawkins, now Orlando. All of them had taken from me, in one way or another.

What made Ollie's actions forgivable compared with the others?

My stomach churned, and I held down the vomit threatening to rise up and out.

Even the drinking hadn't been fun. Now I could drink

without repercussions in the eyes of the law, drinking had lost its edge.

Fuck, growing older sucked.

Skylar, stop.

I needed to get my bearings and to figure out what the fuck I should do next. Should I go find Ollie and tell him everything and risk him killing his brother in a rage?

Should I tell Leo? See if he cared enough to jump ship from underneath Orlando's thumb and help us bring him—and all those who wanted to harm me and my loved ones—down?

Did I tell Griff, who wouldn't do much about it but would cheer me up inside?

Then there was Clover. She had a violent streak living within her, bursting to make an appearance. Maybe Ollie wasn't the most likely candidate for murder.

Mind made up, I walked out of the clearing, hoping I headed toward the party and not further into the woods in the direction Orlando fled.

Like Alice heading further into Wonderland, I kept going, hoping I would see a sign in the trees telling me which way to head. Or maybe a great big smug smiling cat.

I saw neither.

The trees were telling me something a lot less *Alice in Wonderland* and more *Snow White* when the woods tried to harm her.

Everything became sinister. Otherworldly. Out to harm me.

'Fuck!' I screamed into the world, nobody around to hear me.

After a few paces, something up ahead came into view, resting against a tree.

Slowly, I crept forward, trying to make as little noise as

possible. I didn't want to startle whatever—or whomever—it lurked there.

'Hello?' I called out. If somebody sat at the base of the tree, they would answer me, right?

Nobody wanted to be out here all alone.

It was dark, and getting rather late. Or early, depending on whether you were a glass half-empty or half-full kind of person.

Knowing my wild imagination, it would turn out to be some kind of debris, or maybe a discarded piece of clothing from a student using these woods for privacy.

'Hello?' I called again, louder this time.

I kept walking forward. Kept walking towards what I now could see were a pair of legs and a torso propped up against the tree.

'Ophelia!' Her name ripped from my throat, the force of my shout hurting.

Something was wrong.

Very wrong.

If Ophelia heard me call for her, she wouldn't bite her tongue. The two of us were no longer enemies, but we weren't friends either, and with the way she'd sidled herself up to Orlando lately, it wouldn't surprise me if he had twisted her against me once more.

Either way, she'd never miss the opportunity to tell me to shut the fuck up.

How long had it even been since Orlando left me in the clearing?

I growled out loud in frustration. Pissed I didn't know. Pissed I didn't have my phone on me or even a watch.

My phone had dropped out of my hand during my altercation with Orlando, and I had been in such a daze I hadn't thought to grab it before walking away, and now I didn't want to head back to find it. No chance of finding it, anyway, without a phone to shine a torch from.

How the fuck had this evening gone even worse than I expected? I shook my head, trying to clear the fog settling around my brain.

'Ophelia!' I called again. 'Answer me! A grunt, even. Anything.'

I became frantic again, getting closer to her with each stilted step, every fibre of my being knowing I wouldn't like the sight in front of me.

Have you ever seen the film *Stand By Me*? One of my absolute favourites to the point I could quote every line in time with the characters.

Anyway, there was a scene when they find the boy they went in search of and they get a glimpse of the dead body they'd made the journey for.

Well, Ophelia reminded me of that.

Twisted.

Broken.

And undeniably, definitely dead.

Somebody had propped her up against the tree trunk, her head at a funny angle. This may be the second dead body I'd seen, but it seemed different with Odette. That had all been a blur, one I could barely recall even now the memories of the charity show had returned to me in stages.

Ophelia was different.

Her neck looked like someone had snapped it in anger. Her legs stretched out, pale and odd.

What the fuck?

I couldn't breathe.

Pain shot through my body and my heart tightened in my

chest. A deadly squeeze. My vision blurred, the dreaded black spots entering at the edges, making quick work of taking my sight away from me.

The other times I'd passed out were nothing compared to this.

My legs buckled beneath me, and I crumpled to my knees, careful to not fall too close to Ophelia. My hands grabbed the sides of my head, trying to put pressure on my temples to stop the headache from taking over.

I'd never had a panic attack alone, and the thought scared me so much I panicked even more.

Leaves crackled somewhere behind me.

Shit.

A swooshing sound reached my ears, and as I turned to find out where the noise had come from, a sharp pain started on the back of my head.

Then everything went black.

Twenty-Nine

'STUTTER!'

I blinked ... What happened?

Oh, right. I passed out. *Again*.

No wait. My head throbbed, struggling to recall anything. I'd been on the verge of passing out, yes, but then ... then somebody whacked me around the back of the head and I blacked out.

The moonlit night hurt as my eyes adjusted, my head throbbing.

The voice called out. 'Stutter, you around here?'

A drunk Leo stumbled into the clearing, a bottle of jack fixed tight in his grip, and he came to an abrupt stop a metre in front of me.

'Leo ...' I let his name hang in the air, trailing off into the empty clearing.

Wait, empty?

I sat up way too fast, the blood rushing to my head causing me more pain, but I had to see if I could see Ophelia. Had to get her help, and fast.

'Why are you out here all alone?' Leo asked, swaying on the spot, unaware of my despair.

Surely Ophelia hadn't got up by herself and walked away? The girl's neck hung on by a thread.

'Where's Ophelia?' I asked, snapping my head in every direction. 'Have you seen her?'

'Ophelia? Why would I have seen her?'

'She was here.' I pointed to the tree. A dark patch remained where her head had been, but nothing else. Her blood? 'You sure she didn't pass you on your way here?'

'I'm sure,' he said, narrowing his eyes. 'Are you okay? You seem a little out of sorts.'

Did he know? How had he found me? Had he been watching me?

'Are you sure you didn't see anybody?' I asked, choosing not to answer his question. 'Not even Orlando?'

'I haven't seen Orlando all night.'

I scoffed. 'I find that hard to believe.'

'It's the truth, Stutter.' He took a swig from the bottle in his hand. 'The party got boring, so I wandered off on my own.'

'Pity party for one, huh?' My laugh sounded harsh even to me.

God, when would I stop pitying him? Stop wanting to climb inside his mind and find out what went on in there?

Leo didn't respond. He stood there, gazing at me intently, his eyes raking from my head to my toes, searching for something. 'Shit Stutter, you're bleeding.'

My hand touched the sensitive tingling spot on the back of my head and it came away covered in blood. 'S-somebody hit me. I don't know who.'

'Shit!' Leo crouched down to my level. 'Let me take a look.'

I turned my head so he could assess the situation. 'Is it bad?'

'Not too bad, but we need to get you back to school to have

it checked out and washed properly. Do you think you can stand?'

I nodded, and he stood up, putting his hand out for me to grab, and I used his steadiness to get myself back to standing.

'Can you walk?' he asked, his tone gentle. 'Here, lean on me if you need.' He wrapped his arm around my waist and the two of us began the slow hobble back to Hawthorn.

'Now you've got me alone. Want to fill me in on everything? For real this time.'

'I've not hidden anything from you.'

'No, but you've not gone into too much detail either.'

'What would you like to know?' he drawled, a playful smile appearing on his face. His smile still turned my insides into jelly. He'd been drinking out of the bottle all evening, so maybe he was a little looser tongued than normal.

'Everything,' I whispered in his ear. He shivered, the hand on my waist tightening a fraction.

'Everything's a little vague, Stutter.' We paused, and he turned to face me, his gaze boring into mine. Goosebumps covered my arms, and not just from the chill of the night. 'Where should I start?'

'How about you start by telling me how you got involved with Orlando?'

Because that was the event this all stemmed down to.

'I wouldn't say I got involved with Orlando. Not like I had any choice or say in the matter.'

'No, I know, but you've never gone into detail about the tasks *The Sanctum* wanted from you and whatnot.' I waved my hand, hoping it came across in the casual way I intended.

'So, I've already told you about how ol' Winnie took me to the woods the day I met Orlando for the first time?'

I nodded, silent, egging him on to continue.

He stopped talking and rubbed his finger on his chin before running his hand through his hair.

'Go on,' I urged, looking around to make sure nobody had stumbled onto our spot in the woods.

'They gave me two scrolls. If I didn't follow the instructions written inside, they'd kill Red.' His eyes stayed locked on mine, and he swayed on the spot. 'You know Red and I grew up together? Guess they knew about my relationship with her and wanted to use it as their bargaining chip.'

He shrugged and took another swig from the bottle. Liquid-courage and all.

'What did the scrolls say?'

'One had the Hawthorn family tree, and the other held a letter, telling me I had to help Orlando Hawthorn take his truthful spot as an heir. To help him in all endeavours, otherwise they'd harm all I love and I would never get to enjoy the perks of becoming a real member.'

He shook his head. His eyes shone in disbelief, one we all experienced when trying to wrap our heads around the whole scenario.

'So, what did you do then?' I asked. 'Freak out about this ginormous secret they kept from you all?'

'Oh, yeah.' He chuckled. 'As soon as my parents arrived home a couple days later, I flew straight to my dad's office and demanded he tell me more about our family tree. Within moments I could tell he knew fuck-all. He didn't know about Orlando. If he did, he hid it well. From then on, I knew I was on my own. I met with Orlando a week later, in the hidden corridors of the school, to talk about what help he wanted.'

'And ...?'

'He told me to go along with his plan to ruin Ollie's life and take back what he claimed was rightfully his. He knew Clover was attending the next school year as a scholarship student, after Ollie and I had rigged it so she could return, so only one option remained for me. I needed to make it clear I gave zero shits about her. If I didn't care about her anymore, then neither would Orlando nor *The Sanctum*. I made sure the entire school turned against her and I abused the power being the head of *The Sect* gave me. I treated her like shit, never wanting her to know the truth; never wanting her to know I did it all to protect her.'

'You pushed her away to save her?'

'I did.' His bloodshot eyes found mine. 'Orlando also knew you were going to be the scholarship recipient the next year. Knew Ollie planned to make you suffer for the sins of your father, and he wanted in on it. Wanted to harm you, too, but worse.'

I shivered. I'd known since meeting Orlando—as himself and not as his brother—he wanted to hurt me more than Ollie ever had, but having it confirmed by Leo, standing in the darkness of the woods, alone, was eerie.

'And to be honest, Stutter, I didn't know you then, so didn't think about you being a person with feelings. All I knew, you were the daughter of somebody hated within our circle. None of us knew what you knew about your dad. For all we knew, you could have come along and acted like an entitled cow who had been denied your birthright. So I agreed to help Orlando in taking Ollie's place when you arrived. Agreed to make you suffer if it meant keeping Clover safe. I regret it now. From pretty much the moment I met you, I wanted out. But you don't say no to Orlando.'

'I get it,' I said. And I did. I understood the dilemma they had placed him in and could appreciate he hadn't known me from Adam. I could've come along and been a spoiled brat, or been a plant of Jacob's. He'd done what made sense to him at that moment, and I couldn't hate him for that.

'During the first year, there wasn't much to do. You weren't here yet, so Orlando stuck to the family mansion on the grounds, mainly.' Leo swigged from the bottle, but when no liquid entered his mouth, he frowned. During our conversation, he'd finished it. 'Fuck,' he cursed, throwing it to the floor. It smashed on impact, the shards of glass flying out and landing on the branches and leaves below us. 'Shit, be careful, Sky.'

'It's fine, I'm wearing boots.' I raised my foot to show him my sturdy boots, and I watched him relax at the sight of them.

'Right. So. Shit-all happened that year. During the summer, though, things ramped up a notch.' He looked off, and I could see the cogs turning in his head. 'Ollie was putting his "revenge" plan in place against you with the girls ready for September, and Orlando had tasked me with letting him know everything Ollie planned to do.'

'And ...'

'And I told him everything.' He shrugged. No emotion attached to his actions because his loyalty lay elsewhere back then. 'He got the idea in his head to mess with you. Pretend to be his brother and tell the girls to do worse than Ollie asked. Pretend to be his brother to seduce you. To drug you. And so on.'

'Right. And I guess he knew when Ollie wasn't around because *you* told him when to strike, hm?'

'Yeah,' he said, sheepish. 'If Ollie was with me, I'd let him know. We had to be careful. Couldn't have Orlando being seen by other students who may then see Ollie elsewhere and question shit.'

'Sounds like a pretty stressful operation.' I let out a

sardonic chuckle. I had to give it to them. They'd pulled off some pretty decent black ops shit. Nobody had been any the wiser. I'd never doubted the "Ollie" I spent time with wasn't the real Ollie. Not at the time, anyway. Now I doubted all the shit.

'You've no idea.' He chuckled. 'It gets pretty hard to keep it all straight in your head. I can tell you that much.'

I didn't point out how I too struggled to keep it all straight in my head. 'Then what happened?'

'Huh?' He frowned, his beautiful blue eyes glazed over and bloodshot.

'Well, after school started, you *knew* what happened. You knew who drugged me, drowned me, and stabbed me. How could you stay silent? I thought you felt something for me. We said I love you, Leo.' I ended my sentence in a soft whisper.

'And I meant every single word of it.' He gripped my hand in his, squeezed gently. 'It's complicated.' I could see the stress in his features; sense his inner shame. 'I guess you know I wanted the fake relationship to piss Orlando off as much as Ollie?'

I nodded. Leo had multiple angles. Leo always had multiple angles and overlooking that would be silly.

'I knew Orlando had fallen for you, Ollie too, and I knew both of them were too hard-headed to do shit about it and admit it. Plus, anything to piss Red off worked in my book. Me being unable to be with her didn't mean *Griffin* could.' Leo's hands formed into fists at his sides, his knuckles white.

My stomach swirled in a mix of anger and sadness. Most of this I'd been aware of deep down. Even though I was getting the *true* story, my gut had known the truth all along.

'This is a lot to take in,' I mumbled. 'Maybe we should head back? My head and all ...'

'Fuck!' Leo's eyes widened. 'Why didn't you remind me?' He turned me around and shone his phone light at the back of my head. 'It's not bleeding, but we should get it checked out, still.'

'Thanks, but I want to get in the shower before snuggling up in bed.'

I gestured behind me to the trees. Back to the sort of safety of the school and to Ollie's arms, where I could lay awake all night processing all the information Leo had given me. From here, we couldn't even hear the party sounds anymore. I wasn't even sure if there *was* a party still happening or if it was late and most people had crashed out and burned.

'Sky,' Leo said, and I froze. He rarely used my name. Whenever he did, it meant something. It was more real than anything else he said.

'Yeah?'

'I'm sorry. For being a part of it.'

'Sounds to me like you had no actual choice.' I shrugged, the last remnants of my anger towards him leaving and fluttering away in the wind. Maybe after so many apologies, he'd worn me down, or maybe I was ready to forgive him and move the fuck on. Either way, I wanted my friend back. 'I forgive you.'

Many people would say everybody had a choice in everything they did. You could choose to be good or you could choose evil.

If somebody threatened your life, or the life of the person you cared most about, are you telling me you wouldn't do the bad thing? Wouldn't harm others to stop others from being harmed?

If you could honestly say yes, then you were a better person than Leo or me. A better person than *a lot* of people.

'Thank you,' he said sincerely, reaching out to pull me into a hug. 'For being you.'

He kissed my head, and like an egg being cracked on it, it travelled down and out to all of my limbs, leaving a warm fuzzy buzzing in its wake.

'Come on,' I said, pulling out of his arms so I could place my arm around his waist. 'You need some sleep. I know I do.'

'Ha!' He chuckled, as if it were a lot funnier than it was. 'I've not slept right in this place for some time, Stutter. Doubt it will change now.'

How odd, because whenever Leo acted as the little spoon to my bigger one, he slept soundly.

It seemed cruel to say anything, so I said nothing at all.

THE TWO OF us began our trek back to the academy in silence, and it hit me during our entire conversation that I'd not once mentioned Ophelia to him. Fuck, maybe she had a valid reason for not liking me. I reverted to such a trash human in the boys' company.

'Leo,' I started.

'Hm?'

'Did you follow me tonight?' I asked, hoping he'd take my question and run with it, rather than me having to go into any more detail. I didn't want to guide him to the answer I wanted.

'Follow you?' He smiled. 'Follow you where?'

'Anywhere,' I answered. 'Did you see me with anyone before ...?'

He shook his head. 'No. I wandered off earlier after ... Well, I wanted to be alone. I didn't know you were out this way, too.'

'I stumbled across Ophelia after ...' Fuck, why was it so hard to talk to him now? A few months back, I'd have had no issue opening up to him and telling him what Orlando almost did to me, but now it didn't feel right to burden him with my shit. He already had enough on his plate. 'She was badly hurt, but when you found me, she'd disappeared.'

He glanced my way, but continued walking, saying nothing.

'Do you think we should tell somebody?' I glanced at him as we walked, trying to see whether his face was as worried or concerned as it should be. I saw nothing more than his usual blank, bored expression. The one he used to give me a lot back when I first started coming to school here.

'I reckon somebody already knows,' he said, cryptic as all get out.

'What does that mean?'

'It means, Stutter, if your good pal Orlando did this, he would've already passed it on to good ol' Winnie. It's rare anything happens here she doesn't know about. You'd be best to remember that.'

'Back when you first told me of *The Sanctum,* you mentioned you thought she was in charge when they recruited you.' He nodded in response. 'Well, it makes sense she'd be high up. She wouldn't have told them about Orlando if she didn't think they'd keep it a secret.' I shrugged.

'Stutter, if I'm being honest, I try not to think too hard about it. Messes with my head.'

I understood, but it still seemed a bit cowardly of him—the one word I would never associate with Leo Hawthorn.

When I thought Leo wouldn't say anymore, and we would continue on in silence, he spoke up softly. 'Was it Orlando who hurt you?'

'Huh?'

'The blood on the back of your head. Did Orlando do it?'

Oh, so he didn't know.

'No,' I told him, wanting to ease his worry. 'Not that I know of. I didn't see who did it.'

But I was covering up the ways Orlando *had* hurt me. How he'd been about to touch me without my consent hurt me.

'Are you sure? You're not lying to me, are you?' he asked as he stopped dead in his tracks.

I stopped walking, too, and turned to face him. Our eyes locked, him searching deep into my soul for the truth.

If I turned my gaze away, or gave even the tiniest hint of distress, Leo would pick up on it. I didn't want to worry him in his current state. I kept my eyes as still as I could. Trying to convey everything in that one gaze.

'I'm not lying to you,' I lied.

'If you're sure.'

I nodded and reached out my hand to take his large one in mine. Our connection flowed from my fingertips into his, and back again. We still had a connection; a deep friendship. I hoped he wouldn't fuck it up by doing something stupid. Something like helping a secret organisation harm me or my family. My newly arrived dad. Fucking hell. As if my mind didn't have enough fighting for dominance already.

'Where's Ollie?' he asked, and I shrugged.

'You're more likely to know than me.' I smiled at him tentatively. I lost track of Ollie around drink number five. Least I think I did.

'I thought he'd be glued to your side all night.'

'We're not attached at the hip, Leo.'

'But you are back together?'

A lead weight dropped to the bottom of my stomach. 'We are.'

'I'm happy for you both.' I raised my eyebrow in question, and he chuckled. 'I mean it. You deserve the best in life, Skylar.'

A happy buzz spread through me. The two of us were going to be okay. I could sense it.

Leo had sobered up during our talk and walk, and was once again able to stand upright without swaying.

'Let's get you to bed,' he said, waggling his eyebrows.

I barged into his shoulder and moved to walk ahead of him. 'You wish.'

Thirty

'WHAT ARE WE GOING TO DO?' I asked, my eyes widening in Ollie's direction. 'What do you think happened to her?'

'We're going to do nothing.' His hard tone made me blink. 'We're not getting involved this time. I'd much rather find out who hurt you. You're lucky they didn't bash your skull in the way they did hers.'

'We don't know how she died yet,' I mumbled. It had crossed my mind more than once since my birthday party that the person who whacked me around the head likely killed Ophelia. But why had they killed her and allowed me to live? Or maybe they hadn't. Maybe I was meant to be dead, too.

Wouldn't put it past some fuckers here to still want me dead, Orlando included.

'The school has got away with this shit for too long. They won't be able to hush up another one, right?'

He shook his head, more uncertain than I'd have liked.

'Unfortunately, it's in Ophelia's parents' best interest to hush it up.' He winced.

'Shit like this doesn't disappear. Orlando's out on bail. If he did this, it's enough to put him away for life.'

'It does if you have enough money, babe. You'll learn eventually.'

'Oh, wonderful. Once again, my lack of a trust fund is a problem,' I joked, but even I heard the bite in it, so Ollie must, too.

'That came out wrong,' he said. 'I didn't mean it like that.'

'I know you didn't,' I muttered. 'I also know you're a bit of a dick.'

'I know you want my dick.' Ollie laughed and reached out to grab me and pull me closer. I resisted at first. Pretended I wasn't interested. Had to keep the boy on his toes somehow in this constant battle of wits. We may be a couple now, but I didn't want him to stop working for it—for me.

'Oh, sh you!' I laughed, not letting him get a grip on me, but also not getting any further away from him.

Ollie played along a little longer, but then stopped. 'Sky, I think you're joking because your breathing sped up and you're moving away from me but also not, but after everything ... I need you to say it.'

I leaned into his warmth, his heart beating fast under my hand splayed across his chest. 'Say what?'

I rested my head on his chest, and he stroked my hair, sending tingles through me.

'Say you do want me. Say this is okay. I never want you to feel like you've not got a say in anything like this ever again.'

'I—' My mouth opened and closed like a mindless fish, the words struggling to come. 'Ollie, if I ever don't want something to happen, I'll tell you. I promise.'

'No matter what?'

'No matter what. But if it makes it better, you can check in.'

'It does make me feel better, yeah. I never want to do anything you don't want ever again. I'm so sorry for ...' he trailed off, but we both knew he meant the library. The time I'd said no, and he hadn't listened. 'Sky, you mean the world to me.'

'You're not too bad yourself.' I bit my bottom lip, shy but happy he felt comfortable now voicing his emotions. The Ollie of a year ago barely knew how.

'Why thanks?'

I tilted my head up, and he leaned down to press a bruising kiss against my lips. The butterflies who lived in my belly flapped their wings into a frenzy. One kiss from Ollie and I was ready to rip his clothes off and launch myself at him.

But it wasn't the time or place.

'Ollie,' I said, stepping back to create an inch of space between us. I ran my fingertip down his pec. 'Reckon Winnie's called the police? Would she if she suspected Orlando hurt Ophelia?'

'She has no choice but to, I suspect. She may be in charge of the school, but there's a board she has to answer to and more. Plus, it looks worse for Orlando if she doesn't. Like he has something to hide.'

'So, the police will come here again and question us all?'

'Most likely, yeah.'

'Joy.'

Later that night, I lay in bed in Ollie's arms, awake, staring at the lamp on his bedside table.

His soft snores grounded me, yet couldn't lull me to sleep because my anxiety had spiked to nuclear levels.

But my anxiety wouldn't allow me something as simple as sleep. Not when so much shit took place in my mind.

My dad's arrival, mixed with Orlando's assault, wouldn't leave me be.

Orlando killed Mr Hawkins for his actions towards me, yet when it came down to it, he had also ignored my pleas, ignoring my lack of consent. I couldn't wrap my head around it. I thought Orlando cared about me, in his own weird and twisted way.

Yes, life had treated him poorly, but poor treatment from others never excused acting shitty towards others. An explanation, maybe, but never an excuse.

Thoughts swirled.

Images of Orlando flashed.

How do you hate somebody when you know you should, but you didn't have it in you to feel so strongly towards them?

Love and hate walk a tightrope together, a loss of balance either way descending you into the madness of one extreme.

And maybe something died inside me the moment Orlando put his hands under my clothes without my consent, because now I couldn't find any emotion for him besides pity.

I pitied him.

No hate. No love.

Instead, a vat of sadness sat low in my gut, twisting my organs and making it hard to breathe, or to relax enough to get some rest.

And whenever I stopped thinking about Orlando, images of my dad flashed in their place. Jacob Cooper was a mystery to me, even if I'd learned a little about him from others, and I still hadn't made my mind up about whether I wanted to spend time with him.

Ollie wanted me to—I'd even go as far as saying he was

pushing me to—but he also knew I wouldn't do something if I didn't want to and I could see how much restraint he put on himself whenever the topic came up in conversation.

I tossed and turned in bed, careful to avoid waking Ollie. He mumbled, but didn't wake.

I always found it creepy in films or literature when somebody commented on how peaceful a sleeping person looked, like a corpse somehow still breathing, but Ollie also fit the description. His eyelashes fluttered against his cheeks and the permanent scowl he seemed to walk through life with magically disappeared the moment he reached a deep enough sleep to forget about his worries for a while.

'Ollie,' I whispered, half in hopes he'd answer, half in hopes he'd remain asleep and I wouldn't have to voice the things echoing in my mind.

'Mm,' he murmured. His left arm snaked out from the duvet to drape over me, his hand resting on my hip bone.

'Can I ask you something?'

He mumbled some more. I took it as a sign to continue.

Maybe talking it out loud would help me, even if he didn't reply.

'Am I broken?' The words came out stilted. Small.

It seemed to grab his attention. He moved closer and kissed my bare shoulder. 'Broken?'

I nodded, but said, 'Yeah,' in case he didn't see or sense my movement. 'I don't trust my mind anymore.'

'In what way?'

'I can't explain it without telling you ...' I took a deep breath. I hadn't told him about what Orlando had done at my party yet. The right time hadn't presented itself, and with Ophelia's twisted body being found the next morning, well, I had other things to fixate on. 'Something happened at my party, and I haven't told you yet.'

Ollie shuffled up the bed, so his head rested on the pillow at the same height as mine. 'Okay.'

'Orlando ... he acted ... badly?' The disjointed sentence came out excruciatingly slowly, and I still hadn't managed to get across what happened. It came out as a question, my voice going up at the end, and the use of the word badly didn't even cover it. I tried again. 'No, I mean, yes, he acted badly ...' I pressed the heel of my hand against my eye, wanting to relieve the pressure building there. 'He touched me in a way I didn't like.'

'He fucking what?' Ollie growled, rearranging himself to sit up against the headboard, glancing down at me. 'How? Why?' He shook his head. 'No, don't answer if you don't want to. Are you okay?'

'I don't know. Is it bad if I don't hate him for it?'

Ollie cracked his knuckles. 'Not if that's how you feel. Whatever you feel, however you deal with it, is right for *you* and that's all I care about. I care about you, Skylar.'

I swallowed. Yes, I knew he cared, but fuck, it was nice to have it reiterated at a time like this.

'I know. I'm sorry I didn't tell you straight away.'

'You have nothing to apologise to me for.' He stretched out his arm, and I moved closer to his side to snuggle up against his chest. 'I want you to be comfortable telling me things, sure, but I want it to be in your time. Never rush yourself into anything because you think it'll make me happy, or worse, because you think I'll get mad you kept something from me.'

I breathed out through my nose, my body calming down merely from talking to him. It always surprised me when Ollie had the power to make me feel better. A reminder of sorts—one I needed. 'You're the best, you know that, right?'

His chuckle reverberated through his body. 'No, I'm not. I am trying my best for you, though.'

'I know we haven't been a couple again for long, but I want to tell you how much I like you.'

'You don't—'

'I don't have to tell you. I *want* to tell you. They're two different things.'

'Okay, then.' He leaned down and kissed my head. 'I want the record to state I like you a lot. *A lot, a lot.*'

I laughed. 'Thanks for not pushing.'

'Don't thank me for that. I may not be pushing now, but I have been pushing you to spend time with your dad and I'm sorry. I'm not ready to be around him yet, so it's shitty of me to assume you would be.'

'No, you're right to make me think about it. Without you, I'd push it down so far it'd never resurface.' My hand splayed across his ribs, and I dug my fingers in a little.

We both chuckled, and I snuggled in closer to his side. Once more, I found myself falling for Oliver. I'd wait this time before telling him, though. I wanted to be one hundred per cent sure before I blew everything up again.

'I think I'm ready to see him.'

'Okay.'

'You'll come along and rescue me if I need it?' I asked, batting my eyelashes at him. The boy barely refused me anything, so I was pulling out all the stops to ensure he didn't refuse me this. He hated Jacob Cooper. I only hoped he liked *me* more than he hated *him.*

'Skylar,' he said. 'You don't need me to rescue you. You are more than capable of rescuing yourself, because you're strong and beautiful and you take no shit from anybody.'

His words settled over me; a soothing balm to my scorched and somewhat fractured soul.

'I wish I had as much faith in myself as you have in me.'

'One day baby, you will.'

Thirty-One

JACOB COOPER WAITED for me at the entrance, dapper in his shirt and trousers. The fact he'd shown up at all surprised me.

I didn't know why, but I guess I expected him to not show. The fact the man was even walking around this town—this campus—like he'd never left shocked me.

He'd stolen a lot of money, allegedly, and the reactions his name received at the fashion show told me he wasn't well liked around these parts.

Plus, the fact the entire student body had bullied me because of his actions also let me in on his popularity status amongst the elite.

Exiting the doors, I prepared myself for the day ahead.

'Hey, Skylar,' Jacob said when he spotted me. His eyes were the same shade of blue as mine, but they had wrinkled lines at the edges, adding an air of approachability. Friendly. 'You okay?'

'H-hey,' I said, timid, my stutter rearing its ugly head. I knew it would. I'd not been put in a situation like this for some time, and even though my anxiety and nerves had improved, they were still bubbling under the surface. Especially when already apprehensive. And meeting my dad for the first time? My apprehension went into overdrive. 'I'm good, thanks. How are you?'

His smile made my heart stutter. 'I'm good, thank you. Ready to go?' he asked, putting his sunglasses back on. They were black aviators, and they made him even cooler.

On the rare occasions I'd imagined my dad growing up, I hoped he was cool, but deep down I'd assumed he was a low-life. If Cora wouldn't talk of him, well, then you knew he had something wrong with him. She'd married *Andy* after all.

'Yeah,' I replied, rinsing my hands together in front of my waist. 'Where are we g-going?'

He hadn't told me the plan for the day, just that he wanted to talk to me off of school property so nobody would overhear us.

I found that hard to believe. The part about not being over-heard. I swore the town of Beurre had eyes and ears every-where. I hadn't been in town much since starting at Hawthorn, but nothing had changed since the days I went to the local high school and lived on the Hollowdale estate.

'We're going to a little cafe down the way. I used to go there a lot back when I went to Hawthorn. Also used to go with your mother back when ...' he trailed off and I tried to mask my surprise.

Mum had never mentioned him, not once—not until the Mother's Day we spent with Lottie and Leo. I suppose I'd never thought about the things they liked to do together. That they spent much time together, even. Guess I always associated it as a brief dalliance resulting in the unwelcome present called me.

'You did?'

'Yeah,' he said, my confusion lost on him. 'When we first started dating.'

I laughed. I couldn't imagine it. Couldn't see it in my mind. Even in the short time I'd spent with Jacob Cooper, I could tell how different the two of them were. *Are*.

Dad grew up wealthy and his life had been easy—well, maybe not easy, but it had been easier than those who had none.

'Bet you looked a right couple together.' I chuckled. An image of him in an expensive designer suit with Cora standing beside him sporting a large over sprayed bouffant and a skin tight snake print dress entered my mind clear as day.

'We were definitely something,' he said, grinning too. 'Your mother came into my life during my rebel phase.'

'Makes sense,' I said, having already come to the same conclusion. 'Bet your parents didn't approve of her one bit.'

'That's an understatement.'

The two of us were now by his car, a sleek Mercedes that no doubt cost a lot more than any I'd known somebody to own, and he unlocked the doors for us to get inside. It worried me that being stuck in such a small space with him could stifle me, but I had to put on my confident pants and try to dampen my anxiety.

I took my place in the seat and waited for him to get in and start the engine before I spoke again.

'How did you and Cora meet?' I asked once we were on the road heading across town to this small cafe he'd spoken of. He didn't comment on the fact I called her *Cora* and not *Mum*.

'It's a funny story, actually,' he said, his entire face lighting up. Like a creeper, I couldn't take my eyes off his face, watching as his expression changed with each syllable. 'I was trying to escape the life I'd been born into, as you do, and I came down the hill into Beurre to get away from it all. When I was sitting at a bar, alone and nursing a whiskey feeling sorry for myself, this bombshell walked through the door and every eye in the place turned to her.'

'Sounds like Mum,' I said, surprised he'd referred to Mum as a bombshell. A bomb sounded more like it, debris and decay doing its best to get miles away from impact.

'Cora made people take notice.' He chuckled.

'Still does,' I said. I couldn't deny it, no matter how my relationship with her was. These days she came across as more of a caricature of herself, but at the age of eighteen, she had to have been a better sight. 'You should've seen her when she arrived on Parents' Day my first year at Hawthorn.'

My dad laughed, lines appearing on his cheeks, and his eyes wrinkled at the corners—such a human gesture—endearing him to me. Ever since he'd burst on to the scene, I'd been trying to come to terms with his appearance in my life. How it would work in the long run. Would we grow into a rela-tionship, or would he fall off the face of the earth again the moment I got comfortable?

I didn't want to get my hopes up too much.

'I can imagine everybody took notice,' he said, then continued the story, his eyes glazing over slightly. 'So, she entered the bar and came over to me. Asked me why I sat there oozing misery.'

'Sounds about right,' I said. The car came to a stop, and I glanced out the window. He parked the car on the high street, outside a cute coffee joint with sofas and armchairs called The Lounge. Cosy and bright. It also happened to be mine and Griff's favourite spot. 'Me and Griff come here a lot.'

'Really?' I didn't need to know the man to know he was chuffed. 'Me and Damien used to come here. Looks a little different now, I'll admit.' Jacob exited the car, and I followed suit, an odd sensation trickling through me at being out and about with a parental figure.

'The entire town has changed a lot over the years,' I told him. 'A lot of businesses have cropped up, and then disappeared as fast as they arrived.'

'This place used to be up and coming.'

'Well, it isn't now.' I raised my eyebrows, wondering how the town must have been years before. The town had been full of crumbling buildings my whole life, exteriors covered by cracked or fading paint, and an overall sense of decay.

'Still feels like coming home,' he said, his tone nostalgic. 'Suppose I didn't realise how much I missed the place until I came back.'

I followed him into the cafe, and we made our way to the sofa seating area. The moment we were both sitting down, things became even more awkward. The car ride over hadn't been too bad, which probably had something to do with the fact we were both staring ahead, briefly glancing at one another in turn, before our attention went back to the road. Now we were face to face; nowhere to hide.

The waitress coming over made things even more awkward. I glanced at the menu and decided what to order. Cheesy chips and a Diet Coke would be perfect, and right now, I needed some comfort foods to help me with the situation.

'So you have you missed it?' I asked him after the waitress had gone back to the counter. 'The town?'

What I meant: have you missed me?

'There's a lot I've missed,' he said. 'The town, my family, *you*. It's hard though, because this place also holds a lot of memories for me and not all of them are good. There's so much I need to tell you, Skylar.'

The waitress arrived with our drinks, and the two of us fell silent. Yes, Hawthorn may not be a safe place to talk, but the cafe may not be either. Best to be on our guard.

'I don't even know where to start,' he said, bewildered but determined. 'I guess you know about mine and Millie's affair.' I nodded, wanting him to continue. 'It wasn't sordid the way people think, at least not at the start.' He sighed. 'We were together from ages thirteen to eighteen. Thought we'd be together forever, honestly. But then she ended things, and I met your mum …'

He left the gap in the middle alone, skipping past it.

'After I left your mum, I moved away for a bit,' he said, sheepish. I liked how he didn't say "after I left *you*", but we both knew what he meant. 'I left Beurre and travelled; saw the world. Five years later, Millie left me a hysterical voicemail telling me about Damien and Eliza and how I needed to get back as soon as I could. I'd been off the grid and the numbers I didn't have blocked were Cora's and Millie's. By the time I returned, I'd already missed the funerals.'

His entire demeanour reeked of regret and despair. My heart went out to him. Yet, I hated myself a little for having sympathy so quickly. This man left me with nothing—nothing but an uncaring mother and her alcoholic husband—and I needed to remember that.

'She wanted to leave Henry, but we couldn't …' he trailed off, then changed the conversation. 'What do you know about *The Sanctum*?'

At his mention of *The Sanctum*, my drink had gone down the wrong way and I nearly choked.

'Err …' I paused, unsure what to say. What did we even know? Not much. It shocked me he'd got into it so fast. I respected it, though. I appreciated those who didn't beat around the bush. 'We know they're the adult version of *The Set* and *The Sect* and they rule the underground.'

'That's half of it,' he said. 'They've got a lot more sway, though. Most of the important people in the country have dealt with *The Sanctum* at some point or another. Politicians. The police. Every major business person. All under their thumb.'

'Guess that explains how Ms Hawthorn covered up those murders,' I mumbled, mulling the thought over in my mind, but speaking out loud.

'What murders?' Jacob asked, his brow furrowed.

'Three girls who were a part of *The Set* when I joined school. There's one original girl left now.'

It was the first time I'd said it out loud, and when I did, it hit me how fucked my life had become. Even back at my old school, nothing similar had happened. I mean, there had been some minor issues, like knife crime, but nothing in the way of murder.

I felt so disconnected from it, though. Maybe because someone had also attacked me multiple times and had stabbed me. When these things weren't a part of your life, they seemed extreme and worth worrying about, but now I lived it. Disassociating from it became as easy as breathing.

'And how ...'

Once again, we paused when the waitress came over to the table and deposited our food in front of us. The smell of the cheesy chips made my mouth water. I smothered them in salt, vinegar, and tomato ketchup, then watched as Jacob did the same.

We shared a look. *Great minds think alike.*

I waited for Jacob to continue, but he'd taken a mouthful of his food.

'How did they die?' I finished his question for him. Jacob nodded, swallowing his food.

Hm, how did I sum this up? There was one word for it. One word which could answer all.

'Orlando.'

'Orlando?' Jacob repeated, pausing his fork in front of his mouth.

'Yeah. He's Millie's son.' Saying it aloud tasted off in my mouth. 'Well, I know he murdered one of them for sure. The other two … well, the evidence hasn't presented itself yet.'

'But the one you know about, you have proof?' he asked.

'If being stabbed in the gut in front of the dead body of the victim is proof, then I've got plenty,' I deadpanned.

'What the fuck? Skylar, are you okay?'

'Yeah,' I said. 'Don't worry about it.'

'Don't worry that somebody stabbed you?' He put his fork down and narrowed his gaze. 'Sky … can I call you Sky?' I nodded. 'Sky, of course I'm going to worry about you.'

I scoffed, not meaning to, but unable to hold it in. 'Of course.'

'I didn't know.'

'A shame in a way, because having you find out about it made up half the motive.' I sighed.

'So Orlando killed those girls?'

'One of them,' I said, but then remembered my birthday party. Shit. 'Okay, definitely two of them.'

'You need to get away from him, Sky.'

'Oh, so you think now you've reappeared, you can tell me what I need to do?' I asked, crossing my arms, raising an eyebrow at him. Giving him a hard time on purpose.

Now he wanted to act like a dad, huh? Not on my watch.

'It isn't safe for you here.'

'You've had no problem with me being here for the last eighteen odd months, so why do you care now?'

'I didn't know you were here.' His eyes widened. 'I thought you were still under Cora's care. Safe, and far, far away from the harm of Hawthorn.'

'Yeah, 'cause I was so safe and away from harm at home.' I chuckled. The man was deluded. Which, yeah, of course he was. He'd gone *off the grid* to get away from his problems. Nobody sane did that shit.

'What's that supposed to mean?' His fingers went to reach out and graze mine, but he stopped himself, instead letting his hand rest in the middle of the table, his raised fingers twitching.

'Nothing,' I mumbled, not wanting to talk about my home life. I didn't want to let him walk into my life and take over, acting like a parental figure.

He hadn't earned the right.

But I hoped one day he might. If he played his cards right.

'Back to *The Sanctum*,' I said, changing the subject away from Orlando and what I needed to do. 'What were you going to say about them?'

'They ruined my life,' he said simply. No embellishments. No dramatics.

A cold, simple truth. *His* truth. One he believed with his whole being.

The question: why?

Thirty-Two

OLLIE and I were huddled together in an alcove, killing time before we headed off to our next lesson, when Leo stopped in front of us and coughed.

'Stutter. Oliver.' He nodded at us both in turn.

'Leo,' Ollie said, his tone making it clear how little he appreciated the interruption. 'What can we do for you?'

'I've got some news you both might find interesting.'

'And that is …' I said, joining the fray. These two weren't fighting, but they also weren't back to being best buddies, either. Which, understandable. Especially now Ollie and I were together *again*.

'There's a meeting of sorts tomorrow evening, if you catch my drift.' Leo's gaze darted around and paused when a large gaggle of students passed, laughing and joking about something unimportant compared to everything going on in our lives.

'Go on,' Ollie urged when the coast cleared once more. 'Spit it out.'

'I'll text a time and a place, but make sure you stay hidden. I'd rather you leave Griff and Clo here, so there's less chance of you getting caught.' Leo's eyes narrowed on mine and I tilted my head in acknowledgement. I would also rather they stay back.

No need for us all to go down with the ship.

'I mean it, don't get caught. I won't be able to step in if you are.'

'We understand,' Ollie said. 'You're treating us like we're stupid, mate.'

Leo's wince my way made me smile. 'Don't worry, Leo.' I smiled wider. 'I know you only think *one* of us is stupid.'

He smiled back. 'All members are required at this meeting, so it's an important one. I'll be in a fuck ton of trouble if they find out I've blabbed to you, okay?'

'Your secret is safe with me,' I said. 'Let us know and we'll be there.'

'Don't let me down, Stutter.'

'Never.'

WHY DID it not surprise me that *The Syndicate* planned to meet in the woods?

The frigid night air chilled my bones as Ollie and I stood and waited for them to arrive. We'd got there early to get a hidden spot, but now all we could do was wait, and fuck me, I hated waiting.

Patience may be a virtue, but it wasn't one of mine.

'Do you think it'll be much longer?' I asked.

We were crouched down behind some kind of rock forma-tion Leo had told us about. I hoped we were hiding on the right side of said rocks, otherwise we'd be revealed the moment they arrived.

'Bloody hope not,' Ollie replied. 'I didn't think it would be this cold after midnight, seeing as it's May. Swear it isn't usually this chilly at night this time of year.'

'Global warming,' I said, the typical response of a Brit caught up in a conversation about the ever-changing weather.

'Must be.' Ollie nodded.

God, what shit small talk. Ollie and I were better than this. I wracked my head for a topic that wasn't boring as fuck, but nothing came to mind.

'What time did Leo say in his text?' I got out my phone to check, as if I hadn't already read the message a gazillion times.

MEETING'S AT THE ROCK AT 1 SHARP, DON'T BE LATE AND **DON'T** GET SEEN!

Lucky for me, Ollie knew what he meant by The Rock. All I thought of when I heard the phrase was about the wrestler turned actor. Well, technically, I suppose he'd been an actor all along, hadn't he?

'One sharp,' I said. 'And it's ten to.'

'Not much longer.' We went back into a comfortable silence.

The shuffle of cloaks on the leaves came ten minutes later, like clockwork.

Showtime!

Figures appeared, and thankfully for us, we'd chosen the right side of The Rock to hide. Would've been a bit awkward otherwise. I held in my snigger at the thought.

You know, the sight in front of me looked like it had been

taken from a movie about a secret society, or the way I imagined an old religious sect would've behaved years gone by when they were trying to eradicate the plague or witches or whatever issue they had.

Leo was right about one thing. You couldn't tell who was who.

They were all hidden by the hood, a black endless pit where a face should be. A shiver ran down my spine. I didn't like this one bit.

My eyes locked on to Ollie's unnerved ones. Nice to see he took it all so seriously. These people were behind a lot of shit, and had known about Orlando long before his reveal, yet stayed quiet for their own gain. But what did they want?

Jacob Cooper had arrived, but so far they'd made no move against him.

'Welcome,' a voice intoned from the group. They were standing in a circle, because, *duh*. The cliches of my life killed me. If anybody else was telling my story, I'd laugh at them. The speaker took a step forward. 'Thank you for meeting tonight on such short notice. As I'm sure you're aware, Jacob Cooper is once more in our midst.'

Murmurs and head nods followed the statement.

'According to certain members, he has returned to spend time with his daughter and will make his way between his base and the school frequently.'

Will he? News to me.

When he left me on the steps of the school after our day together, we decided not to rush anything and to take a break from anything too heavy. I invited him to the school for Father's Day, but there were still a few weeks left.

'What are you implying?' Another voice piped up. A

female's. Sounded like Winifred to me, but the wind whistling through the trees meant I couldn't be sure.

'Why move away from our previous methods? We've dealt with Coopers effectively in the past. I don't see why we can't employ the same tactic.'

The same tactic?

Did they mean ...?

My hand covered my mouth, needing something to stifle my realisation. The article headline we found in Hawthorn House flashed through my mind.

A person in the circle stumbled, catching my eye.

Leo.

Even in a heavy cloak with no way of deciphering features, I knew him from his posture. The way he carried himself. All of it.

He couldn't hide from me.

'And what do you mean?' Leo's voice carried through the clearing. 'Some of us weren't around back when you handled the Coopers.'

The group bristled. Fabric rustled.

I smiled.

The other members must be aware of who spoke. Just because Leo had never seen them didn't mean they hadn't recruited him without knowing his identity.

'If Jacob Cooper plans to drive around town in the same vehicle, then things should be easy to arrange. Cars have trouble every day.'

Well, guess my dad will have to hire an unfamiliar car every time he wants to leave his base for the foreseeable future.

Then the implication settled in my gut. Poor Griffin. We'd have to tell him what we learned, but I didn't want to be the one to break it to him. It probably should be me, though. They were my aunt and uncle, too.

'I'll get it arranged,' somebody said.

'Thank you,' the leader replied. 'Next on the agenda, Skylar Crescent. A member has put forward the idea we stop targeting her and spare her if our plan against Jacob succeeds. With her dad dead, she'll be a living Cooper and could one day join our ranks.'

Anger burned. I would *never* join their ranks. They'd have to kill me to keep me quiet about their heinous shit.

Steady on, Skylar. That's what they've tried to do the last two years!

'I say we see how things go with Jacob first before we make any big decisions.'

Orlando.

His voice sounded distinctive, and so much like the voice of my boyfriend. The boyfriend huddled down beside me, seemingly as murderous as the bastards in front of us were.

Orlando wasn't sticking up for me, but he wasn't being a total prick against me, either. Everything about him was such a contradiction all the time, and it gave me a headache trying to keep up with it all.

The rest of the meeting, they discussed mundane things about people I didn't know. During certain sentences, Ollie's eyebrows would climb up into his forehead, so I reckoned he understood a lot more about it than me.

The air turned colder; the night brightened into morning, and my bum became numb.

The crouched position hurt, and I breathed a sigh of relief when *The Sanctum* and their cloaks crunched away, leaving no proof they were even there.

'Are you okay?' Ollie whispered once he was certain they were gone.

'Yeah, I think so. Are you?'

He nodded, reaching his hand out for mine. Mine went willingly, slotting into the spot I now thought of as mine. 'Let's get you back in the warm. We can wait until the morning to talk to Griff and Clo.'

'Sounds good to me.'

Thirty-Three

'CLO, do you think I'm a little too reliant on Ollie?'

'In what way?'

My head tingled as the hairbrush made its way through my lilac curls, and I shivered at the sensation. Clo had agreed to straighten my hair for me and I wouldn't pass up the chance. I'd already made her brush the same spot five times because it felt so nice.

'I don't know. I guess the word I'm seeking is codependent?'

It crossed my mind more and more lately. Ollie and I spent most of our time together, and at first I thought little of it, but now I realised maybe it was too much, too soon. We did this the last time round and then when it turned out he'd betrayed me the whole time, things hurt a lot worse than they would have if I'd kept some distance between us.

Being in love made you do some pretty funny things. Things you said you'd never do.

'I suppose you are,' Clo said, running her fingers through my hair. 'And if I was talking to somebody else other than you, I'd say it was unhealthy.'

'But?'

'But it's you and Ollie, and I don't know, but this shit seems inevitable for you two.'

She stopped playing with my hair and leaned down, turning on the straighteners with a little beep.

'Inevitable doesn't mean healthy,' I said. 'I guess I don't even know what a healthy relationship is. Can't say I've been around any.'

'Me either, come to think of it.' She parted my hair into sections. 'I wouldn't say my parents are healthy.'

I didn't want to startle her by pointing out she'd mentioned her parents of her own volition without being forced into it by somebody else, so I stayed silent and waited for her to continue.

'They're still together because they've got too much history to end it, I think.'

'Sounds a pretty poor reason to remain married,' I said.

Clover seemed lost in her task. She picked up a strand of my hair with her left hand; the straighteners gripped in her right. 'So many people stay married for the wrong reasons. It's weird, but I think the one decent marriage I've seen is the one between Edward and Lottie.'

Jeez! Did Clo feel alright?

Mentioning both her parents and Leo's parents in the same conversation without something setting alight was a miracle.

'Don't think I've spent enough time with Edward and Lottie in the same room to pass judgement on them. I've mainly spent time with Lottie when he isn't around.'

'Lottie's lovely, and so many people think she married Edward for his money, but it's not like that at all. She loves him, you know? Unconditionally.'

'Guess I've never thought about it.'

If I was being honest, I didn't think about other people

often if they weren't in my direct eye line. Well, what a lie. I thought about them a hell of a lot if anxiety was attached to said person or a situation involving them. Then I thought about nothing *but* them.

'Edward and Lottie make decisions together. They both love Leo and want the best for him, no matter what. Can't say the same for my parents.'

'All I've got to look at is Cora and Andy, and nobody is ever going to aspire to be like them.'

Clo was around halfway through my hair now, and the repeated motion of the straightener calmed me.

Talking of Cora and Andy, I hadn't heard from Mum since my birthday. Lucky for me that she even remembered it. She called and told me she loved me and wished for me to have the best day and to get everything in life I deserved. The whole time, all I could wonder about was how much she'd had to drink before dialling me. She'd called at ten in the morning ...

'Least your mum loves him,' Clo said. 'Even if he is a massive arsehole.'

'My mum's never had the best judgement.' I sighed. 'Sometimes I wonder if Cora acts the way she does because of her life and all that's happened in it, and then when I think about it, I think maybe I'm a little harsh on her.'

'Oh, really?'

'She didn't get along great with her parents, and I think her opinions bothered them. Extremely over opinionated, you know? So she sought out love wherever she could find it. I've always thought that's how she ended up hooking up with Jacob. He was rich and flashy—the complete opposite of a woman trying to escape her life, with barely more than a few quid to rub together.'

'Sounds a little sad.'

'It is a little sad, but I suppose my anger and hatred towards her has always overshadowed everything else. I always got jealous of the girls who had good relationships with their mums and could tell them everything. Go to them for advice.'

'No need to be jealous of me and my mum, then.' Clo gave a small laugh. 'I've never been able to go to her about anything, and when she wants to talk to me, it's to dictate my life or to tell me I'm doing something the wrong way.'

'Are we bonding over our shitty mothers, Clover Luck?'

We both chuckled.

'Why yes, Skylar Crescent, I think we are.'

'I'M PRETTY SURE my dad hid some stuff back from me.'

I couldn't put my finger on why, but something didn't add up. Or maybe he hadn't actively hidden stuff, but chosen to not speak of it, which ... okay. It had been our first time properly meeting and talking and getting to know one another, so maybe he didn't want to bog it down and make it all heavy and miserable and dark.

'Maybe he saved some stuff for next time, in case it didn't go well. To ensure there even would *be* a next time,' said Ollie.

I nodded. Ollie made a good point, as usual. Sometimes I wished he'd be a little less right all the time. His head could do without being inflated even more.

Good thing I loved him, wasn't it?

'Maybe. Do you think I should reach out to him and arrange another meeting?'

'Do you want to?'

I shrugged. 'I don't know. After what we overheard at *The Sanctum* meeting, I texted him a warning, and lucky for me, he didn't ask how or why.'

'How did he reply?'

'He thanked me and said he hoped to see me soon.'

'Will you invite him to Father's Day?' Ollie asked, running his fingers along my shoulder blade. 'If you don't, Winifred will do it for you as an official school invitation or some bullshit.'

'She does have a habit of sticking her nose in where it isn't wanted.' I chuckled, the image of Mum and Andy arriving unannounced at my first Parents' Day here. At the time, I was certain it had been the boys and the O girls who invited them, but maybe not. 'But yeah, I already decided to ask him. Do you think it'll be super awkward having your dad and Edward here too?'

'Undoubtedly.' Ollie smiled, a glint of mischief flashing in his blue eyes. 'My dad and yours will have to get used to spending time together. We're together, after all, and I'm sure there will be events they both need to attend in years to come.'

My heart dropped. Was Ollie hinting at something ...?

I shook the thought away. Focusing on a future which may never come to pass wasn't worth it. Not yet. Not when we needed to stop those who were trying their hardest to harm us, or worse.

'It might take some time,' I said. 'The two of them don't have the best history.'

'No, but if I can get over it for your sake, then Henry can get over it for mine.'

I'd be lying if I said I wasn't happy to hear Ollie say he could get over his hatred of my father for my sake. The fact he would put something so serious aside to keep the peace made me smile. In his eyes, my dad was one of the many reasons his mum hated her lot in life—one of the reasons she no longer *had* a life.

'I understand if it takes some time,' I said. 'I'm not sure how I feel about him yet, either. It's weird to go from being a girl without a dad to a girl with one.'

'You'll take it in your stride, Skylar, the way you do everything else. Jacob Cooper is lucky you're giving him the time of day.'

Ollie's words soothed me, but they also didn't ring true in my heart. 'I suppose.'

'There's no *suppose* about it!' Ollie kissed my cheek. 'It's within your rights to refuse to see him, yet you haven't because you're the bigger person.'

'Yeah, yeah,' I said, brushing it off. I needed to change the topic. Too much praise so early in the morning would go to my head, even if it came from Ollie. 'Now, what do you say about staying in tonight and not having dinner with the rest of the school?'

'And ditch Griff and Clover?' Ollie smiled. 'I like the way you think, Ms Crescent.'

Thirty-Four

THE NOTE CAME under my door before breakfast.

> *Skylar Crescent,*
> *Your presence is requested on Saturday night at midnight in the*
> *pool house.*
> *Do not tell anybody.*
> *Come alone.*

I read it, then re-read it, until I could recite it off by heart.

My first instinct told me Orlando had written the note and slid it under my door, but I couldn't be sure without either asking him or going to the meeting. Since my birthday, I'd given him a wide berth and avoided him at all costs. He hadn't tried to talk to me or get me alone, either. Which, now I had time to sit down on the edge of my bed and think about it, was pretty fucking weird. To go from wanting to get me alone all the time to not going anywhere near me … well, it was a little odd, wasn't it?

Maybe remorse filled him after his actions at my birthday party. *Hmm.* Somehow, I doubted that.

The note made it pretty clear not to tell anyone, but maybe I could tell somebody.

Not Ollie though. He wouldn't understand, and he'd force me to allow him to come. Or worse, go in my place—maybe without even telling me.

Maybe I could text Leo? He'd at least be able to tell me whether the note came from Orlando. Suppose it was a trap? Would be silly of me to walk into it blindly.

What to do? What to do?

Not like I had to decide straight away. Saturday was another four nights away, so plenty of time to weigh up the pros and cons.

Right?

AT LUNCH, I still hadn't made my mind up about what to do.

At dinner, I was none the wiser.

Same for breakfast the next morning.

No, all I did was replay the note in my mind and think of different ways I could handle the situation. For a brief moment, I thought of telling Griff, but squashed the idea straight away. Griff may be good for a lot of things—plus he was family—but keeping a secret wasn't his strong point. It would pain him to keep things inside, and I wasn't mean enough to make him.

During my free period, I needed to grab some bits for my room, so I said my goodbyes to the boys and Clover and set off on my own.

When I walked alone, I got distracted by the most stupid things. The way my feet stepped against the floor, or a fixed point in the distance, or a cloud resembling a hippo. It meant I entered my own little world, unaware of everything going on around me, oblivious to it all.

A hand gripped my shoulder from behind, and I jumped in the air. Literally, my feet must have made it at least an inch off the floor. 'Shit!'

'Sorry,' Leo's gravelly voice said, calming my heart rate down a fraction. 'I didn't mean to startle you.'

'It's okay,' I said, placing my hand on my chest where my heart lived. 'Didn't hear you coming, that's all.'

'What were you thinking about? You seemed pretty occupied. I called your name twice.'

'Oh,' I laughed. 'It always amazes me how little I pay attention. I didn't hear a thing.'

'Well, now I have your attention. Can I talk to you, in private?' He nudged his head towards an empty classroom and I nodded.

'Where's ...'

'Orlando?' Leo asked. Our telepathy still worked, even though we weren't a couple anymore, fake or otherwise. 'He's busy. Winnie demanded his presence in her office.'

'Sounds serious,' I said. 'How are things going?'

'Do you care?' he asked, sullen, but then he must have realised how moody he sounded because he kept talking before I could answer. 'Sorry, that was shitty of me. I'm good, thanks. Well, as well as I can be with all this crap going on all the time.'

'Feels like there's never any letup, doesn't it?' I laughed. 'The moment I think things will become smooth sailing for a little while, everything blows up in my face, or so it seems.'

'Are you okay?' he asked. It sent a shot of thrill through me whenever Leo cared about me. I doubted it would ever go away, no matter how much time went by.

'I think so. Everything's been a little ... odd.' Why was I downplaying it for Leo's sake? 'No, odd doesn't cover it. Everything's fucked.'

He chuckled. 'Sounds about right for this place. How are Griff and Ollie doing with ... everything?'

'What part? The fact that Griff's parents were murdered or the fact both their parents were mean-spirited bullies who pushed a girl too far one day and regretted it for the rest of their lives?' I crossed my arms. 'They're both dealing with it in their own way. Which means Ollie's not talking about it, but brooding at night when he thinks I'm asleep, and Griff is cracking even more jokes than usual to hide the sadness.'

'Not a surprise,' Leo said. 'They've never handled things in the most mature of manners.'

'I want to agree, but I also know the two of them are struggling, so I want to be kind and give them grace.' I bit my bottom lip and sniggered. 'But yeah, you wouldn't find a picture of them in the dictionary alongside mature.'

We laughed at the boys' expense. Leo ran his hand through his hair, tousling it further. 'Sky, are we good?'

I frowned. 'Me and you?' He nodded. 'Yeah, why?'

'Checking, I suppose. I know I've said sorry and you've accepted my apology, but it's hard to know how to act around you now.'

'I would say act the way you did *before,* but to be honest, I don't want you to go back to treating me like something not worth your time.'

'I could never do that. Not now, I know you better.' Leo's hand hovered in the air between us, wanting to comfort but not knowing how. 'Another apology is on the tip of my tongue, so blink twice to stop it from coming.'

My heart twinged at his hand hovering in the air, afraid to

reach out and touch. Bittersweet sadness overwhelmed me. The one way to pause the melancholy in the air was to blink twice, real exaggerated like, to make him laugh.

Blink. Blink.

Leo responded the way I expected, by barking out a chuckle, and the tension dissipated with it.

The note entered my mind once more, and I took a deep breath, knowing my course of action may be foolish. 'If I tell you something, will you keep it a secret?'

'I suppose I deserve your scepticism, even if it is a dagger through my heart.' He playfully grabbed his chest, a soldier wounded in battle. 'What's up?'

'I got a note through my door yesterday morning,' I said. '*Typed.*'

Translation: typed so I couldn't decipher who it came from. 'Saying?'

'Asking me to go to the pool house at midnight on Saturday, and pretty sure we both know who it's from.'

A smile danced on his lips. 'Is it the location or the time giving it away?'

'Bit of both,' I said, a similar smile on mine. 'The real question is whether I should go?'

'What's your gut saying?'

'It's teetering on the edge, changing its mind each minute. I'd love to find out what he wants, and why he thinks a note and secrecy makes a difference to him asking me in person.'

'Ever since your birthday, he knows he can't approach you without issue.'

'So he told you about what he almost did to me?'

Leo nodded. 'He did, yeah. What kills me, Stutter, is the fact we walked back to school together after he did that and you said nothing about it.'

I tutted. 'Let's not make this about you and your feelings.'

'Shit, I didn't mean—'

'I know. I didn't tell you because I hadn't processed it yet and wasn't sure how I truly felt. It wasn't anything against you. *Not* that I have to justify myself.'

'Sky, forget I said anything. I'm acting like a douche canoe.'

'Yeah, you are, but I'll allow it.' His hand, no longer hovering in mid-air, had returned to his side. It took everything in me to stop myself from reaching out and taking his hand in mine. Not in a romantic way, more in a friendship way. Best not to confuse things, though, when we were already in such a precarious spot.

'Why are you telling me about the note?'

'I trust your guidance. Do you think I should go?'

'What does it say, word for word?'

I put my hand into the inside pocket of my blazer and removed the note. 'Here, peep it for yourself.'

Leo took the note, careful not to touch my hand, and read it. His brows furrowed and I couldn't take my eyes off the creasing of his forehead.

'You've already broken the rules by telling me,' Leo pointed out. 'And you haven't told anyone?'

I shook my head. 'Nope.'

'I'm touched,' Leo said. 'Do you want me to hang around in the corridor linking the pool house to the hospital wing, so if anything goes wrong, I'm there?'

The idea of Leo being nearby to rescue me if I needed it warmed me. How on earth could he be such a good guy but also such a liar at the same time?

'Probably a good idea. What will you do if it is Orlando, and he catches on?'

'I'll bullshit him the way I have for the last two years. He's never caught on before.' Leo chuckled. 'I think you should go.'

'Yeah?'

'Yeah, I do. I wouldn't tell Ollie or Griff either. Nor Red. Seems silly to involve them and cause a fuss for nothing.'

I agreed. I had no plans to tell the others. Fuck, I hadn't had plans to tell *Leo* either. 'Plus, I wouldn't want them to get hurt. What if it isn't Orlando?'

'Who else could it be? Would Ollie do something like that?'

I thought about it. 'Narh, I don't think so. Our history with the pool house ... I doubt he'd put me in a similar position again willingly.'

'Right. I forgot.'

Forgot the time I nearly drowned? Or the time Ollie nearly drowned?

Either way, it pissed me off a little that he could forget either event. They were kind of a big deal.

'Okay, well ...' I trailed off, no longer wanting to talk to him. 'I best be off. Will you spy on the pool house entrance for me so if it isn't Orlando, you can raise the alarm?'

He nodded. 'It's the least I can do.'

'Thanks. I'll see you later.'

'See you later, Stutter.'

Thirty-Five

I COULDN'T TELL you the amount of times I changed my mind about going to the pool house at midnight on Saturday night. At least fifty.

The reason fear hadn't overtaken me had to do with the knowledge Leo would be watching and lying in wait in case anything bad went down. My own personal avenger.

WHAT IF I ARRIVE BEFORE WHOEVER IT IS?

Leo's reply made me smile.

I'LL BE WATCHING, AND IF IT ISN'T HIM, THEN I'LL GET OLLIE

That settled it then. I would show up and hope Orlando walked through the door, and if he didn't, well, I'd cross the bridge when it came to it.

'Why can't I stay with you tonight?' Ollie's pen hovered above his paper. 'I've got used to you being my heater.'

'Oh, so it's nothing to do with wanting to spend time with me?' I widened my eyes and opened my mouth as if in shock. 'I'm a warm body, am I?'

'Shut up.' He laughed. 'You know you're a hell of a lot more than that to me.'

'Pft.' I crossed my arms across my chest, pushing my boobs up in the process—on purpose. Ollie's eyes travelled lower. 'What am I then?'

'You're my girlfriend.' His eyes met mine. 'And if you tell Griff I'll murder you, but you're also my best friend.'

'I'm your best friend?' I tried to keep the wide smile off my face but failed. Something about his words had touched a nerve, in a good way. 'I sort of want to tease you about it, but I won't because you've made me feel good.'

'Tease away,' Ollie said. 'I've got nothing to be ashamed of.'

'It becomes even less fun now you've given me permission.' Somehow, my smile got even bigger. 'Don't tell Clover, but you're my best friend, too.'

'Really?' He dropped his pen and put his hand on top of mine. 'Do you mean that?' The way his tone turned all soft and vulnerable had my insides turning into mush.

'I do,' I said. 'Why would I lie?'

'I don't know.' He shuffled in his chair. 'Maybe for my benefit.'

'No reason to do that.' I shrugged. 'I wouldn't lie to you, especially not about something so serious.'

No, I lie about other things that are probably more important.

'If you're sure.'

'I am.' His hand squeezed mine, and I turned my hand so it was palm up and squeezed back. 'Now, I need to get this essay done before Monday, so if you could keep the distraction to a minimum, I'd appreciate it.'

'Yeah, yeah.' He picked his pen up again. 'So, tonight?'

'I need a night in with Clo. Since everything went down between her and Griff, she's obviously not staying out anymore, so has been all alone. Don't want her to become some kind of ghost haunting the place.'

'I highly doubt Clover would choose to haunt *Hawthorn*, of all places.'

'You speak true.' I pointed my pen at him in accusation. 'But if she did, you would be to blame, and I can't have that on my conscience.'

'We can't have that at all,' he said. 'I could spend the evening with Griff and then spend the night alone, I suppose.'

'You suppose?' I laughed.

'I'm not thrilled about it,' he chuckled. 'But it would do us good to not spend every waking moment together. Or so people would say.'

'Codependency as teenagers isn't a good look.'

'Says who?' Ollie demanded. 'Who's been filling your head with such bullshit?'

'Nobody,' I said, evading the fact it was Clover who said something. Ollie wouldn't take kindly to me listening to her for any relationship advice, seeing as all her relationships had blown to smithereens. 'It's what people will say, isn't it? We're too young to spend this much time together.'

'People may say it, but as long as you don't think it, then I don't give a shit. If we enjoy spending time together, that's all that matters.'

'I agree.' And I did. 'But I'm still staying in my room tonight.'

'Yeah, yeah, I know.' He smiled, the wrinkles at the corners of his eyes making me smile. I loved to see him so happy. It made a massive change from last year. 'Remember, you can sneak into my room at any time.'

'If I miss you that bad, I'll take you up on the offer.'

THE POOL HOUSE was empty and dark when I arrived.

The staircase on my right drew my eye, but I couldn't let myself get distracted. Somewhere up there, Leo watched and waited, keeping an eye out for me—keeping me safe. Or as safe as I could be in this place.

The idea Leo still cared about me enough to watch over me was bittersweet. It also gave me hope. Maybe once all this mess was done and over with we'd return to being real friends. Ones who didn't toe the line of a relationship to piss people off.

The pool room was even quieter than the rest of the building.

The waves of the pool reflected on the ceiling; the calm before the storm. I wandered around, taking in the surroundings, hoping Orlando showed soon.

Hoping Orlando actually showed up and not one of those cloak wearing Sanctum members I didn't know.

The door opened, and unlike previous times, I turned to look at whoever had arrived.

'Little One,' Orlando said, closing the door behind him with a gentle *click*. 'You came.'

I stayed put, letting him walk closer to me. 'I came.'

'Alone?'

I exaggerated and turned in a circle. 'Can't see anyone else here, can you?'

'No.' His little smile unnerved me. 'Unexpected, though. Thought you'd rope in my dumb as rocks brother or my even dumber cousin.'

'I didn't tell them a thing about it.' I spoke the truth. I

hadn't told Ollie or Griff a thing. 'The note said not to tell anybody.'

'You've never been one to follow instructions.'

'I've also nearly died multiple times, so I'm sure you can understand why I like people to know where I am.'

'You're safe with me,' he said. 'Always.'

My laugh filled with scorn. 'A bit rich coming from you, isn't it? The last time we were alone you tried to ...' I trailed off, unable to voice the word. I suppose if I was honest, I hadn't come to terms with it yet. 'Wouldn't call that safe.'

'Which is part of the reason I wanted you to meet me here tonight,' he said. 'I want to apologise.'

'You could have apologised in broad daylight where there were witnesses,' I pointed out. 'Makes it all a little shady boots the way you always want to hide things.'

'Not gonna lie, Little One, but I didn't fancy getting punched by my brother in front of witnesses.'

'He wouldn't punch you.'

Orlando laughed. 'No need to lie to me. I think we both know how much he'd love to deck me.'

'Can't blame him for it,' I said. 'Plenty of times I've wanted to deck you.'

'Lucky for me you haven't. Even if you'd be well within your rights to.'

'So, are you going to then?' I took a step closer. 'Apologise?'

Orlando took a matching step to mine, bringing us closer together, but still not close enough to touch. I wanted to keep enough distance, just in case.

'I've built it up now, and whatever I say won't be good enough.'

My heart twinged, but I stood my ground. There was no way I was letting him off the hook so easily. 'That's the amazing thing about apologies, Orlando. The ingredients needed to make it effective are the words I'm sorry.'

Suppose he'd never had to say it often enough for it to stick in his brain.

'I am sorry,' Orlando said, his hands wringing in front of his waist. 'I don't think I can put into words the extent I'm sorry.'

'Would it be mean of me to force you to try?'

'I deserve that,' he said, 'and I know you're teasing me, but you're right. I should at least try to explain some things to you —it's why I asked you here alone.'

'Okay.'

'Can we sit down?' He pointed to the seating, and I nodded, following him over there. When I sat, I left space between us. I even went as far as sitting in the row above him, so I had the higher vantage point. 'I'm sorry for how I acted the last time we were alone together. There's no excuse for my behaviour and I won't sit here and bullshit you with a reason for it.'

'How big of you.' I rubbed my knees, hoping to put some kind of sensation back into them. The weather outside may be warming up, but fucking hell, the pool room cooled down when empty, with nobody there to fill it with body heat. 'Because you're right, there is no excuse. I do have a question for you, though.'

'Yeah?'

'What went through your head?' I tilted my head, assessing his reaction to my words. 'When you pushed me up against the tree?'

'There isn't an easy answer, and the answer I have, well, I'm not sure I want to voice it to you.'

'Why?'

'You'll think the worst of me.'

I chuckled. 'Hate to break it to you, but I sort of already do. Not sure you can sink any lower, in my opinion.'

'Nice to know you don't feel the need to lie to me.'

'I'm trying a thing where I tell the truth ...' A thought entered my mind. 'Well, except for not telling Ollie or Griff where I planned to go tonight.'

'You didn't tell them?'

'Do you think we'd still be alone if I had?' The image of the two of them bursting through the door made me laugh. 'They'd have shown up like some second-rate action heroes ready to rescue me.'

'You don't need rescuing from me.' Orlando's voice was barely audible, and I had to lean forward to hear him better. 'At least, not anymore.'

'Well, what's changed?' Because in my head, nothing had and most likely never would. Orlando didn't know how to change. He'd never had an excellent role model in his life to show him the way of things. No, neither had Ollie, but at least he was learning.

Orlando shrugged. 'I've seen the error of my ways.'

'More like you know you're not getting anywhere in your revenge plot to steal your brother's life, and you never will if you continue to alienate everybody.'

'I deserve Ollie's life as much as he does. A split second decision gave me my life and him his. A fifty-fifty chance and Millie picked me to give away to her sister. It could have easily happened the other way around.'

'But it didn't, and that's not Ollie's fault, no matter how much you want to make it his.'

'Whose fault is it, then? Who's to blame?'

'Millie Hawthorn,' I said. Millie had caused this animosity

and hadn't even lived long enough to see how it played out. 'She made the choice to do what she did. Nobody else.'

'No matter what you say, Little One, I still want to see my brother suffer, and *that* I won't apologise for.'

I stood up abruptly.

'Suit yourself,' I snapped. 'Thanks for the apology, but I must be off now.'

'You don't have to leave.'

'Yeah, I do. You can fuck off if you think I'm gonna stay here while you're chatting such shit about Ollie and how you want to see him suffer.'

For the first time, I didn't hold back when speaking to Orlando. Kept nothing inside. He deserved my ire and so much more and I was bored with giving him the benefit of the doubt all because his life was harder than Ollie's. Fuck, my life was hard yet I didn't come to Hawthorn ready to ruin the lives of those more fortunate than me!

No, I came to Hawthorn to improve my life and get into a decent university. Something the bastard in front of me had attempted to prevent at every turn.

'The next time you think of sending a note requesting my presence, know I won't show up, but someone else will.' I moved closer to the door, keeping my eye on Orlando the whole time. 'I understand wishing for a better lot in life, and I understand being mistreated, but you can't constantly weaponise it.'

'Little One,' he called, standing up from the bench. 'You're the one person I can talk to.'

'Maybe so,' I said, my hand gripping the door handle. 'But it doesn't mean I have to listen to it any longer.'

Thirty-Six

AFTER MY EVENING meeting with Orlando, I decided not to tell Ollie or Griff a thing about it.

I weighed up the pros and cons, and what did I gain from telling them? Nothing, that was what.

When I left the pool room, I went to the corridor and found Leo, waiting patiently the way he said he would. I thanked him and he walked me back to my room. We didn't talk much, except for me to tell him what Orlando wanted to see me for.

Now, Ollie and I were in History together, listening to the teacher drone on about some war or other. Well, I say listening, but I took not one word in. My head was floating in the clouds and I'd paid little attention to my classes all day.

'Are you okay?' Ollie whispered out of the corner of his mouth. 'You've not written anything down.'

I nodded my head. 'Yeah, sorry, just living in my own world.'

'Good thing you can share your boyfriend's notes then,' he said with a quiet chuckle. 'I'm gonna think you're using me soon.'

'If I was, it wouldn't be for your notes.' I let out a barking laugh, and the teacher snapped their head in my direction, putting their pointer finger against their lips. Ah, the universal sign for shut the fuck up. We all knew it well.

A knock came at the classroom door.

Mrs Wood called out, 'Yes?'

The door creaked open, and when my eyes glimpsed the person standing on the other side, my heart sank. *Shit.*

Detectives Smith and Saunders were standing there and both of them had dark, serious expressions on their faces. Ms Hawthorn hovered behind them, a smug smile playing on her grey features.

'Hello, Mrs Wood. We're sorry to interrupt your lesson.'

'No problem, detectives. What can I do for you?'

Detective Smith took a step into the classroom, surveying the area looking for something, or *somebody*, in particular.

'Oliver Brandon,' he called out, locking eyes on Ollie in the seat beside me. 'Please stand.'

Ollie pressed a bruising kiss to my cheek. 'God, what do they want now?'

The chair screeched as he pushed back from the table.

'Oliver Brandon, you are under arrest for the murder of Ophelia Rogers. You do not have to say anything. But, it may harm your defence if you do not mention when questioned something which you later rely on in court. Anything you do say may be given in evidence.'

Ollie's jaw dropped, but he remained silent. Knowing these bastards, they'd use anything he said to aid their case, even if it were to say goodbye to me.

He placed his hands out for the detective to put hand-cuffs around his wrists. The thing that let me know he was pissed? The change in his breathing. Everything else in his outward appearance remained calm and in control. It impressed me. Ollie always seemed to have it together in front of other people, yet behind closed doors he let me see his true self.

CODE RED. **O**LLIE**'**S BEEN ARRESTED FOR **O**PHELIA**'**S MURDER**!** **C**ONTACT THE LAWYERS **ASAP.**

I texted the same message to Leo and Griff, tapping the message out under the table so the teacher wouldn't see. I don't think they'd penalise me at a time like this, but Ms Hawthorn would, the old witch.

My phone lit up in my hand—a message from Griff.

SHIT! **O**N IT, **C**LOUDS

I was at a loss, not knowing what else I could do to make things better. Messaging the guys was my only move.

'Ollie,' I called to him as he reached the door beside the detectives. 'I'll get this figured out, okay? Trust me.'

He nodded, his face determined yet grim. I blew him a kiss as he went out of view.

Fuck me, could things get any worse?

'T**HEY** **MUST** **HAVE** some sort of proof, otherwise they wouldn't have arrested him,' Griff said. 'We need to figure out what they've got on him.'

'They've got forty-eight hours to charge him,' Clo said, pacing in space between the middle of our beds. 'So I don't think we need to worry yet.'

'Clover,' Griff said, in a tone that made it a clear reprimand.

'I'm just saying,' she said, not sounding anywhere as chastised as she should. 'These detective dickheads have questioned us all plenty over the last two years, and they're as clueless now as they were then. If they can't see the Orlando-shaped criminal in front of their eyes, then nothing we do can change their oversight.'

'I think we should get Leo in here,' Griff said, not for the first time. 'It makes sense to tackle this together. He'll know more for sure. This has Orlando written all over it.'

'I'll send him a message.' I got my phone out. 'Wait, what if he's with Orlando now and he sees it?'

'Well, don't put anything suspicious, so if Orlando sees it, he won't think much of it.'

'Okay.'

HEY, COULD DO WITH SOME OF YOUR SHINING OPTIMISM RIGHT ABOUT NOW IF YOU'RE AROUND?

I pressed send, then threw my phone on my bed like a child. Why was I nervous? Probably had to do with the fact I hated rejection and if Leo rejected me, I think it'd push me over the edge. Especially at a time like this, what with Ollie being arrested and all.

It sounded so wrong in my head.

Arrested.

Not even asked in for questioning like in the past, but arrested.

Leo's knock came within five minutes. He called through the door, 'It's me.'

Griff let out a jovial laugh when he opened the door. 'Of course it's you. The only other person it could've been got hauled off by police a few hours ago. Not sure if you heard?'

'Leave him alone,' I said. 'Leo can't help it.'

Did I even believe my words? Could Leo help being under Orlando's thumb? Probably not if he wanted to keep us all safe. I'd attended a meeting. I'd heard the way they spoke so callously about ending a life. They meant what they said and if Leo didn't play ball; well, I doubted I'd have a beating heart for much longer. Same went for Clover.

'Please don't stick up for me, Stutter. I deserve the shit.'

'You're right, you do.' Clover nodded her head as if it was all decided and we could move on now Leo's shit status had been determined. 'So, what do you know?'

'About ...?'

'Don't act obtuse, it doesn't suit you. What do you know about Ollie being taken in?'

'Since Sky's birthday, I wouldn't say I'm in the fold.' Leo's gaze seared into mine. 'Oh, and somehow they knew I gave you the heads up about going to Hawthorn House while they were out.'

'Reckon they have cameras?' I asked. 'Would make sense, I suppose. At the entrance, at least.'

Leo shrugged. 'Probably. Doesn't matter now. What matters is that Orlando no longer trusts me the way he used to.'

'And who's at fault?' Clover snapped. I rolled my eyes, already bored with having the two of them in the same room together. It got so tedious, their constant animosity. Sure, I understood it, but it didn't mean I had to like it.

'The people at fault here are Winifred, Orlando, and *The Sanctum*. We need to remember and stay united, not divided.' I sat back down on my bed, having stood when Leo arrived for a reason unknown to me. Maybe it was an unconscious want— to hug him and act like things weren't fucked between us. 'And we can all agree it's because of them they've taken Ollie in, yes?'

The group nodded or mumbled their agreement.

'Alright then.' I clapped my hands together. 'Now the question we need to answer is how?'

'Not why?' Griff asked, scooting back on my bed so his back rested up against the wall. Since he and Clo split, my bed was his go to seat these days.

Which left Leo in an awkward position. He hovered in the middle of the room, as did Clover, who had stopped her pacing and looked from left to right. If he chose my bed, it may come across like the three of us were against her, but if he sat on hers, he could end up pissing off everyone in the room.

I patted the bed next to me, making the choice for him. I'd rather Clo be pissed at me than anybody else. Leo came willingly and sat beside me, a large enough gap between us for it not to be improper.

'We know the why,' I said once the awkward moment ended. 'They hate him and Orlando wants his life and blah blah blah. No, the *how* of it all is most important now.' I ran my hands through my curled locks, breaking apart the knots that had formed during the day. 'Where was Ollie when Ophelia left the clearing?'

Blank stares came back to me.

'What?'

'None of us know.' Griff winced. 'He disappeared around the same time as you.'

'Oh.' I shook my head, thinking back to the party, and how we left things before I wandered off. 'So he's unaccounted for?'

Griff nodded.

'Not ideal.' My small laugh sounded false. 'You reckon that's what they have on him?'

'Well, yeah, plus the fact he and Orlando share DNA.'

'But Orlando doesn't have an alibi, either?'

Leo coughed and shifted on the bed, the mattress depressing to the point I nearly flew off. 'He says he was with you …'

'Why haven't the police questioned me about it? Surely they're not taking the prick's word for it?'

'But there's a witness,' Leo mumbled.

'People can't tell the two of them apart most of the time!' I stood up, too mad to stay still, needing to pace to keep the darker thoughts at bay. 'And in the dark in the woods? Per-lease!'

'They were wearing different clothes,' Clo pointed out. She was sitting on her bed, back pressed up against the wall, watching Griff and Leo apprehensively. 'It's not like before where Orlando's worn the same as Ollie to throw us all off. He doesn't have to anymore. He's out in the open these days.'

'Don't I know it,' I grumbled. My head was getting a little dizzy from the small space I had to pace in, but it didn't stop me. 'Let me guess, the witness is you?' Mine and Leo's gazes locked, and he didn't even need to answer, because I could read the truth in his expression. 'Of course it is.'

'I got questioned, and I told my truth,' he replied, tactful as ever. 'I saw Orlando follow you around the time they were asking about. I didn't lie about that.'

Okay, so he had me there. But … 'Why wouldn't you talk to me about it first?'

'They didn't give me time to. Orlando summoned me to Hawthorn House, and the detectives were there waiting for me.'

I scoffed. 'Why would he have given you time to? He *knows* he wasn't with me.'

'In my defence,' Leo put his hands up, 'I thought he *was* with you. I saw him storm away not long before I bumped into you.'

'You were pretty drunk,' I said. 'But it had to be longer than you thought.'

'If I go to the detectives and tell them I've changed my version of events, they'll assume I'm doing it to save Ollie.'

'True ...' I rubbed my temples, the ache setting in. Being a student at Hawthorn was never simple. 'Okay, so they don't know where he was and they may have his DNA linking him to Ophelia. Anything else?'

Leo's face scrunched. Jesus, was there anything more he could add to make it even worse?

'Yes, Leo?' I crossed my arms.

'It may have to do with the fact Orlando told them Ollie would do anything to make him disappear. Everybody knows Orlando is out on bail, so any crime would have him locked up with no chance of freedom until trial.'

'So, they think this is Ollie's revenge?'

'Suppose so.'

Thirty-Seven

'DO YOU THINK KANT HAD ISSUES?'

'Do I think Kant had issues?' I repeated Griff's question, raising my eyebrows in his direction. 'In what sense?'

Griff shrugged. 'I don't know. Think you'd have to have them to become a philosopher, right?'

'He was a philosopher back when things had less explanation than now, but yeah, I'm sure he had issues. The man believed it's always wrong to lie, so I'm sure that caused him some aggro.'

'Clouds, you believe it's wrong to lie.'

'Not going to make speeches or write essays about it, though,' I pointed out. 'Plus, I believe it's wrong, yeah, but there are times where I still do it.'

'Most people lie. Or maybe they hide or disguise the truth to make it more palatable.'

'Suppose you're right.' I guess he'd given me the segue I'd been waiting for. I wanted to tell him the moment I got back from *The Sanctum* meeting, but life got in the way.

Mainly my boyfriend being arrested for something his identical twin brother did and is now framing him for. 'There's something I wanted to tell you, but I haven't known how.'

Griff paused his writing and turned his head. 'Okay … Nothing too serious, I hope?'

I opened my mouth, then closed it again. *That's it, Skylar. Resemble a fish, why don't you?*

'Sky?' Griff asked after a minute of me being unable to push the words past my lips. 'Is everything okay?'

'So, you know how Ollie and I hid during the *Sanctum* meeting?'

He nodded. 'Yeah …'

'They said something about your parents.'

'What about them?'

'They confirmed their deaths weren't an accident. I'm sorry.'

Tears flooded his eyes, and he gulped. 'What are you sorry for? Not like you killed them.'

'I should've told you sooner,' I said. 'Things have been busy, but that's no excuse. Ollie and I wanted to tell you together, but we never got the chance.' Tears filled my eyes, matching his. I hated seeing Griff sad. 'I am so sorry, baby boy.'

His voice cracked. 'It's not your fault.'

I pulled him into a hug, ignoring the stares from the other students in the lesson. Lucky for us, the bell rang to signal lunch and everybody filed out.

'Can we stay, sir?' I asked Mr Sommers. 'We'll close the door on our way out.'

'Of course,' he said, putting his things into his briefcase. I sent a smile his way. He was by far one of our nicest teachers. 'Please close the door, otherwise who knows what I'll come back to.'

'I promise,' I said, waving him out the door. I focused my attention back on Griff. 'Do you want to stay here, or shall we head to the dorms?'

'Can we stay here a while?' Griff whispered. His bottom lip wobbled, and the tears in my eyes grew thicker. 'I don't think I'm ready to go through the halls yet.'

'We won't move until you're ready,' I said, pulling him into a deep hug. 'Well, that's not strictly true. We won't move until we get kicked out.'

His chuckle vibrated my body. 'Thanks, Clouds.'

'No problem. I've always got your back.'

'It's nice to have it confirmed,' he murmured, leaning back a little. 'I've always thought something was fishy about it all.'

The freckles on his scrunched-up nose caught the light. Griffin Cooper was a thing of beauty. His picture should come beside the dictionary definition so everybody can witness it for themselves.

'But I never thought I'd find out the truth,' he continued talking, unaware of where my thoughts had run off to. 'I was supposed to die too.'

'There's no way to know for definite.' I gripped his forearms. 'They didn't mention you, plus, they tampered with the car itself so they had no way of knowing who would get hurt.'

'Can't decide what's worse. An attack intended to take us all out, or one where they hoped for one and anyone else was an added bonus.'

I winced. His anger wasn't misplaced, and having nothing to do or say to make it better didn't sit right in my gut.

'I'm so glad you're alive, Griff, and I'm gutted I'll never get to meet my aunt and uncle.'

'Thank you,' he mumbled. 'And thank you for telling me the truth, even though it was hard.'

'I hate that I had to.'

'I'll have the veggie burger with chips, please.' I handed the waiter my menu and leaned back in my chair.

The dining room was pretty quiet for a Wednesday night. Orlando and the last remaining O girl were sitting with Cordelia and Celia at their usual table, holding court over the school in a way they seemed to get a kick from.

'What a bastard, sitting up there all smug and smarmy,' I said, bitterness filling my mouth at the sight. 'Acting like he isn't in the process of getting away with murder.'

'He's out on bail for another crime,' Clo said. She got out her lip balm and pouted, covering her lips in the stuff, before putting it back in her blazer pocket. 'Another *murder*.'

'Exactly!' I screeched. Heads turned to our table. A flush covered my cheeks. Even though since joining Hawthorn I'd come under a lot of scrutiny, and had a lot of attention my way, I still hated being in the limelight. Usually, I had Ollie by my side, which softened the blow a little, but with him gone, things were off-kilter.

I sent an evil glare Orlando's way.

'Stop trying to antagonise him, Sky,' Clo said, handing her menu to the waiter as he made his way around our table. 'He's not worth it.'

'Easy to say, but harder to do. It's like I can't help but think about it all the fucking time. And whenever I try to stop and think of something else, my brain somehow links it back to him, or to Ollie, or to the current situation. Fuck, the other night I lay in bed thinking about cute cat videos, then about cat milk, then about dairy products in general, then cheese, then the word turophile, then the time Ollie joked about my love of cheese the week I learned said word.' I took a large gasping breath, not having taken one while talking.

Griff and Clover both gawked at me open-mouthed, pausing in their actions. Clo had a lip balm halfway to her lips, and Griff was mid chin scratch.

How to explain my brain to somebody who didn't understand? Or didn't have the same way of thinking?

'Well,' Clo said, breaking the silence, 'that's a lot.'

'Yep. It's constant. A whirring in my brain I can never turn off.'

'Sounds painful,' said Griff. 'I can always distract you if you think it'll help?'

'I am sort of intrigued,' I said, and I meant it. The idea of Griff attempting to distract me amused the fuck out of me. 'How would you distract me?'

'For starters, I could tell you about the time Clover ...' Griff continued talking, and I nodded in what I believed were the right places, but the words weren't going in.

The side of my head burned; a certain someone's eyes on me, no doubt.

It was hard to ignore somebody when they took up such a large presence in your day. Every time I walked down the corridor, his booming voice or barked laughter filtered into my ears, or I spotted him standing with the girls all hanging off him like flies on honey.

Leo took the empty seat to my right, catching me off guard and dragging me out of my darkening thoughts.

'Hey.'

'Hey ... You lost or something?'

He chuckled. 'No, funny enough. Thought I'd come and ask you something in person rather than sending a text.'

'Ask away.'

I ignored the disproving stares from across the table.

Leo had come and talked to us when Ollie got arrested and told us all he knew. To me, that meant he was on our side. Even if he hadn't voiced the sentiment yet.

'Will you meet me tonight?'

'Where? When?' I frowned. 'Stop being cryptic.'

'You know where and when.' He got up and went over to the staff table.

I shrugged at Clo and Griff's questioning faces.

Suppose I was off to the secret tunnels at midnight.

Thirty-Eight

LEO OPENED the door to the tunnel the second I knocked.

'Stutter. Fancy seeing you here.'

I narrowed my eyes. 'Yes, fancy seeing me at a location at the time you requested.'

'I wasn't sure if you'd show up.' He shrugged, opening the door wider so I could step inside the small space alongside him. 'We've not been friends lately.'

'We're not *not* friends.' There didn't seem to be a better way to put it. I didn't dislike Leo—I just didn't know if I could trust him. And trust was super important to me when it came to friends and those I let in. My whole life I hadn't had anyone close who wanted to know me, and now I did. Well, it made sense I wanted to trust them.

'But you still don't trust me,' he murmured.

'Are you a mind reader?'

The two of us headed further into the hallway, one behind the other, until we reached the intersection. His shoulders moved from his laughter. 'No. I just know you well.'

'Yeah, I suppose you do.'

My tone didn't hold any of the sorrow it would have a

couple of months ago. Things were slotting back into their correct place. When I thought of mine and Leo's brief relationship, I chose to remember the happy times. Not much point in dwelling on the past when so much was happening in the present, right?

'What did you want to talk about?' I asked, crossing my arms across my chest. The stance of somebody who meant business and wasn't leaving the tunnel until we'd resolved everything between us. 'And why couldn't you talk about it while the others were around?'

'Because it sounds silly.'

'Leo, nothing you say ever sounds silly.' Even the thought of it was absurd. Leo Hawthorn was the furthest thing from *silly.* 'You're overthinking it.'

'Maybe, but I didn't want to risk it.' He took a deep breath. 'I know I'm a broken record and I've said it all before, but I can't go on knowing you think poorly of me.'

'Huh?'

Well, that was unexpected.

'I know you said on your birthday you believe I didn't have a choice in what happened to me, and I know I've said sorry more times than I can count, but ...'

'But?' The frown remained on my face. 'Leo, I can't do or say anything more than I already have. I forgive you. I accept your apology. I know you did what you thought was best and tried to change the course of things when you realised you loved me.'

It was the first time since we split up—if you could call a massive betrayal resulting in us not talking for weeks a mere break up—I mentioned the word love. The two of us had tiptoed around it in the months since everything blew up, neither wanting to broach the topic first.

I had loved Leo, and he had loved me. Even if we hadn't outright said the words, we'd made it clear we were falling and if things had continued, it would have been a full-blown love affair.

Fortunately—or unfortunately, I suppose, depending on who you asked—things didn't continue.

'I'm not worthy of your forgiveness.'

'That's a you problem,' I said, gently. 'I can't help or dictate how you feel.'

His responding sigh depleted his whole body. 'I know. It's a hurdle I haven't figured out how to cross yet, but it's one killing me inside.'

'Is there anything I can do to make it any better?'

'You've already done so much. Sky, you're nice and supportive and understanding and forgiving when I deserve none of it.'

'I don't think that's the truth of it. You're making me sound a much better person than I am.'

'Well, that's how I see you,' he said, his eyes kind.

'And I don't see you as harshly as you see yourself, so I guess we're even.' I put his hand in mine. 'Leo, we're good, I promise. So no more apologies and no more tiptoeing around me, okay?'

'Okay.'

'I mean it,' I said, reprimanding. 'And I expect you to help us brainstorm a plan for the upcoming ball.'

'Not sure what I can do. *The Sanctum* will all be there.'

I stared at him blankly. Any second now ...

'Oh.' He laughed. 'Yeah, sure. I'll see what I can come up with.'

'Once Ollie's back, we can figure out our plan of action.' And I meant it, because in my head, no reality existed where

Ollie didn't come back. He couldn't go to prison for Orlando's wrongs. He couldn't. 'I don't want to do anything until he's here, too.'

'I get it.' Leo's hand twitched.

'I suppose you know about what our parents got up to while they were here?' I changed the subject, then corrected myself. 'Well, not your mum. She's a sweetheart, as always.'

'She sends her love.' His teeth shone when he smiled. 'I think she loves you and Clover more than she loves me.'

'That's not true!' I chuckled. 'The woman dotes on you. She'd do anything to make you happy, Leo. Wish my mum would act the same way towards me.'

'Cora's a funny one,' he said, and I rolled my eyes. Did he mean funny *ha-ha* or funny *odd*? Both counted, actually.

'I used to hate her so much, but now, I don't know what emotion I have.'

'What's changed?'

'Meeting you guys, coming to Hawthorn, meeting my dad … All of it has made me question and overthink about everything. Yes, she's still crap and has a scummy husband, but I think she's trying?' I shook my head, the confusion causing a headache. 'I can't fault her for that.'

'How are things going between you and your dad?'

Leo took his hand from mine and slumped down to sit on the floor, his back pressed up against the wall. I followed him, my aching feet ready to have a little rest.

'Alright, I guess.' I picked at the drawstring on my hoodie, folding the aglet within the cord and then unravelling it again. 'I'm not sure I'll get used to having a dad who wants to talk to me. We've been texting, and I called him one time to warn him to never drive his car anywhere, but it's still early days.'

Leo nodded, understanding. 'It must be weird building a

relationship with him now at your age. Fuck, I struggle sometimes with my dad and I've known him my whole life.'

'Edward's intimidating to be fair.'

'Believe it or not, he's mellowed out in the last couple of years.'

'Really?' I tried to imagine an even more intimidating Edward, but couldn't. He had always been nice to me, but I could tell he was a man used to getting his own way, and fast. 'No, you're right, I can't believe it.'

'He keeps calling, trying to find out what I know of Orlando's plans and of *The Sanctum*, but I keep ignoring him. I'm not sure what I'm even allowed to say to him.'

'How come he isn't a member?'

'From what Orlando has said, and let's take it all with a pinch of salt, he left. Didn't want to be a part of it all anymore. Same with Henry.'

'When?'

'Not long after they were recruited. It must all tie into whatever happened when they all went to Hawthorn.'

'But *what* happened?' I sighed. 'I feel like we're no closer to knowing than we were before my dad showed up and we started snooping in houses and infiltrating meetings, etcetera.'

It was all so fucking frustrating!

The closer we got, the further away we managed to slide in some roundabout, twisted way.

Bet Orlando and his wicked mother constantly laughed at us behind our backs. I still didn't understand the dynamic between the two of them—not sure I even wanted to understand—and as of late, Orlando had been keeping his distance from me. No doubt for some nefarious reason.

'There has to be a way for us to figure it out. The article we found in Hawthorn House spoke of a girl dying, right?'

I recalled the article in my mind. 'Yeah, Sandy Parks. It said *The Set* and *Sect* were outside the bathroom she died in.'

'And named our parents as being complicit,' Leo added. 'In case anybody at school didn't know who they meant.'

'If it's anything like now, adding their names wasn't necessary. Whoever wrote it wanted their crimes to be known to everyone. Reckon that's why The Hawthorn Herald school newspaper got sacked off?'

'Must be. Can't have something like that falling into the wrong hands.'

'Like the police?'

'Them.' Leo nodded. 'But also the parents of Sandy Parks. I did some digging, and she was a scholarship student.'

'Sounds familiar, doesn't it? Some jumped up Hawthorns, bullying somebody because their family isn't rich enough for their liking,' I said. My stomach soured. 'They do say history repeats itself if people don't learn from it.'

'In our defence,' Leo said, putting his hand in the air, open palm facing me, 'your family, at least one half of it, is pretty fucking rich.'

'So it was justified?' I laughed, without humour. 'You guys make it hard to forget when you act so entitled and justified in what you did to me.'

'No, it doesn't. At all. And for the record, we are trying to be better. Or at least I am. I'm assuming Griff and Ollie are, too.'

I reached out and put my hand on his forearm, intending it to soothe him. I wanted him to know how much I could tell he was doing all he could to change.

'Forget what I said. It was shitty of me. I know the three of you have remorse for what you did and that you've changed. I'm being sensitive.'

'Well, you do have a lot going on.'

I tutted. 'An understatement of sorts, but it also downplays everything you have going on. How are you? *Really*?'

'I ...'

'We're in *private* private, Leo,' I said with as much emphasis as possible. 'Nobody need ever know.'

He sighed, his body slumping further down the wall. 'I suppose I'm not used to talking about myself.'

'Take this chance and run with it because who knows when you'll get it again.'

He cracked a tiny smile. 'Everything's wrong. Out of my control. Like I'm spiralling and there's nothing to be done to stop it. If I don't do as they ask, they'll hurt you all, and I could never live if they did. If they kill me, then so be it.'

'Don't even joke about that!' The thought alone turned my innards into twists and turns. 'Nobody is killing you anytime soon, Leo Hawthorn. We're both going to live long and fulfilled lives and in thirty-plus years, we'll reminisce back on all this absolute *bullshit* and laugh our arses off.'

Leo didn't seem convinced about the future I painted. 'I hope you're right.'

'When am I ever wrong?' I'd been wrong a bloody lot in the last eighteen months, but not like I was about to point it out. 'Whatever happens, we'll be side by side and face it all together.'

'Is that a promise?'

'No. It's a vow.'

Thirty-Nine

OLLIE

ARRIVING BACK AT HAWTHORN, the thing I wanted most was to see my girl. Hug her. Hold her. Whisper all the things in her ear, and never let her go.

Being apart from her during such a tumultuous time pained me physically.

All because of my stupid fucking *brother*.

The bastard had set me up, probably with the help of his fucking awful mother, and I couldn't wait to see the smug look on his face wiped off when I showed up for breakfast in the morning.

I'd messaged Skylar while in the car on the way back and had expected her to be waiting for me at the bottom of the school steps, but it wasn't Skylar who waited for me.

No.

It was Leo.

I got out of the car and made my way over to him.

'Where's Sky?'

He nudged his head towards the school. 'Waiting in your room.'

277

'And she's not here because …'

'Because I asked her to stay in your room and said I'd meet you instead.'

'And you did that because …'

'Because I wanted to talk to you, of course.'

'Of course.' The two of us walked up the steps in unison. 'But why?'

'I wanted to ask what happened while you were gone. Orlando's been tight-lipped about it all, which is shady enough, and I don't like being in the dark.'

'No,' I said, a tad dry. 'You prefer to keep other people in the dark.'

'Are we still not over that?' Leo asked, and I wanted to punch him in the face—again. It seemed my previous punch wasn't hard enough to make a point. 'I've said sorry.'

'Have you?' I wracked my brain, unable to recall the apology he spoke of. 'Did you speak it out loud, or was it all in your head?'

Leo rubbed his jaw. 'Look, mate, if I didn't … I'm saying it now.'

'Saying what?'

Leo's shoulders moved with the force of his responding sigh. 'I'm saying sorry, alright?'

Most people wouldn't take his words as an apology, and usually I wouldn't either, but after a night in prison for something I didn't do, let's say I was a little out of sorts.

And by out of sorts, I meant a lot more forgiving and understanding than I normally would be.

On any other day, I'd never let him get away with something so half-hearted.

'Alright. Water under the bridge and all that shite.' We continued walking at a slow pace. 'Not much happened. The police were wankers as usual and kept accusing me of killing Ophelia and had DNA to prove it.'

'So, how are you out here and not still in there?'

'I pointed out how their DNA evidence isn't from finger-prints and without those there's no way of knowing if it was me or Orlando they were after, and seeing as Orlando is already out on bail ...' I let the sentence hang in the air. 'Well, they were uncertain enough to let me go for now. That, and our lawyers got involved and maybe my dad paid money or something. Didn't stick around long enough to ask once they told me I could leave.'

'But they'll be back?'

'With bells on.' I shook my head, my frustration towards the situation creeping into my mind and getting the better of me. Everything right now was a constant battle. Orlando, Winifred, *The Sanctum*. Even my relationship with Skylar to a degree was a battle, but mainly because I kept opening my mouth to tell her I loved her, but something would come along and interrupt us. 'Wouldn't surprise me if they tried to find a way to take both of us. Or maybe they'll see who offers more money and decide, corrupt bastards.'

Leo nodded, understanding the way the Hawthorn police worked.

Hard to remember a time in my life when people weren't rotten to the core. Maybe they always had been, and I was too young to realise.

But the one person I could rely on to never act rotten was Skylar, and as much as mine and Leo's conversation was important, it still wasn't where I wanted to be.

'Contact your dad and get the best lawyers on it, in case they come for you again.'

I nodded my agreement. 'Already done. Dad's hatred

towards Winifred is the strongest it's ever been, so for once he's on my side with no fight.'

'A miracle.'

Leo's dry tone made me smile against my will. It was a miracle. One I doubted would repeat anytime soon.

'A miracle indeed.'

I LEFT Leo at the entrance to the student rooms, the black door at the end of the hallway beckoning me. Calling to me in a way I couldn't ignore a moment longer.

Skylar waited for me inside, which was all that mattered.

Other students milled around, but I ignored them all. Nobody would find my behaviour unusual, because I usually ignored everybody, anyway. It was rare somebody was worth my notice in this shit hole, after all.

Skylar waited for me on the other side of the door, already dressed in her nightdress ready for bed.

She squealed when she saw me. *Damn.* My heart kicked up a notch.

'Yay, you're back!'

She ran into my open arms, and I hugged her tight, breathing in the scent of her. It grounded me, being so close to her. Fuck, I loved her.

I wasn't sure if she also loved me too.

'How was it? How are you? Are you okay?' All her questions ran into one another, coming out in a jumble of gibberish. 'Did they hurt you? Were they wankers? Are you okay?'

'If you'd take a breath, maybe I could answer one of your questions.' I chuckled.

She laughed back. 'Yeah, sorry. I've hated not being able to talk to you. See you. It sucked.'

'It sucked hard,' I agreed. 'But I'm back now and everything's all good.'

'You mean *for* now?'

I nodded. 'For now, yes. I'm sure tomorrow will bring another battle of sorts.'

'It's tiring, isn't it?' she asked. 'Always fighting battles.'

The question was rhetorical, but I inclined my head. Of course, it was fucking tiring. We needed a distraction, and I had the perfect thing in mind.

'Come shower with me,' I said, a cheeky grin on my lips. 'I need to wash the dirt off.'

'I can wait here,' she said. 'No need for me to come.'

'I don't want to leave your side,' I said, batting my eyelashes at her playfully. 'I've missed you, Sky. In more ways than one.'

I raised my eyebrows at her suggestively, hunger stirring in my belly as I pictured myself pressed up against her in the shower.

Skylar smiled and rolled her eyes. 'You just want to see me naked.'

'I'd never turn down an opportunity to see you naked,' I said. 'But I promise it isn't about that.' Then I coughed, unable to lie to her wide-eyed gaze. 'Well, not entirely.'

'Fine, I'll bite.' Her voice was light, but an eagerness lingered in her eyes and the smile on her lips matched mine.

We both stripped on our way to the shower, leaving a path of clothes in our wake as we walked to the ensuite, a sense of ease settling between us again that made me sigh in relief. Our connection grew stronger every day, and I was so fucking lucky to call her mine.

Leaning into my shower, Skylar turned on the water, letting it warm up before getting in. I'm sure she also did this to give me a better view of her bum, which I appreciated. Giving it a slap, I growled instructions in her ear to let me in. She was under the warm water and I was chilly—never a good look.

Sky shivered lightly but obeyed without question, moving further into the shower to make room for me. Honestly, I was just glad I didn't have a huge shower, so there was nowhere for me to go but up against her soft skin.

Her body stayed still as she faced me, anticipation and curiosity on her face as she watched me. Smirking, I pressed a firm kiss to her lips as I reached past her for her shampoo. I continued devouring her lips and tongue as I popped it open and poured it on to her lilac hair, already soaked from the hot water pouring down.

How did I get so lucky?

I ended the kiss and moved Skylar into a better position so I could focus on washing her hair. This delayed gratification would make it better for both of us, so I did my best to ignore my hunger for her pressed against me, focusing on my fingers instead.

'Are you sure you're okay?' she asked, her voice mumbled. 'I should be the one pampering you.'

'Don't be silly,' I replied. 'You're the important one. No matter what happens.'

She reached up and stopped my hands and turned to face me. I bit down the laugh bubbling up at the view of her foamy scalp. She bit her bottom lip and smiled.

'Yeah, yeah, I look funny. But being serious for a moment,' she said, taking my hands in hers. 'You're important as me.' Then she blinked and shook her head, the bubbles in her hair flicking out and landing on my chest. 'To me, you're the *most* important, okay?'

I swallowed. It hadn't got easier to hear nice things from her about me, but I loved hearing them, nonetheless.

'Okay?' she repeated, more forceful, this time. The conviction in her tone made me love her more ... but now wasn't the time to tell her.

My voice broke when I said, 'Okay.'

Sky nodded with determination.

'Good.' She turned around once more, putting the front of her body under the spray of the water. 'Now, get back to massaging my head.'

'Yes, sir.'

We fell into a comfortable silence, and when Sky turned to put her head under the water to wash off the shampoo, she smiled shyly at me. 'You're pretty perfect, you know that, right?'

'You may have mentioned it once or twice.'

I put some body wash on a washcloth and placed it on her body, starting at her shoulders. My hand made a circular motion, sweeping across her collarbone, down each arm and back again, before moving to her breasts. I circled around them first, ensuring everything got coated in soap before moving my gentle attention to her nipples, already gathered into stiff peaks that had me aching to tug at them with my teeth.

Instead, I played with them with my other hand, amazed at how soft and smooth they were with the soap.

'Don't stop,' she murmured.

I hadn't planned to, but hearing her voice the command had me growing harder. There was something extremely sexy about Sky asking for what she wanted. Demanding it, in fact.

Back when I met her, she would never have uttered such a sentence.

Her newfound confidence was so fucking attractive it almost hurt to watch.

I continued to wash her, turning her around so she could lean back into me as I worked. Soft moans of enjoyment left her lips. 'Mmm.'

In a slow tease, I trailed my hand down ...

I placed the cloth down on the corner shelf and touched her pussy with my right hand, grazing my fingertips across her sensitive flesh, hoping to elicit another moan from her lips.

As soon as I brushed against her clitoris, finding it with instinctive precision, Skylar arched against me, panting with need. 'Ollie.'

I put one finger inside her tight walls, and then followed it soon after with a second, picking up speed.

'Yes?' I bit at her earlobe and moved us so we were both under the warm water, Skylar's back pressed up against the wall tiles. 'Come for me, baby. I need you to fall apart while I hold you up.'

Her pleasure mounted faster as I spoke, using my thumb to rub her clit as I continued to move my fingers. When Sky came, her moan had me nearly coming too. The way she choked back a scream while trembling in my arms was pure heaven.

I didn't give her long to recover, moving her so her tits pressed up against the wall, her head turned towards me, eyes dazed but still hungry. Her back arched; her body ready for me.

'God, you're too damn sexy for your own good,' I growled, thrusting my cock inside, giving her no other warning. She was already slick from her recent orgasm and tight with need. It was a damn good thing I knew how to hold myself off, or I would have finished in seconds from how perfect she was.

As I moved inside her, awed at the way she gripped my cock, she whimpered, a wordless beg for more. For me to give her another release. *Mine,* I thought to myself fondly, grabbing her hips to pull her tighter against me. *All mine.*

Her sounds of enjoyment increased as I moved faster, harder, my breath coming in controlled bursts as I did my best to bring her to climax before I got there myself. Thankfully, as I teetered on the edge, Skylar let out a long, high pitched 'Fuck!'

Her walls clenched around me so hard I wouldn't have been able to fight off my own even if I tried. Grunting, my body released its load, pulsing for longer than I had anything to give.

Flipping Skylar around to face me, I put my forehead on hers, catching my breath for a moment before kissing her adoringly, my hands resting on her waist. She kissed me back, and it hit me like a bolt of lightning that this was the girl I wanted to spend forever with. I didn't know what I'd do without her by my side, and I didn't want to think of a scenario where I would be without her.

I needed to tell her.

And soon.

Forty

THE MORNING after Ollie's return, and our great night of sex and intimacy, a thick, cream card invitation slid underneath his bedroom door.

It read:

> *Mister Oliver Brandon and Miss Skylar Crescent,*
> *You are cordially invited to Hawthorn Academy's Charity*
> *Masquerade Ball*
> *Date: Saturday 2nd July*
> *Dress code: Formal attire*
> *Masks: Required*
> *We look forward to your presence.*

'Fun,' I said, my tone dry, after reading the invitation and passing it over to Ollie. 'Reckon the others have one too?'

'I'd say so. It's odd we're being invited as guests.' Ollie rubbed his chin and my eyes followed the movement, fixated. 'Maybe our parents have paid our fee.'

'Fee?'

'It's a charity event, Skylar,' he said, as if his words were all the explanation needed. Stupid rich-all-his-life bastard.

'And that means ...'

'That means everybody in attendance will have paid an exorbitant fee for their tickets.' He laughed, his eyes wrinkled in mirth. 'I forget how little you know about this life.'

'Oh, ha, ha. Laugh at the scholarship kid.'

He stopped his laughter. 'I'm sorry.'

'I'm teasing you,' I said. 'You're not wrong, in a way. I don't know much about this kind of life. How exorbitant a fee are we talking here? And who would have paid for me?'

'Your dad or mine,' Ollie said. 'No idea of the exact amount, but we're talking in the thousands.'

'The thousands?' My tone was incredulous, because *I* was incredulous. Even after the time I'd spent around the kids here at Hawthorn—and their parents—I still couldn't get over how much money they waved around when it suited them. There were people who lived on the estate I grew up in who had barely enough money for bread and milk, yet these people had never known a day of true hardship in their entire existence. It soured my stomach.

Was I part of the problem? Had I acted grateful enough for all I now had?

Becoming a student at Hawthorn wasn't something I asked for, yet somebody footed the bill for my time here.

'Yep, and the money all goes to a charity of the school's choosing, which means a charity of the *parent's* choosing.'

'Right ...' It all sounded a little dodgy to me, but what did I know? Not a lot, let's be honest. 'So, are we going to go?'

'Yeah.' Ollie threw the duvet off himself and sat upright. 'Somebody has gone to great lengths to invite us. Can't disappoint them.'

'And I suppose we'll need to look the part?' I tried to keep my tone light, but underneath, I was a little giddy. One thing I rather liked about this new life I found myself in was the opportunity to dress up and act fancy. It still made my eyes water to know how much my formal dresses cost, but the moment I put them on, it became easy to forget such a slight detail.

Ollie, knowing me well enough now to see through my bullshit facades, smiled. 'I suppose so. What a heavy task that will be for you.'

I sighed, playing along. 'Tis a heavy burden, but one must make the most of it.'

'Yes, you sound *so* put out by it.' Ollie laughed. 'I'll arrange an appointment for you. We've got a couple of months.'

'Thank you.' I sat down on the edge of the bed and leaned forward to place a grateful kiss on his lips. 'Have I told you how much I appreciate you?'

'You may have mentioned it once or twice, yeah.'

'Good.' The invitation remained in my hands and I couldn't help fiddling with the corners of the card, folding and bending them over. 'Maybe we could use this ball to our advantage?'

'What have you got in mind?'

'I haven't figured that part out yet.' I waved the invitation around. 'But this could be the chance we've all been waiting for.'

'Are you suggesting ...'

'*The Sanctum* will be in attendance, right?' I smiled, the certainty of my words growing. 'So, why don't we make a plan of sorts?'

Ollie moved closer to me. 'We can talk to the others later. See what they think?'

'Don't see why they'd be against it, but sure, I'll message them all in a bit.' I moved off the bed and put the invitation down on the bedside cabinet. 'We didn't have any plans tonight, did we?'

Ollie shook his head, his dark hair ruffled from sleep.

'Nothing we can't postpone until after we meet with them.' His eyebrows waggled, and I laughed at his implication. As if we hadn't spent enough *alone* time together since he got back from prison on Friday night. We hadn't seen anyone since he got back, too wrapped up in each other, but that needed to change if we were to get ahead of the game.

'If there's time. You know we won't be able to meet until much, *much* later. Can't have any eyes on us and we don't want to be spotted by Orlando or Ms Hawthorn.'

'Those two rats will have scuttered back down to the sewers by then.'

The image made me smile.

'We can hope.'

'So, we all got the invitations, yes?'

My gaze travelled across the room, taking in the sight of Clo, Griff, Leo, and Ollie standing in front of me.

Clover had a bored expression on her face, but I doubted it was from being around us—more like boredom from us being targeted all the time.

Griff had his usual cheeky smile plastered on his face, more than ready for the scheming to take place.

Leo, who could match Clover for the most bored expression in the room, stood silently, hands clasped in front of his waist. He wore grey jogging bottoms and a white T-shirt and even though my deeper fondness for him had dissipated, I could still appreciate how mighty fine he looked.

Then there was Ollie, the happiest I'd seen him in a long while, which was an enormous surprise seeing as his week had been more than a little trying.

'To the masquerade ball?' Griff asked, and I nodded. 'Yep. And we all know I don't have any parents who would've paid for my ticket.'

'They were from *The Sanctum*,' Leo said, as casual as anything and bloody hell it made me want to deck him. My emotions were always so up and down where he was concerned, never knowing whether to be happy we'd sorted shit out or mad he was still a vexing bastard on the daily.

'You know this for definite?' Ollie asked, his body turning in Leo's direction.

'I do.' Leo blinked, not one bit threatened by Ollie's stance or glowering eyes. 'They're planning something.'

'Like?' I said, stepping in before Ollie could. 'How do you know this?'

'No idea what.' Leo shrugged, nonchalant. 'I know, because they said so at the last meeting. They want all of us to be there, including the parents. '

'Wonderful,' Clo muttered. 'Assume my parents don't make the cut?'

'No,' Leo said in a clipped tone. 'They don't.'

I rolled my eyes. The two of them could sort their squabble at a later time. There were far more important things to deal with than their shared history.

'Cut it out,' I snapped. 'Bigger fish to fry over here.'

I gave Clo a stern look, and she raised her eyebrows in response.

Yeah, yeah, Clover Luck. Act like you've got no idea why I'm reprimanding you.

I continued talking, giving neither of them time to say anything. 'If they want our parents there too, then something sinister must be afoot.'

'Afoot?' Griff's grin grew. 'Are you well, Clouds?'

'Am I well?' I asked, his change of direction confusing me enough to sidetrack my thought train.

'Yes,' he replied. 'Only it seems you've swallowed some kind of old-timey dictionary.'

My laughter came out as a harsh bark. 'An old-timey dictionary? Honestly, Griff, I wonder about what goes on in your head sometimes.'

The word afoot wasn't too old-fashioned, right?

I didn't think so, but then again, maybe it was? Eurgh! Now I wanted to get my phone and search for the origin of the word. I'd have to do it later, if I remembered.

' ... *Sanctum.*'

Fucking hell. I needed to pay more attention to the conversation going on instead of my own mind. No idea who had spoken, but I hadn't heard a word of it.

'Sorry, what?' I asked, my voice sounding loud to my ears.

Griff scrunched his nose. 'What part?'

'Err, all of it?' I gave them what I hoped to be an impish grin.

'I asked whether there's anything we can do if *The Sanctum* targets us at this thing,' Griff said. 'If they don't talk of their plan in front of Leo, then we've got no heads up. Plus, it could be anything.'

'True. However, we could try to use the crowd to our benefit,' I said.

Ollie came closer and took my hand in his. He pulled me to

his side and placed his arm casually around my waist. I couldn't decide if it was his version of staking a claim or whether he wanted to touch me and craved physical contact the way I did. I hated how it made me more aware of Leo, though. Like I was rubbing it in his face or something.

I know, I know. It was silly of me to think like that, but I couldn't help it.

There was nothing to do but get over it—and myself. *I'm not special.*

'What you got in mind, Stutter?' Leo said, unaffected by Ollie's new position next to me.

'Well,' I chuckled, 'I sort of hoped the five of us could figure something out together.'

'So, you're hoping to use my brains for your own gain,' Griff said, in between bites of a strawberry cable. It must have been a tough one, as he yanked it with his teeth so hard I thought they would break if he kept going.

'Yep, pretty much,' I confirmed. 'My brains want to sit this one out, thank you.'

'How about Ollie asking you to dance in front of everyone?' Clover asked. 'Once you're dancing, Orlando will butt in, I'm sure of it.'

'Okay ... And then?'

Clo shrugged. 'I don't know. Piss him off somehow. Rile him up. Get him to admit something or reveal *The Sanctum.*' She shrugged again. 'I'm sure you can think of something.'

'It's not a poor plan,' Ollie said.

'It's not a *good* one either,' Leo said.

Clo saw red. She snapped, 'Got a better idea, boring bollocks?'

Which shut Leo right up, because instead of snapping

something inane back, he kept his lips pressed tight together in a thin line.

A smile crept on to my lips. I couldn't help it. Sometimes watching the two of them was like watching a train wreck—one you couldn't look away from, no matter how hard you tried.

'Let's be civil,' I said, before the situation could devolve further. I clapped my hands together. 'Let's make a plan.'

Forty-One

THE END OF JUNE ARRIVED. Which meant, you guessed it, exam time.

Finally, we would sit our final exams to determine how good of a life we'd have when we left the halls of Hawthorn.

And I was so ready to ace everything. I'd been studying—somewhat—and I knew I would do better than I had the previous June in my mocks. It also absolutely baffled me to realise it had been an entire year since the failure of those exams. So much had happened before them, but a lot had happened afterwards, too.

It had been an entire year since I had come back to school, revenge plan in hand—a poorly attempted revenge plan that never took off, but we move.

And now my dad had shown up and wanted to spend time together. Get to know me. *What the fuck?*

'Are you nervous?' Griff asked me as we were lining up to enter the hall for our ethics exam. As long as the question wasn't one about a topic I hadn't focused on as much, I had high hopes.

'I am more than ready,' I told him. I put my hair into a high ponytail, meaning business, and swished it in his face to make him laugh. 'I want to be done.'

'I feel you, Clouds.' He nodded, serious. 'Once these are over, we've got the masquerade ball, and then we're scot free. Away from this bullshit, this place, and everyone in it.'

'You think so?' I asked, sceptical. And I had every reason to be. I doubted Orlando would leave us alone once we left the school. That *The Sanctum* would leave us alone once we were off school grounds. They seemed pretty determined fuckers.

'I know so.' He chuckled. Ms Hawthorn came to the front of the line and gave a speech about the behaviour she expected from us while we were taking the exam. The line hushed. And then it was time to enter the hall.

Time to take my seat and write non-stop for three hours straight.

And then after, I had another four to go. Then I was done.

And a weight lifted.

Father's Day.

I didn't join last year, seeing as up until not so long ago, my father lived outside the picture, but now I had one excited to attend.

Lucky for me, I wouldn't have to face the day alone with Jacob as my sole company.

Ollie and Henry were coming, as were Leo and Edward. Unfortunately for us all, Orlando was joining them.

Henry's genius idea, apparently.

He believed it would be a great way for both him and Ollie to meet Orlando and talk as a family and get to know one another. As if we didn't already know enough to want to keep our distance from this newfound member of the Hawthorn/Brandon clan.

When Ollie told me of his father's plans, I laughed. Poor Henry. He could act so ... wrong ... sometimes.

'Does your dad think it's going to work?' I asked Ollie, not turning to face him.

I took myself in from head to toe in the full-length mirror in Ollie's room, and fixed some platinum hoop earrings into my ears that Jacob gifted me for my birthday. They were the most expensive gift I'd received—excluding my necklace from Ollie—and I loved them. But no matter how much I love them, and appreciate the present, I wouldn't allow Jacob Cooper to buy me. The man could win me over with his actions and words in the normal way, thank you very much.

'It would seem so,' Ollie replied, coming into view in the mirror image of the room. 'Seems to believe if he talks to Orlando, things will get all cleared up and one day we'll become like one big, happy family.'

'Miracles do happen.'

'Yes,' Ollie agreed. 'And so do disasters.'

I laughed and turned to face the real him. 'Promise me no matter how bad today gets, we're in this together, okay? As a team.'

'You and I are the best team there is.' He came over to me and placed a kiss on my lips. 'You look stunning. This dress is beautiful, like you.'

My dress was another vintage inspired full skirt design, and I loved it. It had billowed sleeves to be worn off the shoulder, and the most striking turquoise check pattern. It complimented my light purple hair really well, and I loved it. It had been a gift from Ollie for today, and I was thankful he had such impeccable taste and knew me well enough to get it right without my input.

I took him in from head to toe for the first time since he got changed and whispered out, 'Fuck.'

He chuckled, and I fake punched him in the arm.

'Like what you see, baby?' he drawled. His top lip curled up, amused by my reaction. The fucker knew he looked good and could turn me into a puddle, and he used it to his full advantage—frequently.

'You know I do,' I said, taking him in once more. He wore trousers teamed with a suit jacket, which he knew I liked, but he'd gone one further. The trousers and jacket were *grey*.

Damn!

There was something perfect about a guy in grey. I couldn't tell you what, just that I bloody loved it. It was a major turn on.

'Are you sure we have to go?' I asked, reaching down to squeeze his bum to pull him closer, so our bodies pressed flush together. Every contour beneath me had me wanting to undress him right then and there. 'We could bail. My dad did a good enough job of it for the last eighteen years, so not like he wouldn't deserve it.'

'We do,' he said. As always, he got a kick out of me, and how much I wanted him. Me wanting to stay in rather than face the music with his dad and brother.

Could you blame me?

'Spoil sport.'

'Come on, you.' He removed my hands from behind him and pushed away from me. 'Henry's waiting for us at the main entrance and I'd rather get there before Jacob arrives.'

I sighed and took in a deep breath, trying to calm down my newly appeared nerves. I'd been fine while I put my makeup on and got dressed, but the closer it got, the more apprehension filtered in.

'Do you think it's gonna be a total disaster?'

'Oh, yeah. Big time.'

I laughed. 'Okay ...' I took one last look in the full-length mirror to check nothing had changed in my appearance. 'I'm ready.'

'Let's do this shit.'

HENRY WAITED for us outside at the bottom of the stairs leading into the main building. He seemed more tired than the last time I saw him, which made sense. The last time we'd seen one another was at the New Year's Gala, and *let's be honest*, a lot had happened since then.

His hair had grown longer and unkempt, but it was also a lot more silver than before.

'Oliver,' he greeted, holding out his hand to Ollie, who didn't take it. 'Skylar.'

He nodded his head at me in greeting, and I smiled back at him. Since the Orlando shit happened, I sort of felt sorry for him these days?

Yeah, he'd acted creepy towards me, and he had beef with my dad, but aside from that, he was a hurt man who wasn't sure what was what anymore. And no part of me blamed him.

'Hello, Father,' Ollie greeted. Cool as ice. It always surprised me how frosty the two of them were together. I suppose I thought things would improve now they'd opened up a little, but things were the same as before.

I stayed silent, doing my best to not shuffle from foot to

foot to have an output for my nervous energy. The tension rose the longer we stayed here, and I wasn't sure if I should make the next move.

Lucky for me, somebody else stole the limelight.

'Hello,' Orlando boomed from the top of the staircase, a wide smile on his face. A smile that put me on guard.

It was the definition of untrustworthy.

The three of us froze, staring up at him. After a beat, I walked towards Orlando, and after seeing me do so, Ollie and Henry followed suit. They shuffled up the stairs slowly, but at least they *were* coming.

'Little One,' Orlando murmured, inaudible to the two Brandon men still making their way to us. 'You look sublime.'

'Thank y-you,' I stammered back. 'You look good too.'

He wore a similar suit to Ollie, but in a darker grey, and I bet he somehow found out what his brother planned to wear and picked his outfit out accordingly. I shook the thought away. Surely he wasn't *that* sad?

'Dad,' Orlando said, holding his hand out to greet Henry when he got to the top. Shock crossed Henry's features in a flash. Maybe like me, his mind travelled back to New Year's, to the time before the real Ollie had shown up. Or maybe he noticed how different Orlando acted toward him when compared to Ollie.

'Hello,' Henry choked out, taking Orlando's hand in his and shaking firmly. 'Good to see you.'

Shit. This was the first time they were meeting, wasn't it? Properly, I mean, and not in some piss-poor showdown.

'Brother,' Orlando greeted Ollie, holding his hand out to him. Ollie recoiled and stepped closer to me.

'Hi,' he said in a clipped tone. I'd never heard Ollie use the word "hi" in all the times I'd known him. It sounded, *I don't know,* weird. Too un-Ollie.

'Well, isn't this nice?' Orlando said, taking each of us in one by one. 'Waiting on one more, are we?'

I rolled my eyes at him. God, he could be such a dick. 'Jacob text to say he was running a little late, so he'd meet us inside.'

Henry's eyes widened, but he said nothing.

'Let's get this over with,' Ollie said, grabbing my hand and pulling me towards the open school doors, not waiting for the other two. Once we were a couple of paces ahead, Ollie whispered, 'Keep an eye on him. I don't trust him one bit.'

'I don't either,' I agreed. 'But there isn't much he can do in front of all these people, is there?'

Wishful thinking and all that. Of course, he could do a lot of shit in front of this many people. There'd been a fuck ton of people at the gala and he still masqueraded as his twin for the entire evening with nobody being any the wiser. He only came clean because Ollie broke free and spoiled his fun.

'Watch him,' Ollie repeated, urgency in his tone. I nodded and squeezed his hand to tell him I understood.

When we entered the main hall, shock shot through me at how unrecognisable it had become.

It had transformed into some kind of lads' den.

There were large screens all along one wall, each one showing a different sporting event. Then, in the far corner, a section was set aside with video consoles and games, and there were already a couple of students playing with their dads in lush—most likely expensive—gaming chairs.

The vibe was so different to the one on Mother's Day, and instead of an Afternoon Tea, today's option was an outdoor barbecue. Which, yeah, probably catered to the dads more than small sandwiches and different flavours of heated water.

Heck, it probably catered to half the mums more, too. My mum bloody loved a good barbecue.

Ollie and I stopped once we reached a seating area. Orlando and Henry joined us not long after.

'Shall we go grab a beer?' Henry asked the three of us, and the boys nodded, scarily in-sync.

'I'll stay here,' I announced to nobody in particular. 'Make sure we keep the seats.'

'Thanks, Sky,' Orlando said, acting the perfect gentleman. 'Would you like anything?'

'I'll get you a drink you like, okay, baby?' Ollie said, standing to join them, giving his brother a dark look. He didn't like Orlando addressing me at all.

'O-okay,' I said. 'Thank you.'

Ollie nodded, gripping his hands together in front of his stomach. I sensed his agitation from my seat, but I knew I couldn't go to him. He needed to do this without me.

'Come on, then,' Henry said over his shoulder, as he headed towards the bar on the far side of the hall.

I got comfortable in my seat, watching the three of them walk to the bar together. I wouldn't tell them, but they all walked similarly. It was in the way they carried themselves. Confident. Cocksure. They knew what they wanted and they wouldn't stop until they got it.

'Stutter,' Leo greeted me, taking the seat opposite. His father, Edward, took the seat next to him and I smiled at them both. 'You're looking well.'

'Hey! Thank you. Scrub up pretty nice yourself,' I said to Leo before I turned to Edward. 'How have you been?'

'I've been well, thank you, Miss Crescent. Lottie sends her love. She's rather gutted that she couldn't come.'

'Never had Lottie down as a barbecue goer,' I said. 'And please, I think you can call me Skylar now.'

'Of course, Skylar.' He rubbed his hands together, getting comfy. 'Where's your dad?'

'Not here yet. Henry, Ollie, and Orlando are over there.' I nodded my head towards the bar. 'It's the first time …'

Leo's eyes widened, picking up my thought. 'Yeah, Orlando mentioned he was joining his dad and brother today.'

'What's that little shit doing here?' Edward's jaw clenched. 'My sister mentioned nothing about it.'

'Yeah, but your sister's a bitch,' Leo said, bored. *Ah, bored Leo. How nice it is to see thee.* 'Winnie tells you things only if she's going to benefit from them.'

'Don't talk about your aunt like that,' Edward said, sounding tired. He rubbed his face with the palm of his hand, as if the weight of the world lived on his shoulders. 'She's family.'

'I'll stop talking about her when she stops ruining shit,' Leo mumbled, glancing out of the window.

'Watch your tongue, son,' Edward snapped. He took a sip from his drink, and the uncomfortable tension sitting in the air had me fidgeting even more. 'People may overhear you.'

My gaze trickled back to the bar, pretending not to be paying attention to Leo and Edward's tense exchange. The three Brandon men were making their way back to us, each with a drink in hand. I spotted Ollie had won the battle to get me a drink.

'Here you go, babe,' Ollie said as he handed me a tall glass of lemonade and violet flavoured gin. My favourite.

'Thanks,' I replied, moving on the seat a little to make room for him next to me. He took the spot willingly and slung an arm around my shoulder, pulling me closer. 'You handled that well.'

'Hello, Edward,' Henry said, shaking Edward's hand. The two of them both wore black suits, the epitome of wealthy business executives, and I could see the crow's feet at the corners of their eyes—one of the few features on their faces showing their age.

'Hello, Henry.' His tone hadn't changed from when he spoke to Leo last. Guess I'd always assumed the two of them were friends, but thinking about it, maybe they weren't. They were family, sure, but being family didn't mean you liked one another.

The yearbooks we'd found earlier in the year told us they were pals back then, but a lot had changed in the time since. Edward had lost two sisters, and Henry had lost his wife, who happened to be one of those sisters. Tragedies could change even the strongest of friendships.

'Uncle Eddy,' Orlando said, a wide smile on his face. He brushed his hand through his hair, and I reckoned it was a way to come across as nonchalant and carefree. He was taunting him, though, being disrespectful. Orlando was going to act like he hadn't pulled a *literal gun* out on the man the last time they were in the same room.

Edward's free hand clenched and unclenched at his side.

'Hello,' Edward said through gritted teeth, not wanting to respond to Orlando, but not seeing a way out of doing so.

The tension was palpable, everybody in the vicinity on edge and unsure of what to do and how to act, and the six of us fell into one of the most awkward silences I'd ever experienced in my life.

Forty-Two

THE ROOM WAS a large hub of movement and sound, what with all the other pupils and their fathers dotted around the large hall. It was overwhelming to a degree, but Ollie's hand on my arm reminded me of why I was here.

So when the room went silent, we all noticed straight away.

All heads in the room turned to the door as each person tried to see what caused the commotion. Or at least what had caught everybody's eye.

'Ah,' Ollie whispered beside me, able to see the door better, being taller than me.

Henry's face went pale, the colour draining from it.

Guess that explained who had arrived.

My body moved before my brain caught up with the action. I stood up and made way closer to Jacob, to meet him halfway. Everybody's eyes were on him, and I wanted to show my support. Make it clear he was welcome here—invited.

'Sky,' he said, his voice gruff and filled with emotion. 'Thanks for inviting me.'

He opened his arms, and I went into them, being pulled into one of the tightest hugs I'd ever been a part of. His arms were so warm it made me sweat, but I didn't pull myself away. Most people I kept at arm's distance, but it seemed I'd decided my dad could be an exception to the rule.

'No problem,' I said. 'Glad you could make it.'

'You and everybody else, I'm sure.' He chuckled.

I stepped out of his hug. 'I think some people are turning our way.'

Funny, Sky. Bit of an understatement, too. *Everybody* looked our way, and the hall stayed as silent as when he came in.

'Let them,' Jacob said. 'You ready for this?'

'Ready as I'll ever be,' I said. The two of us made our way back to the table where nobody had moved a muscle. Well, not entirely true. The muscle in Henry's top lip moved, as did the twitch in Edward's eyebrow.

When we reached the table, I took my place at Ollie's side and Jacob sat down in the spare seat next to Orlando.

'Jacob,' Henry said, his tone dark and his eyes narrowed. Edward's expression matched. Both of them were pissed, even though they knew he was coming. I suppose it wasn't easy to be around somebody with so much bad blood swirling between you. 'Nice to see you.'

Slowly, the sound in the hall picked up once again, although I reckoned it was a way for them to hide the fact they were still staring over here. *If I were them, I'd be doing the same thing.* People liked to deny it if asked, but everybody had a nosey streak. It was the reason cars slowed down to bog at a crash on the hard shoulder.

'Henry,' Jacob said back. 'Edward.' He nodded at them in turn. 'Is Griff coming?'

'He's coming any moment now,' I said. 'He made it clear he wouldn't miss the barbecue for no man or woman.'

Jacob laughed, but the others all remained silent, sipping their drinks for something to do.

I got out my phone while the adults glared at each other and tapped out a quick message.

HERC, JACOB'S ARRIVED. YOU GONNA BE LONG? x

His reply was instantaneous.

BE THERE IN TEN, CLOUDS x

' ... had to come see my daughter.' Jacob was finishing a sentence I hadn't heard the start of, but it raised my back up and I couldn't place my finger on why. He made it sound as if he wanted to come of his own volition and not just because Cora had called him and practically demanded it.

'Pretty sure your daughter's been alive for eighteen years,' Leo drawled, contempt dripping from every syllable. 'What made you crawl your way out of the gutter now?'

I covered up a cough at Leo's words. Nice to know he still had my best interest at heart, even if we'd been on shaky ground of late.

'I'll have you know I lived on a lovely island, Leo. Not a gutter at all.'

My stomach squirmed. I fidgeted in my seat, the hem of my skirt becoming extremely interesting, a sense of shittiness creeping in. While he'd been sunning it up on an island, I'd struggled to make ends meet and have enough food to fill my belly. Nausea swirled in my gut, and I had to fight the urge to flee the room.

'Well, while some of us were tanning in the Bahamas, others were working in a supermarket to put food on the table,' Ollie growled, placing his arm around me to pull me tighter.

Jacob's face fell, and he didn't need to say anything for me to know he felt guilty about rubbing his exile in my face. It was as if the two of us had an instant connection. An instant piece of string entwining us together, every thought and emotion clear as day.

I hated it as much as I loved it.

'I'm sorry, Skylar,' he said, his eyes earnest.

I swallowed and mumbled out, 'I know.'

I *did* know, but it didn't stop it from hurting.

'What are you doing here?' Edward said through gritted teeth, having had enough time to collect his thoughts. His face went as red as a pillar box, struggling to keep his calm. He'd already been mad at Orlando's presence, so no wonder this had tipped him over the ledge.

'My daughter invited me.' The word *daughter* went through the group like a shockwave, or maybe it was the word *invited*.

'No,' Edward said. 'I don't mean today.'

'What's so urgent you've appeared out of your hole?' Henry spat, his displeasure clear. 'Millie's death wasn't urgent enough.'

Ouch. Low blow.

Everybody shuffled in their seats, not sure what to do or where to focus their gaze. So sod's law meant Griff arrived right then.

'Hey guys!' he said cheerfully. 'How's everyone ...' he trailed off as his eyes landed on Jacob. He'd known Jacob would be here, but it must be different coming face to face with somebody who was the spitting image of your dead dad.

Jacob's facial expression was equally affected. His eyes widened, and he stared at Griff awed. The first night he arrived, Griff hadn't stuck around long, rushing after me when I fled, so they'd spent barely any time in the same vicinity.

'Griffin,' he whispered, tears forming in his eyes. Tears he didn't wipe away.

'Uncle Jacob,' Griff whispered back, his voice cracking. 'Hey.'

'I—' Griff was at a loss for words, and I couldn't blame him. I hated seeing him so bereft of his usual self. It was super rare for Griff to be at a loss for words.

I moved up in the seat to sit on top of Ollie's lap to make room for Griff.

'Come here,' I said, patting the seat next to me.

In a daze, he stumbled towards me and sat down. I reached out and squeezed his thigh, and he grabbed my hand in his and didn't let go.

For so long he'd gone without family, and now he had a cousin and his uncle back. I couldn't imagine the emotions running through him.

'Thanks,' he mumbled, and I nodded, happy I could be here for him. Could be the support he needed.

'The barbecue must be ready now,' Leo said, drawing the attention of the group away from Griff and Jacob, who were still staring at one another, lost in their moment. 'We should head out.'

Everybody grumbled out a 'yes' and we all moved to stand as one.

Griff kept his hand tight in mine, and we made our way out of the hall to the cooking food. It smelled amazing, but I'd lost my appetite.

Suppose the idea of spending the day with people who hate each other would do that to a girl.

'So, Jacob,' Edward said, holding a pint out for Jacob to take. The gesture seemed friendly enough, but I could see the serpent under it. 'How did you fund your lavish lifestyle? It's been, oh, I don't know … about thirteen years since we saw you last.'

'Yes,' Henry continued. 'You left a week before your brother died, if my memory's correct.'

I watched Jacob wince, but he stood his ground, not letting the two men walk all over him. 'Unfortunately, *circumstances* prevented me from returning for the funeral.'

Yeah, *circumstances* had prevented him from returning. One of those circumstances being Cora, I assumed. Or maybe me. The others … well, they weren't clear to me yet, but they would be in time.

'Didn't prevent you from returning after,' Henry grumbled under his breath.

He was talking about the affair Jacob had with Millie for the five years after the twins' deaths. In some weird way, the affair made sense to me. Both Millie and Jacob lost their twin in the car accident—one we were pretty certain wasn't an accident—and they sought comfort in each other.

Plus, Jacob and Millie had been together while attending Hawthorn together, so I can imagine the bond between them, not to mention the chemistry, already existed between them.

'Things were complicated,' Jacob said. 'They still are. But I knew I couldn't leave Sky here to fend for herself any longer amongst you vultures.'

'How gallant of you,' Edward said. 'And I suppose you

made this decision after your daughter had nearly drowned, been stabbed, and whacked over the head?'

The group fell into silence—me included. I hadn't realised Edward knew as much as he did, but maybe Lottie or Leo told him.

Not to mention we all knew Jacob's answer. He'd decided *after* I got hurt, not before. Before those things happened to me, I doubted I was even a blip on his radar while he got a tan and lived his life to the fullest somewhere exotic.

'A pity you've arrived and made her life even more complicated,' Henry said. 'If you cared a smidge about your daughter, you'd have stayed away.'

Jacob laughed. 'Sorry, but am I getting parenting advice from the man who didn't know his wife gave birth to two living twins?'

I winced at my dad's words. Yes, he had a point, but it wasn't the time nor the place to point it out.

Orlando, smug as fuck at how things were playing out, ate his food in silence. To him, we were the entertainment. He loved drama, after all. It surprised me he hadn't yet intervened to cause even more of it.

'Did anybody want any more food?' I asked. 'The coleslaw's banging.'

'No, thank you,' Edward said. The others all muttered similar things, and I shrugged. More fool them.

The pasta salad called my name.

And I must follow the call.

Forty-Three

AFTER FATHER'S DAY, I went straight back into prepping and cramming for my exams.

I spent every spare moment thinking about all the required topics, and when I wasn't thinking about school, I thought about *The Sanctum* and the upcoming masquerade ball.

Jacob texted me Father's Day evening to thank me for inviting him and without putting more thought into it, I replied and asked him to meet me at Hawthorn House the next weekend. Winifred and Orlando were leaving the grounds for a meeting with Orlando's lawyer in London, leaving the place empty.

Jacob agreed to come within minutes of me sending the message.

So for the next week, I knuckled down, attended my exams and worked my absolute hardest to write as much as possible on each booklet. Quite hard to do, to be honest, when all I could think about was whether somebody was going to attempt to kill me and my friends at the upcoming charity event.

'So,' Ollie said, taking my hand as we left the hall after our History exam. 'Your dad's coming tomorrow, right?'

'He is. He called me last night to say he'd arrive around midday.'

Ollie frowned and pulled me into an alcove. 'He called?' I nodded. 'Where was I?'

'Shower,' I said. He'd tried to pull me into the shower with him, but I hadn't wanted to. 'He video called me, which was a first.'

'How'd it go?' His fingers rubbed soothing circles on my wrists.

'Weird. I've never had a relationship with a parent like that. Cora rarely remembers to send a text, let alone video call me.'

'But even though it was weird, it was good, yeah?'

'I'd have told you if not.'

'Would you?' Ollie squeezed my hands in a comforting gesture. 'Because you didn't even tell me he called.'

There was a small amount of reproach in his tone, and I batted my eyelashes in hopes of defusing his mood. Ollie could be such a moody bastard, but more and more, he seemed to be calming down.

'You want the truth?' I asked, moving my arms to wrap around the back of his neck. Ollie nodded, and I moved my hands up the nape of his neck into his hair. 'I had every intention of telling you, but then you came out of the bathroom all mighty fine and wet in a towel and I forgot everything but how much I wanted to kiss you.'

'Well, I can't be mad at you,' he said, although he didn't sound like somebody who couldn't be mad.

I raised my right eyebrow in his direction. 'You sound pretty mad.'

'Nope. How can I be mad when my girlfriend's looking at

me like that?' His smile was beautiful. So beautiful I couldn't help but smile back.

'Is it me or is the word mad sounding odd in your head?' I laughed.

Maybe I was the one going mad.

Ollie kissed my forehead with so much affection I swooned. The glint in his eyes spoke a thousand words. 'Where are we meeting your dad again?'

'Hawthorn House,' I replied, like we hadn't spoken of it multiple times since last weekend. 'Leo told me it would be free.'

'Did you want me to come?'

'Do you *want* to come?' I asked back, genuinely wanting his response. I wanted him there, but only if it wouldn't make him too uncomfortable. Or worse, have him start a fight or argument with my dad. 'Because you don't have to if you don't want to. I promise I won't get pissed about it.'

'I promise you, it's fine. It'll be fine.'

He sounded like he was trying to convince himself as much as me. Ollie wouldn't take kindly to me pushing him to admit something he might not be ready to admit yet.

'As long as you mean it.' I scratched my fingers against Ollie's scalp and he let out a moan.

'I do. Now, if you've finished talking about the topic, can we head back to my room?' he asked, a wicked sparkle in his eye. 'There's much more to discuss.'

'Oh there is, is there?'

'Mhm.' He nodded. 'Lots to talk about.'

I moved my face an inch closer to his. 'Yeah?' I murmured, my lips brushing against his.

'Yeah,' he whispered back, his lips touching mine. 'Lots.'

And then we were kissing in the alcove, and I forgot where we were and what we'd been talking about.

'THANK you so much for meeting me here.' Jacob opened the door to Hawthorn House wide, and I stepped inside, Ollie close behind. Jacob turned around and walked towards the sitting room with the gigantic fireplace. 'Leo let me in.'

'Leo's here?' Ollie asked.

It shouldn't have surprised either of us, but apparently it did. He spent a lot of time at the house on the grounds with Orlando and it made sense he was comfortable here from all the summers and holidays spent here as a kid.

'He is,' Dad confirmed. 'Should he not be?'

Jacob's face fell. *Eurgh, damn my heart for sinking alongside it.* He'd appeared so happy to see us—or should I say me—when he opened the door. Yet now his face had fallen like he'd stepped on a bee.

'No, no.' I waved my hand. 'Just a surprise, that's all.'

When we entered the room, Leo was already seated in one of the large leather armchairs arranged in front of the unlit fireplace, a tumbler of whiskey gripped in his right hand.

Something troubled him. I could tell from his facial expression and the slight unruliness of his hair, but I doubted he'd voice it without prodding and poking.

And honestly? I didn't have the strength to try. If he wanted to tell us, he would in his own time, and I had to be okay with it.

'Take a seat, take a seat,' Dad said, ushering us over to Leo. 'Would you like a drink? Whiskey, Oliver?'

Ollie nodded. 'That would be lovely, thank you.'

'Skylar?' Dad asked when I didn't reply. I hadn't responded, too busy taking in the scene, and now my mouth opened and closed like a stupid fish.

'A Diet Coke is fine, thanks.' I took the empty seat in the middle of Ollie and Leo. 'Lots of ice, please.'

'Coming right up!' Dad left the room and the three of us stayed quiet, all glancing at one another when the other wasn't looking. It was pretty comical, to be honest. The three of us were acting like children, but luckily for me, it wasn't awkward.

More like funny.

Jacob returned with my drink and took the last remaining armchair. He placed a tumbler of whiskey for himself on the small circular table in the middle of us. 'Will Griffin be joining us?'

'He's got something on this morning, but he said he'll come by in an hour or two,' I said. 'He can't wait to talk to you more in depth.'

'I'm excited to spend time with him, too. He looks so much like my brother.'

I laughed. 'He looks more like you than I do.'

'I'm sure you wouldn't appreciate me telling you how you've got the majority of your features from Cora?' Dad smiled, raising his glass to his lips.

'You've picked up on things quickly,' I said. 'I've been told my whole life how much I resemble her.'

Ollie reached over and placed his hand on my knee. 'You might, Sky, but that's where the resemblance ends. For starters, you'd never wear your hair in a bouffant.'

Jacob frowned, but the rest of us let out a chuckle.

'Definitely not like the ones she's so fond of,' I said. 'I'm not sure how Mum dressed when you knew her, but recently her tastes have been rather ... eclectic, to say the least.'

Jacob got more comfortable in his chair, a fond smile playing on his lips. 'Any examples?'

'We don't want to scare you,' I said, trying to recall some of her most recent fashion faux pas'. 'But there was a time not too long ago where she wore socks and high-heeled sandals. We were all frightened, yet somehow still in awe of it.'

'Cora brings that out in people.'

We all nodded at Jacob's words. My mum brought out *a lot* in people, usually none of it good. No, often she made people experience despair and hatred.

'It is quite a skill,' I said. 'But enough talk of my mum. There are plenty of better, more exciting things to talk about.'

'I wouldn't say exciting,' Leo said in a dull voice, 'but there are *other* things to be talking about.'

My dad put down his glass and clasped his hands in front of his stomach, resting his full weight on the back of the chair. 'You sound like you have a topic in mind, Leo.'

'There are a few things we think you can shed some light on,' Leo said. 'Things like what happened here when you went to school with our parents.'

'What happened here ...' Jacob trailed off, his brow furrowing. 'A lot happened here if I'm telling the truth.'

'We've got something specific in mind,' Ollie said, joining the conversation. 'A girl died here, in your last year, I believe?'

Dad's head turned Ollie's way. 'Hm?'

'Sandy Parks,' I said. The moment the name hit his ears, my dad slumped in his chair. 'She died in the girl's bathroom.'

'I know the name.' Jacob gave a swift nod of the head. 'What do you want to know?'

'What happened to her?' I sat up straighter in my chair,

eager to learn the answer. 'We found some articles upstairs in a locked chest and one of them was from the Hawthorn Herald after it happened.'

'*Ah*, the Hawthorn Herald.' Dad's eyes widened. 'Blasted newspaper. The students who ran it didn't like us one bit.' He laughed. 'Because of all the rules, I suppose.'

'You mean the rules of *The Set* and *The Sect*?' I'd forgotten my dad had been one. Fuck, if he'd stuck around, I would've been a member of *The Set* without question. I'd like to think I wouldn't be as bitchy as them, but who knew? If I grew up surrounded by life's luxuries the way they all had, maybe I wouldn't be any better.

'I do. I'm sure you know them.' His smirk reminded me of Griff. 'Reckon they haven't changed much in the years since.'

'They're still bullshit, if that's what you mean,' I said.

Me and my dad shared a warm smile. 'That's what I mean, yes.' He sat a little straighter once more, and I hoped it was in preparation to tell us the truth. 'Okay. I'll tell you what happened, but I don't want any interruptions until the tale is told. Do you understand?'

The three of us nodded.

'Sandy Parks was a scholarship student here at Hawthorn and the daughter of the English teacher and, for the most part, kept herself to herself. Most likely in fear of what would happen to her if she didn't.' Jacob paused, choosing his words carefully. 'No matter how hard she tried, though, it didn't stop the wolves. Rich kids can be particularly cruel when they want, especially to those they believe beneath them.'

His eyes softened my way, and I averted my gaze, not wanting to see the pity in his. I knew what he meant. It had happened to me not so long ago, after all.

He continued, 'I'm unsure what Sandy did, or what she

said, but Millie and Eliza took offence one day and then I suppose it sort of became open season.'

I gulped at the image filling my mind.

Poor Sandy Parks. I could relate more than the others in the room to what she went through.

'It started off harmless enough,' Jacob said. I winced at his wording. I doubted any of it was *harmless*. 'Mostly words hurled at her in the halls or statements written on the toilet walls.' *Ah,* as I said, none of that could be classed as harmless. I kept my tongue. Nothing I said now could change the past. 'But things escalated in our last year and there was no escape for Sandy.'

Jacob turned to Ollie. 'Before I tell the rest, I want to make it clear to you. I loved your mother, Oliver. Millie is the love of my life and talking poorly of her isn't something I'm comfortable doing. However, in this story, Millie doesn't come out of it smelling the best. I want to remind you she was a brilliant woman and a splendid mother, regardless of what comes next.'

Ollie and I locked eyes, and I reached out to squeeze his hand in mine, hoping my support acted as a comfort to him. Whatever came next no doubt would make Millie come across as pretty evil—a girl died no matter what happened—and Ollie already struggled with the image he held of his mother.

'I understand,' Ollie murmured. 'Please, go on.'

Jacob took a deep breath, steeling himself. 'One day, Millie took it all too far. Told us all she'd planned a prank for Sandy and we needed to work together so she would flee to the girl's bathroom on the second floor of the English building, the way she did whenever something happened. Whenever any of us asked what the prank entailed, she and Eliza did their twin thing and refused to say anything. They'd just smile and act coy.

'So, the day came, and we did what they asked of us, and Sandy fled to her sanctuary.'

'To where the girls waited for her, you mean?' I spat, unable to stay silent. My blood boiled at the callousness of it all—at the matter-of-fact way my dad told it.

'Yes,' Jacob said, his eyes downcast. The shame radiated from him, but I didn't pity him in the slightest. A girl *died*. 'To where the girls waited for her.'

'Then what happened?' Ollie asked, steering the conversation back on track after my interruption.

'I don't know. I know what Millie and Eliza said afterwards, and what Winnie has alluded to over the years.'

'Which is?' I snapped, bored, waiting for an answer.

'The girls forced her onto a chair and convinced her to put a noose around her neck. They kicked the chair away and left the room for a moment, to scare Sandy not to harm her, but while they were gone, they got distracted and returned too late to save her.'

'How did she get distracted?' Ollie asked, confusion swimming in his face. 'Or should I say, *who* distracted her?'

'Three guesses who,' my dad said darkly.

'Winifred,' Leo said, his tone even darker.

'Precisely.' My dad nodded his head. 'Then she covered it up. She hid the truth and made sure the girls never got penalised for their actions.'

'So they'd forever be in her debt,' I said, understanding Winifred's motivations well enough after all I'd learned during my time at Hawthorn.

'Precisely,' Jacob repeated, his eyes softening my way. 'And as the saying goes, the rest is history.'

Forty-Four

ORLANDO

'THE MASQUERADE BALL is in a week. I hope you've been preparing yourself.'

I was in Mum's office, walking close to the walls, inspecting all the photos and trinkets she'd placed there. Didn't want the bitch to think I was giving her my full attention.

But I was.

Because the Masquerade Ball would be when *The Sanctum* arrived and showed their faces. Faces I was still yet to see even though I'd attended meeting after meeting for literal years.

'Preparing myself for what, exactly?' I asked. My tone was petulant, and I knew it would tick her off something rotten.

Winnie needed knocking down a few pegs if you asked me. Nobody ever asked me, though. They barely glanced at me if they could help it.

'As you are aware,' she said, her tone one of ice. '*The Sanctum* has invited your brother and his friends.'

'I think they plan to kill them.'

'Kill them?' I asked, turning to face her. 'Bit drastic.'

'Need I remind you, *you've* also been trying to kill them?' Her lips pursed together.

'I only tried to kill Sky and Ollie.' A memory swirled into my mind. *That didn't sound right.* 'And Griff and Clover.'

'Exactly,' she bit out. 'You *tried,* but you *failed.* Which is why *The Sanctum* needs to step in and clear up your mess.'

'Well, if *The Set* was still whole and not half murdered, then maybe *The Sanctum* would have had others on its side to do their dirty work.'

'Yes, well, *somebody* couldn't stop themselves from killing those girls, could they?'

I rolled my eyes, wanting to get away from her piercing gaze.

My mum blamed everybody else for their issues. For the things in their life going balls-up. She always had.

In her mind, it was Millie's fault. Or Jacob's fault. Or Skylar's fault.

Even *my* fault.

But never hers.

'Why do they even want to kill them?' I asked, for maybe the umpteenth time this year. 'Seems counter-intuitive.'

'Never you mind,' Mum said. 'You can ...'

She continued talking, but I stopped listening. I usually stopped listening whenever she spent forever talking about something I couldn't give zero shits about. Which basically was everything the woman ever said.

'Are you even listening to me?' Mum snapped. My eyes went back to where she sat behind her large desk. She thought herself so important, but to me, she looked like somebody playing pretend.

'Always.' I smiled. 'Not like you give me any choice, is it?'

'When *The Sanctum* arrives, Orlando, you have to do everything I say. Stay silent and follow orders. Don't show me up like you did at the gala.'

'Will you stop going on about the gala?' I shouted, my anger rising. 'I get it. I'm a big disappointment to you and your little society friends. Bore me later.'

'You're right, you are a disappointment to me. So, get out of my sight,' she replied in a clipped tone, dismissing me. I took one last look at her, hoping for some kind of reaction, but she'd already glanced back down at the papers on her desk.

Bitch.

One day, she'd get what she deserved..

A slow, and painful, demise.

'ORLANDO, WAIT UP!'

I found Little One lurking a little further up the corridor, hiding out in an alcove. Had she been waiting for me to leave Mum's office?

Doubtful.

But hope filled me regardless. I hadn't seen much of her since we spoke in the pool house after I'd sent her that note. Any time I caught a glimpse of her in the halls, or the dining room, I had to fight my instincts to not stare at her the whole time.

Skylar Crescent had a hold on me, and it seemed I couldn't do anything to break said hold.

I sauntered over to where she waited for me and she took me by surprise when she pulled me in closer to her body.

'I heard raised voices. Everything okay?' Sky said, giving me a tight hug.

She stepped back, putting a good amount of space between us, and assessed my face.

'Yeah ...' My scepticism rocketed sky high. Since when did she care about me enough to stop me in the corridor and hug me?

I'd only ever had this kind of reaction from her when she thought I was my brother—and only because she hadn't known at the time it wasn't her boyfriend in front of her.

'It sounded like the two of you were going at it.' She shrugged. Her blue eyes were open wide and honesty swam in them. She reached out to rest her small hand on my bicep.

Alarms started blaring in my brain.

What was she playing at? It may be everything I wanted, but I wouldn't be played as a fool. I wasn't a mug, even when it came to her.

'Who set you up for this?' I snarled, grabbing her hand and pulling it away from me. 'What game do you think you're playing?'

'N-no game,' she stuttered, her face no longer as sure as it had when she called me over. She blinked multiple times in fast succession, and her heart rate increased within the space of a few seconds. 'Am I not allowed to care about you?'

'Not like you have before,' I muttered. I was acting surly, and I knew it, but the roles were usually reversed. Sky usually wanted to know what I was playing at or what my true motivation was.

'I care about you,' she said, daring to replace her hand back on my bicep. 'You may not believe me, but I do. You've done some shitty things and I won't ever forget them, but I've forgiven you for them.'

She shrugged, running her hand through my hair, brushing

it back from my face. A tingle ran through me, like a bolt of lightning, and I jolted back from the electricity of it.

I wanted her.

I craved her.

And I'd been playing the long game.

Because I wanted her to pick me. I didn't want to decide for her, which was something I'd considered more than once.

Taking her captive and keeping her locked away until she had no choice but to love me was an image that played in my mind daily.

Huh. Maybe I needed to tell her my overall goal.

'Little One,' I whispered. 'You know what I want, right?'

'In what sense?' She tilted her head, her gaze so intent on me all I wanted to do was kiss her.

But I didn't kiss her.

No.

I had some control over myself still. Instead, I spoke.

'In life,' I said. 'What I want for my life.'

She squinted up at me, craning her neck to look me in the eye. Even though I couldn't hear her thoughts, I had a good idea of what they were. Sky was pretty predictable, even if she didn't realise it.

'I wish I knew.' She sighed. 'I'd help you no matter what it was, you know?'

'I don't think you'd say that if you knew'—I grinned and watched her gulp—'because what I want, Little One, is *you*.'

'Me?' she sputtered, moving back, but not going far, before bumping into the wall at her back. 'What do you mean?'

'I want you to be my girl. Not Leo's. Not Oliver's. But mine. I want to wake up next to you. Watch you as you fall to sleep. Be there when you have nightmares—'

She cut me off in a sharp tone. 'Nightmares given to me

because of you! Memories from when you stabbed me. Drowned me. Drugged me.' She poked my chest, emphasising in between each sentence. 'The nightmares would never end if I woke up and saw you.'

What she didn't realise was that a feisty Skylar made me want her even more and showed me the spunk underneath her usual calm exterior, and gave me a glimpse of the girl I wanted by my side forever more.

'Are you attending the Masquerade Ball?' she asked, changing tact.

I frowned. 'Do I have a choice?'

'Guess not.' She chuckled. 'Not like any of us do, really.'

We both fell silent. We were in the same position, but for different reasons. Neither of us had a say in what was to come. All we could do was show up and hope we left intact.

Mother made it clear she expected me to be there. Stay silent, and do as she said. Do as *The Sanctum* said. And for years, I'd allowed her to tell me what she needed from me without ever questioning her motives.

'So, the ball ...' she trailed off.

'Guess I'll see you there?' I joked, trying to lighten the dark cloud surrounding us. We both knew we'd see each other there.

'I'll be the one in a mask,' she teased, biting her lower lip. Damn. I wanted her.

'I'll be the one in a tux.' I smiled. Sky laughed. Easy. Carefree.

And it only made me desire her more.

Forty-Five

THE NIGHT before the masquerade ball, the atmosphere between us all was rather sombre as apprehension about the next evening filled us all.

We had a plan, that wasn't much of a plan, but it was better than having nothing.

'Sky,' Ollie whispered and placed a kiss on my temple. 'It's time to get some rest, okay? We can worry more in the morning.'

'I can't help it,' I whispered back, pressing my back harder against his front as he spooned me. 'Every possible scenario and outcome is flashing through my mind and every time it replays, the worse the outcome becomes.'

He placed another tender kiss, this time on my head. 'Sky-lar, I won't let anything bad happen to you. Ever. You have my word.'

'But what if something happens and you can't control it? I doubt *The Sanctum* will ask your permission before trying anything.'

Which was what worried me most, and what kept me awake well past midnight. There was no way of knowing what they had planned. Leo, who had been told so much over the last few years, was being kept in the dark now. Probably because they knew he'd chosen to talk to us and wanted to be careful in case he was no longer as under their thumb as they believed.

'I know it's hard, baby, but we have to have faith things will work out for the best and in the way we want them to.'

I turned around in Ollie's arms and moved an inch back so I could take his face in. 'Who are you and what have you done with my boyfriend?'

He chuckled. The room was dark, but I could faintly make out his face. His long eyelashes as he blinked drew my attention.

'You make me hopeful, Skylar Crescent.' His top lip lifted into a smirk of sorts. *Fuck, he was so beautiful all the time.* No matter how many times I saw him, I never got bored with the view that greeted me. 'And there's something I need to say to you.'

My mind started racing. Of course, I doubted he was about to end things between us or anything equally as drastic, but my mind didn't always function under the umbrella of logic and fact. My anxiety spikes were unnecessary most of the time, but I couldn't exactly control them.

'What?' His eyelashes fluttered from my whispered question.

'Skylar.' Ollie blinked and placed his hands firmly on my hips. 'I love you.'

I blinked back, so many emotions washing over me. Hearing those three words leave his lips—knowing this time they were real and genuine—had tears filling my eyes.

Oliver Brandon loves me.

And fuck, do I love him, too.

'You do?' I whispered.

'I do.'

A tear travelled down my face. 'I love you, too.'

Ollie blinked, his features relaxing the moment I said the words. 'I want to be cool about this and act like you haven't made my day, but I don't think I can.' His hands, still on my hips, pressed in a little harder. 'I am so lucky to have you in my life.'

'You are.' I bit my bottom lip, stifling my giggle. 'I'm glad you're finally realising it.'

He chuckled. 'You think I hadn't before now?'

My heart beat faster. The *thump-thump* of it registered in my ears, while the rest of the room remained deadly silent. I pressed up onto my tiptoes and kissed Ollie's lips, the taste of my tears mixing with the taste of him.

'I've got a question,' I said. At his frown, I added, 'Nothing too bad, I promise.'

His body loosened under my arms. 'Okay. Shoot.'

'Do you remember when you said to me that our first Valentine's Day together was when you doubted your plan because you were falling for me?'

'Yes?'

'Well, when did you know you'd fallen?'

He sighed, blew out a deep breath, and said, 'It's complicated.'

'Talk to me,' I said, my tone gentle but the words a demand. 'I promise nothing will change for us now. I'm all in, O.'

'You are?' he asked, and I could see the doubt fluttering across his face. His voice was low and gritty, and his eyes were taking all of my face in.

'Course I am,' I replied, certain. I knew it would take some time for him to believe me. For him to understand I was all in now, no ifs ands or buts.

Ollie's eyes were bright blue and shining with love. I'd never seen eyes like it before. My heart swooned and if I'd been standing, I would have gone weak at the knees. 'I'm all in, too. In case you didn't already know.'

I beamed at him, teeth all on show, and his face mirrored mine. It had been nearly an entire year since the events of the fashion show and so much had changed since.

'Believe it or not,' he said, 'I am more than happy I arranged for you to get the scholarship here, because it was everything I wanted but never knew I needed.'

Fuck. I had dropped down dead and gone to heaven.

'You're everything I need, too. Which is why I can't stop thinking about tomorrow and worrying about every single possible outcome.'

'You've got little to worry about.'

'I lost my temper with Orlando the other day,' I whispered. 'I thought it'd be a good idea to corner him and lay the seed for the ball, but then he pissed me off and I saw red.'

'What happened?'

'He told me his one wish in life is to have me.' I scoffed. 'And the fact he can't see shit as it is ... well, I couldn't hold my tongue.'

'You think he'll still cut in to dance, though?'

'I'd put money on it.' I shuffled on the bed and raised my leg to drape over his hip. 'If you make eye contact with him, make it clear you're showing me off and rubbing it in. That'll rile him up like nothing else could.'

'Just remember the plan when you spot me acting like you're a trophy, okay?'

I laughed. 'I'll try my best.'

'Make sure you do.' He kissed my head. 'Right, what can I do to make you fall asleep?'

'Well ...' I thought about it for a moment. 'You could tell me a story.'

'Any particular story?'

He sounded a lot more into the idea than I thought he would be. I only said it to make him smile, not for him to actually do it.

'Hmm. How about a story about a rich bastard who fell in love with a poor student?'

'Don't think I could do a story like that justice.'

'I'm sure you could. Now, I'm gonna turn around again and you're going to hug me and tell me a story, okay?'

'Fuck, I love you.'

'Yeah, yeah, you mentioned.'

My words may have sounded cavalier, but when I rolled over, a huge smile covered my face.

Whatever the next day had for us, I was more than ready for it with a man like Oliver Brandon by my side.

Forty-Six

WHAT WAS it about rich people and masquerade balls?

I swear every film or movie I loved included one—or at least a large majority did—and here I was preparing to *attend* one. It felt as if I were playing in somebody else's life. Could never be mine.

Ollie had kept good to his word and arranged for Clover and me to go shopping for dresses to match our masks so we'd fit in amongst such extravagance. My dad had offered too, but it hadn't seemed right to accept. We still hadn't known one another long and for all I knew, once this was all done and over with, he may fuck off to an island somewhere, never to be heard from again.

My mask was one of the most beautiful things I'd ever seen, made of intricate black lace, and it enhanced my features in such an artful way it surprised me whenever I glimpsed myself in the mirror.

Something I'd been doing all evening.

I chose my dress to match the mask. It was black as night and covered in tiny sparkling crystals. Every time it hit the light, it shimmered and filled me with such joy I couldn't help but have a permanent smile on my face. It had a full skirt and the lace-covered bodice matched my mask, tight fitting to the point I couldn't wear a bra underneath. Lucky for me, the lace hugged me in the right places, so nothing untoward was on show.

Didn't want to send Ollie into a heart attack anytime I moved or somebody looked my way.

Clo entered the suite and took my breath away. Every time I saw her in formal wear, I was reminded of how stunning she was. She stole my breath away—in a totally platonic best friend kinda way. 'You look fucking amazing, Skylar.'

'As if! Look at you,' I screeched in reply, taking her in from head to toe, my excitement and trepidation for the night ahead getting the best of me. If I thought Clover scrubbed up well during our other formal events, then her current outfit blew all of those out of the water.

Her skin-tight silver dress had a high slit up to her thigh and her auburn hair was slicked back in a high ponytail and showed off her sharp cheekbones. *Pure perfection.*

Both Leo and Griff would be in heaven.

'Okay, okay,' she placated me. 'We're *both* amazing! The stuffy people at this ball won't know what hit them.'

'Not to mention *The Sanctum.*' I giggled.

Ah, maybe we shouldn't have had five pre-drinks each, but sometimes, a little liquid courage was nice.

I'd never tell Cora that. She'd be way too proud that her daughter was following in her footsteps or some shite.

'Are you ready?' Griff called as he entered the room, doing his best impression of a boxing commentator. Jeez, the boy scrubbed up well with his tux all tailored to perfection. Clover gulped beside me.

The attraction still hovered between them both—they'd

both admitted as much to me—but neither of them would act on it.

That ship had sailed.

'My gosh,' he said when he saw us both. 'You look outstanding. Beautiful. Perfection.'

Griff's enthusiasm on any day was enough to bring you out of the darkest of moods.

'You are delicious, darling.' I smiled with all my teeth on show. 'We'll be the belles of the ball.'

'What about me?' Ollie asked, entering the room and taking me in from head to toe. 'Am I also a belle of the ball?'

'More like the beast,' Clo said, but unlike anything she would've said last year, she said it with a smile. 'A handsome one.'

'Sky,' Ollie whispered. He came to stand in front of me and brushed the back of his hand along my cheek. 'You are the most beautiful girl I've ever seen. This lace dress should be illegal. I don't know if I'll be able to stop myself from punching everybody who gazes at you too long.'

'Oh, hush.' I laughed. 'Punching people is beneath you.'

'Tell that to Leo!' Griff chimed in and I darted an evil glare his way. We didn't bring up the time Ollie gave Leo a black eye. It was a thing of the past, never to be repeated.

'Maybe if *The Sanctum* show their faces I will,' Ollie mused, as if Griff hadn't spoken. The air in the room soured. Whatever spell we'd existed under for the past few hours had broken. None of us had thought about them all evening, and now, all I could think about was the night ahead and what might happen. Ollie, oblivious to the shattered atmosphere, continued, 'Let's hope it doesn't come to that.'

'Is Leo meeting us there?' I asked. Last I heard, he'd arrive with Orlando. It bothered me, the two of them hanging around together still. Yeah, we all decided it was for the best, so nothing seemed out of the ordinary, but it didn't mean I liked it.

'Yep,' Clo replied and glanced at her phone. 'We should make a move.'

I nodded, and went to follow Clo and Griff, but Ollie pulled me back towards him before I could get closer to the door.

'Wait up,' he whispered. His eyes flitted to the necklace around my neck. It was the one he'd got me for Christmas shaped like the north star, and I loved it. Every time I saw it, I was stunned all over again. It went perfectly with my dress, too. He touched the star. '*This* is going to draw attention.'

'I think this *dress* is going to draw attention.' I chuckled. It felt daring to be wearing something so sophisticated yet sexual. I finally felt my age, in a way.

We were all adults now; time to act like it.

'You're mine,' he drawled. 'That's what matters most.'

Ollie leaned in and kissed my cheek, then his eyes went to my bright red lips.

'That colour on you makes me want to bite them clean off your face,' he said darkly. 'But I won't.'

'I'm glad you can refrain,' I joked. 'Do you think our invitations came from *The Sanctum*?'

'No idea.' He kissed my temple, stepped back, and reached out his hand for mine. 'I'm sure we're about to find out.'

'Let's do this shit.'

HENRY, Edward, and Jacob were standing together in front of the silent auction table, acting their usual intimidating selves.

No part of me expected to see those three in one another's company voluntarily, but there they were.

'Hey, Dad,' I greeted him when we came closer. 'Hello, Henry. Edward.'

The three of them looked over at us, and my dad's eyes filled with tears.

'Skylar.' He brushed his eyes, flicking the moisture away. 'You are … beautiful.'

'Th-thank you,' I whispered. My emotions were all over the place. The man had been gone for the last eighteen years of my life, but he was trying now and I couldn't hold it against him. 'You look great.'

He coughed, and the group fell silent. *Wonderful.* Our awkward display of familial affection had caused everybody to freeze up.

I giggled. These stuffy rich men wouldn't know familial affection if it bit them on the arse.

'Dad.' Ollie nodded. 'Uncle Edward. Jacob.'

It was weird and unusual to see everybody in elaborate masks. Very high fantasy, and very misleading. After watching plenty of films where the mysterious girl was unknown to all because of a mask, I wondered how nobody had known her identity—it always seemed pretty obvious to me sitting at home watching—but now I was living it, I understood a bit more. I barely recognised anybody.

What a mind fuck.

'So,' Griff said, cutting through the tension. 'We all ready for some food, booze, and silent auctioning?'

His infectious smile had me beaming right alongside him. No matter what, the boy made me happy.

'Can't wait,' Clo said, sounding miserable. She'd never

been one for parties, and a school sanctioned party was the worst of the worst in her eyes.

'Oh, come off it, Lady Luck. We'll have a splendid time.' Griff grabbed Clo's hand and pulled her in to twist her out again into a spin. Lighthearted and free. 'Okay?'

'Okay,' she replied, still rather begrudgingly, but with a smile of sorts. 'If you say so.'

Edward, Henry, and Jacob stayed silent on the fringe of our small group. They were serious, and their facial expressions told me they were watching out for something. What? Or rather, who?

'Why are you all so on edge?' Ollie asked. Lately, he seemed able to read my mind, and it freaked me out. Maybe it was because we spent so much time together.

'Son,' Henry said, not answering Ollie's question. His eyebrows dipped, and he searched for his next words. 'Was the invitation you guys received for tonight ... unusual in any way?'

'Are you asking if *The Sanctum* sent our invitation too?' Griff asked, no longer joking around with Clover, putting his rarely used serious face on.

'So you got them, too.' Edward nodded. 'As we expected.'

'They invited you, too?' I asked, pinning my gaze to my father. When he'd told me he was coming tonight, I thought little more about it. And when I had, I'd thought maybe he was coming to make an effort now he'd come back into my life. 'Makes sense. I suppose that they'd want all of us here together.'

Well, it looked like we were none the wiser about any of it.

What they wanted. *Why* they wanted us.

None of it.

Leo and Orlando entered the ball and in a moment of déjà vu, everybody in the hall stopped talking and turned to face them to watch as they made their grand appearance. I scoffed at the pageantry of it all.

As if these parents were still happy to let a murderer amongst their midst and their children. It sickened me how money had warped all the people in this room so much they were happy to cover up the murders of innocent—albeit bitchy—teenagers.

'Surprised he showed his face,' Henry mumbled.

'I'm not,' Edward replied, talking out of the side of his mouth. I stepped a little closer. 'Not if he invited us here.'

'You don't think?' Henry rubbed his jaw. Any time Henry made a gesture so similar to one of Ollie's, my stomach flip-flopped, the oddness of it surprising me.

'Maybe. My son has told me a little about what he's been doing these past few years, and I believe there's something not right here about *The Sanctum*. We know they exist, but surely not to keep the identity of a secret heir hidden. When we were members, I never got the impression they'd give a shit about something like that.'

'That was a long time ago,' Henry said. 'We've got no clue what they do now.'

My dad joined in. 'Except for trying to kill teenagers.'

Forty-Seven

THE DINNER TOOK PLACE, and there were no issues. The food was fancy, and I hated it all.

Orlando had been placed on our table and it was as awkward as you'd imagine it to be. Conversation was stilted, but mostly, people were too busy eating to get into it, which I was super thankful for. Food had so many purposes in this life and I appreciated every one of them.

'We can get a pizza delivered when this bullshit is over,' Ollie whispered in my ear during the main course, and I nodded enthusiastically.

He knew how to talk dirty to me.

Once the dessert plates got cleared away, Ms Hawthorn made her way to the centre of the stage, and her appearance made me pause.

She wore an ill-fitting grey dress; the material bunched up around her hips like a dress you'd see in an Edwardian book, and a grey mask which showed the depth of her grey eyes and grey hair she'd pulled back into the most severe bun I'd ever seen her sport. Miss Havisham come to life in front of our eyes.

'The silent auction tables are available along the back wall,' she said, pointing in their direction. 'There are many prizes to be won, and all the money raised is for charity, so don't be shy.'

Some parents cheered, while others politely clapped. Our table had pretty sombre occupants, and we did neither. All of us were either watching Ms Hawthorn with narrowed eyes, or were darting our gaze around the room to seek those who may wish to harm us.

I'd been certain something would have happened already.

Plus, members of *The Sanctum* wouldn't wear their cloaks to a soiree like this. Nope. They'd blend in.

Damn, even the most unsuspecting person could belong to the secret society that had plagued us for the last two years, and we'd be none the wiser.

'Would you like to dance?' Ollie whispered, his tongue darting out and touching my ear, causing goosebumps to trail down my arms. Everything about him—every action, every glimpse, every touch—made me fall even further in love with him. My heart was fit to burst thinking of it; of him.

'I'd love to,' I replied, hoping my smile came off flirtatious, and not like an illness. This casual flirting malarkey had got easier, sure, but it still didn't come naturally to me. It was like I was playing pretend, and not doing an excellent job of it.

'If he sees us dancing,' Ollie whispered. 'It won't be long until he asks to cut in. Bastard won't be able to stop himself.'

I turned my focus to the silent auction tables and nodded absentmindedly. It wasn't much of a plan, but it was something. It also made my stomach flutter funny when Ollie asked me to dance, knowing he asked not because he wanted to but because he wanted to rile up his twin.

'We're off to dance,' I announced to the table. Orlando's devilish stare landed on me, and I tried to keep my face neutral. I turned my attention to Clover. 'You coming?'

'You know it,' Clover said. She stood and pulled Griff with her. He gave a half-grimace, which I supposed could be classed as a smile in some circles. 'Can't let you two steal all the attention.'

We laughed good-naturedly and left the table, while Orlando's stare burned a hole in my back. It was well known now how he wanted to be in his brother's position. Wanted to be the one holding me close, flush up against his chest.

'You reckon this'll work?' I asked, as quiet as I could to be heard over the music. Ollie's azure blue eyes stared back at me, so much love and affection swimming in them, I nearly burst into tears at the emotion he was showing me. So much had changed since we met and sometimes it took me by surprise. 'Because now we're here, it all seems rather flimsy.'

I wanted *this* to be over. And by this I meant all of it. *The Sanctum*, Orlando's bullshit, being at Hawthorn, having to worry about whether somebody was going to make an attempt on my life anytime I left my dorm, to name a few things.

Oh, and I wanted to be happy. Healthy.

And I wanted both of those things to take place far, far away from Hawthorn.

The band played a slow song from their position on the stage, and the two of us waltzed in time to the music. Ollie was such an elegant dancer. It seemed I never had enough time to appreciate his skill before something or *someone* interrupted us.

Within moments, a small cough came from behind. Like clockwork, set to happen.

'Can I cut in?' Orlando asked, falling right into the trap laid out for him.

'No,' Ollie replied.

'No?' Orlando laughed, a deep chuckle making my insides twist. 'And why is that?'

'Do you need me to lay it out for you?' Ollie mocked. 'I rule this school. I rule over *you.*'

The plan was simple. Create a scene and draw all eyes in our direction. Which, knowing Orlando's reaction to all things me, shouldn't be too difficult.

The anger on his face already told me he was putty in our hands, ready to be moulded whichever way we chose.

'*You?*' Orlando scoffed. 'You rule over nothing. You're delusional.'

'I'm the delusional one?' Ollie laughed. Loud. Barking. Attention-stealing. 'You seem to believe Skylar wants to be with a nobody like you. Heck, even your own mother didn't want you. Told everybody you'd died. How does that feel? To be so unloved and rotten, even your mother wanted you gone before you could ruin more lives.'

'You think you're so special, don't you?' Orlando spat. 'There was a fifty-fifty chance of what twin she gave away. I'm sure if she had based it on personality, things would be different around here.'

'Are you questioning my mother's judgement?' Ollie's eyes narrowed on his twin. It always seemed odd to watch the two of them so close together. A mirror image without the mirror.

'*Our* mother,' Orlando corrected. 'And yes, yes I am.'

I rolled my eyes at the pissing contest the two of them had entered. Even at a time like this, they couldn't help themselves. A compulsion of sorts. *Idiots.*

'No. *Your mother* is standing somewhere in this hall.' Ollie made a show of standing taller and searching over the heads of the crowd, seeking Ms Hawthorn. 'No doubt embarrassed by you and the spectacle you're once again making of yourself.'

Orlando stood frozen at Ollie's callous words, flung at him when he least expected it. His face rearranged into something ugly. A sneer on his perfect lips, cold enough to turn my stomach.

He pulled a gun from his waistband and the crowd formed around us gasped. One woman screamed in terror so loud my hands went to my ears involuntarily.

For fuck's sake.

It was like the New Year's Gala all over again. Same position. Same people. Same stupid bullshit.

Yes, there had always been a possibility things would turn violent, but it would've helped us all if Leo had told us Orlando still had access to a *fucking gun*!

It would be nice to work with all the information for once. Was that too much to ask?

I didn't know where to look, or where to turn, but I knew I needed to keep my calm. It would be stupid to ruin things now, not with *The Sanctum* so close to being revealed. Or maybe they'd remain in the shadows and watch it all play out, and decide what to do later down the line when things were clearer. Orlando may not be important to anybody besides Winifred.

Ollie and I stayed where we were. United, hands grasped together, staring Orlando down. Yes, I was terrified—I assume most people would be if they had a gun pointed their way— but something told me I wasn't the one in danger. No, my terror was for Ollie and what could happen to him if Orlando lost his temper and decided killing his brother was worth the inevitable prison time.

Orlando had nothing to lose, after all. He was already out on bail, and it was a matter of time until they arrested him for

Ophelia's murder. Which made a guy pretty reckless in my books.'

'Do you think that's a good idea?' Ollie asked, his voice a low growl. Nobody liked being threatened, especially in the middle of a masquerade ball.

'I do.' Orlando threw his arms back, an over-the-top gesture showing off to the growing audience. People screamed as the gun in his right hand swung when he moved, sweeping across the crowd. 'Everybody in this room needs to be taught a lesson. For years, they've been allowed to get away with their heinous crimes and nobody has called them out, so it's time somebody does.'

The way Orlando acted so casually while wielding a weapon in his hand scared me more than anything coming out of his mouth. His face told me he wanted nothing more than to shoot Ollie dead. If he was gone, and out of his way, Orlando probably thought he'd have a better shot at taking his brother's place.

A better shot of winning *me*.

But one thing he'd never realised was that I was not some prize to be won. I never had been, and I never would be, no matter what tactics he employed, nor how desperate his actions became.

'You're wrong,' Ollie said. 'The only people in this room who need to be taught a lesson are you and those who go by the name of *The Sanctum*.'

'And what do you know of *The Sanctum*?' Orlando barked. 'You know nothing, Oliver.'

'Maybe.' Ollie gave a casual shrug. 'But there is one thing I do know.'

'And what's that?' Orlando couldn't help but ask and fall

into the carefully laid trap of a question. 'Because from the time I've watched you, I've realised you know little.'

Ollie's eyes scrunched at the corners, amusement dancing on his features. 'I know you have no position of power. Not here and not within *The Sanctum* either. You're a lackey for those higher up than you.'

Where the bloody hell were Griff and Leo?

I braved glimpsing away from Ollie and Orlando for a second to search the room, eager to find my friends amongst the masked faces crowding the dance floor. Griff and Clover were behind us, watching it all unfold, ready to back us up with a moment's notice.

Leo stood by our parents on the edge of the dance floor. I caught his eye on my perusal and he tilted his head and gave a little shake. *Not yet, Skylar. Let it unfold.*

I turned away. Ollie and Orlando were still facing off, not having moved a muscle in the brief time I stopped paying them any attention.

If one of them wasn't holding a gun out to the other, I would laugh. The two of them had similar stances. Similar faces. Similar *everything*.

Even after knowing of Orlando's existence for a while, it still unnerved me how easy it was to mistake one for the other —the police had managed it enough times.

'A lackey?' Orlando laughed, matching his brother's deep bark. 'There are many names I'd expect you to call me, but a lackey isn't one of them.'

'Now I know for a fact you are delusional,' Ollie growled, staring his brother down, not letting the weapon faze him in the slightest. 'If you're not a lackey, then have them reveal themselves right now. Demand they show their faces and come into the light.'

Orlando's face soured, but whether it was at the demand or the realisation he had less power than he'd like to portray, I couldn't be sure.

'You do not give demands around here, boy.' Ms Hawthorn's voice gave me a chill. She always came across as stern and grey, but now, as she removed her grey mask and walked into the centre of the dance floor, I saw cruelty.

I saw a woman who wanted chaos.

Everybody around the circle removed their masks, too, as if the spell of the evening had lifted in her one move. The band had stopped playing when they realised nobody was dancing or paying them any attention.

Nobody in the hall talked. They were all patiently waiting.

'No, you're correct,' Ollie said icily. 'That would be *The Sanctum*, wouldn't it?'

'Oh, Oliver dear. You think you're all so clever.' Winifred smiled. 'But *The Sanctum* won't be showing their faces here tonight.'

Her smile grew wider. Thin lips pushed up and teeth on show.

The cat who got the cream, the canary, and the curious.

What kind of bullshit bomb was she about to drop?

Forty-Eight

'*THE SANCTUM* NO LONGER EXISTS. Or at least not in the way you think.'

'What do you mean, it no longer exists?' Ollie spat. 'We *know* the members are here.'

'One day last week, all the older members were sitting around a dinner table, talking and having a laugh. Then the next, they slumped in their seats.' Winifred shrugged. 'Seems they all drank poison.'

When I looked around to see how the others here were taking the news, I spotted Leo. I hadn't seen him slip back into the crowd. Even he appeared stumped at the announcement.

Griff slumped beside me. 'Now we'll never know whether they wanted to kill me.'

'Oh, you foolish boy.' Ms Hawthorn turned her piercing gaze to Griff. '*The Sanctum* didn't want to kill you.' She laughed again, setting my teeth on edge. 'I did.'

'You did?' Griff answered.

She cackled, evil personified. 'All three of you were meant to die in the crash. I convinced the other members we needed to eradicate the whole Cooper line.'

'You sound like you're in charge,' I said, finding my voice

for the first time since Ms Hawthorn entered and became the centre of attention. Hoping my words would stroke her ego to the point she'd answer me honestly without too much thought. 'So why would you kill them all?'

'My whole life, I've had to listen to others. Follow instructions. Sit there, be silent, and do as I'm told.' She locked eyes on each person before moving on to the next. This was personal for her. 'Well, not anymore. I decided enough was enough. I wanted what was mine. What should have always been mine!'

'And what is that?' Ollie said.

'The Hawthorn legacy,' she shouted, her voice cracking. 'The school, the money, all of it! It should have been mine. I'm the eldest and tradition always dictated that the eldest got it, regardless of gender, after an addition a hundred years ago, but no! My stupid parents didn't trust me. Thought I'd squander the lot and fuck it up for everybody. So they gave it to *Edward* instead.'

I squeezed Ollie's hand in mine, my anchor in the tough times, and from the hatred exuding from Winifred's face, we were about to hit some rough sea.

'Then my younger sisters were born, and things got worse. Everybody loved Millie and Eliza. Adored from birth they were.' She took on a mocking tone. '"*Oh, look how beautiful they are. The twins will have everybody fighting over them.*" People wouldn't stop going on about how loved they were. Including our parents.' Her venom surprised even me.

'What did you do?' Edward roared.

'I don't know what you mean,' Winnie said, playing coy. What a bitch. 'If you're asking about whether I killed our dear mother and father, then you would be correct.'

Ollie bristled next to me, the fate of his grandparents

settling over us all. Damn, Winifred was even more cold-hearted than I thought.

'God, woman, why?' Edward's face melted into one of complete horror. His bloodshot eyes filled with tears. Learning of your parents' fate this way, in front of such a large crowd, was cruel and calculated. Something Winnie took pleasure in.

'An inheritance doesn't exist if people are alive. I needed the Hawthorn money passed down to the next generation, even if it meant I saw a small fraction of it.' She smiled wider.

'Did it make you happy?' Leo said, watching her with narrowed eyes.

'For a time,' she said, gesturing around the vast hall, 'but like everything else, it goes away.'

'I still have my part of the money,' Edward replied, 'so you must have been doing something wrong, Winifred.'

She cackled with derision. 'I *did* do something wrong. I helped you brats cover everything up!'

'What we did?' Henry looked at Ollie, then Orlando—who hadn't spoken since his mother had taken over the floor, but still held a gun to Ollie's head—and then to Edward. Winnie must be referring to what happened with Millie and Eliza back when they were members of *The Set*. The prank gone wrong; the one she helped covered up as a suicide. 'That was years ago.'

'And I've never forgotten it!' she screamed, spit flying from her mouth. She turned to my dad. 'How do you think Jacob Cooper "stole" Hawthorn money? Because I let him! I shoved it into his greedy grasp and told him to never return, no matter what happened. I wanted Millie's life ruined worse than the way she ruined that poor girl's.'

Jacob stepped forward, having hidden behind the others during the rest of Winnie's speech. His face told me all I needed to know. This was the truth of what happened, and of why he left. Winifred paid him off to leave Millie.

He'd already left me long before.

'And now he's back, ready to ruin everything I've achieved.' Winifred's grey eyes glared at my dad, her hatred for him evident to all.

'I've returned because of your actions,' my dad said. His eyes were sorrow-filled, and I knew he had remorse for his part in everything. For leaving me. For leaving the love of his life alone in a cold world. 'I also left for the same reason I've returned. You told me if I didn't leave, you'd kill my daughter. Now I know you've been trying to kill her the last two years, anyway.'

Winifred shrugged, little care given. 'You'd left her with her shit-for-brains mother ten years before you took me up on my offer.'

The dig towards Cora hit me in a place I never expected— my heart. Yes, I could think poorly of my mother, but having it come from this evil witch was *not* okay.

Winifred also had a valid point. Jacob disappeared from my life within a couple of months of me being born, yet he'd stuck around Beurre for a bit if he had time to have an affair with Millie.

'And you, of all people, know why,' Jacob growled. He moved into the centre of the circle and swept his gaze on everybody watching. 'This woman,' he spat, 'has been threatening our children's lives since they were born. I left Skylar at Cora's, because Winifred Hawthorn told me she'd kill her if she ever stepped foot on Hawthorn ground.'

I gasped alongside every other person in the room watching this shit show unfold. All of this was news to me. Ms

Hawthorn had never hidden the fact she hated me, but no part of me ever believed she wanted to *kill* me.

Ollie tightened his grip on my hand, keeping us rooted to the spot, which was as much for his benefit as it was for mine.

Jacob continued talking. 'She threatened Edward, Millie, and Eliza, too. If we ever told the truth of what happened when we were at school, she'd kill our children.'

'But why?' I whispered, confused. It was so extreme. So drastic. Why on earth would this woman want us all dead? Even for her, it seemed *a lot*.

'Why, Miss Crescent?' she asked, her beady eyes locked on mine. 'They killed an innocent girl, and came running to me to help them. Snivelling little brats wanted me to make it all go away. Millie even went as far as blaming me for distracting her.'

Edward, Henry, and Jacob all looked geared up to rush her, but then, as one, they remembered themselves and held back.

God, I'd love to wipe the smile off of Winifred's face.

I *hated* her smarmy smile. The way she took joy in revealing the secrets and lies she'd been complicit in. It made me sick.

No wonder Orlando was so fucked up.

This woman had been his role model. The person to show him the way of the world and teach him about other people's emotions and needs.

For the first time in a while, I understood the full extent of Orlando's childhood and upbringing. Of how twisted his mind was inside—and who had made it so.

It was all making sense why he thought murder to get what you wanted was okay.

'Did you shoot Griff at the gala?' Edward asked, his hands clenched into fists at his sides.

'Yes, yes,' she said, amused. 'It was all me.' Her smile split her entire face in two.

I'd never seen the woman before me. Not the way she acted at that moment, anyway. I'd always found her uncomfortable, and from the first time she laid eyes on me, I knew she didn't like me, but I didn't realise how deep it ran.

She despised me.

She despised all of us.

'Why did *The Sanctum* kill Olivia?' Orlando asked, lowering the gun in his hand an inch.

Winifred narrowed her evil eyes on her son, disappointment oozing from every pore.

Orlando had told me he didn't kill her, but I hadn't believed him. I'd given him a hard time about it, actually. Been a bit of a bitch. Yet he'd told the truth the whole time.

My heart dropped.

'We needed to frame Skylar, and you handed me the perfect opportunity when you took *that girl* back after the gala, pretending to be your brother.'

'Why did you *need* to frame me? It didn't even work. You hushed up the murders with the police. Paid them off. Why do that if you wanted to frame me?'

'Because she wanted it to get back to me,' Jacob said, shaking his head. 'Wanted to torment me and have me believe all the steps I'd taken to keep you away from this life had been fruitless. If I knew you were in danger, or needed help, then she knew I'd come.'

A gunshot rang out throughout the hall, shocking everybody. My head frantically snapped around, my heart beating out of my chest, searching for the sound. The last time I heard gunshots, Griff and Clover got hurt.

Henry lowered a gun down. He'd fired the warning shot into the high ceiling to get everyone's attention.

'This is beyond ridiculous, Winifred. You've stood before us all and admitted you killed Eliza and Damien. Killed the poor girl, Olivia. Attempted to frame my son and his girlfriend. Corrupted my other son—one you never even told me existed.' He took a deep breath and paused, collecting his thoughts. 'I'm sorry, but you can't leave this room. I forbid it.'

Winifred scoffed. 'You forbid it? Oh, please, Henry. Are you going to stop me?'

If I didn't want the woman gone, I'd be a little impressed. She was being held at gunpoint, yet still acted like it was a normal day—a normal conversation.

A small part of me admired that.

'We're all going to stop you,' Ollie said, moving to join his father, not caring Orlando had a gun trained on him the whole time. I'd never seen Henry and Ollie so united; so in sync. They both widened their stances, a metre gap between them, and stared down Ms Hawthorn. 'Nobody in this room is going to let you leave.'

'You won't get away with this,' Henry spat.

Hysteria settled into her features. 'My whole life I've been overlooked. There was always somebody prettier. Somebody wealthier. Somebody with more brains, or more brawn. Well now, I will win. It's my time to shine.'

It was pitiful.

My feet unstuck from the floor, and I went to move over to where Ollie stood with Henry when Leo grabbed my arms from behind, taking me by surprise.

'Don't, Stutter,' he whispered in my ear harshly. 'He's a big boy. He can look after himself.'

'He wants her dead,' I whispered back. 'We can't sit here and watch this.'

'She wants *you* dead,' he reminded me. 'And has tried to kill you multiple times.'

He was right. She had, and during the course of the evening, had shown no remorse for it. No, if anything, she seemed pretty proud of it all.

I locked my feet to the floor once more, turning my attention back to the stand-off happening in the middle of the room. Everybody forgot the charity effort now. All eyes were on the unfolding drama. Masks off—literally and figuratively.

'You won't kill me,' Winifred cackled. 'You haven't got it in you, Henry dear.'

Henry's face changed in a split second and his intention became clear, the gun gripped firmly in his palm, pointed at his sister-in-law. He pulled the trigger, and after a flash, the bullet found its place in Winifred's chest.

She fell, crumpling to the floor, shock covering her face.

Of all the things she expected, it was never that.

'Mum!' Orlando roared, falling to the floor to put his hands over the blood gushing from the wound. Red stained and covered his hands. The gun clattered to the floor, forgotten.

The guttural sound from deep in his throat rang out and reverberated around the hall, the high ceilings causing it to echo.

The pure emotion gutted me. I wished things were different, and I could rush over to him and pull him close. Hug him tight, until no breath remained in his body.

The room's occupants waited with bated breath to find out whether Winifred had breathed her last.

Orlando let out one last wail. He pushed himself to standing, his angry gaze locked on Ollie like a bull at a red flag.

'You,' he seethed in a low and deadly tone. 'You did this.'

Ollie said nothing. Must be weird to watch an unhinged version of yourself staggering towards you. Leo still had a firm grip on my arm. His fingers no doubt would leave bruises, and I couldn't do anything to stop whatever Orlando had in mind.

I felt lost. Like a weak girl bullshitting herself. One who said she couldn't do anything but could if she applied herself.

I didn't know *what*.

'You will pay!' Orlando's gaze searched the floor. He found the gun and scrambled for it before anybody else could. Once again, he raised it and aimed at Ollie.

My heart stopped beating. The blood in my veins turned to ice.

'No!'

I screamed, my heart threatening to leave my throat. The sickness and nausea swirled around with the dinner and alcohol I'd consumed, dragging me under.

Then everything happened as if in fast forward. Not slow motion, the way things told us life-changing events were.

Orlando pulled the trigger.

Henry leapt in front of Ollie.

Pushed him out of the way.

Took the bullet with Ollie's name on it straight in the heart. The ultimate sacrifice.

My jaw dropped to the floor. My heart was beating erratically, and my vision struggled, those black spots clouding the edges once more. I fought them off. I couldn't pass out now. Not when Ollie was still in Orlando's path of wrath.

'The knife,' Leo whispered in my ear. 'Ollie's unprotected. Go!'

I stumbled forward, tripping on the skirt of my ball gown, as my dad and Edward went to Henry's aid.

How had this night descended into chaos so fast?

We'd known it was going to explode, but we'd been so sure we'd come out on top, victorious.

In a nervous gesture, I brushed the skirt of my dress, checking the knife was still in its place at my thigh. *It was.* Sighing in relief, I scrutinised Orlando, my heart breaking at the sight of him.

Like Oliver, he looked destroyed. The mother he'd been given through some luck of the draw was lying dead at his feet, her blood covering his shoes, his shirt, and his hands.

I was in between Ollie and Orlando, but it was the latter I turned to face.

'Little One,' he croaked out, his voice breaking as much as my heart. 'Don't do this.'

My eyes filled with tears, the gut wrenching emotions hurting me more than anything else ever had.

My hands shook as I removed the knife from the hidden holster on my body and I gripped it tightly in front of me.

'I have to,' I whispered. 'You've left me no choice.'

'Sky,' Ollie said from behind me, taking a step closer, his shoes clicking on the floor. 'Are you sure?'

A tear left my eye and trailed down my cheek. I turned my eyes to Clover. Then Griff. And, finally, Ollie.

'He'll n-never stop,' I stuttered. 'He wants your life. He wants *me*. He always has.'

'Little One,' he whispered, reaching out and grabbing my wrist to pull me closer. 'Do it. It's only fair,' he whispered in my ear. 'It was all me, Skylar. I stabbed you and drowned you and drugged you. I love you.'

I whimpered and pushed the words from my heart past my lips. 'I love you.'

Then I reared my hand back and lunged, the hot sticky blood coating my hand in seconds.

Orlando grunted as I held him up, allowing the blood to cover my dress. I glanced down, the blood on my clothes and my hands settling like a second layer of skin.

Out, damned spot. Out, I say.

It was as if the world had reduced to nothing. No words entered my head. No sounds. Orlando and me, alone. The sins of the past washed away.

My heart pounded in my chest, threatening to leave it.

Numb. Lost. *Whole.*

'Skylar!' Ollie's voice sounded as if it was coming from behind a door. Or a wall. One I couldn't penetrate. 'Skylar!'

His face appeared in front of mine. I watched his mouth move, but the words were still foggy.

'We've got to go!' He shouted in my ear. 'Fire!'

Then it registered. The smell of smoke. The distinct smell of something burning, and then the heat of the air. The physical smoke in the air.

The smoke in my lungs. The black bleeding into my vision.

Then …

Nothing.

FIRE AT HAWTHORN ACADEMY

**A fire broke out at Hawthorn Academy late on
Saturday evening.**

*The firefighters who went to the scene believe the fire started
in the school's old hospital wing and spread from there. By
the time the fire force arrived, both the hospital wing and
the pool house were unable to be saved.*
The administration building also suffered some damage.
There were four fatalities and a number more casualties.
*Headteacher, Ms Winifred Hawthorn, lost her life, as did
her son, Orlando Hawthorn.*
His body is yet to be recovered.
*Henry Brandon, father of Orlando and brother-in-law of
Winifred, tragically lost his life in the same evening.*
Their deaths aren't being treated as suspicious.

Epilogue

GRADUATION. A day I never thought I'd see.

Yet here it was and I couldn't be fucking happier.

'You really are so very beautiful, Skylar,' Ollie said, placing a deep kiss on my lips.

'Thank you.' The blush at his words rose on my cheeks. Ollie's praise had always been something I craved, but now, after everything we'd been through, it mattered even more.

My dress, a knee-length 1950s style find with a full skirt and Bardot shoulders, made me feel a million pounds. The moment I saw it at a vintage store in London, I had to have it.

'Shame it'll be covered by a stupid gown for most of the day,' I said, my hands travelling down the bodice, touching the fabric with reverence. 'You scrub up well, too.'

'In this old thing?' he joked, holding the lapels of his suit jacket and straightening them out.

Damn. He looked hot. *Really fucking hot.* Good enough to eat kind of hot, and I wanted to climb him then and there, but I knew my mum waited downstairs for us with my dad, of all people.

Stranger things have happened.

If you told me when I started at Hawthorn that I would

finish my scholarship with two parents who cared about me, then I would have told you to stop smoking drugs or whatever you were doing, causing you to hallucinate and alter reality.

The question that had run through my mind all morning left my lips unbidden. 'It's odd, isn't it? That we're here?'

Ollie paused in his fidgeting, and his eyebrows raised, scrunching up his forehead. 'Here as in Hawthorn? Or here as in graduation?'

'Both?' My voice went up at the end so it came out sounding more like a question.

Ollie stepped towards me and placed his hands on my shoulders to ground me. It was something he'd started doing often, and I loved it. I think it grounded him as much as it did me. Something we both needed.

He placed a kiss on my head, before resting his defined jaw there, pressing into my skull slightly.

'Hm,' he mused, taking his time to answer. 'Guess it is a little odd, but I knew we'd get here.' His tone was so confident, I moved my head from underneath his chin and looked up into his eyes in question.

'You did?'

'Sure did. Things were a little hairy at the start of the year, I'll admit. At the start of your scholarship, I *definitely* didn't see us getting here, but even then, in my gut, I guess I always knew we'd be here in the end.'

I hummed, not believing him. 'Well, I didn't.'

'Not that hard, babe. You struggle to see something even when it's right in front of you.' He smiled, hinting at his teasing, and his eyes sparkled at me.

'Hey!' I nudged him with my sharp elbow. 'You didn't know about *him* either.'

Ever since the events of last month, neither of us had

mentioned Orlando's name. I couldn't decide if it was a denial, or whether it was a way for us to move on, but either way, he barely came up in our conversation. It was easier to talk about anything else. To move on without the shadow of him lingering over us for all eternity.

'I'd never seen him,' Ollie said, the answer an obvious one in his eyes.

'Oh, yeah, yeah.' I nudged him again, but straight after I wrapped my arms around his waist, so they joined at his back. 'Well, I'm sorry I didn't know you had an evil twin lurking about.'

'You're more than forgiven.' He leaned down and kissed my lips. A kiss holding the promise of *more*.

'Thank fuck.' I bit my lip, once again my dirty mind going back to all the things we could get up to if we didn't have to attend our graduation ... 'Come on, my rents are waiting downstairs.'

I unfurled my arms from around him and placed his hand in mine to drag him along behind me. The longer we spent upstairs, the longer we were putting off the inevitable, and I didn't want to put off graduation any longer. I *wanted* to graduate from Hawthorn Academy and get the fuck out of dodge. It was always my plan and to see it come to fruition? Well, victory was sweet indeed.

Graduating alongside Ollie, Griff, and Clover was nothing short of a miracle in my eyes. Multiple events and circumstances over the last two years had made me believe we'd never get to, and now we were able to, I wanted it to be done and over with.

Ollie ushered his hand out towards the door. 'Lead the way, baby.'

He didn't need to tell me twice.

The two of us left Ollie's suite and made our way to the front lawn of the school where the chairs and stage were set up. The weather was lovely, thank fuck, otherwise this wouldn't be much fun. A soggy outdoor graduation? No thanks.

The fire at the Masquerade Ball started in the hospital wing and burnt the building and the pool house down to the ground before the fire could be stopped. It broke my heart to see the hospital wing go. Yes, we had our differences, but it was a huge part of the history of the school and of what it once was during the war.

The pool house could rot in hell for all I cared. Too much bad had taken place there for me to see it any other way.

By the time the fire reached the main building, the fire-fighters had arrived. They rescued me soon after arriving, but they left Orlando until last.

They never located his body.

It was still surreal, the entire end of the evening a blur. A nightmare I hadn't woken from.

Was I at fault? A murderer? According to the reports, he died of smoke inhalation and it was no fault of mine, but he and I both knew better. He'd given me a choice and had honoured my decision, had honoured *me*.

Our graduation gowns were being held in the hall for us and it gutted me that my gown would cover up Ollie's jacket. The way his shirt stretched across his broad shirt should be illegal. All hard muscles and straining buttons. *Fuck.* Maybe the gown was a good thing after all.

Cora's face split into a wide smile, stretching across her entire face when she spotted me. If she'd given me the same smile a year ago, I'd have wondered what she wanted from me, but now I saw it for what it was: genuine love and affection.

Bloody weird, right?

'Oh darling,' she said, dragging out the word to make it the longest word known to man. 'You look ab-so-lutely ah-mazing.'

'Thanks, Mum.' I still found it hard to act normal around her. Even though we'd sorted our differences, it would be a while before I forgave the past. If I ever did.

'My baby, graduating.' She wiped a tear making its way down her cheek, small flecks of mascara clinging to its path. 'Skylar, I am so proud of you. You know that, don't you, darling?'

I nodded, letting her pull me in for a hug with her outstretched arms. Her perfume nearly knocked me out. It was so strong I could *taste* it.

'Yeah, Mum,' I said. And the thing surprising me the most? I sort of meant it.

'Skylar,' Jacob said, moving from his position off to the side to stand in front of me and Cora. 'You get even more beautiful every day.'

'Thanks.' It came out even more uneven and awkward sounding than when I answered Mum. Jacob and I were still on uneven footing. Whatever way you sliced it, he had still been absent for eighteen years of my life, and I couldn't bypass that just because he was here now.

One person who wasn't here was Andy. When I was in the hospital getting checked out after the fire, Mum came. She'd seen the fire on the news and called Lottie, who sent a car round for Mum to bring her to me. While there, I opened up about what had happened on the day I left home for Hawthorn.

• • •

'MUM,' I said, scared to voice my thoughts, but knew this was my chance to talk to her without interruption. 'There's something I need to tell you.'

'What's up, darling?' she said, interested at what I had to say for once.

'There's something I have to tell you about Andy.'

'What?'

I took a deep breath, steeling myself for the difficult conversation ahead. 'He kissed me, the day I left to go to Hawthorn.'

'Why didn't you tell me before?' she asked, her expression one of genuine shock. She squeezed my hand, encouraging me to continue.

'I left for school pretty much straight after, then I barely saw you without him afterwards. And when I did ... guess I didn't know how.' I tried to shrug it off but was unable to because of being hooked up to the IV still. 'And Andy told me you wouldn't believe me.'

'I'm sorry he made you think that,' Mum said, her eyes shimmering with unshed tears. 'I wish you'd told me, darling.'

Tears leaked out of my eyes, an overwhelming rush of emotion surging through me at her reaction. I hadn't expected her to believe me. Hadn't expected her to be so nice about it.

'I promise I'll do better, Skylar.'

AFTER OUR CONVERSATION, she kicked him out of her house and threw out his stuff. It had shocked the shit out of me. I hadn't expected her to do anything with my words, but I was so fucking glad she did.

'Shall we go get our gowns?' Ollie asked me, stretching his arm out towards me so I could walk into it. I went willingly, a smile covering my face.

'Yeah,' I replied, then looked at both of my parents. 'We'll be right back.'

The two of us went into the main entrance of the school, and those gargoyles were staring at us as we did so. I would miss those pesky little guys.

Clover, Leo, and Griff waited in front of the hall entrance for us, each with a big smile of their own.

'You ready to do this shit, Clouds?' Griff asked me, his cheeky grin covering his face. It had taken a while, but his smile had returned, and I hoped it would be permanent from now on.

'You bloody know it,' I replied. 'I am beyond ready to never step foot across this threshold ever again.'

And I meant it. Even coming back in ten years would be way too soon for my liking. Even without the dark cloud of Orlando and Ms Hawthorn lurking above the place, it still felt wrong. Even if Leo owned the place now.

Didn't have that on my bingo card, that was for sure.

'You and me both,' Clo said, looping her arm in mine and walking us into the hall. The gowns were all arranged on rails behind a desk, and one of the teacher's volunteers helped each of us into a gown in our size. It was meant to be oversized, but this was beyond, and I imagined I looked a little stupid in it. It swamped me and I swore it made me appear shorter.

Clo, who was shorter than me, looked even more like she was wearing a large parachute tent. You know, like the ones we used to run and hide under in primary school during PE lessons?

'We look ridiculous,' she giggled, her smile wild. It was nice to see her so carefree. Now everything about her past was out in the open she'd relaxed a lot.

'We do,' I said. 'Wonder if the boys look as silly as we do.'

'Nah.' She shook her head, her red curls bouncing with the

motion. 'They'll look like some kind of heavenly beings or some shit.'

I laughed at the image she painted in my mind, but I agreed with her. If those boys managed hotness in those tiny swimming speedos, I knew they could pull off graduation caps and gowns. Although Ollie might get a little precious if it messed up his hair.

'I'm so happy we're here, Clo. Together.'

'Me too. And if you tell anybody I said this, I will kill you, but you're my best friend, Sky. My life wouldn't be the same without you in it.'

My eyes welled up, but I pushed it down. 'You're mine. Hawthorn's good for something, ay?'

Ollie and Griff came back into our eye line and a smile came to my lips. As expected, they were gorgeous. Not that I'd ever tell them I thought of the word gorgeous in relation to them. They preferred to be called sexy or hot. Well, Griff preferred to be referred to as a Greek god, causing us all to roll our eyes in unison; a collective unit.

'Hey,' Ollie said, pulling me into a tight hug. His hands travelled south to my bum, and I tilted my head up.

'Hey there,' I replied, the playful smile still firm on my lips. 'Man, when I thought you couldn't get any sexier.'

He chuckled and squeezed my arse. 'Sky, you look beautiful, don't get me wrong, but you do also sort of resemble a yurt.'

'A yurt!' I shouted, chuckling, before schooling my features into a frown. At least he said a yurt and not a regular old boring tent. 'Piss off.'

'You wouldn't want me to go anywhere, would you?' His eyes glinted with humour as he placed a kiss on my lips. I returned the kiss, an enormous wave of love for him rushing through me. It happened a lot recently, and I wasn't mad at it.

I hummed, dragging out his torment. Or at least attempting to. We both knew I was full of it. 'I guess I'd be sad if you left.'

'Come on, fuckers.' Griff called over his shoulder as he left the hall, Clo by his side, the two of them having resolved everything broken between them. They were best as friends and thank fuck they'd realised it. 'We've gotta move!'

'Leggo, baby,' Ollie mumbled, and placed one last kiss on my forehead.

I took a step back and spotted some of my lipstick staining his lips.

'Wait, come here,' I said, and discreetly tried to take my red lipstick off his mouth. 'Apparently, my lipstick isn't as matte as I'd have liked.'

He smiled, and heat prickled inside me. *Fuck sake.* Not now.

'I'd like to see your lipstick smeared somewhere else,' he drawled, a salacious smile on his lips tempting me to ditch this thing and get him alone. I poked him in the stomach to stop this train from derailing off the tracks.

'Ouch!' I shook my hand, hoping the pain would disappear with the motion, but it didn't. 'That hurt.'

'Next time,' he said, amused, 'accept it and move on.'

'Yeah, yeah,' I replied, not able to hide the smile gracing my mouth. 'Let's go.'

'GRIFFIN COOPER!' Edward Hawthorn called out from his spot in the middle of the stage behind a podium. Even though he didn't want to own the school, he was still acting head until Leo took over at age twenty-one. Our class was small, only forty of us graduating, which meant the ceremony would be short, thank fuck. I didn't have the patience to sit through a long, drawn out thing.

Griff strolled across the stage, cocksure as always, and stopped to receive his diploma and handshake from the guest speakers who were here to talk motivational words at us. I cheered loudly, clapping my clammy hands together, happy for Griff.

Edward opened his mouth once Griff passed, and called, 'Skylar Crescent-Cooper!'

I took a large lungful of air and made my way across the stage, tears pricking the corners of my eyes.

I'd done it.

Somehow, I survived this shit show and was getting everything I ever wanted.

'Woo!' Cora called from her spot in the front row of parents. 'You've done it, baby!'

'Well done, Skylar!' Jacob hollered from next to Mum, both of them standing and clapping and making the most noise they could. I rolled my eyes at them, acting embarrassed by their behaviour, but I was thrilled. I'd never had parents who cared. And now, from the disaster I'd experienced here, I had two.

I shook the lady's hand and received my diploma, then stood and posed for the photographer positioned in front of the stage.

Moving back to my seat in the front row next to Griff, I smiled at Ollie sitting on Griff's other side. His eyes were warm as he smiled back at me, and whispered a quick, *Congrats, baby.* I sat down and waited for the next name I cared about to be called out.

I didn't have to wait long.

'Clover Luck!'

Griff and I stood up the moment Clo appeared on the stage, cheering as loud as we could. Her parents weren't here, and if I ever got the chance, I'd give them a strong piece of my mind.

Regardless of what had happened before, they shouldn't be missing out on her enormous achievements because of it. They didn't deserve her.

In the row for parents, Cora stood and clapped as loudly for Clo as she had for me. Lottie Hawthorn stood next to her, cheering as loudly as Mum. At some point, somehow, Mum and Lottie had become … real friends? Yeah, I didn't understand it either.

But they were both happy, so who was I to judge?

It made me so happy to see them embracing Clo and loving her the way her own parents should. Cora had stepped up in such a short amount of time, and yeah, part of me waited for the other shoe to drop, but I hoped that wouldn't be the case.

'Go, Clo!' I called out, cupping my hands around my mouth so it would carry further. 'Woo!'

In my peripheral, I spotted Leo standing with the members of staff, and he clapped as heartily as us. Nothing had happened between the two of them since *The Sanctum* had disbanded and Orlando was no longer holding shit over Leo's head, but maybe one day it would. I wasn't getting involved. The two of them would sort it out in their own time. I sensed it in my bones.

After posing for her picture, Clo made her way back to the rows of seating for students and took her seat. I leaned forward to smile at her, and she beamed back, shaking her head in disbelief.

My eye caught Ollie's as I leaned back and he winked,

warming my already overheated cheeks. He moved his arm and placed it across Griff to take my hand in his briefly. After a quick pump, he removed his hand and went back to sitting properly.

Griff chuckled in between us, and whispered, 'Do I need to move?'

I shook my head at him and shh'ed him.

The rest of the ceremony continued, but I didn't take any of it in. I tried my hardest to not cry, but everything was overwhelming, and I was the happiest I'd been in so long.

I never expected to be so content.

My life was more than good. More than great.

It was fucking fantastic!

Afterword

Thank you so much for finishing Skylar's journey at Hawthorn
with me.
I truly appreciate each and every one of you.

If you would like to join my newsletter to stay up to date with
my upcoming projects, then scan the QR code below.

Acknowledgements

Thank you so much to everybody who stuck by me during the journey that has been Hawthorn Academy rewrites!

The list contains, but is not limited to:
- Megan
- Cress
- Fiona
- Billie
- Els
- Jess
- Jess
- My family

And of course to you reader, who has stuck by me throughout it all.
Thank you.

About Katie Lowrie

Katie Lowrie is a Brit who loves to read and write.

A list in no particular order of her greatest loves:

- Henry VIII and the Tudor era
- Her baby cat, Cress
- Musicals
- Disney
- Cheese

She loves to stalk people online (in a good way) and understands if you do too.

[instagram] instagram.com/katielowrieauthor

[goodreads] goodreads.com/katielowrieauthor

[facebook] facebook.com/katielowrieauthor

[bookbub] bookbub.com/authors/katie-lowrie

Also by Katie Lowrie

Hawthorn Academy Series:

Disorder

Disease

Disturbed

Rebels of Hollowdale High:

Haven at Hollowdale High

Hero of Hollowdale High

Heirs of Hollowdale High

Re-Imagined Series:

Key of Cunning (**Dark** Billionaire Romance)